Praise for Susan Ouellette's Wayw

"Every once in a decade you read a book like *The Wayward Spy*, which is thrilling, addictive, and sends you reading more thrillers, but you'll go back to this stunning book by Susan Ouellette and reread this tour de force." —***The Strand Magazine***, *a Top 12 Book of the Year*

"[A] gripping debut and series launch . . ." —***Publishers Weekly***

"She has walked the halls of the House Intelligence Committee and the CIA and knows those institutions as very few novelists do."
—**Dr. Mark M. Lowenthal**, Former CIA Assistant Director for Analysis

"*The Wayward Assassin* is one of the best books I've read this year. The action is gripping, the plot full of twists and turns [that] draws you into a roller coaster ride. A must read that should be on every thriller fan's bookshelf. Ouellette has hit this one out of the park."
—***The Strand Magazine***

"Ouellette, herself a former intelligence analyst for the CIA, imbues the exciting action with authenticity. Readers will want to see more of the wily Maggie . . ." —***Publishers Weekly***

"VERDICT: An enjoyable spy thriller from an authentic source."
—***Library Journal***

"I couldn't turn the pages fast enough . . . I hope to see much more of Susan and Maggie." —**Tim Suddeth**, Killer Nashville

•THE WAYWARD SERIES•

THE WAYWARD ASSASSIN

•THE WAYWARD SERIES•

THE WAYWARD ASSASSIN

Susan Ouellette

CamCat Publishing, LLC
Brentwood, Tennessee 37027
camcatpublishing.com

This is a work of fiction. Names, characters, places, and incidents are either products of the author's imagination or are used fictitiously.

Hardcover ISBN 9780744304787
Paperback ISBN 9780744305258
Large-Print Paperback ISBN 9780744305234
eBook ISBN 9780744305265
Audiobook ISBN 9780744305319

Library of Congress Control Number: 2021947069

Cover design/book design by Maryann Appel

5 3 1 2 4

For Dan.

For giving me the time, space, and encouragement

to keep on going.

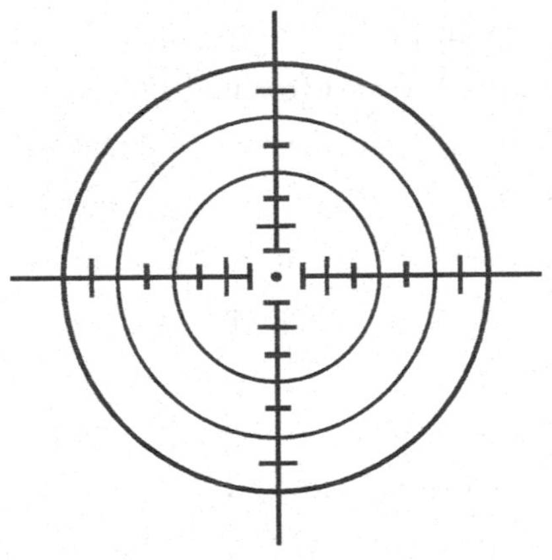

CHAPTER ONE

CIA Headquarters, August 16, 2004

Maggie Jenkins strode across the parking lot to the sidewalk that led her past the "Bubble," the CIA's white, dome-shaped auditorium. Just ahead, she paused at the bronze statue of Nathan Hale, the first American to be executed for spying for his country. A half dozen quarters lay scattered at his feet, left there by superstitious CIA employees hoping to garner good luck before deploying overseas. She fished around in her purse for a quarter, which she placed carefully atop Hale's left shoe.

In just a few minutes, Maggie would learn whether her six-month deployment to the US embassy in Moscow had been approved. Even though Warner Thompson, the CIA's deputy director for operations, had advocated on her behalf, there were several others, including an Agency psychiatrist and a team of polygraphers, who were not convinced that she should be stationed overseas. *She's not ready yet,* the shrink had opined, as if she were a piece of fruit not quite ripe enough for picking.

"Wish me luck," she said to the statue as she turned for the entrance ahead. The CIA's headquarters comprised two main buildings, both seven stories high, which were linked together by bright hallways with large windows overlooking a grassy courtyard. Maggie worked in the original headquarters building (OHB), which had been built some forty years earlier during the height of the Cold War. From the outside, OHB was a concrete monstrosity with no aesthetically redeeming value, at least in Maggie's opinion. It reminded her of Soviet architecture—heavy on the concrete, light on the beauty.

And other than the expansive marbled foyer and the posh seventh-floor executive offices, OHB's interior also was nothing to write home about. Every floor between the first and the seventh looked exactly the same—drab, hushed, windowless hallways lined with vault doors. Behind those heavily fortified doors sat rows of cubicles, a few conference rooms, and cramped offices here and there for mid-level managers.

Maggie pulled open the heavy glass entry door and ducked into a pristine lobby gleaming with white marble-clad walls. Ahead, the Agency's logo covered a massive swath of the gray-and-white checked granite floor. To the right stood the Memorial Wall, which was emblazoned with black stars honoring dozens of Agency officers who'd perished in the line of duty. Maggie stopped and bit down on her lip.

The wall was an awesome, solemn reminder of lives given in the defense of freedom. Every time she walked past it, the sharp points of the eighty-fourth star—Steve's star—ripped another gash in her heart. He'd been working under cover, so no outside friends or relatives had been invited to the ceremony. Warner had sat with her, stoic, as she clutched his hand and stared at the parade of speakers, not hearing a word they said.

She turned her gaze from the wall, slid her badge through the security turnstile, and offered a polite hello to the officer manning the front desk. She bypassed the elevator that she took every day to the fourth floor and made a beeline for the spacious employee cafeteria. In the far corner sat Warner Thompson, nose buried in the *Washington Post*.

"Morning," she offered.

Warner rattled the paper and folded it lengthwise. "Coffee?" He pushed a Styrofoam cup across the quartz tabletop and smiled at her. His full head of hair had grayed considerably since last year, but it worked on him, enhancing his gray-flecked eyes and tanned complexion.

"Thanks." Maggie sat.

"You ready?"

"I guess." She sipped the coffee, still piping hot and perfectly sweetened. Warner knew her well. "What do you think they'll say?"

"There's no reason they should deny you the posting."

"The psychiatrist thinks I'm obsessed with Zara."

"He has a point." Warner leaned forward, elbows on the table. "I told you not to bring her up in your evaluation sessions. If she's still alive, we'll find her, Maggie. I promise."

"There's no 'if' about it." She waited until a man with a breakfast tray settled at a nearby table, then lowered her voice. "I saw her fleeing the farmhouse in Georgia. Who do they think set fire to the place after I escaped with Peter?"

Warner winced, obviously uncomfortable with the reminder of Peter, his former case officer, the one who'd been intimately involved in the murder of Steve, another case officer, and his protégé, nine short months ago. That Steve also had been Maggie's fiancé made saying what he had to say all the more difficult. "The point is, the Agency needs to think that you've moved on from what happened in Georgia before they send you to such a sensitive overseas posting."

"Moved on? Warner—"

He raised a hand to stop her. They'd had this discussion dozens of times since the previous November. Maggie had made it perfectly clear that there was no moving on, no closure, as people said these days, until she found Zara. "You know what I mean. You have to toe the party line and say you believe that everyone involved in Steve's murder is dead. Period."

"I still don't understand why they won't at least consider the possibility that Zara got away."

Warner rubbed his forehead. "Because the Agency wants this to go away. A star operations officer was murdered by a terrorist and the terrorist is dead. It's a simple, straightforward narrative. They don't want the press finding out that another Agency employee and a senior US congressman were involved in Steve's death. Everything is about the war on terror, Maggie. If the media found out that CIA and elected officials were mixed up with terrorists, there would be hell to pay."

Maggie quoted the Biblical phrase inscribed on a wall in the CIA's lobby. "The truth shall make you free." She snorted. "The truth, unless it's too embarrassing?"

Warner exhaled and shifted in his seat. "Both of us are lucky that the FBI investigation didn't uncover . . . everything."

He was right, of course. Last year, Maggie had destroyed classified documents and withheld other evidence from the FBI to protect them both. And Warner had been entangled, albeit unwittingly, with a Russian who had ties to both Zara and the congressman. Had the FBI known any of this, neither of them would be CIA employees today.

Maggie waved to a coworker who stared from the nearby coffee station. Warner didn't frequent the employee cafeteria, so his appearance was sure to raise eyebrows. She'd grown accustomed to sidelong glances inside the Agency's walls. Everyone recognized her. The media had splashed her face all over television and the internet after Congressman Carvelli's death. There were some who whispered about her using her fiancé's death to advance her career. Fortunately, they were in the minority. Most who knew about her role in uncovering the terrorist plot considered her a hero, a designation she refused to embrace. Her actions may have saved thousands of lives, but her motivation had been personal—to clear Steve's name.

He was no traitor, and she'd proven it.

Maggie glanced at her watch. "We'd better go."

Warner nodded. They grabbed their coffees and headed for the elevator bank.

"Remember, you believe Zara died in the fire at the farmhouse," Warner reminded her on the way up to the fourth floor.

"That's what I told the shrink last session, but then he talked to the polygraph people." Since leaving the House Intelligence Committee to return to the CIA earlier this year, she'd endured three marathon polygraph sessions. Every time, the stupid machine registered deception in her response to questions about whether she intended to violate government policies for her own benefit. "Now he thinks I'm up to something."

Warner shrugged. "Aren't you?"

Maggie laughed despite herself. "Always."

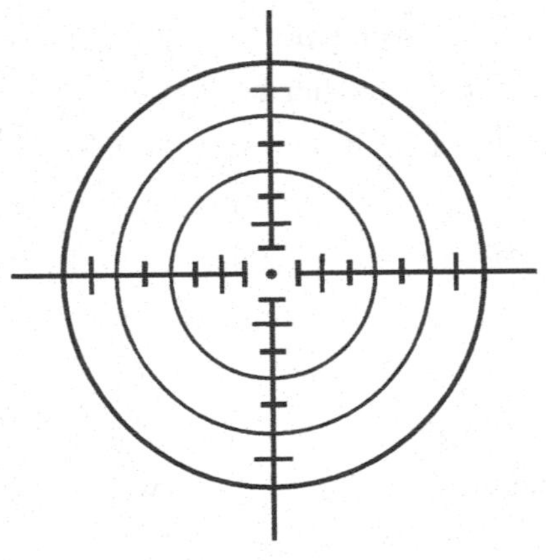

CHAPTER TWO

Vladikavkaz, Republic of North Ossetia, Russia, August 16, 2004

After the man left her alone in the mosque's office, the young woman tugged off her emerald-green hijab and shook out her raven hair. Initially, he'd refused her request to use the computer, but once he realized she was connected to Imran, he'd relented. Even though he wasn't a Chechen himself, it was clear that he knew better than to cross such a powerful man.

She logged into the joint email account Imran had set up for them and checked the draft folder. There were two messages waiting. Undoubtedly, he'd be annoyed that she hadn't responded sooner, but it hadn't been safe for her to travel for several days. Reports of Russian patrols had kept her even further underground.

The first message confirmed that the operation was on as scheduled. The second gave her an address and the name of the target. She pushed back in the chair and exhaled. The likelihood of her surviving this wasn't great. Imran had to know that. If she was going to die a *shahida* during this operation, why had he agreed to an even bolder operation next month, an operation she had devised and was supposed to lead?

She started to respond to the second email but quickly deleted it. Replying broke protocol. Instead, she was to respond via a new draft email in the same folder.

I was unable to travel for several days. Thank you for the information. I will check back once a week for the next two weeks for further instructions. If we can speak on the phone, I'd like to discuss the second operation.

She clicked out of the email account, navigated to the history tab, and deleted the file just as the man returned.

"Your hijab," he gasped.

She stood, tossed her hair, and eyed him from head to foot.

"You must wear the hijab in the mosque."

She draped the silky fabric over her head, wrapped it around her neck, then across her face, covering all but her eyes. As she passed by the man, she brushed against him and leaned in close. "I saw how you looked at me. You'd like to see even more, wouldn't you?"

The man stammered and backed away. "Go . . . please go."

She never used the same computer twice, but she was tempted to return next week in tight jeans and a low-cut blouse. Touching a finger to his lips, she smiled as said, "No one has to know."

With that, she turned and walked down the hall, through the lobby, and out into the warmth of an August afternoon. Inside the Skoda, she pulled off the head covering and tossed it in the backseat. Imran had warned her about making an impression on people. She was supposed to fly under the radar, but men were so easy to play that she couldn't help herself.

Powering up the car, she set off for the drive back to the safe house.

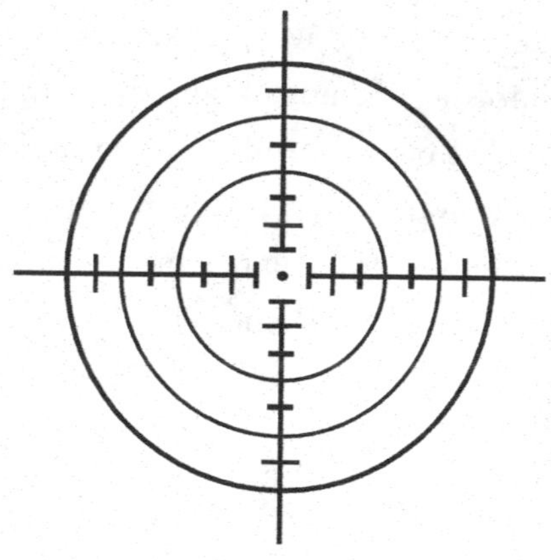

CHAPTER THREE

CIA Headquarters, August 16, 2004

The elevator door rattled open, depositing Maggie and Warner into a nondescript hall with off-white walls and a gray-speckled tile floor. Fluorescent lighting above lent an institutionalized feel to their surroundings. Thick metal doors with keypads above the handles lined both sides of the hallway. Black placards with room numbers were the only markers to guide visitors to their destination. They stopped in front of the third door on the right. Maggie keyed in the combination, waited for the click, and pushed open the door.

The sound of clacking keyboards rose from behind cubicle walls. Ahead was the main conference room for the Office of

Russian and European Analysis. Maggie went in first. At the head of the large, oblong table sat her boss, Jim Carpenter. A middle-aged man whose soft midsection betrayed a fondness for pastries and too little time for exercise, he had been Maggie's boss when she worked at the Agency before she accepted a role with the House Intelligence Committee several years earlier. He was smart, dedicated to knowing everything he could about the former Soviet Union, but his frumpy appearance and academic demeanor ensured that he would toil away in middle management for the next twenty years.

To Carpenter's right, Dr. Hansen, the Agency psychiatrist who'd been assigned to her, peered over bifocal rims. Next to him sat a younger woman, midthirties, mousy brown hair pulled back in a severe bun. She looked vaguely familiar.

"Good morning, Maggie. Warner, I didn't know you'd be joining us." Jim Carpenter flashed a forced smile as Warner entered the room.

Maggie's stomach tightened. Carpenter wasn't good at hiding his emotions. She sat and folded and unfolded her hands.

"Maggie, there's no question you are the most qualified applicant for the analyst position in Moscow," her boss began. "I think it would be an excellent opportunity for you to immerse yourself in Russian culture and language and to help the embassy with some rather delicate upcoming negotiations and terrorism concerns."

A smile spread across her face. She straightened in the chair.

"However," said Dr. Hansen, "we continue to have concerns about your readiness to live and work in Moscow."

The smile vanished. The shrink was the definition of a wet blanket.

"You remember Ms. Smith, the chief of our polygraph group?"

Maggie squinted at the dour woman. That's where she'd seen her. Two polygraphs ago, she'd come into the testing room to explain that shouting at the polygraph administrator was not going to get her through the test more quickly. The polygrapher had been coming at her with the same question asked in a dozen different ways for over an hour. She'd finally snapped.

"If I may," Warner said, "what are your concerns?"

"Ms. Jenkins claims to be over the trauma of last year." Dr. Hansen studied a notebook on the table in front of him. "And while I have seen improvements, her polygraph results are problematic."

"Polygraphs, in general, are problematic," Warner replied. "People with a conscience, like Maggie, tend to have the most difficult time passing the CIA's polygraph exam."

It was true. When she first applied to work at the Agency, she'd been sent to see a different CIA psychiatrist after her polygraph indicated deception. The doctor, a lovely older gentleman took one look at her file and said, "You're Catholic. You feel guilty about everything. Don't let the bastards mess with you." He'd sent her back to the polygraph room, and sure enough, she passed the exam and reported to CIA orientation the next week.

"She had difficulty answering questions about the shooting of Congressman Carvelli, isn't that right, Ms. Smith?" Dr. Hansen cocked his head and eyed Maggie.

"She did—"

"Surely, you've reviewed the FBI's summary report fully exonerating Maggie in the congressman's death." Warner pulled a folded piece of paper from the inside pocket of his suit jacket.

"Ms. Jenkins fired the gun multiple times. It was excessive force, in my professional opinion," protested Dr. Hansen.

"You've got to be kidding me." Maggie seethed.

"It was self-defense." Warner waved the sheet of paper. "You have a problem with that, take it up with the FBI."

The first full day in the hospital after the congressman's death had been a nightmare. FBI agents cuffed her to the hospital bed as if she were a flight risk and questioned her for hours after her shoulder surgery. Eventually, she called the nurse for more pain killers and pretended to pass out. Once the ballistics report came back, proving that Carvelli had shot Warner and her first, the FBI withdrew their agents and sent in terrorist specialists to hear what Maggie knew about the looming al-Qaeda attack.

Ms. Smith interrupted her thoughts. "Mr. Thompson, with all due respect, Ms. Jenkins continues to show deception on one other area of the test."

Maggie settled her gaze on Smith. They'd been over this so many times already. "You think I'm going to go rogue because last year I took it upon myself to solve my fiancé's murder."

"Your polygraph results—" persisted Ms. Smith.

"With all due respect, Ms. Smith," Warner intoned, "last year, Maggie uncovered a major terrorist threat. She literally helped save thousands of lives. Probably more. That experience wasn't without trauma."

Maggie had only recently convinced Dr. Hansen that she was over the trauma. She gave Warner a little warning kick to the ankle.

He flinched but continued. "Your relentless questions about whether Maggie is pursuing her own agenda rather than that of the US government naturally would cause a physiological reaction. A spike in blood pressure, respiration, and heart rate. Am I right?"

Ms. Smith pursed her lips.

Dr. Hansen frowned. "Well, yes, that's the usual response to stress."

Maggie locked eyes with Jim Carpenter. He nodded and raised his eyebrows. "Nobody knows Maggie better than Warner does," offered Carpenter. "And personally, I think she's ready for this deployment."

Hansen and Smith exchanged glances.

"Our concerns about Maggie remain and will be noted in the official record."

Maggie concentrated on not rolling her eyes.

"That settles it, then," her boss said with a grin. "Maggie, you're off to Moscow."

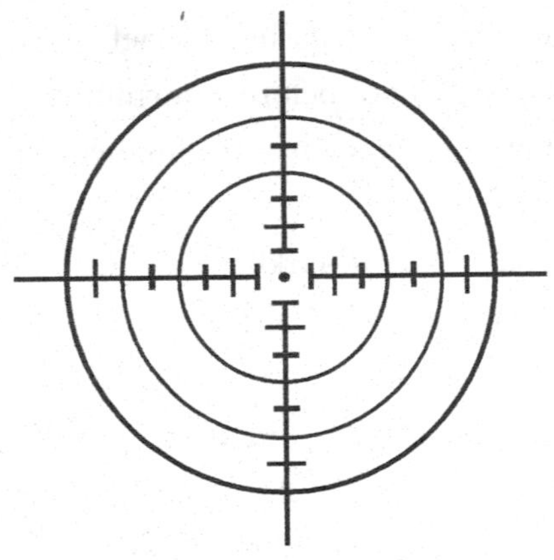

CHAPTER FOUR

CIA Station, US Embassy, Moscow
Wednesday, September 1, 2004

Maggie burst into the CIA station chief's office on the top floor of the embassy. He looked up from his laptop, phone to his ear, and mouthed, "What?"

She snatched the remote control from the corner of his desk and hit the power button. Three televisions hanging on the opposite wall lit up in unison. One was tuned to Russian news, the others to British and American channels. The Russian channel ran video of soldiers forming a cordon around a school in Beslan, a town some one thousand miles south of Moscow.

The British channel cut to two terrorism experts arguing about whether the breaking news from Beslan was terrorism-related. The

American station, meanwhile, flashed a brief story about a security concern at a Russian school before returning to coverage of the Republican National Convention and a hurricane barreling toward Florida.

"I'll call you back." Bob Markham dropped the phone into its cradle and stood. "What's going on?"

"There's a situation at a school in Beslan."

Markham frowned. "What kind of situation?"

"It's the first day of school. Always a big deal in Russia. The kids dress up, bring flowers to their teachers."

Bob turned to her. "Why are all those soldiers there?"

The video feed switched angles, capturing adults with anxious expressions trying to see beyond the uniformed men. "That's what I'm trying to figure out." Maggie shook her head. "They wouldn't go after a school, would they?"

Markham looked confused. "Who?"

"The Chechens."

Markham paled.

A graphic reading "Possible Hostage Situation at Russian School" scrolled across the screen on the British channel. Maggie turned up the volume. According to reports, gunfire had been heard coming from the school grounds. Several people claiming to be inside the building told police that militants had forced everyone into the gymnasium.

"Do we have any assets in the area?"

The station chief shook his head. "You know we focus mostly on Moscow. On Putin."

She squinted at the television. "We need to get a team down to Beslan. Figure out if this is the Chechens. Or maybe al-Qaeda."

"Better if we just watch from here. At least for now."

"But Bob, if it's the Chechens, I know how they operate, I should be there—"

"Maggie, you're not going anywhere."

Three hours later, the CIA Operations Center in Langley sent Moscow station the first images from inside the school, no doubt intercepted from Russian communications channels. Maggie scrolled through the photos on her desktop computer. Heavily armed men in green camouflage and black ski masks towered above hundreds of frightened children and adults crowded together inside a gymnasium. Then came a photograph of an armed woman wearing a flowing black abaya and a niqab that covered all but her eyes. Maggie gasped, clicked on the mouse, and zoomed in.

Is that you, Zara?

Her heart beating faster, she picked up the phone and dialed. What seemed like an eternity later, someone finally picked up.

"Warner? It's me." Maggie's words tumbled out before he could answer. "Sorry to wake you."

Warner mumbled something incoherent then cleared his throat. "Everything okay?"

She offered a quick rundown on the situation in Beslan. "It's the Chechens." She walked around her desk, stretched the phone cord to the breaking point, and shut her office door. "I'm sure of it."

"What?" His voice was gruff with sleep. "Where is this happening?"

"Beslan. In North Ossetia." She gripped the phone tighter. "West of Chechnya."

Warner fell silent for a moment. "Do we have anyone in the region?"

"No. I think we should send a team."

"Why?"

Maggie wanted to tell Warner about the photo, but if she did, he might not go along with her plan. He'd worry and make her stay in Moscow. Later, once she got to Beslan, she'd tell him she thought Zara was one of the terrorists. "We could offer the Russians assistance. Food, water, medical help. Meanwhile, we'll really be there to collect intel on Russian police and military tactics."

"That's not exactly an intelligence priority."

"But terrorism is. And, as we both know all too well, the Chechens have ties with al-Qaeda. We should be there. On the ground."

Warner grunted. "I'll talk to the director and then call the secretary of state. Perhaps we can pull something together under the guise of a State Department mission."

Maggie exhaled, relieved. The station chief might not listen to her, but he'd have to follow orders coming from Washington. "I have to be on the team."

"I don't think that's a good idea."

"I'm the expert on Chechen terrorism, Warner. That's why I'm in Moscow."

Silence.

"I know these people better than anyone else."

He sighed. "Promise me you'll be careful."

Maggie returned to the computer and stared at the woman in the photo. "I promise."

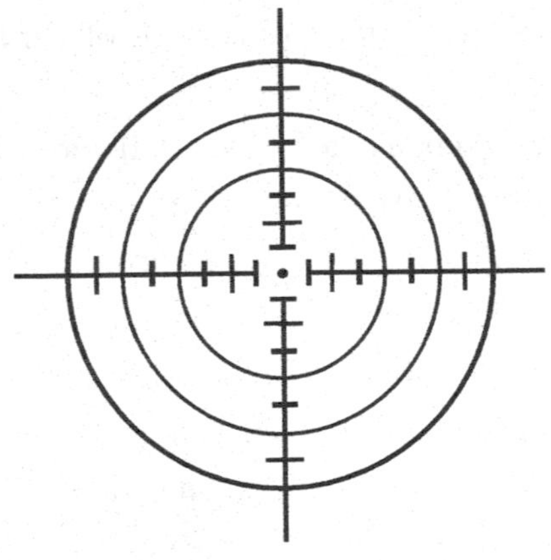

CHAPTER FIVE

School Number 1, Beslan, Russia
Thursday, September 2, 2004

Zara Barayeva slipped and fell on the blood seeping across the floor like a crimson oil slick. Viscous warmth coated her fingers and clung to her abaya. She scrambled to her feet, swiped her hand across the black fabric, and scanned the bodies lying closest to the gymnasium exit. Initially, all she saw were children—but there, in the corner, was a woman, slumped on her side. She was considerably larger than Zara, but she'd suffice.

With the grace of the ballerina she'd once trained to be, Zara leaped between lifeless figures with twisted limbs. She shoved the woman's left shoulder with her foot, forcing the corpse onto its back, arms spread wide. A gaping wound on the side of the woman's face added a splotch of color to the coarse fabric of her frock. It was the perfect touch.

Zara rolled the woman onto her side and undid a line of buttons that ended at the waist. With considerable effort, she tugged the beige dress off fleshy arms, over corpulent hips, and around stout ankles. Zara tore off her abaya, the black garment that covered her clothes, and the niqab, the veil that hid all but her wide, olive-colored eyes. Tangled, damp raven hair fell forward, clinging to high cheekbones and an elegant neck. She pulled the dead woman's voluminous dress over the tight red sweater and black cotton skirt that had helped her breeze into the school, no questions asked, two days prior. The abaya and niqab had been hidden here weeks ago, along with guns, bombs, detonators, and other instruments of terror—or liberation, depending on your viewpoint.

She balled up the billowing black garments and threw them to the floor. Zara had been instructed to blow herself up, become a *shahida*, a martyr for Allah. Naturally, she'd agreed to sacrifice herself for the greater cause, but she had no intention of keeping her end of the deal. Instead, she'd spent weeks planning her escape from Beslan. And now was her chance—she needed to act quickly, during the height of chaos.

She scanned the room, her gaze landing on a girl in a navy-blue dress. She was five or perhaps six years old, sitting alone amid a sea of lifeless bodies, crying for her grandmother.

Zara ran to the child, picked her up, and deposited her outside the gymnasium entrance where she'd stashed her knock-off Ferragamo purse hours before. Just inside the door stood what remained of a cache of grenades. The number of dead was already sufficient to send the message that Chechnya would stop at nothing to achieve its independence, but she needed to distract the soldiers swarming outside—Russians—who would become instant heroes for killing her, a Chechen terrorist.

In one deft move, she snatched a grenade, pulled the pin, and hurled it to the center of the gymnasium, where it landed amid dazed, disheveled schoolchildren who had the misfortune of being collateral damage in a greater struggle.

Zara sprinted toward the exit, pausing only long enough to scoop up both the girl and her purse. Shrieks, groans, and desperate pleas for help punctuated the explosion behind her as she fled from the building to the madness outside.

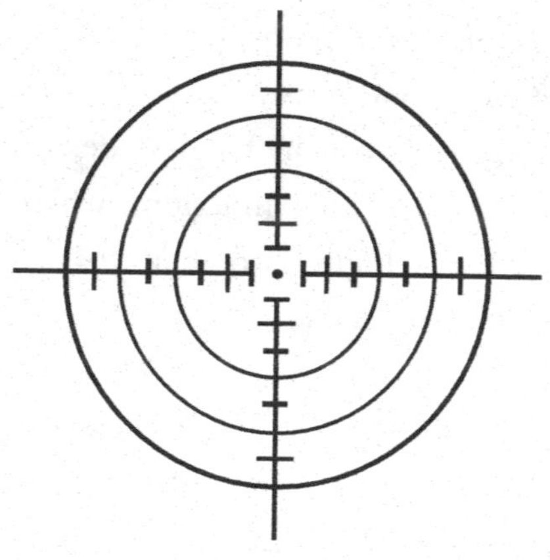

CHAPTER SIX

North Ossetia, Russia
Thursday, September 2, 2004

On the thirty-minute drive from the Vladikavkaz airport to Beslan, the four-member team went over the latest situation report. Twenty-eight hours into the school siege and dozens of hostages had been freed, predominantly women with infants. Dozens more, mostly young men, had been killed. And the terrorists had made their demands known. Chief among them—all Russian troops out of Chechnya.

In the backseat of the Range Rover, Maggie's body buzzed with adrenaline. She'd barely slept, and when she did drift off, her dreams had been fraught with vivid images of Zara, reliving their violent encounter last year. Next to Maggie sat Jennifer, a petite, middle-aged State Department official whose portfolio included humanitarian affairs. Her presence lent legitimacy to the group's ostensible mission—to provide whatever assistance they could to Russian emergency workers. As did the presence of the driver, Dr. McAuley, a physician from the US Embassy in Tbilisi, who'd driven several hours to pick them up from the airport. In the front passenger seat sat Tom Merrick, a brash, young Moscow station case officer who was traveling under diplomatic cover.

As Dr. McAuley navigated through rural areas on the outskirts of Beslan, Maggie's palms grew damp. "We almost there?"

"Five minutes," Tom replied.

Five minutes grew into twenty after they were stopped at a police checkpoint. It took Jennifer's fluent Russian and quiet manner to finally convince the police that the group had arrived with Moscow's permission. By then, perspiration was rolling down Maggie's back, dampening the gray T-shirt she wore.

"Remember," Tom intoned, "stay near the car unless I direct otherwise."

The young case officer seemed to think he was in charge. Circumstances, not some guy right out of CIA training, would dictate Maggie's actions.

Dr. McAuley pulled the SUV onto a patch of grass about one hundred yards from the school. Russian troops eyed them suspiciously.

"Help me unload?" Jennifer called from the tailgate. Inside were ten cases of bottled water and an assortment of American snacks, from bags of pretzels to energy bars. "I'll start distributing these to the military men."

The doctor grabbed a large bag of medical supplies. "I saw a medical tent on the way in. I'll see if I can help."

"Wait a second," Tom began. When he realized no one was following his directive, he turned to Maggie. "I'm going to take a look around. Stay here."

Maggie threw him a look but said nothing as she pulled the embassy's Nikon SLR camera from a supply bag stashed under the backseat. She slung the strap over her neck and drew closer to the school. A sudden explosion sent her scrambling back behind the SUV, where she sank to the ground, hands shaking, breaths coming in jagged gasps.

This isn't Tbilisi.

And the terrorists weren't holding her hostage this time. With trembling fingers, she pulled a copy of the photograph from her back pocket and reminded herself why she was here. Because the woman inside that school might be Zara.

Maggie had never accepted the official report that all her Chechen kidnappers were dead. She'd seen Zara fleeing the farmhouse where they'd held her captive; she was sure of it. And the Georgian government hadn't been able to positively identify the remains found in the dilapidated structure because it had burned to the ground after Maggie escaped. Someone had set the house ablaze.

And now here she was, in Beslan, within striking distance of where the woman in the photo—Zara, maybe—held hundreds of children hostage.

As she peered around the Range Rover's bumper, another explosion rocked the brick building that stood just beyond a grove of towering Russian elms. Every ounce of common sense told Maggie to stay put. But the least she could do was document the situation for later analysis. She stood and pulled the cover off the camera lens.

• ★ ★ ★ •

Russian troops blanketed the schoolyard. If there was any chance of escaping, Zara would have to blend in, look like the other distraught young mothers. The dead woman's dress wasn't helping. It fit like a circus tent, slipping off her shoulders, getting caught underfoot. She lowered the child to the ground and slid out of the garment. In all the confusion, no one noticed her tossing the dress aside.

The girl stared at Zara, still wailing, "*Baba! Baba!*"

Zara grabbed the child's disheveled ponytail. "*Tvoya babushka mertva.*" Zara had no idea if her grandmother was dead. It made no difference.

The girl stopped screaming for a moment. Then her silence turned into shrieks as she absorbed Zara's words. "*Nyet! Nyet, babushka, nyet!*"

Two soldiers heard the girl's cries and urged Zara to run to them.

Before she could move, the force of an explosion sent her careening into the girl, whose head hit a concrete barrier with a hideous thud. Life seemed to drain from the child with every ounce of blood that seeped through the fissure in her skull.

Zara rolled the girl onto her back. Her eyes were blue and wide with shock. Zara scooped her up, determined to look the part of a devastated mother. But the soldiers were running toward the building, ignoring her. This was her chance.

• ★ ★ ★ •

Maggie crouched behind an abandoned police car, trying to catch her breath. Smoke and dust hung like a low fog around the school.

She pushed tangled auburn hair from her face, raised the camera, and took a picture of boyish Russian soldiers smoking cigarettes at the perimeter of the school grounds. Fierce scowls failed to conceal their despair and fright.

Maggie swung the lens toward the school, forty yards ahead. Her finger froze over the shutter button. She zoomed in on a boy clad only in underwear. He dangled, then dropped from a blown-out window. Tears soaked the dried blood on his face, sending pink rivulets trickling from his cheeks to his gaunt chest. Maggie wanted to rush to him, usher him to safety, but her legs felt like lead.

There was movement inside the school. Several more children tumbled from the window, all in various states of undress. Early reporting indicated that the temperature inside the school had risen to a sweltering 100 degrees. Maggie snapped photo after photo, hoping that a terrorist would move into view. That Zara would appear before the camera lens.

A commotion near the school entrance drew Maggie's attention from the window. A woman in a red sweater and black skirt emerged from the smoke, clutching a limp-bodied child. The camera whirred and clicked as Maggie snapped a series of photos. The woman glanced over her shoulder at the soldiers, who conferred in small huddles, their fingers fluttering over Kalashnikov triggers. She ran farther from the school until she was about ten feet away from Maggie, where she stopped and lowered the little girl to the ground.

Maggie sensed the woman's desperation and shoved aside her fear. Russian words she thought she'd forgotten tumbled from her lips. "Stay with your daughter. I'll get help," she called.

The woman glanced over her shoulder, her eyes locking with Maggie's. She tilted her head and squinted, confusion drawing her eyebrows together.

Maggie stepped out from behind the car and brushed a damp auburn curl off her forehead.

The woman's brows shot up in recognition.

Maggie approached, her legs suddenly weak. She'd been right. "Zara?"

The corners of Zara's mouth curved up into something between a sneer and a smile. Maggie glanced at the child, who was moaning on the ground, her small, dirty hands reaching up, begging for help.

She charged, but Zara was faster, evading Maggie's flailing arms and sprinting away.

"*Ostanovite!*" Maggie screamed. "Stop her!"

Maggie began to give chase, but a cry from the child halted her in her tracks. She hurried back and knelt. Blood had stained the girl's blonde ponytail a muddy crimson. She touched the girl's cheek. Enormous baby-blue eyes stared up, unfocused and unblinking. Gently caressing the child's damp, dirty face, she said, "It'll be okay." Thick eyelashes fluttered in response before closing.

"Somebody help!" No one moved in their direction. "Dr. McAuley!" Cradling the child's head in her lap, she placed a hand on the girl's neck. No pulse. No breath. Maggie began chest compressions, not stopping until a Russian medic arrived and took over. But it was no use. The little girl was gone.

Maggie looked around, but of course Zara was long gone. She ran over to a group of Russian soldiers, asking if they'd seen the woman in the red sweater. They shrugged in reply. She scanned the countryside just beyond the school grounds. Zara had vanished. Again. As she made her way back toward the school, she spotted a black purse on the ground just beyond where the little girl lay, a white sheet now covering her torso like a discarded tissue. Amid the shouting soldiers and rising smoke, Maggie scooped up the purse. As she fumbled with the clasp, a soldier carrying a bloody and dazed boy of about six or seven grabbed Maggie's arm and handed her the child. Blood oozed from multiple locations on the boy's arms and legs. She dropped the purse, cradled the child's head against her shoulder, and hurried away in search of Dr. McAuley.

• ★ ★ ★ •

Zara slowed from a run to a trot, then finally to a walk. She needed to catch her breath and gather herself. How the hell had Maggie Jenkins found her? Up until this moment, everything had gone exactly as planned. The Russians, the Americans, and the Georgians all thought she'd been killed by the man who'd freed her captive, Maggie Jenkins. She hadn't let her guard down completely, but lately, she'd felt more confident that she wouldn't be discovered.

Now she had to assume that she'd been compromised. There was no way to know how extensive the damage was, which meant there was only one solution. She had to eliminate the most immediate threat and then proceed with her original plan. Nothing, not even Maggie Jenkins, would derail her.

Zara took a few deep breaths and tried to focus. Soldiers might be in pursuit, so a speedy escape was essential. She looked herself over—thanks to the abaya she'd worn inside the school, her clothes were clean. That wouldn't do. After two days of a siege, she should look filthy, like the hostages. She took her left hand, which was covered in the girl's blood, and smeared it across her face, sweater, skirt. *That's better.*

She averted her eyes from two policemen running toward her. They shouted something about a medical treatment area. One of the men, a gangly blond, grabbed her arm. She pretended to be disoriented. He shoved a plastic bottle into her hand and dashed away to catch up with his colleague. Zara smiled and took a swig of cold water. She'd been plotting revenge, dreaming of the moment she'd exact it. Surviving this day could mean only one thing—she was destined to succeed.

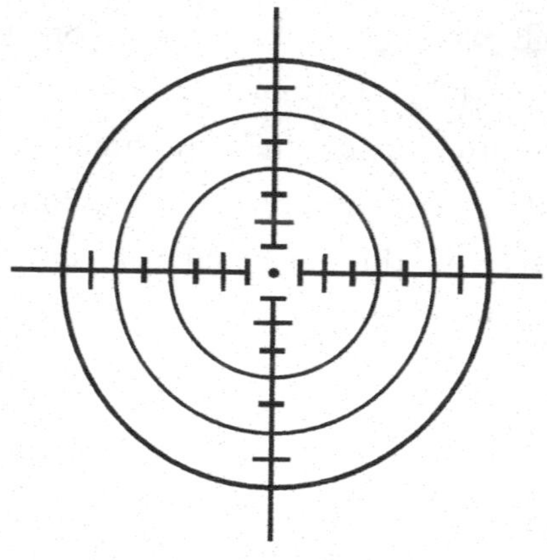

CHAPTER SEVEN

Just outside the medical tent, Maggie peeled off the latex gloves Dr. McAuley had provided her. She felt so useless, only able to clean and bandage superficial wounds while the doctor worked with local medics on the more seriously wounded. All around her, children cried for their mothers and mothers for their children. Desperation permeated every face, survivors and rescuers alike.

Despair hit her in waves. All the blood, terror, and chaos. And all for what? She'd let her chance to get Zara slip away. The chances of finding her again were next to zero. She had to tell Warner. Maybe there was a way, maybe the CIA could find her.

Maybe—the sudden appearance of Tom pulled her from her thoughts.

"There may be as many as eight hundred hostages still in the school," he said as he tried to catch his breath.

"Eight hundred?" There was no way Dr. McAuley and a half dozen Russian medics could handle that volume of people. As it was, the wounded were lying on brown army blankets on the ground.

He nodded. "I'm trying to get more information on the terrorists. See if there's an angle we can work. Maybe they have family that will talk them down."

"They're fanatics, Tom. Nothing will get them to surrender."

He tilted his head. "Clearly you don't understand the art of negotiation."

"You think you can negotiate with them?" She swiped at the sweat beading on her forehead. "You can't. And I know that because I know one of the terrorists."

His eyebrows shot up.

"Zara Barayeva."

"Zara who?"

"Barayeva. She's a known terrorist. Long story short, I saw her fleeing the school." She waved a hand in the air between them. "I was this close to her."

"And you're just telling me this now?"

"It just happened," she snapped. "But she's already gone. Vanished."

"Stay here."

"Excuse me?"

He raised a hand. "I'll handle this."

"Handle what?"

"Zara Barayeva." With that, he turned and sprinted back toward the school.

"Arrogant little—" she muttered.

"Maggie?" It was Dr. McAuley. "There's another bag of bandages in the car. Could you get it for me?"

"Of course." She made her way back to the Range Rover, her throat parched and head pounding. Rifling around in the rear compartment, she found the extra medical supplies in a duffel bag also containing two satellite phones. She tossed one of the telephones into the backseat, slammed the rear gate and glanced over to the right, where the little girl's corpse lay. The white sheet fluttered in the breeze, leaving most of the child's body exposed to the hot sun. Maggie pictured a frantic mother searching for her missing child, stumbling across her, abandoned in a dusty field. She dropped the supply bag and approached. "I'm so sorry, sweet girl." Gently, she tucked the edges of the sheet under the child's lifeless limbs and over her blood-soaked hair.

She straightened, blinking away tears, and caught sight of the purse lying a few feet away. Inside were lipstick, a hairbrush, chewing gum, and a coin purse. But no wallet or passport. Upon closer examination, she discovered an interior pocket containing a tattered envelope and a folded newspaper clipping. She slid the envelope from the pocket. It was addressed to Zara Barayeva, 32 Revolution Avenue, #211, Grozny.

Zara tested the door on the dilapidated Lada. She smiled and glanced around. No one had bothered her since the policeman who'd handed her a water bottle. She slipped into the driver's seat, silently thanking her older brother for teaching her about cars when she was just a teenager. If only he were still here to teach her more. Her fingers worked fast, finding the right wires. Ramzan would be proud of her. The car choked to life.

The plan was to head south to Georgia. From there, she had several options, which she'd sort through after she arrived. She tried not to think about the Jenkins woman—it was too much of a distraction.

There'd be time to deal with her later.

Zara drove up two blocks and took a left. "Damn it," she cursed under her breath. Ahead in the middle of the road was a military truck teeming with Russian soldiers. A stocky, dark-haired man with a cigarette dangling from the corner of his mouth eyed her. He nodded to the men in the truck.

Zara slowed the Lada. A story came together quickly in her head. As the car rolled to a stop, she cranked down the window.

"Can you help me?" she implored. "I don't know which way to go. I need to get to Vladikavkaz to pick up my mother."

"Identification, please." The soldier's gaze darted to the empty passenger seat, then to the backseat. He didn't come across as the compassionate type.

It wasn't until then that she realized her purse was missing. She couldn't afford more mistakes like that, but at least her travel documents were safely stashed in Tbilisi. "I lost my purse at the school." She dug her fingernails into her palms, but the pain wasn't enough to produce tears. "My niece was inside. We can't find her." She dropped her head into her hands. "I have to go get my mother."

"No one leaves Beslan. Identification."

"Please!" She looked up at him. "My name is Nadia Andreyeva. My niece, Ludmilla, she's only eleven."

A thin, brown-haired soldier approached the car and whispered something into the man's ear. The burly soldier nodded. "Open the trunk."

Officially speaking, there was no crime in the Soviet Union, so older model cars had no locks. If this trunk had one, she was screwed. When Zara stepped out of the car, both soldiers' eyes dropped to her tight skirt. *Rossiiskie sviny*. She gave the Russian pigs a demure smile and walked behind the sputtering vehicle. She ran her fingers under the trunk lip and found a latch. The trunk creaked open.

The soldiers peered inside. Empty. The second solider, a lanky kid who looked too young to be in uniform, smiled at her. "We're not supposed to let anyone out of town. But we understand how difficult this is for your family." His eyes rested on her chest.

"*Spaciba*." She flung her arms around his neck and thanked him repeatedly between manufactured sobs. When his hand wandered too far down her back, she pressed against him before pulling away. "Will you be here when I get back?" He was under her control. Completely.

"*Da*." He looked at his comrade and smiled. "Waiting right here for you, Nadia."

"I'll hurry back." She slammed the trunk and slid back into the car. Had it not been for the truckload of soldiers behind them, she would have grabbed one of their guns and shot them both dead. Instead, she mouthed, "thank you," and drove away without directions to Vladikavkaz.

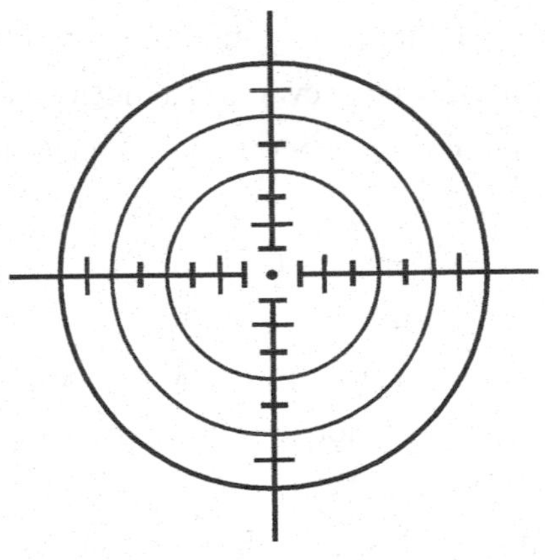

CHAPTER EIGHT

With a final glance back at the dead girl's body, still lying on the ground near the Range Rover, Maggie stuffed the envelope back into Zara's purse and retrieved the medical supplies. From inside the car, she grabbed her backpack and placed the purse and satellite phone inside, along with several bottled waters and energy bars. Then she pulled the camera strap over her head and fumbled with the camera, finally managing to eject the memory card, which she slid into her pants pocket.

Back at the medical tent, Dr. McCauley sat in a folding chair guzzling water. Jennifer, the State Department official, sat off in the distance under the shade of an oak tree.

"Here are the bandages. Do you need anything else?"

He shook his head. "They evacuated the first group of patients. All we can do is wait for more people to escape or for the terrorists to surrender."

"I don't think they'll surrender."

He pressed his lips together.

Maggie left him to his thoughts and stepped outside. Soldiers stood in small groups while local police manned a makeshift perimeter around the school. Why weren't they doing something? She gnawed on her lip. None of these soldiers looked like special forces. They had the physique and undisciplined demeanor of new conscripts who'd rather be anywhere else. And speaking of inexperienced, where the hell was Tom? He'd better be gathering intelligence on how the Russians planned to end the siege.

She sank to the ground and opened her backpack. Pulling the envelope from Zara's purse, she extracted a single sheet of paper—a handwritten note dated November 3, 2002. It took a moment for her brain to process the Russian. Even then, she couldn't translate every word.

But she got the gist of it.

It was a condolence letter to Zara, thanking her for her brother's dedication to Chechnya's freedom. The author regretted that Ramzan had perished in the gas attack perpetrated by the vile Russian imperialists.

Ramzan? Had Zara mentioned another brother? She wracked her brain. *Yes*, she thought. Zara told her that her mother and brother had been killed by the Russians. They'd talked about it last year as her younger brother, Dhokar, lay dying of a gunshot wound.

Maggie shook off the memory of the dilapidated farmhouse and the tinge of sympathy she'd felt for Zara. The dead child lying near the Range Rover and the dozens of wounded Dr. McAuley had treated served as a harsh reminder that Zara was an unrepentant killer willing to harm even the most innocent.

She cracked open a bottle of water and skimmed through the letter again. Gas attack? Ramzan must have been one of the terrorists involved in the Moscow theater siege. More than a hundred hostages had died, either at the hands of the terrorists or from the gas that *Spetsnaz* troops had pumped into the theater. Next, she pulled the wrinkled newspaper clipping from the purse. Embedded in a report about the theater siege was a grainy black-and-white photograph of Yuri Markov.

Maggie didn't know the former KGB man personally, but Warner did. From what she could decipher from the article, Markov had praised the Russian government for killing Chechen rebels, something he'd been stridently advocating ever since Boris Yeltsin fired him in 1999. She made a mental note to ask Warner what he knew about the old KGB boss.

She retrieved the satellite phone from her backpack and dialed Warner's cell phone. No answer. "Ugh," she grunted in frustration. Maybe he was at the office. She glanced at her watch and did the math.

It wasn't even 5:00 a.m., but it was worth a shot.

"Warner Thompson."

"What are you doing in the office?"

"Couldn't sleep. Wanted to be here in case anything developed over there."

"Well, there have been developments. I found her."

"Who?"

"Zara. She was inside the school."

"In Beslan?"

"Yes." Maggie nodded vigorously. "I didn't recognize her at first, but then she saw me, and took off. I couldn't catch her because the little girl was—"

"Little girl?"

Maggie closed her eyes as if it would help her forget what she'd seen. "Warner, I have Zara's address. I found it in her purse."

"Whose purse? The little girl's?"

"What? No, Zara dropped her purse when she ran off. Warner, I—"

"Where's the rest of the team?"

"I'm with two of them. The other, Tom, one of your new operations officers, is running around like he owns the place."

He grunted. "You're positive it was Zara?"

"One hundred percent. Look at the photos from inside the school. The woman."

"I saw those. There's only one woman and most of her face is covered."

"Damn it, Warner, I saw her up close. No veil. It's her." She checked her jeans pocket for the camera's memory card. "In fact, I took of couple of pictures of her."

"Any way you can send the photos?"

"I don't think so. I don't have a laptop and," she scanned the surroundings, "I doubt I could find an internet connection around here."

"I'll call the embassy. Have the station chief pass this information to his counterpart at the FSB. Maybe they can find Zara."

She slung the backpack over her shoulder and stood. "There's nothing else I can do here. I'm going to head into the town, find out if anyone saw her."

"Take Tom with you."

Maggie swiped at the dirt on her pantleg. "Okay." She disconnected and returned to the tent. "Have you seen Tom, Dr. McAuley?"

"No. I think he's off doing his spy thing."

"If you see him, let him know I went into town to follow a lead."

• ★ ★ ★ •

Maggie flashed her US Embassy identification card at the Russian police officers guarding what passed for a barricade about a hundred yards from the school. A stout, middle-aged officer with a face drawn from exhaustion pushed himself off a wooden trestle that tottered precipitously in rcsponsc.

She pointed to the street just beyond them, and raised the satellite phone. "*Amerikanskoye posol'stvo.*"

The officer frowned but let her pass.

She wove her way around several police cars blocking the road leading to the school. Just ahead, a small crowd of people gathered. Elderly women sobbed into handkerchiefs. One wailed, shaking her fist at the sky. A thin, unshaven man spoke with a smartly dressed woman who recorded his words on a mini cassette recorder.

Maggie approached a young woman at the edge of the crowd. "*Vy govorite po-angliyski?*"

She shook her head but tapped the shoulder of the woman next to her.

"English?"

"Yes." The woman tilted her head and studied Maggie.

"I'm looking for a woman who may have passed through here forty-five minutes or an hour ago. About this tall." She raised her hand to her chin. "Straight black hair. Black skirt and red sweater. Attractive."

The woman spoke to several others around her in rapid Russian. They all shook their heads.

She turned to Maggie. "Sorry."

"Thanks, anyway." Hands on her hips, she surveyed the rest of the crowd. "One more thing. Can I rent a car here?"

"Today?" The woman raised an eyebrow. "Business is not open. Everyone knows someone in the school."

"How far is it to Grozny?"

"Not even two hours away."

Maggie ran a hand through her hair. "That way to the town?" She gestured over her shoulder."

The woman nodded.

Maggie trotted away down a wide road lined with hulking, Soviet-style buildings a half dozen stories tall. Minutes later, she found herself in a central square ringed with pastel-colored prerevolutionary buildings. Clusters of ordinary Russians huddled together, speaking in hushed tones.

Police officers stood along the far sides of the square, their alert eyes scanning for danger, as if the siege at the school might suddenly descend on the town center.

She sat at a table outside an empty café and called Warner again. "I think I should go to Grozny."

"What? Don't tell me you think Zara would go home."

"No, of course not, she's not stupid. She knows I recognized her." She glanced around the square. To the right was a dusty, mustard-yellow Lada with a taxi sign on the roof. "But maybe I can get a lead from family or neighbors."

"Let the Russians handle that."

Maggie tapped her fingers on the metal tabletop. "No one in Grozny is going to talk to the Russians. And after today, the Russians will treat every Chechen like a terrorist."

"It's a war zone, Maggie."

"Technically, yes, but all the recent skirmishes have been Chechens ambushing Russian troops. I'm just going to check Zara's apartment. I'll be in and out in a half hour."

"Is Tom going with you?"

"He's off somewhere. I can't find him, and I don't think he has a phone." Not that she'd looked. But the last thing she needed was a rookie case officer to tag along and try to dictate her every move.

"I don't like this, Maggie. Not one bit."

"I know. I'll call you when I get there."

Maggie disconnected the call and approached the taxi. Inside, an obese man sat slumped in the driver's seat, eyes shut, mouth agape. Maggie tapped on the window. He startled, forced open one eye, and mumbled something unintelligible behind the glass.

He cranked the window halfway down and squinted at Maggie.

"Grozny. Chechnya. *Skol'ko?* How much?"

The man cleared his throat, a rattling, low sound emanating from his chest. "Grozny?"

Maggie nodded.

"*Nyet.*" He waved her off.

She fished around in her backpack, extracting a crisp hundred-dollar bill.

The cab driver's eyes widened. He pushed open the door, and swung his thick legs to the pavement, his gaze locked on the small fortune Maggie held.

"Vy govorite po-russki?"

"Nemnogo."

She held her forefinger and thumb close together. With much effort, her Russian had improved vastly over the past year, but she'd pretend otherwise. That way she could avoid answering questions about why she was going to the capital of Chechnya.

"Maggie!" Tom, the young operations officer was striding across the road in her direction. "What the hell are you doing?"

"I'll be back in a few hours. Any questions, call your boss."

The taxi driver snatched the American bill from her, opened the rear passenger door, and smiled. "Grozny."

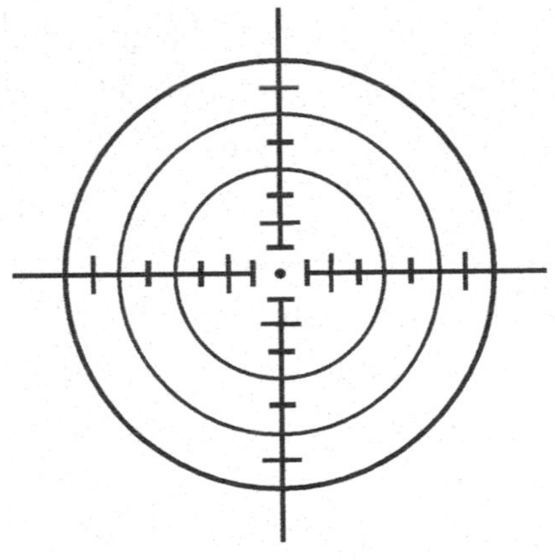

CHAPTER NINE

CIA Headquarters
Thursday, September 2, 2004, 5:00 a.m.

Warner paced the length of his office, pausing only to take a sip of coffee, wishing he had some bourbon to add to it. It was too early to start drinking, but Maggie had a talent for pushing his stress level into overdrive. According to the latest intelligence, the former president of a neighboring republic in southern Russia had been allowed into the school to meet with the terrorists. Maybe this mess would end quickly. Then the Russians could hunt Zara and Maggie could return to the safety of the embassy. But for now, he couldn't relax, not with her pursuing her fiancé's assassin. A woman everyone thought was dead. Everyone except for Maggie.

After the events of the past year, Maggie had a reputation at Langley. Multiple reputations, actually, depending on who you asked. Many who knew about her role in uncovering and helping to thwart a terrorist attack against the United States viewed her as a legend in the making. But there were others who considered her a loose cannon liable to ignore the rules when they got in her way. The truth lay somewhere in the middle—she could be both heroic and reckless. It was the latter character trait that had kept him awake most of the night.

He sank into the chair behind his desk and took a final swig of coffee. Bob Markham, his station chief in Moscow, wouldn't be happy to hear about Maggie's trip to Grozny. And if the ambassador found out, he'd blow a gasket. Perhaps it would be best to keep him out of the loop for now.

Warner swiveled and stared out the window while he waited for the secure call to connect. In another hour, the rising sun would illuminate the first hint of fall color on a handful of red maple trees outside.

"Bob, I got an update from Maggie."

His man in Moscow didn't take well to the news about Maggie. "Why didn't Tom go instead? He's the operations guy, not Maggie."

"Apparently, he was off doing his own thing."

"No wonder he didn't answer my calls," muttered Markham.

"Look, I'm not thrilled about this, but Maggie knows Zara better than anyone. She's just going to ask some questions and get out."

Markham exhaled loudly. "Let me know the second you hear from her. If the ambassador finds out that someone on his official delegation has left Beslan—"

"She should be back in four or five hours. I'll keep you posted."

Warner hung up and rubbed his eyes. He'd feel a whole lot better with backup in Grozny. Just in case. Tom was probably too green. And headstrong. Maggie wouldn't listen to someone like him because she was even more stubborn. He began to flip through his Rolodex.

"Yuri!" he breathed. A former high-ranking KGB officer who now split his time between New York City and Washington, DC, Yuri still had strong ties with Russian intelligence. And an even stronger influence with the Russian mafia. No doubt he could send someone to put eyes on Maggie. He pulled out a card marked only with a phone number and the letter *Y*. Then it occurred to him. He was due for his periodic security reinvestigation. Which meant a polygraph awaited. He couldn't expect to pass the polygraph if he enlisted the aid of a foreign national, much less a former KGB bigwig, to track down a CIA intelligence analyst. They always asked about contacts with foreign nationals. He drummed his fingers on the desk. There had to be someone he could trust. Someone close by.

His gaze shifted to a group of framed photographs on the built-in mahogany bookcases behind the desk. *Roger Patterson?* Roger had quit the CIA just weeks before the 9/11 attacks out of frustration over increasingly tight restrictions around recruiting assets. He and Roger had come to blows several times over his efforts to recruit agents with known human rights "issues," as the politicians called them. Warner abhorred these restrictions as much as Roger, but his hands had been tied. Congress threatened the Agency with funding cuts if it continued to recruit individuals with violent backgrounds. Roger had found these restrictions inane and tendered his resignation. But now, after a stint at a buttoned-up Ivy League MBA-run government consulting firm, he was back, working in the CIA station in Tbilisi,

Georgia. In the wake of Steve Ryder's murder and the scandal that ensued, several seasoned operations officers had turned down the assignment to fill the post. That's when Warner approached Roger. It took much persuasion—lubricated by expensive liquor and a sumptuous dinner at Red Sage—to convince Roger to return to the Agency and help clean up the mess in Tbilisi.

Warner found the number and dialed.

"Patterson."

"Roger, it's me."

"Me, who?"

"Warner."

"You must have the wrong number. I don't know anyone named Warner."

"Roger—" He exhaled loudly. Patterson was one of the best operations officers he'd ever managed. But he was also the most infuriating. "I need your help."

"I'm here to serve, boss."

"I need you in Grozny, stat."

"This have something to do with the Beslan siege?"

"Yeah. One of our analysts arrived in Beslan today. She's on her way to Grozny to follow a lead."

"An analyst?"

"Maggie Jenkins."

"Steve Ryder's fiancé? The analyst who played spy, killed terrorists, and saved the world?"

"The one and only. She's quite capable, as I'm sure you've heard, but I'd feel a lot better with you at her side."

"Glad to ride to the rescue, but you realize Chechnya's a five-hour drive from here?"

"I do. The sooner you hit the road, the better."

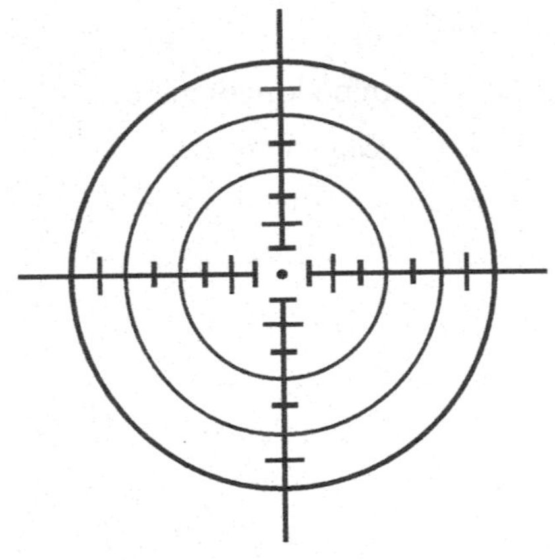

CHAPTER TEN

The Chechen Republic, Russia
Thursday, September 2, 2004, 2:30 p.m.

On the way out of Beslan, they'd stopped at a service station for gas, an oil top-off, and air for the tires. The Lada moved more quickly, but not by much, than its driver, who'd chatted at length with the gas station attendant. Finally, he'd returned to the car and driven along a highway that wound through several increasingly remote villages. A radio station covering the Beslan story droned on incessantly. One report provided a lengthy overview of both the first and second Chechen wars for independence from Russia. Thousands of Russian and Chechen forces and possibly up to 100,000 civilians had been killed in the first war, which ended with a peace treaty in 1997. The second war broke out two years later and while it was still ongoing, there were no longer major combat operations in Chechnya. Instead, some Chechens had turned to asymmetrical terrorist attacks, including, as the report pointed out, the hostage crisis at the Moscow theater. Throughout the news stories, the driver muttered repeatedly to himself. The only words Maggie caught were *Putin* and *Chechenskiy.*

In the distance, the outlines of a city formed. Soon, the taxi was bouncing over gaping potholes on the approach to Grozny. Minutes later, they passed the first of innumerable abandoned buildings whose skeletal remains were held together with pockmarked concrete walls. Several structures were nothing but burned-out shells with balcony railings hanging like broken limbs. On the side of the road, a dark-haired boy with serious eyes jumped from one large chunk of concrete to the next.

Maggie watched the boy disappear behind a partially collapsed wall. As they drew closer to the center of the city, the change was stark. Several apartment buildings had newly whitewashed façades, the road was smooth, and an outdoor market was crowded with women and children. This was the Chechnya the Russians wanted the world to see.

But then, suddenly, ahead was more devastation. Buildings with blown-out windows and doors that dangled precariously above uneven sidewalks. Trash skittered and danced along the dusty roadside. To the right, hundreds of Russian soldiers milled about the crater of a vacant lot. Chairs and tables lined the perimeter, serving as an outdoor dining hall for the dirty, haggard conscripts.

Just beyond them, the driver slowed to a stop at a checkpoint where heavily armed Russian soldiers surrounded the car. They examined the driver's license and spoke to him outside of the car.

Moments later, they directed Maggie to exit on the opposite side. She produced her personal passport and explained, "*Ya zhurnalist.*" If they searched her backpack, they'd find her embassy ID and official passport and quickly figure out that she wasn't, in fact, a journalist. Pasting on a pleasant smile, she shifted from foot to foot and glanced at her watch as if she were late for an appointment. After a few minutes of discussion with the driver, one of the men, a well-built man with dark hair and bright blue eyes, returned her passport.

Inside the car, she exhaled and caught the driver studying her in the rearview mirror. That could've been a disaster.

Just past the soldiers, the driver pulled to the side of the road and pointed to the left. "*Prospekt Revolyutsii.*"

Revolution Avenue. Zara's street address. If she found her, then what? Alert the Russian soldiers who could've easily detained her back at the roadblock? She shook her head. What had she been thinking? She should've stayed in Beslan. After all, the rational side of her knew that Zara wouldn't dare return home. It was preposterous to think otherwise.

"*Devuskha? Prospekt Revolyutsii.*"

"Yes, sorry. *Da.*" Maybe Warner was right. One of these days, the Russians would catch up with Zara. She briefly considered having the taxi driver turn around and take her back to Beslan. But that might attract even more unwelcome attention from the soldiers. Better that she act the part of the journalist and at least check out Zara's address. Looking around for a few minutes couldn't hurt.

"*Tridtsat' minut,*" she said to the driver as she pulled another hundred-dollar bill from her backpack and waved it in front of her face.

His eyes widened and locked with hers in the rearview mirror. He turned in the seat and reached for the crisp American currency.

Maggie slid it in her backpack. "Thirty minutes," she repeated. "*Tridsat' minut.*"

Maggie walked along Revolution Avenue, garnering curious stares and wary glances along the way. She pulled together her cover story—she was a freelance journalist doing a story on how the war with Russia had devastated entire Chechen families.

Zara's apartment building was about a dozen stories tall, and although it was in better condition than the structures down the street, it'd obviously taken some direct mortar hits. Even if Zara wasn't here, someone might know about her role in Beslan. And certainly everyone would know that Ramzan had died in the Moscow theater siege and Dhokar in Georgia last year.

Just then, a petite woman in black polyester pants and a gray blouse emerged from the apartment building.

"Excuse me," Maggie called in Russian.

The woman eyed her warily.

Maggie held up her hands. "I'm sorry to startle you. I'm a journalist interviewing families who've been affected by the war."

The woman clutched a denim purse to her side.

"I want to make sure the world knows what's happened here. Do you know anyone who might want to tell their story? Maybe a family that lost a son?"

"Everyone has lost someone." Her voice was little more than a whisper. "That's what happens in war."

Maggie stepped closer and lowered her voice.

"I sympathize with the Chechen people."

The woman glanced over Maggie's shoulder. "No Russians with you?"

"No Russians." Maggie pointed to the building. "Do you live here?"

"Yes."

"I'm looking for someone you may know. A woman named Barayeva. She lost both her brothers in the past two years." Maggie held her breath.

"Zara's been away a long time," the woman said, glancing over her shoulder.

"What about her family?"

"There's only an aunt left." The woman's gaze jumped from one end of the street to the other. "Everyone else was killed."

"When's the last time you saw Zara?"

The woman's eyes narrowed. "I don't remember. If you'll excuse me, I must go."

Maggie stepped toward the woman. "Wait, please," she said, hoping she didn't sound desperate. "It's very important that I find Zara."

"You shouldn't be asking about her around here." She turned to leave.

Maggie grabbed her by the sleeve. "Why not?"

She shook free of Maggie. "The Russians always seem to be looking for her."

"So she is alive?" Maggie had just seen her with her own eyes, but now she knew for certain.

"Last I heard. Why are you so interested in her?"

"It's such a tragic story. The world should know what the Russians have done here, don't you think?"

"Of course. But even if you could find Zara, I don't know that she would talk to you. She's not the same girl she used to be. Not after her mother died." The woman shook her head. "Killed in a bombing at her school. And just a few months ago, her father was caught in crossfire between the Russians and Chechens." She shook her head again. "One brother died in Moscow and another died last autumn. They're all gone."

"That's awful." If they'd been talking about anyone other than Zara, Maggie would've meant it.

"It is. The only person she has left is her aunt. The old woman is lost without her niece to help her."

"An aunt?"

"Yes. Tries to get by selling bread at the market."

Maggie tried to contain her excitement. "The market in the city center?"

She pointed to the right. "Yes. About one kilometer that way."

"What's her name?"

"Natalia Barayeva." The woman sighed. "Poor soul."

Maggie scanned the marketplace. People—mainly desperate-looking women—hawked wares, from old blankets and worn clothes to potatoes and homemade preserves. Several tables away stood a round, older woman with sad, deep lines cutting across her face. On her table sat lumps of thick-crusted bread. Maggie bypassed a small crowd surrounding a table covered with potatoes and turnips. She pulled out her phone and snapped a quick shot of the woman.

"Natalia Barayeva?"

Dull brown eyes settled on Maggie's face. "*Da.*"

Maggie repeated the cover story she'd told the woman outside the apartment building.

"I don't know anything."

"Is Zara Barayeva your niece?"

"No." Tears filled her eyes. She looked behind Maggie as if she expected someone to be watching them.

"Look, I know you are Zara's aunt. When's the last time you heard from her?"

The old woman squinted in confusion. "Who are you?"

Maggie explained again that she was a journalist.

Natalia's wrinkled face softened. "You're not Russian."

"No. I'm American."

"She was such a beautiful little ballerina. But now there is no ballet." She shook a meaty fist in the air. "Do you see what the Russians have done to us?"

"I understand you've lost many family members?"

The woman's arm dropped. "Yes. My brothers, my nephews." She leaned on the table as if she'd fall without its support. "I'm all alone."

"But you still have Zara," Maggie prompted.

"Not really."

"Did she move away?"

"I see her sometimes, but—" she cut herself off and glanced around the marketplace.

Maggie leaned in closer. "But what?"

"I can't say any more. Zara will get angry."

Maggie's heart rate picked up. "How much for your bread?"

The woman shrugged. "Whatever you can pay, I accept. The war has made it so hard."

Maggie placed a twenty-dollar bill in the woman's sweaty palm.

She looked at it, confused at first. Then a smile creased her round face. "I can give this to Zara. For London."

"She's going to London?"

The old woman's hand flew to her mouth. "I'm not supposed to tell anyone. What have I done? The Russians, they will find her and kill her."

"I am not with the Russians. I am American. Many of us side with Chechnya."

The woman, her hand still on her mouth, kept shaking her head, her eyes darting around frantically, as if looking for someone to come out of nowhere to punish her.

Maggie put her hand on the woman's shoulder to calm her down and focus her. "When is she leaving? You can tell me, I won't tell anyone."

The woman stared at the American money in Maggie's other hand.

Maggie offered her another twenty dollars. "When is she leaving?"

"Today. She phoned and said she might not be back for a while." Her dark eyes filled with tears. "She's all I have left."

"If I know where she's staying in London, I can find her, tell her to come home."

Natalia shrugged. "If Imran lets her."

"Who's Imran?"

"Her boyfriend. She says he's a very important man."

Maggie tucked away the name Imran. "May I see her apartment?"

Before Natalia could answer, Maggie noticed that the lanky blond man selling used magazines at the adjacent table was hurrying toward her with one hand inside his black leather jacket. In the next moment, his arm was raised. The sun glinted off something in his hand. She hesitated only a moment before upending Natalia Barayeva's solid wooden table, diving behind it just as gunshots exploded nearby. The old woman crashed to the ground next to Maggie, an arm hanging loosely at her side. Blood spread across the synthetic fabric of her blouse like a blooming flower. Screams broke through the stunned silence.

"Please help me," the woman moaned as she swiped at her tears with bloodstained fingers.

"It's okay, Natalia. Help will be here soon."

"Tell Zara." She closed her eyes. "Please tell Zara to come home."

Maggie opened her cell phone again and snapped two quick photos of the injured woman. "I will, Natalia. I'll tell her." She peered up from behind the table. Two men were fighting with the blond man for control of his gun. Dozens of Russian soldiers materialized, weapons raised.

Maggie sprinted from the square all the way past Zara's apartment. Not surprisingly, her taxi was gone. She turned down a narrow alley that led to another running behind the apartment building. A metal fence separated the alley from a vacant lot. After a pause to catch her breath, she scrambled over the fence and lowered herself into what remained of a bombed-out building's basement. The shock of the eight-foot drop sent a jolt up her feet into her shins. "Ouch," she muttered. Over in the corner, she slipped into a small, closet-like space with three intact walls and a partial ceiling of sorts formed by a fallen chunk of concrete.

She dislodged the backpack from her shoulder and scoured inside for the satellite phone.

"Maggie, you okay?"

"Yeah. If you don't count the fact that some Russian guy just tried to kill me."

"What?"

"He missed. I don't suppose anyone can come get me?"

"We're trying to get ahold of Tom. But I was worried, so—"

"Warner?" The connection had cut off. "Warner?" Maggie yelled louder, as if that would help. She stared at the phone, but of course that didn't help either and so she redialed. Nothing.

"Come on," she muttered as she punched in the numbers again and again. She was about to give up when suddenly the phone buzzed.

"Warner?"

"Yes, you okay?"

"I am now. You were saying?"

"I dispatched a case officer from Tbilisi to come get you."

Maggie stiffened. Tbilisi had been Steve's posting. "Oh."

"He should be there by seven. Can you hold out?"

She looked at her watch: 5:42. "It's not like I have a choice. Where do I meet him?"

"Stay hidden. I'll send him to you."

She emerged from her hiding spot and looked up. There were a couple more hours of daylight, if that. "Okay, I'm in the basement of a shelled-out building directly behind an apartment building at 32 Revolution Avenue. About a kilometer from the central market square."

"Revolution Avenue," he repeated. "Sit tight."

"I will."

"Please do. You can't keep running off and doing your own thing. One of these times, it's going to cost you."

Hasn't it already? "I'm sorry, Warner."

"We'll talk about it when this is over."

"Sure. In the meantime, I have reason to believe that Zara's heading to—" The satellite phone emitted a series of beeps. "Warner?" The display screen faded to black. The battery was dead.

She swore and turned to her makeshift closet, pausing just outside of it. Unease passed through her. Claustrophobia was something she'd never experienced until last year, when she'd been locked in a closet before her first encounter with Zara. She sank to the floor just outside the space, thirsty, famished, exhausted. And defeated. Zara was gone. At least for now. If there was a bright side, it was that surely someone, a police or intelligence agency, would be able to find Zara in London. If that's where she was, in fact, going.

A little after 7:00, a sudden scuffling shook Maggie from a dazed state. She stood and hoisted the backpack over her shoulder. There it was again, a scuffle of something against the dirt and crumbled concrete surrounding the building's basement. Flattening herself against the wall, she peered up.

"Maggie?" It was an unfamiliar voice.

She snatched a jagged sliver of glass from the floor and crept along the wall. To the right, at the edge of the foundation, stood a tall, dark-haired man with chiseled features. He looked like Paul Newman—minus forty years, plus fifteen pounds of muscle.

"Anyone home?" he called.

Definitely an American accent. She stepped into view.

"Maggie, I presume?"

She nodded.

"Roger Patterson." He glanced around behind him. "Directorate of Operations. I believe we both know Warner."

She ran Roger's name and face through her mental databank but came up empty. His was a face that she'd remember. And she didn't think Steve had ever mentioned someone named Roger. But that didn't mean they hadn't known each other. The case officer cadre was a small, elite fraternity within the Agency, which meant Roger probably knew her life story. Everyone else seemed to. Sometimes she felt like she was starring in her own reality show while thousands of CIA employees watched.

"Come on, let's get you out of here." He waved her toward him.

She scanned the area and trotted over to a debris pile comprised of plaster, brick, concrete, and dirt. Standing precariously atop the heap, she lifted her arms. "Help me up."

Roger dropped to his knees and reached his hands down into the basement. Maggie clasped her fingers around his wrists and used her shoes against the wall to push herself upward as he pulled. With a final grunt, Roger yanked her to the top edge of the wall. She swung both legs over and shook out her arms.

"I've heard a lot about you," he said.

As she pushed hair out of her face, she found herself staring into crystal blue eyes lit with a hint of mischief. He smiled a disarming, dazzling smile.

Maggie flushed. "Thanks for coming to get me."

"The pleasure is all mine."

"I . . . um." She brushed dirt from her sleeves. "I have to get out of here."

"My car is a block from the market square." He pulled a black scarf from his back pocket. "Cover your hair. You look foreign."

Maggie draped the scarf over her head, securing it with a knot at the nape of her neck, kerchief style.

They turned into the alley that led to the market, Roger leading the way. Russian soldiers surrounded the perimeter of the now empty square. One of the soldiers took interest in them, signaling to a comrade to follow him.

"Are they looking for me?"

Roger grabbed Maggie by the arms and spun her around so her back was to the soldiers. Loud enough for the Russians to hear, he switched to Russian, begging for Maggie's forgiveness and pledging his undying love.

Maggie stared at him, bewildered. "Don't turn around," he hissed. Placing both hands on her cheeks, he leaned in, and kissed her, pausing only to utter words of contrition as the soldiers passed. "I'm so sorry, my love." He resumed kissing her.

Maggie gave in to his lips, surprised by his tenderness. But then it was over, as fast as it had begun. The soldiers had returned to their post on the far end of the square.

Roger dropped his hands from her face. "We're clear. Act like we are lovers who just made up." He clasped her right hand in his left. "Let's go."

Maggie followed, too flustered to utter a word.

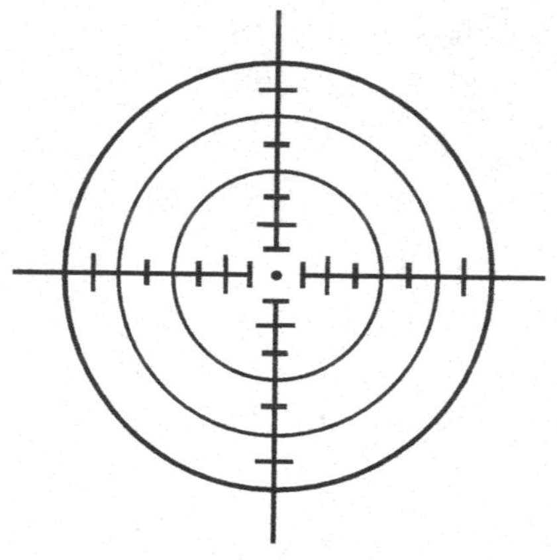

CHAPTER ELEVEN

London
Thursday, September 2, 2004, 4:00 p.m.

Imran Bukayev poured another cognac to toast his success. He was starting to feel the liquor's effects, so he capped the bottle and lowered it into its hiding spot inside a vase. Now that he was becoming more devout, he felt guilty for drinking. His new Saudi friends certainly wouldn't approve. Liquor was *haram*, forbidden, in Islam. But he was weak. After all, he'd lived most of his life like a Soviet. Then, as a Russian. It wasn't until the past ten years that he'd begun to view himself as a Chechen. And now, as a Muslim, a servant of Allah. He downed the cognac, savoring the warmth as it slid down his throat. He vowed again that this would be his last taste of alcohol. *Insha'allah.* Allah willing.

The school siege had gone better than he'd dared to hope. In fact, nothing had gone wrong. And even though Beslan had been a soft target, a trial run of sorts, his Arab friends would be impressed. They didn't need to know that external funding and information had helped ensure the attack's success. And he certainly wouldn't reveal anything about the benefactor's identity. That juicy bit of information was too valuable to share. He'd lied to the Saudis, said the money had been diverted from a charity fund established to help the world's displaced Muslims.

Beslan's success meant the upcoming mission would be even more spectacular. The target and timing hadn't been his idea, but after a while, the plan had grown on him. And now everything was about to come full circle, and justice—Allah's justice—would be restored.

Bukayev opened a safe concealed behind a vibrant abstract painting whose color scheme might appear, to the untrained eye, to be the work of a child. He pulled out a list of the Beslan attackers—all denoted in code, of course, and wondered who, if anyone, would survive the siege. Of course, survival wasn't really the point. The goal was maximum devastation. But, still, he would need to know who was alive, and even more important, if anyone had been captured. His people were trained by some of the best in the business to withstand interrogation techniques. Even so, any of them could crack under Russian torture. But if they did, he reminded himself, none of the operatives knew his true name. Except for one—Zara. The one who'd been so instrumental in planning the next attack. With any luck, she was dead.

The grandfather clock in the corner chimed. He grabbed a light jacket and rushed several blocks to the mosque. He had plenty of time before *Salatu-l-Asr,* the afternoon prayer, but he wanted to get there early to reassure everyone. As a spokesman for the Chechen government-in-exile, he would condemn the men who'd taken hundreds of innocent lives in Beslan. But he'd also call on Moscow to cease its endless war against the gentle people of Chechnya. It was Moscow's relentless brutality, after all, that had radicalized some of his countrymen. Decent people can tolerate only so much repression. The solution, he'd argue, was for Moscow to withdraw its troops from Chechnya. Immediately.

The mosque, whose moderate Imam routinely condemned terrorism, provided him with the perfect cover. The men here were vaguely sympathetic to Chechnya's plight, but few had any real interest in politics or *jihad*. Imran's two closest associates—the only ones he trusted from this mosque—acted as his liaison to his true home—the Finsbury Park Mosque. He could never set foot there because it was under constant surveillance by British authorities. Just last year, police had raided it and arrested several men they'd labeled as radicals. Across the street from the mosque, Bukayev smiled and nodded to one of his confidants as he made his way up the sidewalk.

"Omar, *assalamu'alaykum*." He embraced the portly Jordanian.

"*Alaykum Assalam*, Imran."

"How was your week?"

"Excellent. Business was brisk."

Bukayev laughed. "Indeed, it was, wasn't it?" The men crossed the street. Several people were milling around outside the mosque. "I need the technician to do some reprogramming."

The Jordanian lowered his voice. "How soon?"

"As soon as possible. There is another project underway with a slight change in personnel. Time is of the essence." Bukayev locked eyes with Omar before turning away to greet his fellow moderate Muslims.

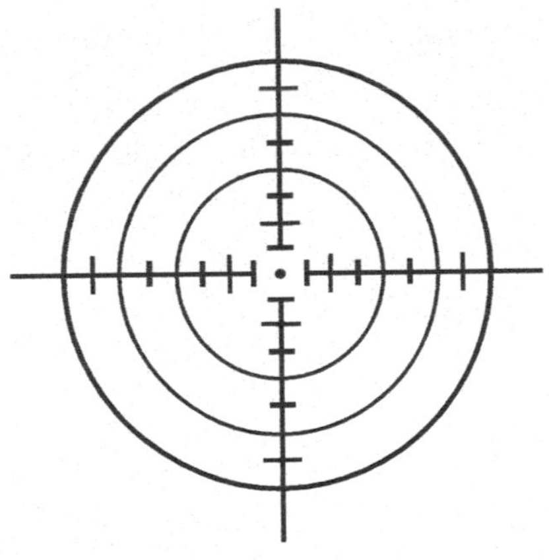

CHAPTER TWELVE

Roger's car, a Honda Accord with diplomatic plates, wound its way west toward Vladikavkaz. At the first military checkpoint, two Russian soldiers eyed Maggie with a mixture of suspicion and salaciousness. She tucked a stray curl under the scarf, held her breath, and looked out the opposite window. When the men began to fire questions at Roger, he pulled two bottles of Stolichnaya vodka and a carton of Marlboro cigarettes from under his seat. The soldiers decided that the contraband goods had more appeal than Maggie and waved the car on.

"Do you always travel with vodka and cigarettes?"

"Pretty much. Russians are suckers for American smokes. And vodka, of course."

Maggie stared out the window as the car careened through the devastated outskirts of the city.

"Can I ask what you were doing in Grozny?"

"Looking for information."

"About?"

"Beslan."

He studied her profile. "And?"

"I'm starving. I don't suppose there are any fast-food restaurants around here?"

"No, but there's water and some snacks in the backseat."

Maggie gulped down an entire bottle of water and munched on a few pretzels. Her eyes grew heavy, and the next thing she knew, Roger was shaking her shoulder as the car shuddered to a halt at the border between Russia and Georgia.

"Your passport, Maggie."

She blinked and looked around, momentarily disoriented. The car's headlights illuminated a sign informing travelers that they were leaving Russia. She handed her passport to Roger. "Will they question me?"

"It won't be a problem. I come bearing gifts, remember? A trunk full of them."

Roger doled out more vodka and cigarettes to the border guards and they were soon on their way. They drove along the Georgian Military Highway, passing through small mountainside villages illuminated only by the lights emanating from the windows of local farmhouses.

"You should come back here in the daylight. There are monasteries, ancient fortresses, gorges, lakes. It's quite beautiful."

"I've had more than my fill of Georgia."

"Yes, of course." He cleared his throat. "I heard about last year. About Steve. I'm really sorry."

Maggie nodded in the dark. She didn't want to talk about Steve, not with the man who had replaced him in the Tbilisi station. "Can I use your phone? I should tell Warner you found me."

"Of course, but you'll have to wait until we get closer to the capital. There's no signal out here."

Two hours later, they arrived in the outskirts of Tbilisi. The capital city's familiar blend of ancient, Soviet, and modern jolted her. She'd been in Tbilisi for fewer than forty-eight hours last year, but the sudden rush of memories was unstoppable, like an invading force with overwhelming power. Maggie leaned her tired head against the window and surrendered to them.

Dima's Restaurant in downtown Tbilisi. Men sweeping up piles of glass that the bomb had shattered. Bloodstained concrete on the spot where Steve died. Drawn to Tbilisi like a drowning woman flailing for the water's surface. She needed the truth. Who killed Steve?

Roger's voice startled her to the present. "Hey, Warner. Yup. The eagle has landed. The package is secure. The prodigal analyst—"

She extended her arm toward him demanding the phone. "Let me talk to him."

"Hang on, boss."

"I think Zara's going to London, Warner," she said the moment Roger had handed over the phone.

"Based on what?"

"What her aunt said. She may have a boyfriend there."

"I'll let London station know immediately."

"I think I should go—"

"No."

"But—"

"Put Roger back on."

She exhaled loudly and handed the phone back.

"Uh-huh . . . yup . . . will do."

Roger hung up and slowed at an intersection. "Who's Zara?"

She stared out at the mostly empty sidewalks.

They rode in silence for the next ten minutes until Roger turned onto Moskovskiy Prospect. "My apartment is a few blocks ahead."

Maggie sat bolt upright in the seat. "What are you doing?" A swell of panic rose in her throat.

"Going home." He flashed a smile. "Don't worry, I'll take the couch. And in the morning, I'm flying with you back to Moscow. Warner's orders."

Ahead on the right stood a looming Soviet-era apartment building. Steve's old apartment building. And the place where she'd narrowly escaped with her life. "Stop the car."

"What's the matter?"

"Stop the car!"

Roger pulled over to the curb and turned to her. "Are you okay?"

She pulled her wallet from the backpack and searched it until she found the scrap of paper with a phone number scrawled across it. Without asking, she snatched Roger's phone and dialed.

It was after midnight. *Please answer, please answer!*

"*Da*?"

"Tamaz? It's me, Maggie."

There was a long pause, followed by a low, gravelly voice, "Maggie? My dear, how are you?"

"I'm in Tbilisi, actually."

"Why? What's going on?"

Maggie heard the concern in Tamaz's voice. Theirs was a friendship borne of tragedy last year when Steve and Tamaz's brother, Josef, were victims of the same terrorist bombing. Unlike Steve, Josef had survived.

"I've been tracking Zara."

"Zara," he breathed.

"I know it's late, but can I stay at your place tonight? I'll explain when I get there."

Roger interrupted. "Who are you talking to?"

She ignored him. "Thank you, Tamaz. What's the address?" She locked eyes with Roger and recited it aloud. "I'll see you in a few minutes."

"Who the hell is Tamaz?"

"An old friend. Please take me to his apartment."

"I'm not taking you anywhere."

She pulled the door handle. "I'll walk."

"Whoa, whoa!" He grabbed her arm. "You win. I'll take you. But I want to meet this Tamaz."

"Fine. Just go."

"In the morning you're going with me to the airport."

She nodded.

He spun the car around and muttered, "If I had any idea you were going to be this difficult . . ."

Ten minutes later, Roger hurried to keep pace as Maggie trotted across the parking lot outside Tamaz's apartment complex. Inside the building, dim lighting cast a gloomy pall over gray tiled floors. They rode in silence to the fourth floor. There, the hall lighting was glaringly bright. Up ahead, Maggie knocked on the third door on the right. Moments later, Tamaz Ashkhanadze appeared, a wide grin replacing his usually dour expression.

After a hug and kisses on both her cheeks, Tamaz waved Maggie into the flat. "Who's your friend?"

"He not my friend," she sniffed. "He was just leaving."

Roger stepped into the apartment behind her. "Roger Patterson. State Department."

The Georgian extended a hand. "Tamaz Ashkhanadze, Ministry of Foreign Affairs."

"Really?"

"Yes. Warner knows him," Maggie spat before Tamaz could respond.

Tamaz's eyes flitted from Maggie to Roger.

"You can go now, Roger. I'll see you in the morning."

Roger raised an eyebrow. "I'll pick you up at 5:00 on my way to the airport."

"Fine."

"Good night, then. A pleasure to meet you, Tamaz."

"Likewise," Tamaz said to the door Maggie had already closed behind her. With any luck, she'd never see Roger Patterson again.

• ★ ★ ★ •

Maggie took in the small but exquisitely decorated living room. "Tamaz, it's lovely." A bright, intricately woven Georgian carpet offset muted eggshell walls. A cityscape of old Tbilisi hung above a sideboard table housing a collection of delicate antique vases. Beyond a hallway on the right was a tiny kitchen with a white double burner stove and a compact refrigerator. In the corner stood a simple wooden table draped with a lace cloth.

"Come sit. I'll fix tea while you explain what's going on." He gestured to the table.

As Tamaz bustled about, Maggie relayed the events of the past week, from Moscow to Beslan to Grozny.

"How can Zara be alive? The official report said all the kidnappers were killed last year."

"I know, Tamaz. But I saw her myself. In Beslan." She gestured toward the front door where her backpack sat on the floor. "I have her purse and photos of her. On top of that, two people in Grozny confirmed she was alive."

He emerged from the kitchen with a tray containing two steaming cups of tea, a loaf of bread, and a block of cheese. "She's a very dangerous woman. Why do you want to catch her yourself, Maggie? Why not get help?"

"I am. Getting help, that is."

"From Roger?" Tamaz asked as he sliced the cheese.

"No. From Warner."

"Ah." His face relaxed.

"I think Zara's on her way to London to meet her boyfriend. That's where Roger and I are flying tomorrow."

She felt terrible about lying but didn't want Tamaz to try to stop her.

"Who's her boyfriend?"

Maggie sipped her piping hot tea. "Imran somebody. I don't have a last name."

Tamaz grumbled, pushed his chair away from the table, and grabbed the receiver from the telephone set on a table in the corner.

"Who are you calling?"

"Josef. He might know who this Imran is. And he should know that Zara is alive."

When his brother answered, Tamaz broke into Georgian before Maggie could object. "Mmmh. Mmmh. Okay." He dropped the phone into the cradle where it landed with a thud. "Josef thinks Zara's boyfriend could be Imran Bukayev."

Zara knew Bukayev? Possibly. Imran Bukayev lived in London. The Agency believed he had ties to terrorists, a point it'd pressed repeatedly with British intelligence.

Tamaz leaned forward, elbows on the table. "I cannot let you go after someone like Bukayev on your own."

"I wasn't planning—" She cut herself short. There was no plan yet. "Warner's involved. And now Roger." She folded and unfolded her hands. "I can't let her get away, Tamaz. For all we know, she's plotting another attack."

Tamaz furrowed his thick brows. "I agree, but this is not your job to chase terrorists around the world."

"But she—"

"I know what she did. It's still not your job."

"The Agency needs my help."

"Please don't do anything foolish, Maggie."

"I won't."

Tamaz stepped closer. His piercing dark eyes locked with hers. "I'm afraid you are blinded by hate for this woman."

His words hit her in the gut. *Am I?* "It's been a long couple of days, Tamaz." She grabbed a few slices of cheese from the table. "I've got to get some sleep. Thank you again for letting me stay."

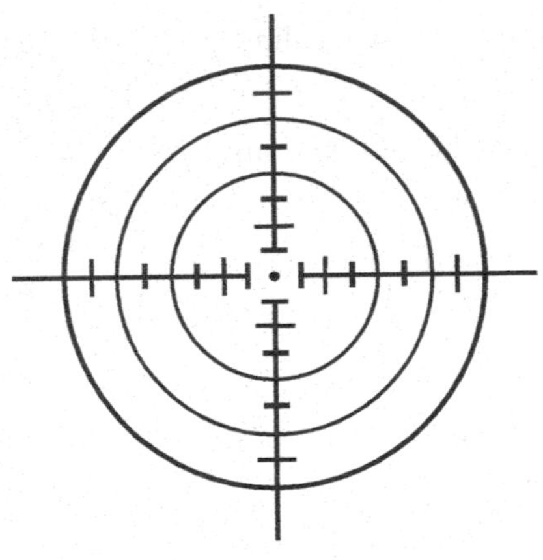

CHAPTER THIRTEEN

London
Friday, September 3, 2004, 10:00 a.m.

Zara clutched her travel bag and avoided making eye contact with her fellow passengers. With all she'd endured to get here, she didn't want to risk making an impression on anyone. After getting past the military roadblock outside Beslan, she'd driven south through the treacherous Georgian mountains. In Tbilisi, she booked a predawn flight to London and waited in the airport, almost certain that there'd be a dragnet out for her. But no one came.

Maggie Jenkins was the last person she'd expected to see outside that school. Zara took it as a sign that fate was on her side, that her plan was better than Imran's. In fact, she'd contemplated calling Imran to tell him what had transpired but decided it was too risky.

Now, she found herself surrounded by Westerners, everyone swaying together with the rhythmic motion of the tube. Zara examined them like a scientist studying a rare species. Most of the people were tuned out from their surroundings—either listening to music or typing messages into tiny cell phones. Westerners had no idea how vulnerable they were. If her bag were loaded with C4 instead of clothes, she could decimate the carriage and they'd never see it coming.

Just like Madrid.

As the train pulled into the Gloucester Road underground station, Zara forced her weary body from the seat and glanced around a final time. She was no expert in surveillance, but she was almost certain she wasn't being followed.

Outside the station, she took a minute to absorb the chaos of London. Honking taxis, screeching buses, seas of people bumping past. Everyone in such a purposeful hurry. Zara knew she had to keep moving, stay alert, remain inconspicuous. Melting into the crowd on the sidewalk, she made her way up Cromwell Road to Gloucester, where she ducked into a corner shop for supplies. After arming herself with a street map, a chocolate bar, and a bottle of water, she got her bearings and proceeded up Gloucester toward his neighborhood.

She'd considered finding a hotel but had a feeling she wouldn't need one. Once he saw her face, learned that she'd survived—and succeeded in her mission—he'd beg her to stay with him. She turned onto Lennox Place and stopped short. The homes' architecture and bright gardens exuded wealth and privilege, the kind she'd never known. What if he'd fallen sway to Western excess, what if he'd lost his fervor? Zara tried to dismiss the doubts clouding her mind as she walked slowly toward his house. She smoothed her hair and straightened the tight gray skirt that skimmed the tops of her knees. Here she was, terrorist extraordinaire, nervous as a schoolgirl on a first date.

She paused outside the front door. Maybe he didn't want to go back to Chechnya because he was too comfortable here. Then again, he couldn't go back. The Russian government had declared him a terrorist enemy of the state. So, here he was, living in posh surroundings, but didn't he deserve it after all he'd given to the cause? Zara fluffed the raven hair she'd just smoothed and knocked on the door.

Imran Bukayev opened the front door a crack. His jaw dropped at the sight of her. "Zara Barayeva," he whispered, as if seeing a ghost. "*Al-hamdu lil-lah*."

"Yes, it's me, Imran." She felt a jolt of excitement the second he spoke her name.

He opened the door wide enough to let her in, then glanced out at the neighborhood and locked the door behind them. "What are you doing here? I thought . . . they're still inside the school. How did you get out?" He brushed the hair from her forehead.

"I had my chance to die, Imran, but I knew you needed me more than Allah did."

Bukayev burst out laughing. "Zara, don't tell me you've ever cared about Allah."

Zara smiled and ran a finger across Bukayev's lips. "You know the only thing I believe in is my cause."

"Hush, my little apostate. I can't fraternize with the likes of you. So just pretend you believe."

Zara gave a coy grin. "So you'll keep me if I lie?"

Bukayev's eyes bore into Zara's. "I fear for you. Allah knows your heart and your motivation."

"You know them even better, Imran." She wasn't about to get sucked into another theological debate with him. When they'd first met years ago, he'd been a nationalistic, secular Chechen warrior. But when the Wahhabi descended on Chechnya, offering their oil money and puritanical brand of Islam, Bukayev had changed. The only bad habit he couldn't shake was Zara. Over the past few days, she'd wondered if Beslan had been his attempt to purge himself of her once and for all.

She brushed by Bukayev to explore the house. The lounge, which was larger than the apartment she'd grown up in, was decorated with chic modern furniture and abstract artwork.

"You feel no shame living with such extravagance while our brothers and sisters hide from Russian bombs and live without electricity?"

Bukayev's overgrown eyebrows shot up. "Are you accusing me of hypocrisy?" He snapped off the flat-panel television mounted on the wall. "If any of this were mine, I'd sell it all to help destroy the Russians."

"Your Saudi friends own this place?" She loathed the Saudis for their misogyny. "Haven't the Brits figured out that you're living well beyond the means of an ex-guerrilla in exile?"

Bukayev lowered himself onto the couch, too weary, it seemed, for the type of full-blown argument that punctuated their relationship. He ran a hand through his mass of unruly gray hair.

"They don't seem to believe Moscow's accusations about my connections to so-called terrorists. And Moscow hasn't helped itself win any allies against me. Some of their allegations are completely outlandish, and the British know it." He snickered and motioned for her to sit next to him. "Of course, some of the charges are true, but they can't prove them. And as long as the Brits think Moscow will execute me, they'll let me stay."

Zara couldn't resist this contradiction of a man. A liar telling so many truths. A jihadist living well among infidels. She stared into his eyes. A smile teased at the corners of her mouth. He, a Wahhabi puritan. She, an agnostic terrorist seeking revenge.

His breath caught in his throat as she kissed him softly. "When I get to America," she whispered, "I will get my justice."

"Zara—" Bukayev started to protest before his voice failed him. She ran her hands across his shoulders and began to unbutton his shirt.

"Finally, for my mother, my brothers." She kissed his neck. "And my father."

Bukayev let out a grunt, seized her arms, and shoved her off the couch.

Zara's head smacked the coffee table before the rest of her hit the floor. She blinked to clear the haze before her eyes and checked her hair for blood. "What the hell was that for?"

Bukayev stood, glaring at her. Shaking hands fumbled at his shirt buttons. "How dare you!"

"How dare I what?" Zara scrambled to her feet. "How dare I what?" she repeated, her voice rising to a shout.

Bukayev's olive skin darkened. "This is not about personal revenge for your family. It's about all the Chechen people. Not that it matters. You're not even part of the mission." He tucked his shirt in. "I didn't think you would survive this week, so I already replaced you with an equally talented assassin."

"But I'm the one who selected the targets. I know all the details. And I'm certainly not dead." She smoothed her hair, careful to avoid the welt rising on the back of her head. "Besides, who else can do the job like I can?"

Bukayev studied her. "I don't know."

She bit down hard on her lip to keep from smiling. He was putty in her hands. "So, I'm back in?"

He exhaled through his nose. "If I let you run the mission and find out that you've deviated from the plan, even the slightest, you're done."

"You didn't even know I survived Beslan." Zara gave a knowing laugh. "Yet you think you can control my every move?"

Bukayev grabbed her left wrist and twisted. "Don't you ever question my authority."

Zara tried to wrench herself free, but his grasp only tightened. "Let go of me, Imran."

He slapped her hard across the face. She stumbled back when he released her wrist.

"Like I said, if you stray from the mission, you're done." His face was twisted in anger. "Do you understand?"

Zara knew she had no choice. She'd have to remain silent about the Maggie Jenkins complication. Imran held the passports, the money, and the details. And he probably did have a substitute ready to take over her role, even though they both knew she was the best one for the job.

She'd never failed him, and she was more committed to the mission than the most zealous jihadist.

"I'm sorry, Imran, I was being selfish. You're right. We must avenge the wrongs perpetrated against all Chechens."

"Very well." Bukayev's face relaxed, but he didn't smile. "It's too dangerous for you to stay here. Meet me at the South Kensington underground entrance tomorrow at noon."

Before Zara could protest, Bukayev's home phone rang twice, then stopped. He ran to the window and moved the curtain aside a fraction of an inch. "You can't go."

"Why not?"

He released the curtain. "That was a warning. I have a friend who checks the neighborhood from time to time." He peered out the window again. "Could be the Russians."

"The Russians?"

"One of these days, they'll come after me. Right now, I think they're trying to intimidate me, let me know they haven't forgotten where I live."

Zara rushed over to him, forgetting his assault for a moment. "They're out there now?" She had to escape. She had to survive.

"Or it could be the Brits. After I complained about the Russians, they started patrolling the area more often."

Zara turned and dashed for the front door.

"Stop!" Bukayev was right behind her. "You can't go anywhere. Not now. If the Brits or the Russians figure out who you are, it's over. We'll both be in the Lubyanka by week's end."

Zara grabbed her travel bag. "I can get away." She flipped her hair away from her face. "I can blend in here. After all, I don't look like a terrorist."

"That's enough, Zara." He snatched the bag and shoved her down the hall. "You're staying."

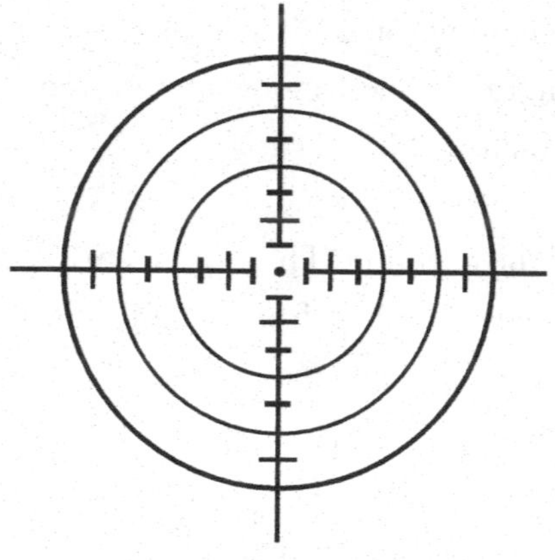

CHAPTER FOURTEEN

At noon, Maggie checked into the Grosvenor Kensington Hotel in West London. Once a Victorian mansion, its steeply pitched roof and ornate gables gave it the appearance of a royal residence. She rolled the suitcase she'd borrowed from Tamaz across the red carpeted floor to the elevator. Aside from the toiletries, two pairs of yoga pants, and three T-shirts she'd purchased at the Novo Alexeyevka Airport in Tbilisi, she was traveling light. The only thing weighing her down was her guilt. When Roger arrived at Tamaz's earlier this morning, he would've discovered that she had already left for the airport and was flying to London, not Moscow. Naturally, this meant that Warner knew too.

She was surprised that he hadn't sent a gaggle of CIA officers to intercept her at customs.

Her room was rather sparsely appointed for such a lovely hotel. A queen-sized bed, two nightstands, a dresser, and a standard hotel bathroom. After a long, steamy shower, she dressed, applied makeup, and styled her hair. After only two hours of sleep last night, what she really needed was a nap. Instead, she clicked on the television, watching in horror the footage from Beslan where two large explosions had rocked the school earlier in the day.

A massive firefight was ongoing between the Chechens, who used children as human shields, and the Russian military, which fired indiscriminately into the school. Hundreds reportedly were dead.

She switched off the remote, grabbed her backpack and the pad of paper on the bedside table, and made her way to the hotel's business office.

First order of business on the desktop computer was an email to Warner letting him know she was okay and that she'd explain herself as soon as her cell phone was charged. Next was an internet search on Imran Bukayev. Some news accounts hailed him as a moderate leader of the oppressed Chechen people. A few lambasted Britain for providing refuge to a known terrorist leader. She clicked through link after link until a tabloid photograph caption caught her attention.

Imran Bukayev, spokesman for the Chechen government-in-exile, exiting his posh residence near Gloucester Street.

She scribbled down the street name and rushed from the business office. As she turned the corner for the lobby, she collided with someone. The backpack flew from her grasp, spewing its contents across the carpet.

"Damn it." She knelt to gather her things from the debris field of receipts, lipstick, coins, and crumpled gum wrappers.

A man squatted beside her. "We have to stop meeting like this."

Maggie paused from gathering her things. "How the hell did you find me?" She snatched her passport from Roger's hand and stood.

"I'm a really good spy," he mock whispered, his rather distracting dimples deepening with his smile. "And Tamaz told me where you went."

Flustered, Maggie moved toward the lobby.

"Where're you going?" He hurried to her side. "How about we grab some lunch? I'll pay, because I'm a gentleman. Even though you owe me big-time for rescuing you yesterday."

Maggie studied his face and decided that his annoying personality canceled out his striking looks. "What are you doing here anyway?"

"I'm keeping you company."

She stopped short. "I don't need company. I need clothes. I'm going shopping."

Roger eyed her yoga pants and T-shirt. "Nothing wrong with that outfit."

She rolled her eyes and resumed walking.

"Seriously, Maggie, you can't go out without me."

She stopped again. "Says who?"

"Says Warner. He's not very happy with you right now."

"I can handle Warner. And myself."

"Let's get something to eat. Then we'll call Warner and talk him off the cliff."

She closed her eyes and took a deep breath. She'd promised Warner she would do what he wanted and she'd already broken that promise once today. Maybe if she calmed him down and gained Roger's trust, she could slip away and try to find Bukayev. "I'm a little hungry myself."

They headed for the Norfolk Bar, a bright, airy pub off the hotel lobby and ordered lunch from a corner café table.

Between bites of his fish and chips, Roger peppered her with questions about Beslan, Chechnya, and Zara. Obviously, Warner had given him the whole story since they'd last been together at Tamaz's apartment.

"I went to Chechnya because I found an address linked to Zara Barayeva."

"The dead assassin you hold responsible for your fiancé's death?"

"She is responsible all right, but she's not dead. Her aunt said as much, just before she let slip that Zara has a boyfriend named Imran."

Roger raised an eyebrow. "And?"

"I think it's Imran Bukayev."

"Ohhh, so that's why you're here. To find the boyfriend."

"And Zara."

Roger put down his fork. "You're an analyst, Maggie. No offense, but you should let the spies handle this sort of thing."

She poked at a salad and considered how much to reveal. "For almost ten months, everyone at Langley insisted that Zara was dead. Everyone except for me. I was right all along."

He chewed on a piece of fried fish. "You knew for certain that she was alive?"

"Believed she was. But I needed proof." She bit into a cucumber. "When I first came back to the Agency earlier this year, they sent me to a psychiatrist, who is convinced I have PTSD."

"Do you?"

Maggie startled. No one had ever asked her that question directly. They just slapped the label on her and treated her like a fragile piece of china. "Maybe a touch," she admitted. But what really set her off wasn't the memories of Steve or her brushes with death. It was the fact that no one was willing to listen to her. "The shrink thinks I'm a loose cannon. A bit delusional. Obsessed with Zara."

Roger tilted his head and studied her. "You don't seem at all delusional to me. Obsessed? Absolutely."

"What?"

"Hear me out. Your obsession proves that you're sane. You were right. She's alive." He leaned in. "Unfortunately for you, the Agency doesn't like being proven wrong. Believe me. Been there. Done that."

"What's that supposed to mean?"

"Long story." Roger balled up his cloth napkin and deposited it on the table. "Look, the best way to get the bureaucrats off your back is to hand them a victory they can take credit for."

"How?"

"We find Zara and the CIA gets great publicity for catching one of the world's most wanted terrorists."

Maggie set down her fork. "Is that why you followed me to London? To find Zara?"

"Originally, I was supposed to deliver you to the Moscow station. But yes, now I'm here on Warner's orders to follow up on your lead. He doesn't want Zara to get away. And I'll make sure she won't. I promise."

"You can't promise that, Roger. You don't know this woman."

He leaned forward and locked eyes with her.

"And you don't know me. When I make a promise, I keep it. And I'm telling you, we will catch Zara Barayeva."

A charge passed through the air between them. Maggie flushed and looked away. She took a long sip of seltzer water and cleared her throat. "How did you prove the Agency wrong?"

"I'll tell you on our second date."

Maggie stared. "This isn't a date."

Roger shrugged. "We're getting to know each other. Have a lot in common. Sounds like a date to me."

"I'm going to my room."

"Was it something I said?"

"I'm tired."

"Why do all the ladies say that to me?"

Maggie rolled her eyes.

Roger asked the waiter to put the bill on his room tab and followed Maggie to the elevator. He pushed the fourth-floor button. "We have adjoining rooms."

She ignored him.

"Where should we go for dinner?" he called as she put the do-not-disturb placard on her room door and closed it behind her.

Maggie sat on the edge of her bed. She understood Warner's impulse to send a minder to watch over her, but did it have to be this Roger character? *Annoying* was the first word that came to mind when she thought of him. Even more annoying, she couldn't get his face out of her mind.

She flopped backward on the bed and groaned.

"Maggie?" His voice was muffled through the door. "I'm running out for a few minutes. Please stay here."

She pushed herself up and checked the peephole in time to see him turn and walk away. *Where is he going?* She pressed her ear against the door, waiting for the *bong* of the elevator. Grabbing her backpack and her phone, she slipped from the room and sprinted for the stairway.

On the ground floor, she cracked open the door and peered into the hallway. All clear. She crept along, stopping when she heard the clacking of a keyboard coming from the business office. Then the scrape of a chair. Maggie dashed across the hall into an alcove housing a vending machine.

Holding her breath, she peeked out and caught sight of Roger leaving the office for the lobby. Ahead, he ducked into the bar. Maggie grabbed an abandoned *Daily Mail* from a table at the edge of the lobby and slid into a lounge chair, newspaper raised in front of her face.

She flipped through the paper, pretending to be engrossed in the latest British celebrity gossip, which was even more outlandish than what constituted tabloid news at home. When she heard Roger call out, "Thanks, chap," she waited twenty seconds before lowering the paper. And there he was, turning right onto the sidewalk outside the hotel.

Maggie made her way to the bartender. "Excuse me, I was in the gym and just missed my boyfriend. Devastatingly handsome American? The one who just left?"

The bartender nodded, uncertain.

"Did he happen to mention where he's going?"

"Ma'am, I'm not sure that I—"

She pasted on a smile. "Oh, never mind. Silly me. He's off to his friend's flat over on Gloucester Street, isn't he?" The street near where Bukayev lived. Where Zara might be hiding out.

"That's right. He asked for directions. It's not far from here. Just around the corner."

What was Roger up to? Whatever it was, she didn't like being kept out of the loop. Especially when it came to Zara. "They're probably already drinking." She rolled her eyes and sighed before brightening. "Might as well take advantage of the situation and spend his money shopping."

Outside, she spotted him walking a considerable distance ahead, phone to his ear. Maggie had no formal training as a spy, a deficit she kept in mind as she followed Roger, a professional with a dozen-plus years of experience conducting surveillance operations. She kept a half-block between them and tried to walk at a casual pace, gazing at the Georgian architecture of the buildings along Gloucester Street. At one point, Roger stopped suddenly and turned himself around in a complete circle. Maggie managed to duck into the doorway of Café Nero before he caught sight of her. After that scare, she dropped back even farther, slipped on oversized sunglasses, and put her cell phone to her ear.

At the next corner, Roger dashed across the street, narrowly avoiding an oncoming double-decker bus. Maggie waited until he disappeared down Lennox Place before giving chase. A quick scan of the neighborhood revealed pristine, brick row homes with small but well-manicured gardens. But there was no place to conceal herself. Roger could easily spot her if she followed on foot. *Smooth move.* Any spy worth her salt would've purchased a decent street map before running around an unfamiliar city. She doubled back to Gloucester Street and flagged down a taxi on her fourth try.

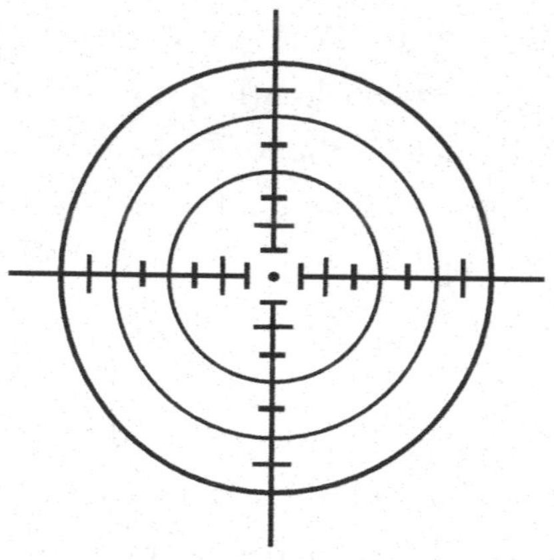

CHAPTER FIFTEEN

In the guest bedroom on the ground floor, Zara awoke to the sound of the phone ringing. Imran had exiled her downstairs after their argument over her leaving his house. As irritated as she'd been at him, she'd fallen into a deep sleep within minutes, exhausted from her journey. Zara threw off the luxurious satin sheets and stole across the blond-wood floor. She leaned into the hall and listened. There was only silence.

"Imran? Is it safe now?" Venturing upstairs might antagonize him. Besides, she could achieve much more through other means. Within seconds, she was undressed and nestled between the cool sheets.

He appeared in the doorway. "I got the all-clear. Whoever was loitering in the neighborhood earlier is gone." His eyes took in the curves under the sheets. "I think you should stay here a few more days."

Zara ran a hand across her neck. "Under one condition."

Imran's voice was husky. "What's that?"

"I think you know." She sat up. The satin sheets slid into a pile around her feet.

Twenty minutes later, Zara stole from the bed and slipped back into her clothes. Imran was dead asleep. She peered under the sheet—he'd put on weight. He wasn't someone she'd look at twice if he were a stranger. But he couldn't resist her, and that gave her power.

Outside, Zara scanned the street for anything suspicious. Not a thuggish Russian in sight.

Roger ducked behind a parked car as a woman fitting Zara's description emerged from Bukayev's fashionable mews house. He reached his phone around the bumper and snapped a photo as she descended the front stairs. As she neared the end of the street, he dashed along the hedges until he was just feet from her. Gloucester Street was teeming with taxis and cars but provided no cover otherwise, so Roger waited, giving her a fifty-yard lead. From there, he assumed a casual pace, pretending to talk on his cell phone. Not once did she look back.

For someone clever enough to escape Beslan, she didn't exercise very good operational security, which would make his job a lot easier.

Then again, maybe part of her OPSEC was looking and acting like an average Western woman. She absolutely didn't look like someone who'd attended a terrorist training camp. Or murdered schoolchildren.

Zara ducked into a coffee shop a block ahead. Roger continued past the shop, crossed the road, and took up position leaning against a lamppost.

•★★★•

Maggie jumped in the taxi. "Lennox Place, please. Quickly." As the cab lurched into traffic, Maggie sank low in the seat, ignoring the driver's curious glances in the rearview mirror.

"Miss?" he said two minutes later, "we're at the end of the cul-de-sac. Where to now?"

Maggie peeked her head up far enough to get a glimpse outside. "Did you happen to see a man walking down the street?"

The driver, a balding man with enormous jowls weighing down fleshy cheeks, struggled to turn around in the seat. "What kind of a man, miss?"

"Sort of black hair with some gray at the temples. Good-looking—" Her cell phone cut her off. It was a Virginia number. Could be someone from work.

"Hey, it's me."

"Who?"

"Roger."

"How'd you get my number?"

"I'm a spy, remember?"

"How can I forget when you won't stop reminding me?"

"Actually, Warner gave it to me."

Maggie sat straight up and scanned the cul-de-sac. "Where are you?" She heard a loud screech in the background. "What's that noise?"

"Oh, that? Just a bus."

"A bus?" She tapped the driver on the shoulder and mouthed, "Bus?" He looked around and shrugged. Maggie motioned for him to drive back to the main road.

"I'm sending you—" Background noise drowned out Roger's voice.

"You're sending me what?"

"A picture. To your cell phone. Call me back when you get it."

Roger hung up before Maggie could protest. Where the hell was he?

"Was that the gentleman you're trying to find?"

"Yes," Maggie snapped at the driver. "Pull over for a minute."

He scowled at her in the rearview mirror as he pulled to the side of the road.

"Sorry I'm so crabby. My boyfriend stormed out of the hotel this morning."

The driver smacked his lips together. "Yes, indeed."

Maggie's phone buzzed, alerting her to an incoming message.

Inside the coffee shop, Zara found exactly what she needed—a public computer. She ordered a latte and smiled at the barista who was tidying the coffee bar. He squinted at her from behind thick black-rimmed glasses. Zara's internet skills had improved rapidly in the past ten months, thanks in part to the teenage boy she'd seduced in Ingushetia, where she'd hidden out for months after the debacle in Georgia last year. All the news reports had said the Chechens in the farmhouse had died, but just to be sure, she kept a low profile for months before returning to Chechnya for a few quick visits.

She typed in a URL, hoping she'd remembered it correctly. The site popped up. Now she had both of the addresses she needed for the next mission. One of the first things she'd do on arrival would be to buy a good street map so she could get a sense of their neighborhoods.

A chime on the door sounded as two teenage girls entered the shop. With a few keystrokes, Zara closed the search window and watched the girls order coffee. They plopped onto overstuffed leather chairs, more interested in gossiping than in using the computer. Relieved, Zara opened a new window. She checked the news headlines but found no mention of a fugitive female terrorist. Two major explosions had rocked the school earlier in the day. Hundreds were feared dead. She smiled to herself because she was not among them.

She checked her watch. *Imran!* He'd be furious if he found her gone. With any luck, he'd still be asleep when she got back.

Maggie gasped at the picture filling the tiny screen on her phone.

"You know, ma'am, the meter runs even when we're parked."

"Huh?" She glanced up at the taxi driver.

"The meter is running."

"It's fine." She stared a moment longer before pushing the redial button. "Roger?"

"Yep."

"Where is she?"

He sounded out of breath. "I'm following her."

"Why are you huffing and puffing?"

"You have that kind of effect on me."

"Roger, could you please be serious!" Maggie realized she was shouting and lowered her voice. "Where are you?"

"I went to find Bukayev's house."

Maggie clutched the phone.

"And I saw a woman come out the front door of one of the houses. It was her."

Her voice rose an octave. "Roger, where is she now?"

"In a café. I'm across the street, waiting."

"A café?" She tapped the driver on the shoulder. "You're at a café?" She swept her hand along the car window and mouthed, "Café?"

Again, the man shrugged. He looked more familiar with pubs than coffee houses.

"This is fantastic, Roger. Now we have proof that Bukayev is tied to Zara. Which means he's probably tied to Beslan too." Maybe the aggravation of dealing with Roger would be worth it after all. "What's Bukayev's address?"

"Maggie—"

"I know he lives on Lennox Place. Just give me the house number."

"I can't." He hung up.

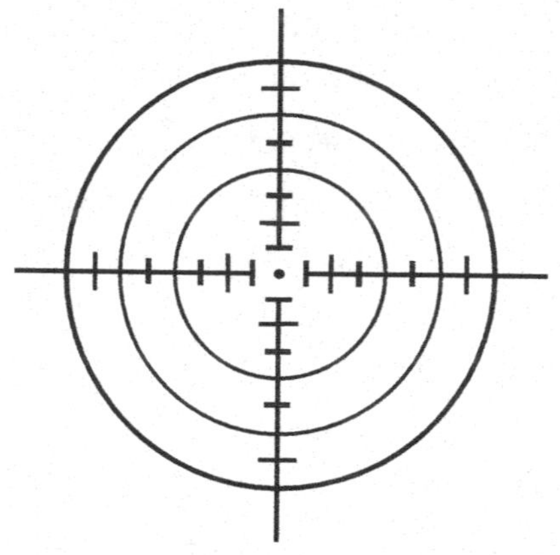

CHAPTER SIXTEEN

McLean, VA
Friday, September 3, 2004, 8:00 a.m.

Warner checked the caller ID twice.

"Maggie!" Even though Roger had left a message that he was with Maggie, it was a relief hear from her. "Where are you?"

"Sitting on a park bench. I need your help."

"I can't believe you went to London—"

"What's the least conspicuous way to break into a house?"

"What?"

"I need to look into something. Roger's off chasing Zara and I need to get into the house where she's staying."

Warner saw red.

He had warned Roger to keep Maggie in check and now he'd left her alone? "Sonofa—"

"What's his deal, anyway?"

Warner had learned his lesson about keeping the truth from Maggie. Still, it might be best to tell her only what she needed to know. "He has a history and a reputation at the Agency."

"Uh-huh."

"A few years ago, he was reprimanded for failing to disclose ongoing contacts with foreigners. And there were issues with him continuing this contact and traveling to certain hot spots without Agency authorization."

"Is that why he left the CIA?"

So, Maggie didn't know the whole story. "As Roger's boss, I had many conversations with him about his proclivity for ignoring the rules."

"Did you fire him?"

"We came to a mutual understanding of sorts. He left of his own free will." At least that's what the records stated. "I hated to see him go. I mean, he broke the rules sometimes, but no one uncovered critical intelligence better than he did. I'm glad he's back."

Maggie shifted gears. "About breaking into a house . . ."

Warner stalled for time as he punched Roger's number into his home phone. No answer.

"Whose house?"

"Bukayev's."

"Do you have proof that he was behind the school siege?"

Maggie's words tumbled out quickly. "Not yet. But at a minimum, he's complicit in harboring a terrorist. If I can get inside his house, maybe I can find evidence tying him directly to Beslan."

She was in way over her head.

"Go back to the hotel and wait for Roger. Please."

"No."

"Maggie, you're not trained—"

"Yeah, well I wasn't trained last year and I survived that, didn't I?" Her tone grew more insistent. "We're close to getting her, Warner."

"I directed Roger to get and keep eyes on Zara. You've brought us this far, Maggie. It's time to let others handle it."

Her tone grew more insistent. "But this may be our only opportunity to figure out Zara's relationship with Bukayev. And whether he's involved in Beslan."

"Look, you can't break into Bukayev's house. You know there's political sensitivity around his presence in London. The Brits have stuck their neck out to defend him against Russia's allegations. If he's involved in terrorist activity, Downing Street will want to handle that quietly."

"So what am I supposed to do? Sit here and wait for . . . what, exactly?"

"I need to alert MI5 that a Beslan terrorist is in London. But I need evidence first."

"Roger got a picture of Zara leaving Bukayev's place," she exclaimed.

"Great, but that doesn't prove that she was in Beslan."

"I have photos, on the camera chip."

"Which photos?"

"The ones I took of Zara outside of the school." She sounded breathless. "Crap, the camera chip is back at the hotel with my luggage. I'll go get it now!"

• ★ ★ ★ •

Roger waited for two minutes after Zara left the coffee shop before crossing the street. Inside were six round café tables. Two were occupied—one by a businessman and the other by an overly pierced, pink-haired girl. In the corner was a computer with a sign on top that read, "Public Access Internet Computer—15-minute time limit." Roger sauntered up to the counter and ordered an espresso. He flipped open his phone and pretended to dial.

"Oh darling, please answer." Roger smiled, admiring his refined British accent. "I just got to the coffee shop. I'm sorry I was running late." He handed a few pounds to the kid behind the counter. "Darling, I swear I wasn't flirting with that woman at the party. I'd never sleep with the likes of her. Please call me back." He slapped the phone shut.

"Your change, sir."

Roger gave a pathetic half smile to the kid. "It's yours, chap." He accepted the espresso. "She can't wait five measly minutes for me? Seriously?"

The kid looked over his glasses at him, then turned away to wipe the counter.

Roger persisted. "She was here just a few minutes ago, wasn't she? Dark hair, past the shoulders. A body to worship?"

"You just missed her." He pushed his glasses back into place.

"Did she happen to say where she was going?"

The kid shook his head. "Never saw her before. She just popped in to use the computer."

"Women," he muttered. "Might as well check my email while I'm here."

Cyber-spying wasn't exactly Roger's forte, but he knew his way around the internet. He clicked on the browser's history. The three most recent pages were all news sites. And all the news was about

Beslan. Any lingering doubts he might've had about Maggie's insistence that Zara was one of the Beslan terrorists vanished. Next, he pulled up a few articles about Imran Bukayev. *Interesting.* He took a swig of espresso and hurried from the shop. Once he got eyes back on the target, he was going to need reinforcements.

For the second time that day, Roger took up residence behind the hedges across the street from a small but elegant brick row house. It wasn't the most comfortable stakeout spot, but it afforded him a perfect view of Bukayev's front door.

Roger glanced at his vibrating phone. A text from Maggie. It would have to wait. He emerged from behind the hedges, walked past Bukayev's house, and turned left just beyond the neighboring end unit. Fifteen yards ahead, he came to a paved path that ran along the back of the homes. To the right was a grove of trees and beyond them, more houses on the adjacent street.

He crept alongside the high brick wall behind Bukayev's house, hoping he'd remain undetected from this vantage point. Much to his frustration, he couldn't see over the wall, but at least it provided him decent cover. Dropping to his hands and knees, he peered through an iron gate leading to a small courtyard. He could see three entryways from the courtyard into the house—French doors to a ground-level family room of some sort, a single door leading to what looked like a bedroom, and on the second level, a small balcony overlooking the yard.

Roger shrank back to the corner of the gate when movement in the family room caught his eye. Through the French doors, he spotted Zara. She held a glass in her hand and was leaning into what looked like a small refrigerator, the kind you'd see in a hotel or college dorm. Bukayev appeared behind her and ran his hands across her breasts. She straightened, turned around and kissed him. Bukayev took the glass and placed it on an end table. He grabbed her wrists and forced her back against the wall. *A little rough*, Roger thought. But Zara appeared unfazed as she arched her back toward him. Bukayev was kissing her neck, when out of nowhere she slapped him. He responded by grabbing her arms and shoving her. She stumbled but quickly recovered, snatching the glass and hurling it just past his head. *So much for foreplay.*

The muffled harshness of their shouts penetrated the glass doors. Seconds later, Zara was in the courtyard, stomping in Roger's direction. He sprang away from the gate. If she opened it, he was a dead man. She cursed Bukayev as he shouted at her from inside the family room.

"You can't keep me prisoner in this house!" Her English had a British accent.

"You have no regard for security. I told you they're watching me, but you just up and left without even asking permission."

Charming couple. Roger was breathing a little easier in his hiding spot. Now if they'd just wrap up the fight and go out to dinner, he could get inside the house.

"I'm sorry, Imran. I'll be more careful." Her tone was conciliatory. "But I can't stay cooped up day in and day out. Taking walks clears my head."

"I understand, Zara. But staying safe is more important."

Roger edged forward and peered through the gate. The two of them were in the courtyard, at it again, kissing and groping. *Doing the terrorist tango.* The make-up sex was about to begin, but how to get them out of the house?

Just then, Roger's cell phone rang. He fumbled for the mute button, but it was too late. He stood and pressed himself against the brick wall that ran behind the houses, then side-shuffled until he reached the end unit, turning the corner just as Bukayev emerged from his courtyard onto the path. *Did he see me?*

Roger ran along the grass toward the street. He peeked around the corner only to find Zara standing outside Bukayev's front door, scanning the neighborhood. They had him cornered. If he ran through the woods, Bukayev would see him, and a casual stroll past Zara was out of the question.

Roger tugged a credit card from his pocket and inserted it into a side window on the end unit house. With a quick twist of his wrist, the lock gave way. Roger threw open the window and dove inside, landing with a thud between the wall and a wing chair.

"Nigel, is that you?" a fragile voice called from upstairs. "I've just finished my bath. I'll be down in a few minutes."

A large photograph of an elderly man—*Nigel?*—and woman surrounded by teenagers and forty-somethings hung over the fireplace mantel. Out the front window, Roger saw Zara and Bukayev in the street, talking, gesturing. He'd given them a scare, but not as big as the scare they'd given him. He pulled the cell phone from its clip. It was Maggie who'd called. She'd almost blown everything.

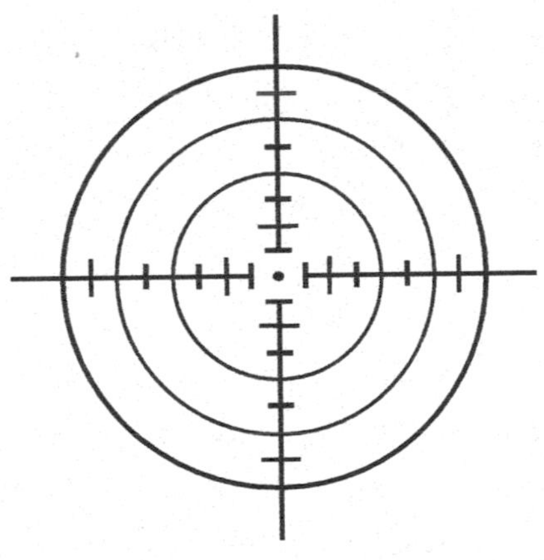

CHAPTER SEVENTEEN

Washington, DC
Friday, September 3, 2004, 12:00 p.m.

Yuri Ivanovich Markov leaned against the cool metal railing and took a final drag from his cigarette before tossing it into the Potomac River. He knew he was being watched; he expected no less. The other man, an accomplished professional, would take every precaution to make sure he wasn't walking into a trap. Yuri laughed to himself. There was no reason for the American to distrust an ex-KGB man. Their respective countries were on the same side these days, weren't they?

The Russian tugged at his sleeve, making a show of checking the time on his Rolex Submariner. He pushed his large frame away from the railing and began a slow stroll along the concrete path that meandered through the park. It was a cool day for this time of year, but most of the leaves still clung to their summer green. Yuri never grew tired of September in Washington, where the weather engaged in a tug-of-war between summer and fall. Today, it seemed, fall had the upper hand.

Yuri neared Hains Point, the far end of a spit of land sandwiched between the Potomac River and the Washington Channel. Through squinted eyes, he scanned the area for anything unexpected. He'd been cautious in his approach to East Potomac Park, changing taxis three times along the way. In this business, one could never be too careful. He watched a man and his son flying a kite just beyond *The Awakening*, the curious sculpture of a half-buried giant. Parts of the giant jutted up from the ground—an enormous arm with fingers curved and ready to clench, a bent knee smoothed from years of children sliding down, and an oversized foot rising from the mulch. Yuri studied the giant's frozen expression—a mix of surprise, agony, and anger. Some pundits thought 9/11 had awoken a sleeping giant. Yuri wasn't so sure.

Sensing the American's presence, Yuri pulled his gaze from the giant sculpture. Their eyes met, but their expressions betrayed nothing. The Russian noted the half-empty bottle of spring water in the man's right hand, the signal that they were free to proceed. Yuri moved first, assuming the leisurely pace of a man reluctant to go home. The American joined him a moment later.

"I'm glad you could make it, Carl." Yuri was more relieved than glad. This meeting was critical to ensuring the success of his plan. Nothing would be allowed to derail it.

"I'd like to say it's a pleasure, Yuri, but it's not."

Yuri let Carl's words hang in the air. The American cleared his throat repeatedly, obviously anxious to fill the silence. Carl was a professional, a case officer by trade. To any outside observer, he'd appear thoroughly relaxed, thanks to years of experience that taught him to blend in, to attract no undue attention. His six-foot frame and slight paunch made him look like any other middle-aged Washington bureaucrat.

He'd never stand out in a crowd.

"We need to talk about this. You can't keep putting me off."

Yuri smiled and looked sideways at his companion. "Let's go this way." He pointed toward the path that rimmed the outer edge of the park. "I always enjoy a nice view of the Potomac." He studied Carl's irritated expression and retracted his smile. "I didn't mean to ignore you these past few days. You know how busy we all are."

"I thought you were retired. Or do your new business dealings consume all your leisure time?"

"Business is excellent." Yuri's old KGB connections served his capitalistic ventures well. In less than two years, he'd built up substantial wealth, purchased several sprawling homes, and indulged himself in modern luxuries that had been unavailable to all but the top echelon of Soviet elites. His only complaint was how much effort was needed to ensure that the FBI couldn't prove he was involved in anything improper. It wasn't like he was trying to undermine democracy these days. Those efforts had ended with his KGB career. But the FBI harassed him nonetheless.

Yuri slowed to watch a lone rower power his boat up the Potomac, cutting a silent line across the dark water.

Carl stopped short. "Yuri, I want out."

Yuri continued to watch the rower. "Out?"

"I never imagined it would turn out this way. Shit, Yuri, all those children." He took a swig from the water bottle. "Didn't you see the news this morning?"

"Collateral damage, Carl. It's an ugly thing." Yuri was more horrified by what had happened than he'd admit. In fact, he was furious. As a condition for his funding the attack, he'd instructed them to keep casualties to a minimum. But children had died—hundreds of them. The point of the siege was to get the attention of the Russian people. To rally them to support an all-out assault on the radical Islamists infiltrating southern Russia and some of the nearby republics. It was bad enough that Russia had lost its Soviet empire at the end of the Cold War. Now, Russians were losing their culture, their very essence. At the rate things were going, it wouldn't be long before sharia law became the norm in certain parts of Russia. Yuri refused to sit back and watch his beloved country be torn apart by two opposing forces—Western liberalism and Islamic radicalism. If he didn't do something to reverse the course, the best and brightest would continue to leave Russia at the first opportunity. He had. And much to his dismay, so had his daughter. How he hated that his granddaughter, Elena, was safer in her American school than she'd be in a Russian one.

"Did you know it would turn out this way?" Carl struggled to control his voice. "Did you know they were going to attack a school?"

"Of course not," he lied. "But honestly, my friend, it will take something of this magnitude to shake Moscow from its complacency. You said it yourself—not enough is being done to destroy al-Qaeda."

"But innocent people died in the process." The American's voice cracked. "What have we done?"

Yuri grabbed Carl's shoulders with his massive hands. "Remember the goal. Never to have another 9/11. Never to let someone else's wife die on a plane hijacked by fanatics. You're doing this for *her.*" He released his grip and lowered his voice. "The unfortunate truth is that there will be innocent victims along the way. But at least these victims will not have died for nothing. They'll motivate the world to hunt down each and every last one of the terrorists."

"Yuri," Carl whispered, "the Agency's investigating, helping Moscow find the Beslan masterminds."

Yuri clenched his fists. It had taken him years to get used to the fact that the Cold War was over. And yet, he still couldn't accommodate the idea of Russian and American intelligence working together, exposing their secrets to each other like giggling girls at a sleepover. Why the hell couldn't the FSB—one of the successors to his beloved KGB—conduct an investigation without involving the CIA?

Carl grew more agitated. "I need out of this arrangement, Yuri, because they're putting me in charge of the investigation. I'm too close to this. What if—"

"They won't find out." Yuri had been meticulous in his use of cutouts—offshore bank accounts, a phony front company, and couriers who'd met their unfortunate demise days before the siege. No one would be able to trace the funding or logistical advice back to him. No one except Carl. And possibly the middleman. He would deal with him later.

The American rubbed his hands across his face, massaging his forehead for a moment. "You know one of the terrorists escaped. What if she can connect us to . . . what happened over there?"

He'd heard a rumor yesterday of an escaped terrorist, one of the black widows, as these women called themselves. Now, Carl had confirmed it. Acid rose in his throat. "You worry too much, my friend." Earlier in the week Yuri had put men in place near each of the terrorists' homes. Just in case one of them bailed out at the last minute. Or survived and returned home. So far, the escaped terrorist had not surfaced. Yuri knew one of the two female terrorists by reputation. She was formidable and would have to be dealt with if it turned out she was, indeed, still alive.

Yuri resumed walking. The American fell in alongside him. "You knew when we agreed to work together that once you were in, there was no way out." He chose his next words carefully. There was a fine line between scaring a man and sending him into an unpredictable state of panic. "If you expose me, I expose you, Carl."

Yuri had friends in high places, particularly in Russian intelligence. Late last year, one of these friends had told him about Carl, a senior CIA official with a prescription-drug problem. At a cocktail party soon after, Yuri cornered him and offered up a passionate discourse on US and Russian reluctance to obliterate their terrorist enemies. He'd played on Carl's grief over his wife's death on 9/11, then casually mentioned his interest in lobbying Moscow to take a harder stance against countries like Iran and Syria. Carl had wished him luck but declined to delve further into the subject. It wasn't fitting for a CIA case officer to discuss such matters with a retired KGB official.

Poor Carl had underestimated the Russian. When Yuri arranged to "bump into" Carl at the American's favorite bar a week later, he resumed the conversation. Carl remained reticent, so Yuri pressed him with an ultimatum. If he wanted to keep his little narcotics problem a secret, he needed to provide information about how closely the CIA was monitoring Chechen rebels. The first classified documents changed hands two days later.

"Look," Carl whined, "I know I can't escape responsibility for what happened, but I'm done. I don't want to meet with you again. Tell whoever you want about my drug issue. I don't care anymore."

Yuri shook his head. Carl had backed himself into a corner, sealing his own fate. "I see. I'll take what you've said under advisement. In the meantime, I assume you won't betray me because if you do, you'll get no leniency for confessing. There's blood all over your hands."

"Is that a threat?" The American was beginning to sound slightly hysterical.

"Not at all, my friend. It's the simple truth." Yuri sighed. "We're doing the right thing and you know it. In the end, lives will be saved."

"You're wrong, Yuri. There has to be another way. Maybe the administration will smarten up and make this war really mean something, maybe—"

Yuri extended his right hand. "My friend, I won't soon forget you." The last comment *was* a threat, and Yuri knew that Carl knew it.

The Russian turned from the American and walked back toward *The Awakening*. Men of courage, he thought, were few and far between these days. He approached the giant, stared at his twisted mouth, and tried to decide how best to clean up this little mess before it spun out of his control.

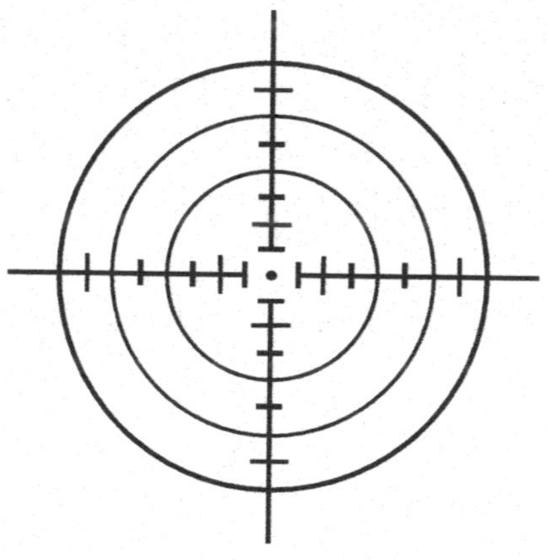

CHAPTER EIGHTEEN

Warner eased his gold BMW onto the winding mountain road. He proceeded another mile, his eyes drinking in the earliest hints of fall color, before turning left at the sign outside Windwood Winery. He double-checked that his cell phone was fully charged.

Moments later, he slipped inside a refurbished barn that had found new life as a spacious wine-tasting room. Other than the tanned, middle-aged woman behind the counter and a napping black Labrador, the cavernous room was empty.

"Good afternoon, sir."

"Good afternoon. Beautiful day, isn't it?"

His gaze drifted to the floor-to-ceiling window, across the open porch, and out to the pond just beyond.

"How can I help you?"

"I'm going to buy a few bottles, but I think I'll have a glass or two first." Maybe a glass of a hearty local red might calm his nerves until he heard from Maggie. And Roger.

"Rough week?" the woman asked, a broad smile revealing deep lines around the pleasant edges of her face.

"You could say that." Warner glanced outside again. "Kind of quiet here. Business pick up later in the afternoon?"

"Always. We'll be packed in a couple hours." Her hand swept toward the empty tables. "But for now, it's just you and another gentleman who's wandering around on the farm somewhere."

Yuri's already here? "Why don't I start with a glass of your Vintner's Reserve?" It was the vineyard's most expensive wine.

"Absolutely." The woman poured him a generous glass of deep crimson wine, recorked the bottle, and set it on the counter.

He carried the glass out to the porch and sat at the far left corner, a spot that offered a view of the gravel path leading from the parking lot. Warner checked his phone, then took a sip of wine, allowing it to run under his tongue before he swallowed. He savored the hint of raspberry as he gazed out at cows grazing in a far field. Then Yuri came into his view.

Warner took a larger sip and stood. The Russian ambled up the dirt path that cut between the pond and a small horse corral, then climbed the porch stairs.

"Good afternoon, my friend." Yuri gestured to the table. "May I?"

"Of course, have a seat." The casual tone of his voice belied the urgency he felt to get back to headquarters. Yuri had said the matter was urgent. He'd better make it quick.

The Russian settled himself into a chair.

"Want a glass? It's fabulous."

"They don't distill vodka here, do they?"

"I'm afraid not," Warner chuckled. Yuri's mood seemed somber. "Is everything okay?"

The Russian lowered his voice. "Yes, everything is fine. But I wish to discuss with you a very sensitive and quite urgent matter."

It probably wasn't a good thing that a former high-ranking KGB officer wanted to discuss a sensitive matter with him. Other than banter about their old KGB-CIA rivalry, they never discussed intelligence matters.

In fact, they'd become friends of a sort after discovering that Warner's daughters and Yuri's granddaughter attended the same elementary school. He took a sip of wine and watched a duck land in the pond.

When Warner finally made eye contact, Yuri began to speak. "It's about the Beslan massacre, Warner. I need your help."

Warner lowered the wine glass. A sense of unease brushed over him. "That's an internal Russian matter. What can I possibly help you with?"

Yuri dropped his voice, forcing Warner to lean across the table to hear. "I fear that President Putin was behind it. If he was, I must expose him."

Warner considered Yuri's allegation for a moment. It sounded preposterous on its face. Besides, according to Maggie, Bukayev might be the mastermind. "You don't even live in Russia anymore. Why would you get involved?"

"Russia will always be my home." He scowled at Warner. "I may be living far away, but I can't sit back and watch my country fall apart."

Warner studied his old Cold War rival. He seemed genuinely upset. "Do you have any evidence that Putin was involved?"

Yuri shook his head. "Just whispers here and there. But you know as well as I do that no government investigation will point to him. He holds all the reins of power."

"You really think the Russian president allowed the slaughter of hundreds of children?" Warner was no fan of Vladimir Putin, but he didn't think him capable of such a horrific act. Besides that, the attack had all the hallmarks of Islamic terrorism. "Why would Putin do such a thing?"

"To gain support for crushing the Chechens." Yuri scratched his neck. "I hate those barbarians as much as Putin does, but the ends don't always justify the means."

"You've evolved, Yuri."

"I'll take that as a compliment." The Russian pulled a pack of cigarettes from his jacket. "Can I smoke here?"

"Afraid not."

"I thought this was the land of the free." He stuffed the cigarettes back in his pocket. "Puritans."

Warner smiled, trying to maintain an air of nonchalance. "Let's go for a walk."

The men left the porch for the gravel path. Warner picked up a pebble and tossed it into the pond, sending ripples across the still water. Nearby, a duck flapped its wings before settling on the shore.

"Why should I help you, Yuri?" This was an unusual request, to say the least. And it would be a firing offense if he handed over a single tidbit of classified information. The Russian had to know that, which meant that something else was going on here.

"Imagine such an attack on an American school. Wouldn't you do whatever it took to find the perpetrators?"

"Of course. But Russia is not my responsibility."

"Perhaps I should be more direct." Yuri folded his arms across the expanse of his stomach. "You owe me, Warner."

Warner stiffened but tried to maintain a neutral expression. Indeed, he owed Yuri a debt of gratitude for providing critical information that helped Warner and Maggie prevent last year's terrorist attack.

In fact, he'd been the one to warn of a female Chechen assassin who had trained with al-Qaeda. That assassin, it turned out, was Zara. And he was certain Yuri knew about his one-time dalliance with a young Russian. Was that what he meant by "you owe me?" Warner studied a flock of Canada geese flying overhead in raucous formation.

Yuri hadn't used this knowledge to destroy him. At least not yet. "Perhaps we can work something out."

The Russian studied Warner before asking, "How so?"

Warner forced his clenched hands to relax. "You share everything you know about Beslan and Putin, and in exchange, the CIA will provide you with whatever information we can." The CIA had not and would not authorize any such intelligence exchange, but he was unsettled by Yuri's unexpected overture and wanted to keep him talking. Maybe then he'd reveal what he was really up to.

"I think it would be best if we worked together on a more personal level, Warner. I don't think the CIA will be keen to share secrets with someone like me. Do you?" Yuri's chuckle turned into a cough so violent that Warner feared he'd hack up a lung.

"You know, you might want to cut back on the smokes, comrade." He paused so Yuri could catch his breath. "Things have changed. Russia and the United States have more in common now.

Perhaps the Agency would welcome your insight. And maybe your cooperation would cast your business dealings in a better light." The FBI kept a close eye on Yuri's mafia activities, but it hadn't been able to pin anything illegal on him.

Yet.

Yuri folded his hands and tapped his fingertips together. "Are you implying that my business is not aboveboard?"

"That's between you and the bureau." He had a feeling Yuri derived great pleasure from messing with the Feds.

Yuri stopped and squinted up at the midday sun. "Perhaps this was a mistake, Warner. I thought we could work out something just between the two of us." He pulled sunglasses from his breast pocket and slid them over his eyes. "I'll remember that the next time you need a favor."

Warner didn't want this conversation to end yet. Not without understanding what was really going on. Maybe if he threw some bait Yuri's way, he'd keep him on the hook a little longer. "I don't know if you've heard, but one of the Beslan terrorists escaped."

"Yes, I heard."

"Rumor has it that it's Zara Barayeva and that she's close with Imran Bukayev."

Yuri swayed on his feet.

Warner extended an arm. "You okay?"

"Yes, yes. It's just . . . hot out here in the sun." He swiped at his brow. "I should be going."

"Enjoyed seeing you, my friend." Warner's voice was light, but his eyes were like steel and locked onto Yuri's. "Talk to you soon." With that, he walked around the enormous red barn and back to his car, where he sat for a moment. It was no surprise that Yuri had heard of the escaped terrorist. The rookie case officer on the ground had taken it upon himself to report Maggie's run-in with Zara to the local Russian army commander. What surprised him was Yuri's reaction to Bukayev's name. He started the car and checked the phone. Still no call from Maggie or Roger.

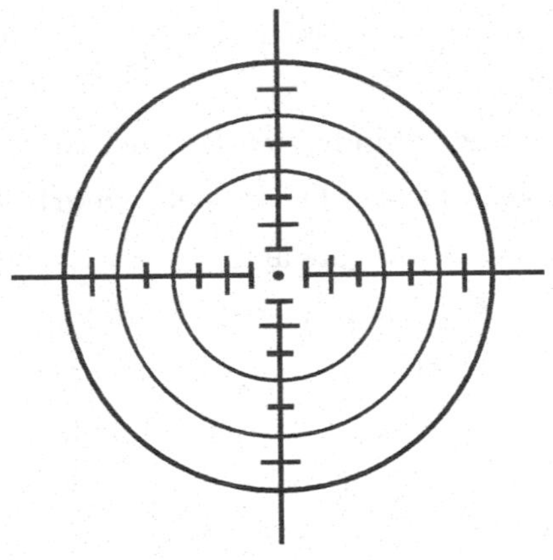

CHAPTER NINETEEN

London
Friday, September 3, 2004, 7:30 p.m.

Maggie's irritation was increasing by the second. The camera chip was missing. Back at the hotel, she'd torn apart her luggage and gone through her jeans pockets a dozen times to no avail. Her call to Tamaz had gone unanswered. The chip had to have fallen out of her pocket when she changed at his apartment. And now, Roger wasn't answering his phone, which left her with no other option. She'd have to figure out which house was Bukayev's herself.

A quick survey of the neighborhood made it clear that it would appear odd for her to stroll up and down Lennox Place—a cul-de-sac—by herself. Even if she played the part of a jogger, she could only make one pass by each house without potentially garnering unwanted curiosity.

A spate of barking behind a nearby fence caught her attention. No cars were parked in front of the stately white brick mews house. Maggie peered over the low gate at the side of the house and caught sight of a Sheltie barking at a squirrel chattering at him from atop the fence. She let herself into the yard. "Come here, boy." The dog trotted over, still yelping. "Hush!" Maggie squatted down to pat him. "Where's your leash?" She stood and peered around the back side of the house. On the rear gate hung a leash. Quickly, she fastened it to his collar and led him to the street, where he took immediate interest in a tree that stood next to the sidewalk.

"Come on, you. Walk." She dragged the dog a few feet before he gave in and started trotting alongside her. To any outside observer, she'd look like an ordinary woman out for a brisk walk with her dog. Unless, of course, she ran into someone who knew this dog or his owner. She looked around but didn't see any curious neighbors. She had to run the risk. To her right were detached homes separated from the street by high, square-cut hedges. Roger said he'd hidden behind hedges, hadn't he? That meant Bukayev probably lived in one of the row houses on the left side of the street. But which one? It wasn't like he'd fly a Chechen flag outside his door. The guy was in the country with the British government's permission, but for all intents and purposes, he was in hiding from the Russians.

Several cars were parked in front of the row houses. Maggie yanked the dog across the street and peered, as casually as possible, into a Peugeot, a BMW, and a Mercedes. Nothing. She stood in the middle of the road and scanned the area. There was no sign of Roger, Bukayev, or Zara.

She swore under her breath, irritated that she didn't have the information she needed and couldn't control what happened next. If she waited to pick up Roger's trail again at the hotel, he might not return for hours.

And Warner couldn't go to British authorities without actual evidence that Zara was a Beslan terrorist.

Maggie tugged on the leash. "Come on, Fido, time to go home."

As she gave the dog a gentle nudge and secured the gate, her cell phone rang.

"Roger?" She shielded her face with her hair as a Bentley turned onto the street.

"Yup, it's me."

"Why are you whispering?"

"Long story."

"I have all day." She stopped walking and leaned against the cold, rough brick of a three-story building on the corner. "Did you get any more information?"

"Yeah, but oh crap, I gotta go. I think Nigel's home."

"Nigel, who's Nigel? Roger, wait." It was too late. He hung up.

Warner tapped the pen on the edge of his desk as he waited for Maggie to answer, which she did on the third ring. "You find Roger?"

"No. In fact, he just hung up on me."

"I hope you're not going anywhere near Zara or Bukayev."

"Warner, listen, I'm afraid I can't find the memory card from the camera."

"You're kidding." He stood and shut his office door.

"Unfortunately not. It was in my jeans pocket and, I don't know, maybe when I changed out of them last night at Tamaz's, it fell out? I left him a message asking him to look."

"Not helpful, Maggie."

"Can't you still alert MI5 about Zara? As I understand it, the Brits can detain a suspected terrorist without evidence. And," she persisted, "we have that photo of Zara leaving Bukayev's house."

He scratched at the stubble already growing along his jawline. "The British maintain that Bukayev is not a terrorist, so the fact that Zara's with him carries no weight. Without the photos from Beslan, they won't move against Zara."

"You sure?"

"I'll double-check with our lawyers, but . . ." He thought he heard cars or buses in the background. "You out for a stroll?"

"My feet are killing me. I've been walking up and down this street all evening."

"What street?"

"I think I found him."

Warner's breath caught. "Who?"

"Roger, sitting in a pub. I'll call you back."

Roger ignored the incoming call from Warner. It could wait until later. If he survived that long. He didn't know what might kill him first—the smoke in the pub, the mug of flat, warm ale, or the exhaustion. Other than the two-hour nap on the flight from Tbilisi earlier this morning, he hadn't slept for almost forty-eight hours. So tired. And a bit buzzed. Or maybe it was a concussion. He rubbed his head and winced. When he'd jumped from Nigel's window into the alley, his foot had gotten caught on the sill. He'd tumbled headfirst to the ground. But he'd gotten away, and that was all that mattered in the end.

After leaving Nigel's, Roger had hidden on the path behind the homes, then crawled back to peer through Bukayev's patio gate. All was quiet inside and out, save for the distant barking of a dog. The lights were on upstairs, but he couldn't see Zara or Bukayev through the windows. Instead of camping out indefinitely behind the Chechen's house, he'd made his way through the adjacent neighborhood to the pub. With his barstool facing the intersection of Gloucester and Lennox, he would spot the Chechens if they came this way.

At first, the ale served as an anesthetic for his wounded head and pride. Then it became a way to drown his sorrows. The third anniversary of Jane's death was eight days away. The pain of losing her was still fresh, if no longer quite as raw. Maybe that's why he felt guilty about his instantaneous attraction to Maggie. She was smart, sexy, and funny. But Jane had meant everything to him and he couldn't let go. For years, he'd been patient, waiting for her to work up the courage to leave her husband, Carl. Then finally, she'd made the decision. To celebrate, he'd planned a getaway in San Francisco, after which Jane planned to tell Carl that their marriage was over. She'd cut short a business trip to New York and boarded United Flight 93. Her life, and his future, ended the moment passengers overpowered the hijackers and crashed the plane into a field in Pennsylvania. As far he knew, Carl Manning remained unaware of his wife's betrayal. But as for Roger, he'd been unable to shake the guilt over leading the woman he loved to her death. If he'd picked another date for the rendezvous, if he'd chosen another location, or if he'd insisted she stay with her husband . . . if, if, if.

Roger took a final swig of ale as his thoughts drifted back to Maggie. In theory, she could keep an eye on Bukayev's house so he could catch a few hours of sleep. But Warner would have his head on a platter if he did that. He was supposed to keep her a safe distance from both Bukayev and Zara. Then there was the fact that Maggie wasn't a trained spy and Zara was a cold-blooded killer. He pushed the mug across the bar.

"Are there any mosques around here?"

The bartender, a bloated middle-aged man with a bulbous red nose, stopped wiping the counter. "Mosques? You don't look like one of those Asian types. I swear, they're taking over London."

Roger nodded and turned his attention to a crowd of boisterous young businessmen whose laughter grew louder with every pint. Something told him it was going to be a hell of a long night.

Maggie slipped behind a double-decker bus idling across the street from the two-story cream-colored brick building. She peered around the rear bumper, coughing away black exhaust that stung her throat. Light spilled onto the far sidewalk through the floor-to-ceiling windows lining the façade of the Hereford Arms pub. Inside, patrons in blue jeans and sweaters drank ale, smiled, socialized. All except for the man at the bar, who seemed content to keep to himself. When he swiveled on the stool, Maggie drew back behind the bus. The straight nose, strong jaw, and broad shoulders—it definitely was Roger. She dialed his number again. He glanced at the phone but didn't answer.

Maggie cursed to herself and slung the backpack over her shoulder. She rubbed her arms against the chill. The day's warmth had disappeared with the sun, but she didn't dare run back to the hotel for a sweater. Roger could make a move at any minute. She still didn't know which house was Bukayev's and he probably wouldn't reveal it. Then it occurred to her. She flipped open her phone and studied the picture Roger had taken of Zara descending the front steps. The photo was tiny, but maybe there was enough detail to point her to the right house.

Zara sat up with a start, alone on a canopied, king-sized bed. "Imran?" She grabbed his T-shirt from the foot of the bed and slipped it on. There was no light coming from the bathroom, so she stole down the hall to the lounge. Not there either. She returned to the bedroom and grabbed a flashlight from the nightstand drawer.

Downstairs was dark. And empty. In the family room, Zara opened the French doors leading to the patio. "Imran?" He'd searched the courtyard after they heard the cell phone ringing earlier in the evening. But it couldn't hurt to double-check things. She tugged on the back gate. Locked. The incident had unnerved her, but Imran was adamant that it couldn't have been the Russians. They weren't that sloppy. In the end, they'd agreed that the ringing phone probably had belonged to a jogger running on the path. Even so, Imran's disappearance worried her. But it also presented an opportunity.

She raced back upstairs to the master bedroom and began searching his drawers. As much as she cared for him, she needed to protect herself first. If she ever got arrested, she could bargain for leniency by giving up the goods on the infamous Imran Bukayev. There was nothing interesting in his dresser, which didn't surprise her. Imran hadn't gotten where he was by being careless. Anything important would be well hidden. But where?

Maggie dashed from house to house, stopping along the way to run her hand along the front-step banister at each one. Most of them were shaped like a mound—rounded on the top, flat on the bottom. Just two had completely round handrails. The house to the left had a hefty door knocker. The one in front of her didn't. She checked the cell phone photograph again. This had to be it. The second house from the end.

She trotted toward the cul-de-sac and turned left at the end house. Behind that house, a paved path ran between a high wooden fence on the left and a thick grove of trees on the right. Using a keychain flashlight stowed inside her backpack to help guide her, she followed the path to the back gate of the second row house—Bukayev's house, where a wrought-iron gate led to a courtyard. She tried the handle. Locked. Maggie scanned the windows. All were dark. With one foot on an iron crossbar, she hoisted herself halfway up the gate. The tricky part would be getting over the spiked top without impaling herself.

Zara padded along the upstairs hall to the lounge. She swept the flashlight beam around the room, searching for potential hiding places. She started with the shelves on the far wall, shaking out each book. Nothing. Next came three vases, two on the shelves and an oversized one on the floor. Inside the second vase was a bottle of Russian cognac. *Really.* Imran knew that liquor was *haram*. An interesting discovery, but not what she was looking for.

In addition to finding incriminating evidence about Bukayev, she wanted to find the documents pertaining to the next operation. If she could take care of logistical issues before she left for the mission, there'd be more time to focus on her personal business. It would be better for both of them if she simply kept silent about Maggie Jenkins.

There was nothing under the sofa cushions, not even a crumb of food. "Damn it," she hissed as her knee met the corner of the coffee table. She squatted and ran her hand under the sofa. Nothing there either.

Maybe he was out tonight collecting the documentation she needed. If so, this snooping was a waste of time. Zara was tempted to turn the lights on for a final look at the room, but if Imran saw them from the street, he'd be suspicious, no matter how good her cover story was. She pulled herself onto the sofa and swept the flashlight around the ceiling and walls. *Maybe.*

There was nothing behind the first painting. The second one concealed a safe. She grinned in the dark and set to work, lowering the painting to the floor. She tugged on the safe handle. Not surprisingly, it was locked, and though the chance of her figuring out the combination was slim, it was worth a try.

Maggie's left pant leg got caught on a spike on top of the gate. She fell with a thud to the brick patio. She rubbed her throbbing hip and stayed crouched and motionless a few moments to make sure the fall hadn't awoken Zara or Bukayev. Then she crawled to the window at the back of the house and tested it. *Locked.* She shined her flashlight around the edges, searching for wires or alarms. She did the same thing with the French doors. There were no visible signs of an alarm system—a surprise, but not a guarantee that sirens wouldn't start wailing the second she broke in. It was a risk she'd have to take, she realized, as her stomach churned with anxiety.

Maggie fished her insurance ID card from her backpack. She tried to slow her breathing and recall what Steve had taught her a few years ago.

They were tipsy after a bottle and a half of wine, but he still refused to tell her exactly what he did on overseas missions. "If you really loved me, you'd tell me one story. Just one." She punctuated her pleading with a long, slow kiss.

"If I told you," Steve began.

"You'd have to kill me," Maggie finished. "C'mon, Steve, I have higher clearances than you."

He smiled. "I know, but you know the rules."

"You're no fun." She put her feet on the coffee table and crossed her arms across her stomach.

"I suppose I could teach you how to break into our house. Then the next time you lock yourself out, I won't have to come to the rescue."

She threw a pillow at his head.

Maggie slid the card into the vertical crack between the door and the frame and tilted it until it was almost touching the door handle.

"Now bend the card in the opposite direction."

Maggie could almost hear Steve's voice directing her every move. A smile spread across her face as the lock gave way, but it vanished just as quickly when she noticed the dead bolt. Opening that would require tools and far more expertise. She cursed to herself, leaned into the door, and pushed down on the handle. To her surprise and relief, the door swung open into Imran Bukayev's ground-floor family room.

Zara spun the safe combination lock to the first two numbers she thought of—19 and 44, the year Stalin began the mass deportation of Chechens to Kazakhstan. Then she paused and strained to listen. What was that noise? Something downstairs? Outside? Imran returning? She dashed to the front window. The street was empty. The house silent.

Zara exhaled and returned to the safe. The third number she tried was 57, the year Khrushchev allowed Chechens to return home from exile. And it happened to be the year Imran was born, en route back to his parents' hometown. His mother had died two days after giving birth, just miles from seeing her home for the first time in over a decade.

The safe didn't open, but she persisted, switching the numbers around in various combinations. Still no luck. *Think, think*, she admonished herself.

Zara tugged on her hair. This was much too complicated. If Imran would only give her the information she needed, she wouldn't have to sneak around. She thought of the cognac. Maybe she could get him so drunk he'd reveal the combination. No, he'd probably pass out first. Resigned to defeat, at least temporarily, she reached down for the painting, then froze. This time, she'd definitely heard something.

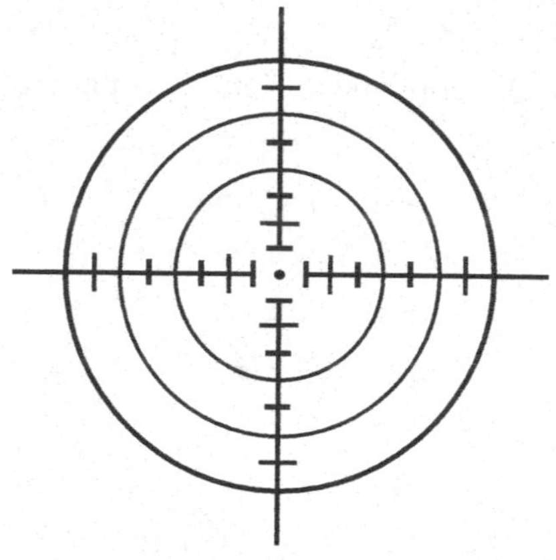

CHAPTER TWENTY

After doing a quick search of the ground floor and finding it empty, Maggie climbed the stairs at a glacial pace, hoping to avoid any creaky floorboards. At the top of the landing, she extinguished the flashlight and stood still. Sometimes at night she'd hear things, things that either weren't there or were innocent house sounds—the heater kicking on, the dishwasher cycling off. Those same sounds must've existed when Steve was alive, but she'd never noticed them. Since his death, the noises had cost her hours of lost sleep, but they'd also heightened her sense of awareness. She listened intently for another minute before deciding it was okay to proceed. The hall was pitch-black, so she felt her way along the wall. When her hand slid from the wall to empty air, she stopped, looked left, and covered her mouth with her hand to silence a gasp. Zara was standing just feet away in the adjacent room, holding a flashlight, her back to the hall. Maggie wanted to charge and deliver a roundhouse kick to her head, but her feet refused to budge.

When Zara started to pivot toward her, Maggie shrank away from the lounge entryway, flattening herself against the wall. Farther up the hall to her left, a key rattled in the front door, sending her heart into wild palpitations. This was it, she'd really screwed up. There was nowhere to hide and no one to help her.

A beam of light suddenly sliced through the darkness. When Zara rushed into the hall and turned toward the front door, Maggie cut behind her into the lounge. She froze in the dark for a moment.

"Zara?"

The woman replied in Russian. "Where have you been, Imran? I've been worried sick."

Maggie clicked on her tiny flashlight and searched for a hiding spot. She dashed over to the first place she saw—the gap between the back of a black leather chair and the front window.

"What are you doing with that flashlight?"

"I heard a noise."

Maggie curled her five-foot-eight frame as small as she could make it and squeezed her eyes shut, the way she had as a little girl when she'd wanted to disappear. Their footsteps got closer. Light flooded the room from an overhead fixture.

"What is this?" Bukayev sounded furious.

Uh-oh.

"I can explain."

Maggie heard the scuffing of shoes on the wooden floor.

"You're trying to break into my safe?"

"Imran—"

"Shut up, Zara."

Maggie winced at the heaviness of the slap.

"Please, Imran."

Thwap. Zara crashed into something. Probably the wall. Maggie made a concerted effort not to look.

"You're off the mission to Washington. I can't trust you anymore."

"But this is to be our most spectacular operation yet," Zara protested.

What operation? Fear clutched at her gut. *Washington, DC?* Maggie crossed her fingers, hoping for details. Instead, Bukayev assaulted Zara with a variety of slurs, the least offensive of which was *slut.* Then he ordered her to her feet. From behind the edge of the chair, Maggie watched him shove Zara out of the lounge toward the back of the house. She waited a few seconds, then scurried to the hall entrance so she could hear what was going on.

Zara was begging Bukayev not to tie her up. He told her to shut up or he'd gag her too. Maggie heard the stomping of his feet before he exited a room on the left. Probably the master bedroom. She ducked behind a tri-paneled decorative screen in the corner and held her breath. Blood pulsed rapidly through her, heightening all her senses.

Bukayev stormed into the lounge, still grumbling about "the bitch." Maggie peeked out from behind the screen and saw why he was so furious. An oversized abstract painting was on the floor, leaning against the wall. Above it was a safe. The painting looked like a three-year-old's artwork to Maggie, but what did she know about the artistic sensibility of nouveau riche terrorists?

Bukayev pulled on the safe's handle. Maggie could see the relief in the man's shoulders as they slumped inward. *Please open it, please open it,* she silently implored. Steve hadn't taught her how to crack a safe, so her only chance to get hold of what was inside was for Bukayev to open it and leave it unlocked. Maggie could see the combination lock, but from this distance, she couldn't make out the numbers.

Bukayev spun the combination dial once, then bent down to examine the painting. He stood and ran a hand through his thick gray hair. Peering around the edge of the screen, Maggie readied the cell phone.

When Bukayev reached for the safe again, Maggie clicked on the video button and aimed the phone at the Chechen as he spun the dial right and left and right again. When the thick metal door swung open, she saved the video—she hoped—and turned off the phone. From her hiding spot, she could see that the safe contained a half-inch-thick stack of papers. Bukayev flipped through them, seemingly satisfied that nothing was amiss.

Then he pulled out a handgun and ran his hand along the barrel.

Maggie closed her eyes and swallowed. To her considerable relief, Bukayev put the gun on top of the papers and closed the safe. Ever so gently, as if handling a newborn baby, the Chechen placed the painting back on the wall. When he turned to check out the rest of the room, Maggie shrank behind the screen.

Bukayev's footsteps stopped. Then came a scraping noise, a clink of something, and the sound of pouring liquid, followed by a satisfied "ahh." He was so close she could've reached out and tapped him on the shoulder. Instead, Maggie blessed herself, hoping it would inoculate her from discovery. There was another clink and the scraping sound again. Then the room went dark, and Bukayev's footsteps echoed away down the hall.

Maggie had to remind herself to exhale, and when she did, her breath came out heavy and unsteady. After waiting another minute, she watched the cell phone video. Maybe she couldn't crack a safe, but she sure could open one with the right combination: *57-44-17.* She heard running water but not a sound from Zara. Quiet was good, but that meant she had to be absolutely silent if she wanted to escape.

Maggie crept a few feet down the hall. Now, all was still on the bedroom front. She returned to the lounge, flashlight in her mouth, and shuffled over to the painting. It was heavier than she'd expected, but she managed to lower it to the floor.

Three spins to the right. Stop on 57. Two spins to the left. Stop on 44. One spin to the right. Stop on 17. *Bingo.* The lever gave way and the safe swung open without a sound.

Maggie ran her hand over the semiautomatic handgun. It looked like a Makarov PM, a pistol used widely by the Soviet army. She'd fired one once at the shooting range. It wasn't her favorite gun, but it would do. The magazine slid from the grip with a muted metallic *swoosh.* Maggie turned the flashlight to the chamber—it was empty. She placed the gun and the magazine into her backpack and rifled through the documents. There were about three dozen pages full of handwritten Cyrillic notes she couldn't decipher. Most likely they were written in Chechen, a language few knew—even Chechens, who'd been forced for decades by the Soviets to learn Russian. She had to hand it to Bukayev. He employed excellent operational security. But it might not be enough to keep his secrets intact. Maggie shoved the papers into the backpack and closed the safe. As she leaned over to grab the painting, the flashlight struck the right side of the canvas. She checked the spot with her finger. The canvas had torn from the frame. *Oops.* Zara would end up paying for that.

Once the damaged painting was securely in place, Maggie doused the flashlight and made her way down the stairs. The house was totally silent. She twisted the lock on the back door and slipped into the courtyard.

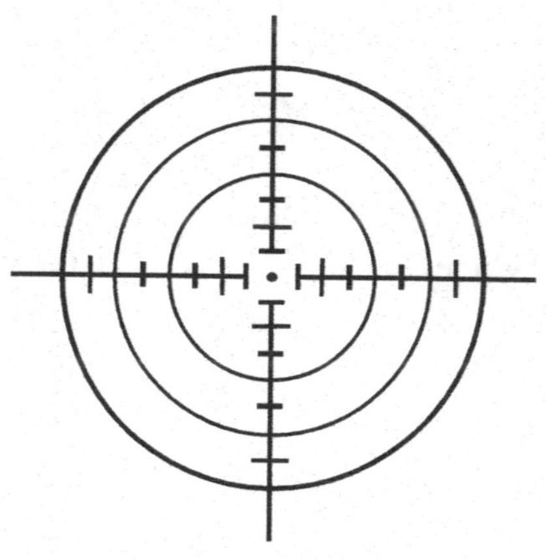

CHAPTER TWENTY-ONE

London
Saturday, September 4, 2004, 12:30 a.m.

Roger leaned against a tree behind Bukayev's house. He'd left the bar a half hour ago and arrived outside the house just as Bukayev had driven up. Talk about a close call. He'd barely managed to dive under Nigel's Bentley before the taxi's headlights hit him. Then there'd been a commotion inside, another Zara-Bukayev knock-down, drag-out, as far as he could tell. If past were prologue, they were having make-up sex right now, which was all fine and dandy for them, but it made Roger's night more miserable. He would have to hide in the woods even longer until he was certain they were asleep.

He pulled out his phone. No messages.

He thought for sure Maggie would be looking for him by now, especially since he hadn't returned any of her earlier calls. Maybe he should give her a ring? But just then, he was distracted by a movement near the path. Someone was scaling Bukayev's gate. It looked like a woman.

Zara?

Roger crept closer.

Zara dropped to the ground.

Crack, a branch splintered under Roger's sneaker.

Zara broke into a run.

Instinct told Roger to hang back, but he'd promised Maggie he wouldn't let Zara get away. He gave chase, surprised at how fast she was. And agile. She weaved through the trees, dodging to escape her pursuer. Despite protesting lungs—he needed to get back to the gym when this was all over—Roger picked up the pace. The gap closed.

He heard her heavy breathing and focused on her backpack. His first swipe at it missed. The second time he held on long enough to throw her off balance. She screamed, fell, and rolled away from him.

Roger lunged, pinning her under his elbow. She struggled and scratched at him. "You're not going anywhere, Zara."

"Get off me, Roger!"

He fumbled for the flashlight in his back pocket and clicked it on. "Maggie?"

"In the flesh. Now get off me before you snap my ankle."

Roger stood and wiped dirt from his pants. "What are you doing here?" He kept the flashlight trained on her face as she sat up and rubbed her foot.

"Quit shining that thing in my eyes."

Roger was rarely at a loss for words, but it took him a moment to regain his voice. "Were you—were you—" he stammered, "were you just in Bukayev's courtyard?"

Maggie pushed herself from the ground and tested her ankle. "Not broken, lucky for you."

"I just saw you climbing over the gate." He pointed over his shoulder.

"Oh, that." A broad smile spread across her face. "I was in his house and that was the safest way out."

"I can't believe you—" His voice rose an octave. "You actually broke into a terrorist's house?" Warner had warned him that she could be a bit impulsive in stressful situations, but *wow*. "Why would you—those two are crazy mother—" Bukayev would've beaten the life from her.

The smile vanished. "You wouldn't answer my calls, so I took matters into my own hands."

"How'd you find the address?" Warner had sent it to him because he couldn't find it online.

"I followed you. Then I used the picture you sent me of Zara to pinpoint the exact house."

"I was handling this, Maggie. I told you I wouldn't let Zara get away."

"Oh, and then I broke into Bukayev's safe."

Roger stared for a moment. "Langley's going to go ballistic. They might even fire you."

Maggie picked at leaves that had taken root in her hair. "They won't."

She didn't know the CIA like he knew the CIA. They'd toss her out on her ass and slam the door behind her.

"Really?"

"They won't because I have the goods on those two." She patted the backpack.

"What kind of goods?"

"I'll get to that. But first, what do we do about Zara?"

"Great question." Roger stepped toward the sound of her voice until he saw the spiral edges of her hair. "And the answer is . . . I don't know. Has Warner contacted MI5?"

Maggie shook her head. "No. He needs the photos of Zara in Beslan and I can't seem to find the memory card. But maybe the documents will give us the proof we need."

"Documents?"

"From the safe."

Roger's temples started to throb. "You took documents from Bukayev's safe?"

"They're planning another attack, Roger. I heard them arguing about some sort of mission. In DC."

"Holy sh—" He stopped himself and rubbed his hands together against the chill. "We have to put those documents back, Maggie. If he notices them missing, he'll destroy all the evidence, send Zara away, maybe go into hiding himself before we figure out what they're planning."

Maggie was silent, then let out a deep breath. "You're right. That's why I want to make copies before returning the documents. Maybe we can get to the embassy and use their photocopier?"

"That'll take too long. We have to put them back as quickly as possible. A guy like Bukayev probably checks his safe every day." He clicked on the flashlight and reached for her backpack.

"What are you doing?" She whispered hoarsely.

He pulled a stack of several dozen papers from the backpack. "I'll shine the light. You take photos of every page."

"Oh, of course." Maggie lined up each page and snapped away.

"When we get back to the hotel, forward the photos to your email. Or better yet, send them to Warner."

"Great idea." She took the last photo and scooped up the documents. "Give me ten minutes. If I'm not out by then, come and get me."

Roger turned the light to his face so she could see how deadly serious he was. "You're not going back in there. Hand me the documents."

"Roger, I know the layout of the house and where the safe is. I've got this."

He threw his head back and stared at dark clouds swirling above in random formation. He had the sense he'd never win an argument with her. Negotiation seemed the better option. "How about we both go in?"

She shook her head. "That doubles the noise factor and doubles our chances of getting caught."

"If you don't let me go with you, I'll call the CIA station chief and tell him we have an emergency." He'd do no such thing, but he also wouldn't let her sneak back into Bukayev's house alone.

She stared at his unblinking eyes. Then, apparently convinced that he'd follow through on his threat, she conceded. "Fine. But only if you stay downstairs and wait for me."

Roger swallowed his pride and said nothing. She grabbed his arm and guided him to Bukayev's back gate.

"Before we go in, let's put all our stuff in the in the backpack."

"Why?"

She frowned at him, hands on hips. "For safe keeping. What if we have to make a run for it and something falls out of our pockets?"

"Unlikely."

"We can't risk leaving any trace behind, Roger."

"Fine," he muttered, shaking his head.

They dropped their phones and Roger's wallet into the pack, and Maggie slung it over her shoulder.

Once they were safely inside the courtyard, Maggie made quick work of the lock on the French door.

"Who taught you how to do that?"

"Shhh!" she shot back.

Roger surveyed Bukayev's family room in the dim light cast by a lamp someone had left on. It was small by American standards but well-appointed by anyone's taste, with its two leather club chairs, a large-screen television and a wine refrigerator in the corner. Maggie lowered the backpack to the floor and signaled for him to wait. With the flashlight in one hand and the documents in the other, she vanished into the darkness upstairs.

Roger paced the length of the room. If anything happened to her up there, he'd never forgive himself. Why'd he let her steamroll him like that? *Come on, Maggie.* Three minutes passed like an eternity. Roger finally exhaled when Maggie returned. "All set?" he whispered.

She nodded then frowned. "I put the flashlight down for a second when I thought I heard a noise. I think I left it at the top of the stairs."

"I'll get it."

Maggie nodded.

Roger climbed the stairs. The flashlight was right where she'd left it. He grabbed it and listened. It would only take a few seconds to scan the lounge and make sure Maggie hadn't left behind any evidence.

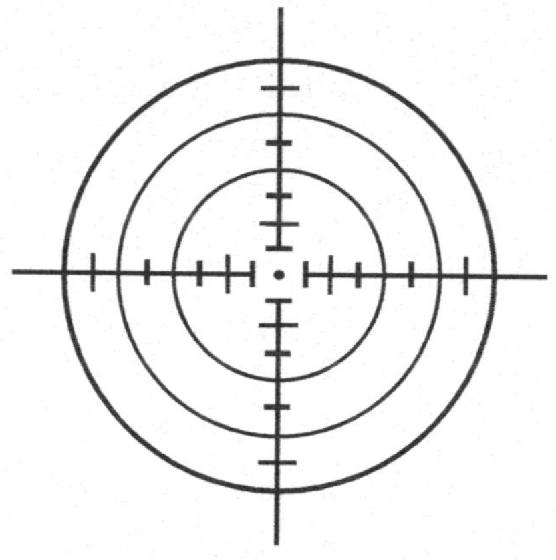

CHAPTER TWENTY-TWO

Maggie had been hiding for a half hour, maybe more. A few moments after Roger went up for the flashlight, there'd been shouting, then a loud crash. She'd grabbed the backpack, ducked into the family room closet, and waited. But Roger hadn't reappeared, which meant one of two things—he was injured or dead. Maggie tried inhaling and holding her breath for a count of five. It did nothing to settle the panic taking over her body. This was all her fault. If she hadn't left the flashlight upstairs, or if she'd made Roger wait outside, they'd have the documents in the CIA's hands by now. For a split second, she considered fleeing. She had all the evidence and she could summon help for Roger. But she couldn't leave him here alone, could she? Steve wouldn't have left a colleague at the mercy of terrorists. And in fairness, Roger probably wouldn't either.

Sudden heavy thuds from the stairwell beyond the family room disrupted her internal debate. Through the crack between the door and the jamb, Maggie saw Bukayev drag a limp Roger into the ground-floor bedroom across the hall. From this angle, only the dirt-crusted soles of Roger's running shoes were visible. When they twitched, relief swept over every inch of her tense body. *Thank God.* He was still alive.

Maggie sank to the floor, bending her knees to her chest to fit herself into the small space. Now the question was, How badly hurt was he? If he was unconscious, she wouldn't be able to drag him out of the house without making a racket. Besides, Bukayev was still in the room keeping watch over his captive. Maggie tried to text Warner an SOS, but her cell battery died in the process. And Roger's phone was passcode protected. Neither development surprised her in the least. Her life of late had comprised a series of events that started off on auspicious notes before descending into chaos.

She shone her keychain flashlight around the closet, pulled the Makarov from the backpack, and let her hands get acclimated to the grip, its weight, and its sights. When it came right down to it, Maggie didn't know if she could kill Bukayev or Zara in cold blood. Then again, she'd fired under pressure before, and at the moment, there didn't seem to be another viable solution. She placed the gun next to her feet, gave up fighting exhaustion, and let her forehead rest on her knees.

• ★ ★ ★ •

Zara's head throbbed. Imran had kept her locked in the master bedroom until 4:00 this morning. Just as she'd finally fallen asleep, he burst into the room and ordered her to get up. She was furious with herself for being so careless. And now everything was in jeopardy. Even seducing him might not be enough to put her plans back on track. She had to lead his mission in Washington, DC. It was the only way she'd be able to get to her targets. And now that she knew where they both lived, she was tantalizingly close to success. If things went well, she'd take out his targets, but her priority was the ones he didn't know about. The only ones she cared about.

She picked at a piece of dry toast. Her coffee was cold. "Imran, I'm so sorry. It was foolish of me to mess with your safe. I know I should trust you, but I wasn't thinking straight. I'm so tired from Beslan."

He frowned at her, circled his hand above his head, and whispered hoarsely. "For all I know, this place is bugged. Don't mention that place in this house. Ever. Do you understand?"

She nodded, afraid if she spoke, she wouldn't be able to conceal her irritation. How dare he speak to her as if she were a child?

He got up from the table to pour himself a fresh cup of coffee but didn't bother offering her any. "You're not scheduled to leave until Tuesday. If I let you go. And I may not. The entire operation might be on hold because of our friend downstairs. I can't even interrogate him. He's out cold."

"You sure he's not faking it?"

"Of course I'm sure." He leered at her like she was some sort of imbecile. "If he wakes up, I've got him tied to the dresser. He's not going anywhere."

"Any identification on him?"

"Nothing."

"Imran, can't we just get rid of the guy? Our plans have been in motion for so long. We can't abandon them now. And you know I'm the only person for the job." She tossed a chunk of dark hair over her shoulder. "Look at me. Like you always say, I don't fit the profile. And I'm an experienced professional."

Imran didn't reply. Zara took this as confirmation that he agreed. He couldn't suddenly substitute some male jihadist. It would never work. She walked over to him, letting her breasts brush his arm.

"Can I show you how sorry I am?"

Imran grabbed her forearm and tugged her toward the master bedroom. She was exhausted, but she summoned the energy to satisfy her distracted lover. It was over quickly, and he seemed less hostile. Zara decided not to push her luck by mentioning the operation again. Instead, she kissed his bare chest and let her hair fan out across him, while her mind wandered.

Less than a week from now, Americans would be reeling. What they were about to do would rip the bandage from the wounds of a still unhealed country.

She smiled.

"What is it, Zara?"

"I want more," she whispered.

"I don't satisfy you?"

"Imran, there's no one better." She lifted her head from his chest. "I just can't get enough of you, and after last week, I realize it could all end at any time. I could have died there."

He played with her hair. "Are you willing to die for me?"

She was willing to die for her own cause, not for his. But perhaps those two causes would merge in Washington, DC. "I am."

He pulled her on top of himself. "I think I believe you, Zara. But you have to follow my instructions to the letter. You have to trust me. And obey me."

"I will, Imran." She kissed his neck to conceal her smile. "Believe me, I will."

"I need you to kill the man downstairs when I'm done questioning him."

She brushed her lips across his. "I'd be glad to."

Maggie listened from the bottom of the stairs. She couldn't hear what they were saying, but there definitely were two voices up there. How long had she been asleep in the closet? It couldn't have been more than a few minutes. It seemed like Bukayev had only just gone upstairs after his long vigil over Roger. Outside, the sky was just starting to shed its heavy darkness.

She tiptoed across the hall to the guest bedroom and swept the light across Roger's still body. This might be their only chance to escape. His arms were pulled tight over his head, bound at the wrists, the rope lashed to the leg of an enormous cherrywood dresser.

She dropped to her knees and touched his chest. "Roger," she whispered. "Can you hear me?"

He remained still, unresponsive.

She patted his cheeks, gently at first, then a little harder. "Roger? You have to wake up." *Please.*

"Mmmm." He twisted his head away from her and moaned.

"That's it, Roger, wake up. We have to get out of here before Bukayev comes down to check on you."

His right eye opened a crack. "Arms."

"Hang on." She crawled to his hands and started to work on the rope, stopping suddenly at the sound of heavy footsteps on the stairs. "Pretend you're still out," she whispered in his ear. She swept the tiny flashlight around the room and sprang toward the bedroom closet, sliding the door shut just as Bukayev appeared in the doorway.

Maggie hugged the backpack to her chest, her heart beating wildly.

"Wake up!" the Chechen commanded.

She flinched at the sound of Bukayev's hand against Roger's face. The Chechen swore and stomped back up the stairs.

Maggie put her ear against the closet door and listened. Roger was groaning softly. She slid the Makarov from the backpack and pushed the door open a crack. Only half the room was visible.

"Maggie!" Roger whispered hoarsely.

"Shhh," she cautioned.

Roger lifted his head a few inches from the floor. "He's gone."

She placed the gun in the backpack and set to work on the ropes around Roger's wrists. "Do you think you can walk?"

"Yeah, it's just my head." He grimaced. "It feels like it's split in half."

She ran a hand over his hair. There was a welt on the back of his skull, but only a spattering of dried blood surrounding it. The area around his right temple looked worse—it was starting to swell and bruise.

"I love when you play with my hair." He tried to wink, but it came across more like a wince.

She fought back a smile. "Give it a rest, Roger, or I will really split your head open." She freed both his arms and helped him sit up.

He shook out his wrists, grabbed the edge of the dresser, and pulled himself to a stand. "We have to get out of here."

"You sure you can make a run for it?"

He nodded, winced again.

She peered into the hall, then hurried to the bedroom door that led outside. Maggie held her breath, gripped the handle, and pushed it down. The door swung in, and Maggie stepped out. Early-morning sun broke over the treetops, scattering soft light across the courtyard bricks. She motioned for Roger to follow.

He glanced up at the upstairs windows. "Let's go." He unlocked the gate and let Maggie exit first. Out on the path, she stopped short and grabbed Roger's arm.

A stout man in an unseasonably heavy overcoat was lumbering down the path, head down, shoulders forward. As Roger nodded toward the woods, the man looked up. His eyes, small and dark under heavy, unruly brows, locked with Maggie's. The corrugated skin of his face betrayed a hard-lived life. He stopped and slid his hand inside the overcoat.

"Maggie," Roger whispered, "run like hell."

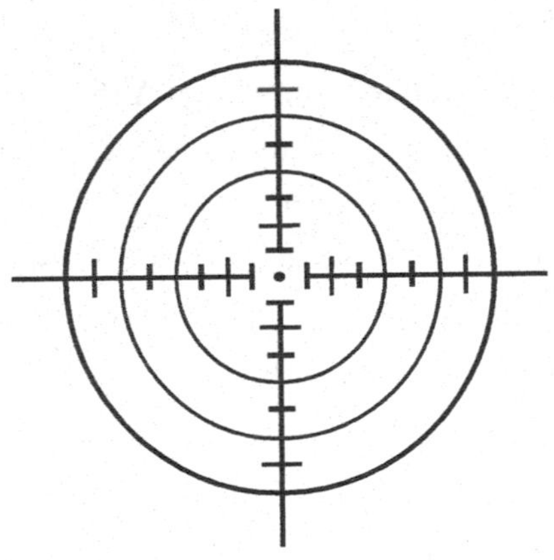

CHAPTER TWENTY-THREE

Zara flew down the stairs at the sound of Bukayev's shouts. She found him in the guest bedroom, clutching a length of rope.

"What happened?" Imran never screwed up. Not when it counted.

He unleashed a string of Russian profanities and tugged at his hair.

Zara pulled the rope from his hands and tossed it on the bed. "Imran, that man couldn't possibly know anything. He never even saw me." The color was rising on Bukayev's cheeks. "Imran, look at me. We can figure this out together."

He turned his black eyes and his fury on her. "This is your fault, Zara. You never should have come here. And if you hadn't put on your seductress act upstairs, I wouldn't have been distracted."

"This is your screwup, Imran, not mine."

His hand came too fast to stop. Zara stumbled and cried out from the pricking sting. That's it. She was done whoring herself out to this man. She was done with his pedantic Islamic affectations. She was done with his cause. Once she got to DC, she'd take care of her targets. To hell with his.

• ★ ★ ★ •

Maggie and Roger tore into the woods, slowing to a jog when they realized the man was running away from them.

"Who the hell was that?" Maggie stopped and rested her hands on her thighs.

"Beats me, but that guy doesn't look like he's from the neighborhood."

"Let's follow him."

"Maggie, no, that's crazy." Roger ran his fingers gingerly across the back of his head. "You've done all you can do."

"What if he has something to do with Zara or Bukayev?" She stood straight and crossed her arms. "In case you didn't notice, she's still not in custody."

"Yes, and we're still alive. Let's keep it that way."

"I can't. I've spent all these months—" Maggie stopped herself short and bit down on her lip.

"All these months doing what, Maggie?"

"Trying to find her, Roger. I can't—" She cleared her throat. "She's not getting away this time." Maggie glanced over her shoulder as she jogged away. "You coming?" She merged onto the path.

Roger joined her moments later, muttering something about her making his headache worse.

"Let's go." Maggie led the way down the path and around the side of the end row house. Her breath produced little puffs of fog in the chilly morning air. She leaned her head around the corner of the house, but quickly snapped it back and turned to Roger, her eyes wide. "You're not going to believe this." She peeked again. The man was at Bukayev's door, his right hand inside the overcoat, his left hand pounding on the knocker.

"Believe what?"

The man pulled a semiautomatic handgun from his coat, slamming the butt of it against the door.

"He's going to kill them," she hissed.

Roger crept past Maggie and took up a position behind a Bentley that was parked at the curb.

Maggie followed. "What do we do?"

Roger shrugged. "If he kills them, we can go home."

She recoiled. Yes, it would finally be over.

But then she wouldn't have the chance to . . . to . . . what? Have the last word? Pull the trigger herself? "She has to pay for what she's done."

He looked over his shoulder. "Death is the ultimate payment."

She opened her mouth to reply but realized she had nothing to say.

The man pounded on the door again, then rattled the knob. He finally gave up, turned, and lumbered in their direction. Maggie and Roger dove under the Bentley, managing to pull their legs into hiding just as the man's thick-soled brown shoes passed by.

Maggie counted to twenty and dragged herself out from under the car. Whatever was going on, she didn't want to miss a second of it.

Roger scrambled out after her. "We have to get the hell out of here."

Maggie pushed her hair away from her face. "I'm not going anywhere." She ran to the neighbor's side yard and turned onto the path. Up ahead, the man stood in front of Bukayev's patio gate. A shot rang out, but it hadn't come from his pistol, which left only one possibility. One of the Chechens was firing from inside the house.

The man flattened himself against the brick wall and looked to his right, locking eyes with Maggie again. "*Ukhohdite!*" He raised the gun and motioned for her to go away.

Maggie had no idea who this Russian-speaking man was, but she wasn't about to argue with his directive. She backed toward the side yard, then turned and ran for the street.

"Roger?" she called. Across the street, a bleary-eyed woman peered out her front door. A thin man with a shock of white hair stood outside the corner house. He squinted at Maggie.

"Miss, was that a gunshot I heard?"

Roger popped up from the street side of the Bentley. "Nigel, get back in the house, away from the windows."

The old man craned his neck toward Roger. "Pardon me, do we know each other? How in the dickens do you know my name?" He crossed his arms over his royal-blue bathrobe and frowned. "I say, are you trying to steal my car?"

"Sir, it's not safe." Maggie pulled Bukayev's Makarov from the backpack and slid the magazine into place. "Please go back inside."

The old man sighed, muttered something about the world going to hell, and retreated into his house.

Maggie joined Roger on the street. "That thug could have shot me back there." She nodded toward the alley. "But he didn't. He told me to go away. In Russian."

"That guy's Russian?"

"Apparently."

"Who the hell is he?"

"Someone sent to kill Zara and Bukayev?" She waved her hand in the air. "I have no idea."

Roger's eyes locked on the black gun. "Where did that come from?"

Maggie didn't bother explaining. There was too much commotion. Up the street, Zara was running, full throttle, her dark hair whipping behind her. Just then, the man in the trench coat tore around the corner of the cul-de-sac. He did his best to catch Zara, but the gap between them grew. The semiautomatic pistol in his right hand pumped in time with his lumbering gait. Bukayev streaked out his front door seconds after the man passed, jumped in his blue Audi convertible, and sped toward Zara. The man stopped for a moment and eyeballed the car as it approached. He watched it pass, never raising the weapon at Bukayev. Instead, he started running again, firing wildly at Zara.

The moment Zara dove into the car, the shots stopped. In the rearview mirror, Bukayev saw the man chasing them, but there was no way he'd catch up now. He looked over at Zara, who was still too out of breath to speak.

"He was after you, not me." It was a statement as much as a question.

Zara nodded, then started to laugh between gasps.

"What's so funny? You could have been killed."

Zara took a few deep breaths. "The Russian army can't stop me, but they think a lone assassin can. That's what's funny."

There were so many things about her that Bukayev didn't understand. Maybe all that mattered was that she was willing to martyr herself, albeit reluctantly and for her own reasons. But he couldn't help feeling that time was running out for her, which meant the mission had to go forward as planned. If not sooner.

"Zara, you mustn't become overconfident. You might be lucky, but you're not invincible."

"Maybe. Maybe not." She turned and stared out the window.

"Zara, this is serious. An intruder broke into my house and escaped. Then an assassin tried to kill you. Someone knows who you are and knows you're with me. I absolutely cannot be tied to Beslan, which means I must not be tied to you."

"It's a little late for that, isn't it?"

He was tired of their constant fighting. The truth was, he didn't need Zara. Imran could have almost any woman he wanted. He simply had to direct Omar to bring him one. Some were more beautiful than others, but they were all young, subservient, and docile. Sure, Zara was more alluring. She was ferocious, irreverent, sensual. But she was also becoming a liability. He needed to ensure that her next mission would be her last.

"You can't go back to the house. The police will be swarming everywhere." He formulated a cover story. "When I go home, I'll tell them I just met you last night. And that the man with the gun was your husband, out for revenge on his cheating wife."

"Where are you taking me?" She tried to comb her fingers through tangled hair.

"The mosque."

"Imran, anywhere but there." She pouted. "I won't be able to think or prepare myself for the mission if I'm at the mosque."

"No." He refused to succumb to her emotional manipulation. "You'll stay at the mosque until I can get you out of the country."

• ★ ★ ★ •

Maggie and Roger raced up the street. Zara and Bukayev were long gone, but the gunman was still in sight. With Roger falling back, Maggie kicked into full sprint mode, desperate to catch the Russian, to find out what he knew about Zara. The pounding of her feet drowned out the curious and concerned shouts of Bukayev's neighbors, who by now were milling about in the street wondering what had happened to their tranquil little neighborhood.

Up ahead, the man turned the corner onto Gloucester Street. Maggie arrived seconds later, only to watch him disappear into the back of a sputtering pea-green taxi.

She collapsed onto a bench and threw her head back. "Damn it!" she huffed. *Not again*. She swiped furiously at a tear that appeared out of nowhere in the corner of her eye.

"You might want to put the gun away." Roger was at her side, sounding even more winded than she felt. "Handguns are illegal in the UK. You get caught with that, you're screwed."

"Right." Maggie wriggled her shoulders from the backpack straps, ejected the magazine, and dropped both pieces inside the pack. Roger looked like he'd gone a few rounds in a bar brawl. Blood crusted on one side of his head, a blossoming black eye, a scraped chin, and silver stubble sprouting across his face.

He touched her shoulder. "You okay?"

"I'm fine." She sniffed and ran her hands through her hair. "What just happened back there, Roger?"

"Obviously, someone sent that guy to kill Zara." He wiped a trickle of sweat from his hairline. "Looks like we're not the only ones who know about her."

"Roger." Maggie stood, her expression panicked, and grabbed his arm. "Sirens. Come on, we should get out of here." She flagged down a taxi and yanked him inside as the wailing grew louder. "The Grosvenor Kensington Hotel, please."

"You should probably stay in my room to make sure I don't die from this head wound."

Maggie offered a tired smile. "You wish. Do you have any money for the fare?"

"You get me into this mess and then expect me to pick up the tab?"

Five minutes later, the taxi pulled to the curb. Inside, Maggie marched to the elevators, pushed the button for the fourth floor, and yawned.

"What's next, Maggie?"

She shrugged. "No idea. It all feels so useless. And I'm just so tired."

Up on their floor, Maggie fished her room key out of the backpack and slipped it into the door. She tried to push the door shut behind her, but Roger's foot and arm got in the way.

He forced open the door. "If you're Bukayev, where do you go? Someplace safe, right?"

Maggie ran a hand through her tangled hair. "I guess." She tossed the backpack onto the bed and grabbed two bottled waters from the refrigerator. "Here."

Roger took a swig.

"She's a Russian citizen but obviously can't take refuge at the Russian embassy."

Maggie plugged in her cell phone, sank onto the bed, and curled onto her side.

"And she can't go back to Bukayev's."

"Maybe he's taking her to a friend's house," she mumbled, her eyes half closed.

He sat on the edge of the bed. "You know that scene in *The Sound of Music*?"

"Excuse me?" She rolled onto her back and eyed him.

"The one where the von Trapps hide from the Nazis in the abbey?"

She rubbed at her face. "Yeah."

"Replace Maria with Zara and the nuns with imams."

She groaned. "That would make us the Gestapo, Roger."

"Okay, forget that part. But don't you see? The only safe place Bukayev can take Zara is a mosque."

Maggie sat up, suddenly more alert. "Do you have any idea how many mosques there are in London?"

His shoulders slumped. "Hundreds."

"We're never going to find her."

"Wait." He jumped up and began pacing. "When I was online yesterday, I saw a profile about Bukayev. It said something about his mosque."

Which mosque?"

"I'd have to look it up, but I'm willing to bet it's low profile."

Maggie's eyes grew wide. "One that British intelligence isn't watching."

"Exactly."

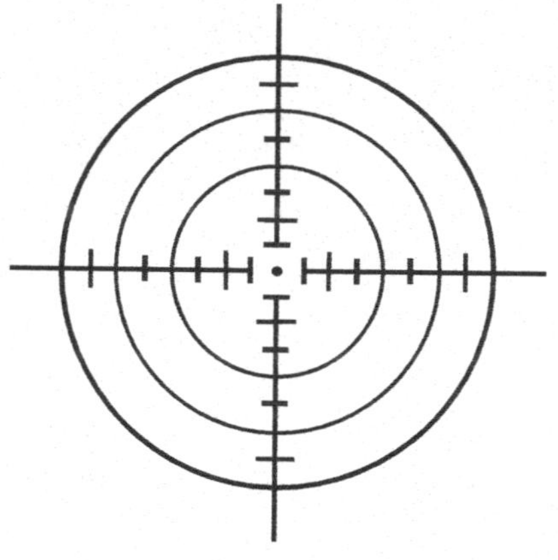

CHAPTER TWENTY-FOUR

Bukayev dialed Omar's phone number. The Jordanian acknowledged the prearranged emergency code and hung up. Things weren't exactly going according to plan, but at least Zara understood her role. And soon, she'd be in safe hands.

Bukayev parked behind the mosque. Allah willing, the police wouldn't be watching the place right now. He handed Zara his sunglasses. "Keep your head down and follow me." It looked like she might protest, but his scowl silenced her.

They hustled up the sidewalk to a rear door partway down an alley. Bukayev knocked twice. Omar opened the door and ushered them in. He ogled Zara's tight jeans and low-cut blouse, his expression a combination of sneering disapproval and brazen lust.

"I apologize for her immodest dress, Omar. You must have something appropriate for her to wear?"

Zara shot Bukayev a look, but she kept her mouth shut.

"Yes, of course, more modest clothes." He stopped undressing Zara with his eyes and led them to a small, windowless room with two oversized brown chairs and a matching sofa. "Make yourself comfortable," he added before scurrying off to find something to cover her sinful flesh.

"Imran, please don't make me stay here." Her eyes were wide and moist, full of panic and pleading.

It was hard to believe that she was more afraid of a mosque than an assassin. "It's just for a while, Zara. As soon as I get your passport and tickets, you'll be on your way."

"Hurry."

"I will. In the meantime, behave yourself. And get some rest."

Omar appeared with an abaya, which he placed on one of the chairs. Both men turned for the door.

"Where are you going, Imran?"

"Things are going to happen very quickly now. You're safe here."

They stepped into the hall. Omar shut the door and locked it from the outside before Zara figured out what was happening.

Maggie grabbed two cups of coffee from the hotel's breakfast room while Roger used the business-office computer to find the article he remembered seeing about Bukayev speaking at a London mosque.

"Found it," he said as Maggie joined him. "We should probably call Warner and let him know."

"As soon as we get a taxi." Maggie handed him a disposable coffee cup as they made their way to the lobby. Once inside the cab, she dialed. "Quick update, Warner. Bukayev held Roger hostage. I freed him. A Russian hitman tried to killed Zara but she got away. We're on the way to Bukayev's mosque. Tell MI5 and call me when you get this."

"Nice message. He'll be thrilled to get it."

Maggie looked at her watch. It was 4:30 in the morning in Washington, DC. "Maybe he's already in the office."

"On a Saturday?"

"Knowing Warner, he's been there all night trying to figure out where the hell we went." She dialed his office number. It rang five times before going to a general voice mail that he probably never checked.

Ten minutes later, the taxi pulled to the sidewalk across the street from the mosque that Bukayev was known to frequent. Were it not for the minaret rising above the brick façade, the mosque would pass for an ordinary office building.

"Now what?" Roger asked. "Do we go in and ask for Zara?"

Maggie looked at her phone. *Where are you, Warner?* "I don't know. Even if we call the police, it would take hours to convince them to raid the place."

The taxi driver studied them in the rearview mirror. "Why would you raid that mosque?"

Roger grimaced. "Could you forget that you heard that?"

The driver shrugged. "The people who attend services here are a friendly lot."

"How do you know?" Roger asked.

"I've been in there. Took a tour. Was curious, I suppose. I'm a Christian of sorts, but I can't say the last time I went to church. Maybe my grandmum's funeral."

Maggie gave herself a looking over. "I'm not exactly dressed for a mosque."

"You could buy something more appropriate right over there, miss." The driver pointed to a store with black, tan, and gray abayas in the display window. Draped around them was an assortment of brightly colored scarves. "Sign says they open at ten on the weekend."

"Great idea." With that, she exited the taxi and dashed across the street to the store. Inside, a saleswoman wearing a vibrant turquoise, yellow, and white patterned hijab approached.

"May I help you?"

"Yes, um, I was hoping," Maggie stammered. "Something simple. I'm just visiting a mosque."

The woman smiled. "I see. Perhaps one of these abayas?"

Maggie nodded and glanced out the window at the cab. She could see Roger leaning forward, chatting with the driver.

"Anything else?"

"No, thank you. I'm sure I'll find something I like." Once the woman left, she placed a hand against the clothing rack to steady herself. Maybe this was pushing things too far. Acting the part of a Muslim woman? She didn't know the first thing about how to behave or where to go inside a mosque. But she'd come this far and she couldn't stop now.

She owed this to Steve. To herself.

Without checking the price or the length, she selected a tan abaya and a matching scarf. In a flash, she was back in the seat beside Roger, pulling the garment over her head. She draped the scarf over her hair, wrapped it around her neck and secured the ends under the abaya's neckline. "How do I look?"

Roger tucked loose ends of her hair under the scarf. "Great, as always, but for the record, I am advising you not to do this. At least not without me."

Maggie looked him up and down. There was no hiding the swelling and discoloration on his temple. "If Bukayev's in there, he'll recognize you immediately. He's never seen me."

"But Zara has."

She smoothed the tan fabric. "If I'm not out in five minutes, you come in." She pulled the gun from the backpack, keeping it out of the driver's line of vision and nodded to Roger as she lowered it back into the bag. "Just in case."

"We can just watch for Zara from here. Follow her if she leaves." He placed a hand on hers. "You don't have to do this."

She averted her eyes. "I know."

"I mean it, Maggie. You're not alone in this anymore. You've done more than anyone could've ever expected. It's okay to let go."

She bit down on her lower lip and blinked rapidly. "I'm just going to take a look around."

"Okay." He squeezed her hand. "I'm right behind you if you need me."

Warner toweled off and studied his tired face in the mirror. Another horrible night's sleep was written all over it. He snatched his phone from the vanity and groaned. Maggie's message was both unclear and alarming. She didn't answer. He tried Roger.

"Roger, what the hell is going on over there?"

"Hang on a second."

Warner heard a car door slam.

"I'm outside a mosque where we think Bukayev is hiding Zara."

"Where's Maggie?"

Roger exhaled. "Inside the mosque."

"What? How could you . . . you let her . . . damn it, Roger!"

"It's been an insane twelve hours, Warner. We took documents from Bukayev's house that may prove his terrorist links." He glanced over at the mosque. All was calm from the outside. "If Zara is in that mosque, I think we have enough for the Brits to detain her."

He clenched his free hand into a fist. "You'd better not let anything happen to Maggie."

"I won't."

"I'll make a few phone calls. I have a good friend in MI6 who can connect me with the right people. What's the name of the mosque?"

Warner wrote down the information, threw on a pair of sweatpants, and flew down the stairs to his home office. Rebecca, his old MI6 friend, had spent her career recruiting Soviet-bloc agents, quite successfully in fact, if you didn't count the rather hairy incident in Berlin twenty years earlier. It hadn't ended well, but thanks to him, Rebecca had made it out alive.

She'd vowed to repay him one day.

That day had come.

He flipped through his Rolodex until he found her card.

"Hello, Rebecca, it's Warner."

"I'm afraid Ms. Wellington isn't home this morning," a woman replied. "Would you like to leave her a message?"

"Is she at the office?"

"I'm sorry, who is this?"

Warner hung up and called the second number.

"Rebecca Wellington's office."

"Hello, this is Warner Thompson from the CIA. I need to speak with Ms. Wellington. It's urgent."

"The CIA? It seems everyone is working this weekend."

"Is she there?"

"Yes, but I'm afraid she's in a meeting."

Warner scratched furiously at his head. "It can't wait. If you would, slip her a note that says 'Berlin 1984.'"

"Okay," the receptionist replied. "Your name again?"

"Warner. She'll know."

"Right. Please hold."

Warner paced before the expansive bookshelves lining the walls behind his desk. A thin layer of dust had accumulated on his full collection of Winston Churchill books. He hadn't noticed because he never had time to read. Or clean.

Finally, after what felt like an interminable wait, Rebecca Wellington's voice came over the line. "Warner, darling, how are you? Everything all right?"

"Rebecca, there's a situation in London right now. The terrorist who escaped Beslan was seen with Imran Bukayev."

"Bukayev? There were shots fired in his neighborhood early this morning, if I'm not mistaken. Hold on." The sound of shuffling papers filled the line. "Yes, right here. In my morning briefing, London police informed MI5 that shots were fired on Lennox Place, which is where Bukayev lives. No injuries reported, but neighbors say they saw him fleeing the area in his car. Current whereabout unknown, at least as of early this morning. I didn't follow up as this is MI5's responsibility."

"That's why I'm calling. I have a couple of people on Bukayev's trail."

"The CIA is conducting an intelligence operation on British soil? Without our knowledge?"

He swallowed. How to explain Maggie in a thousand words or fewer? "Not exactly. I authorized no such operation, but one of our analysts ran off to London yesterday to follow up on some information. Things have sort of spiraled from there."

"Why didn't you call me yesterday?"

"I should've. And I apologize." He scrambled to explain. "Because of the political sensitivities around Bukayev's presence in London, the State Department general counsel advised me to compile the intelligence we gathered in Russia before approaching your government."

"I see."

"I had every intention of doing so, but they . . . this analyst went dark on me for about twelve hours. As soon as I heard from her this morning, I called you."

"It sounds like you have a rogue operative on your hands."

"Yeah, and I'll deal with that. Right now, my priority is getting Maggie out of danger. She's really important to me."

"Oh? Do tell, Warner."

"Not like that, Rebecca. She was engaged to the CIA officer we lost last year in Georgia. Anyway, the point is, she's in a mosque in pursuit of Bukayev and a terrorist named Zara Barayeva."

"I can't just call MI5 and have them raid the mosque. There's a whole set of procedures we have to go through. And political considerations."

"Rebecca," he pleaded, "there's no time for that."

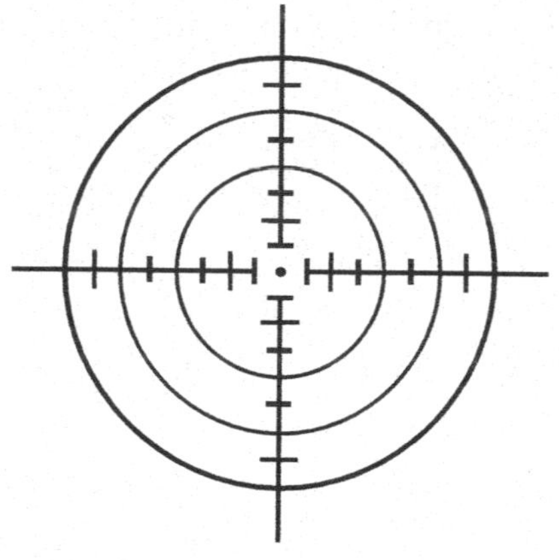

CHAPTER TWENTY-FIVE

Inside the lobby, Maggie nodded to several men who eyed her curiously. "*As-salam Alaikum.*"

"*Wa 'alaikum-as-salam,*" one replied.

She averted her eyes and took in the space. Arabic script in flowing calligraphy dominated the wall to the right. Mosaic tile-work in azure-blue and white marble drew her attention to the prayer hall entrance across the lobby. Zara wouldn't be in there. It was reserved for the men. To the left was a sign in both Arabic and English directing her to the women's section of the mosque.

Checking behind her to make sure the men hadn't followed, Maggie entered a long, dimly lit hall with a series of closed doors lining both sides. The first two rooms she checked appeared to be meeting rooms. Ahead on the left was the women's bathroom with a foot washing basin in the corner. Also empty. At the end of the hall, she tried to open the last door on the right. Locked. Perhaps it was the women's prayer room? She rattled the handle.

"Hello?" came a muffled voice from inside.

Zara? Maggie cleared her throat and donned a British accent. "Are you doing okay?"

The doorknob rattled. "Let me out."

"I can't. You're safer in there."

"Are they looking for me?"

"I don't know, but we should keep you hidden just in case." Maggie fumbled with her phone and dialed Roger. "I think I found her," she whispered, forgetting the British accent.

"Where?"

"Locked in a room near the rear of the building."

Zara pounded on the door. "What's going on out there? Open the door!"

"I need to get the key," she called, British accent back in place.

She returned to Roger. "How quickly can you pick a lock?"

"In seconds. But then what? We detain her?"

Zara pounded even louder. "Open. The. Door!"

"Hang on." Maggie trotted to the end of the hall and pushed open a door labeled "Exit." "There's an alley behind the mosque. Have the taxi drive down it. Then you pick the lock, we grab Zara, throw her in the cab, and take her somewhere."

"Where?"

"I don't know. The embassy?"

"Do you have any idea how many laws, both British and American, that would break?"

"You have a better idea, Roger?"

"This is insane."

"We'll figure it out. Meet me in the alley."

Maggie stepped back inside and returned to Zara's room. "They're bringing the key now." She grimaced the second she realized she'd forgotten to disguise her American accent.

Zara began pounding the door again. And shouting. "Let me out!"

A commotion erupted at the end of the hall nearest the lobby. Two men dressed in dark-wash jeans and black polo shirts advanced toward Maggie.

Maggie averted her eyes. "The woman in this room needs to use the restroom."

"Omar!" Zara yelled from behind the door.

One of the men put a phone to his ear as they advanced. "Who are you?" the other said.

Maggie backed toward the exit.

"Stop right there," he commanded.

Maggie turned and sprinted the final fifteen feet and burst into the alley. Roger was just exiting the taxi. "Go, go, go!" she shouted. "I'm blown."

"Drive!" Roger shouted as they dove into the car. The bewildered driver threw the gear into reverse just as the men emerged from the mosque and began to give chase.

"Go!" Maggie urged again.

"Where to?" A flush spread across the man's pasty complexion.

"Away. Get us away."

She peered around the driver's shoulder. Both men were on their phones gesturing toward the taxi, which had reached the end of the alley. The driver spun the vehicle around and careened into traffic.

"If I lose my license over whatever that was—" He waved a hand out the window.

Maggie pulled two fifty-pound notes from her wallet and offered them to the driver. "For a job well done."

The man wiped sweat from his forehead with his sleeve and grabbed the money.

Two blocks ahead, Maggie slipped out of the abaya and the headscarf.

"Pull over here, please," Roger said.

"Gladly," replied the driver.

"What are we doing?" Maggie asked, her voice shaking.

"We've got to get the documents to Warner."

"Right." Maggie fumbled for her phone. She scrolled to the email icon and clicked to attach the first document. They both watched as the progress bar crept across the screen. After three minutes, it still hadn't attached to the email. "Without Wi-Fi, it'll take hours to send all these pages."

Roger squeezed his eyes shut. "Okay, here's what we're going to do. I'll take your phone to the embassy and use their Wi-Fi. You keep my phone in case you need it. In the meantime, you stay in the car and watch the road. If you see Zara leave, follow her, but don't do anything. Don't let her see you."

Maggie nodded. "Okay, but hurry, Roger."

Roger exited to the sidewalk, leaned into the car, and smiled wearily at Maggie. "I'll see you soon."

She watched as he ducked into another cab and sped off. "Would you mind driving back to the mosque?"

"I'd rather not, miss."

"We can park up the street. I'm not going back inside. I just need to see if anyone leaves."

"Bloody hell," he muttered as he spun the car around, eventually parking a half block from the mosque entrance.

All seemed calm, nothing out of the ordinary. Then she saw it: a black Mercedes sedan edging out from the alley. She could make out a figure in the backseat with long, dark hair. When the woman turned her head, Maggie saw she wore large sunglasses. Two men, the ones who'd chased her, were in the front seat. "Follow that car, please!"

The driver sighed but complied. The Mercedes driver proceeded through traffic without displaying any signs of urgency or distress. The cab was three vehicles back. They followed the vehicle west on the A4. "Where does this road go?"

"Lots of places."

Maggie studied the road signs. "Like Heathrow Airport?"

"Indeed. It's about eight, maybe nine miles from here. But they could be going anywhere west, really."

Once they were three miles from the airport, Maggie was certain. She grabbed Roger's phone and then realized she didn't know his pin code. "For crying out loud!"

"Is there a problem?"

"I hate to ask but could I borrow your phone?"

The driver rolled his eyes and handed his phone to her.

The moment Warner recognized her voice, he jumped right in without a greeting. "I just got off a very unpleasant call with the heads of MI5, MI6, the assistant to the foreign secretary, and our ambassador, who wants you to report to the embassy immediately."

"I can't."

"The Brits are furious. If this story leaks to the press, the entire world will think that the CIA is running covert operations in allied countries."

"Don't we already do that?"

"Not without their permission," he shouted. "And certainly not without the CIA's authorization."

"I'm sorry for the trouble. But we can still get her."

"MI5 is preparing to search the mosque. There's a dragnet out for Bukayev. Whatever you're doing, stop."

"I'm following her. She's a mile from—" The phone cut out. "I lost the call."

"What can I say? Coverage is a little spotty sometimes."

She hit redial. The call wouldn't connect.

"You're not calling overseas, are you?"

"I'll reimburse you."

"Roaming minutes are expensive, you know. I set my phone so it cuts off when I reach my monthly limit. I can't afford to go over that. I'm just a cabbie."

She threw her head against the seatback.

"You used up all my minutes, but at least you've given me some excitement for the day. Can't say that often."

They approached the entrance to Terminal 3. "Don't lose that Mercedes, please!" Ahead, the black sedan pulled to the curb. "Hurry," she urged the driver. Just then a traffic officer stepped in front of the taxi, stopping it to let a group of elderly tourists cross to a waiting bus.

She grabbed her backpack and jumped out of the cab. "Thanks again. Sorry for everything." She turned and ran, bypassing slow-moving travelers, but when she entered the terminal, Zara was nowhere to be found amid the throngs of people. Her eyes darted to every ticket counter, every petite dark-haired woman. Maybe she already had tickets. Maybe she was already at security. Maggie weaved around suitcases, tourists, and tired businessmen until she saw signs for the security checkpoint. Hundreds of people were in line just beyond the initial security desk. And she couldn't join them because she didn't have a ticket.

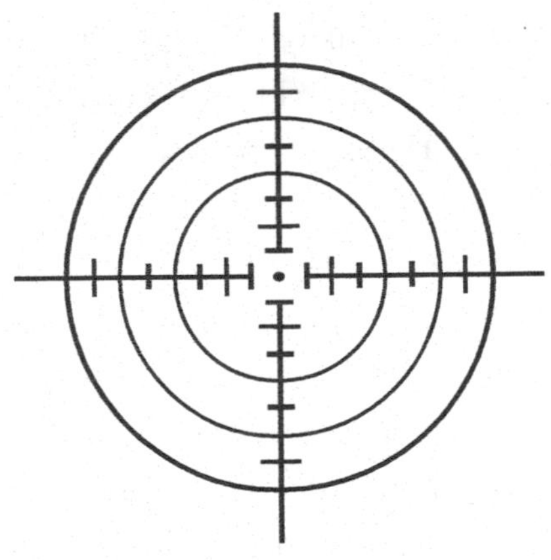

CHAPTER TWENTY-SIX

McLean, Virginia
Saturday, September 4, 2004, 7:15 a.m.

Yuri unleashed a string of Russian curses. "What do you mean she got away? Where is she now?" Things were going from bad to worse.

He listened to his man in London try to excuse his failure. Yuri paid him good money—no, exorbitant money—for these kinds of jobs. And even though there'd only been a few hours to plan the hit, he'd expected nothing short of success.

"Find her. I don't care where she is, in what country, under what circumstances. You find her and finish the task." Yuri's anxiety had risen to full boil after his sources in Chechnya confirmed that Zara had escaped Beslan and his people in London confirmed that she'd been spotted with Imran Bukayev. “And while you’re at it, find out where Bukayev has gone.” The Chechen had been a useful, albeit unwitting, asset. He had to be dealt with before he became a liability.

Yuri couldn’t remember the last time he’d been so angry. He tried to calm himself down. With any luck, Zara hadn’t been privy to the details behind the Beslan attack. No misogynistic terrorist in his right mind would give a woman such information. And he was reasonably sure that the middleman had kept his identity secret from Bukayev. But reasonably sure wasn’t good enough. Yuri had threatened the middleman with loss of life and limb if he revealed his name, but what if the young Chechen didn’t fear him? What if he’d told Bukayev that Yuri was the source of the money and intelligence for the Beslan attack? And what if Zara Barayeva also knew?

Yuri lowered himself into the kitchen chair. This was no time to panic. He had resources at his disposal. One of them was Warner, who owed him for the information he’d provided last year that helped foil the terrorist attack. And since Warner was the one who’d tipped him off about Zara staying in London in the first place, maybe he also knew where she was now. He stared through the skylight at the clear morning sky. He’d have to approach the matter delicately. Raising Warner’s suspicions would be counterproductive.

Adding to his anxiety, Yuri had spent the last hour comparing the photo of the woman in Grozny with online pictures of the Jenkins girl. Her fifteen minutes of fame—earned because of her dead fiancé and the congressman—lived in cyber perpetuity.

It had to be her. She must’ve been in Grozny to chase down leads on Zara Barayeva. What had she learned from Zara’s aunt? He banged the table. And why had it taken his people in Russia more than two days to notify him about all of this?

He called his man in London again. "Was there anything unusual about Bukayev's neighborhood? Could someone have warned him that you were coming after the target?"

His listened for a moment. "A woman with red hair?" He clenched his fist. "Behind Bukayev's house?" The room swam in front of him for a moment. A deep breath steadied him. "How tall? Was she American?" Yuri had never dealt with such incompetence. "You don't know?" He blurted out a string of expletives and hung up.

Two things were clear. First, Maggie Jenkins knew more about Zara than anyone in his organization. Second, he needed to use Maggie to lure the beautiful terrorist out of the shadows.

Maggie clapped shut the prepaid mobile phone she'd just bought from a shop in Terminal 3. Some fifteen miles away, Roger was at the embassy updating authorities on Zara and dealing with Warner's wrath. He'd told Roger in no uncertain terms that since she refused to report to the embassy, she was to return to Washington, DC, immediately before she caused an international incident. And Warner wasn't the only one whose patience had expired. The ambassador was furious that Maggie and Roger had been chasing a terrorist all over London without the State Department's knowledge, much less authorization. She could only imagine how much worse the reaction had been from the CIA station chief.

Warner's order for her to come home wasn't necessary. She was fairly certain that's where Zara was headed anyway. How had she and Bukayev characterized her next mission? *Our most spectacular operation yet?* Something like that. Maggie shifted on her feet and checked her watch again. Every minute spent waiting in the airport was time Zara could use to vanish.

Finally, it was her turn at the ticket counter, where she bought a one-way ticket on the next flight to Washington Dulles International. As she made her way to the security line, she gasped and stopped among a throng of people. *The gun.* She spun around and found a restroom at the far end of the terminal. Inside, she grabbed a wad of brown paper towels, wet several of them, and locked herself in a stall. Using the wet towels, she wiped down the gun and the clip, hoping that would suffice to remove her prints. Next, she wrapped the gun inside the remaining towels and peered through the crack between the stall door and the wall. With the toilets all occupied and no one at the sinks, this was her chance. Maggie slipped from the stall and lowered the concealed weapon into a trash receptacle built into the wall. Someone might eventually discover the gun, especially if security ran K-9 dogs through the restrooms. But there was no place else to dispose of it.

She froze and stared at herself in the mirror. *K-9*s. She'd seen them pacing up and down the winding security line when she was trying to find Zara. If one of them came near her, the dog might alert on her backpack, especially if it was trained in firearms detection. Maggie had no idea if the gun had left behind a detectable scent, but she couldn't take the chance. She splashed cold water on her pale, exhausted face and hurried to the Boots health and beauty supply store she'd passed on the way to the restroom. There, she filled a basket with a toothbrush, makeup, travel size lotions and hair products, a hairbrush, several bars of soap, and a half dozen wash cloths in assorted colors. She grabbed two oversized bathrobes from a corner rack, spritzed her T-shirt and black yoga pants with sample perfume, and approached the counter.

The clerk raised an eyebrow.

"Left all my toiletries at my flat," she explained, donning a British accent.

Moments later, shopping bag in hand, she headed next door to a luggage and travel store, where she purchased a small wheeled suitcase, a faux-leather purse, and a wallet. Back in the restroom, she dug into the backpack, retrieving Roger's phone and her passport and old wallet. She frowned. And Roger's wallet. There was no way to get it back to him now. It would have to wait until she got home.

The young woman at the adjacent sink watched in the mirror as Maggie soaped off her license and credit cards and wiped down her passport and Roger's things with a damp paper towel.

"The baby spit up all over everything," she explained. "Never happens to my husband, of course."

The woman made a face and hurried away.

Maggie washed her hands thoroughly and slid her license and credit cards into the new wallet, which she placed in the empty purse along with several of the beauty products. She rifled through the backpack, checking to make sure there was nothing in it that could lead to her. A half empty bottle of water and unopened bag of pretzels went into one trash can while the backpack and its remaining contents—a sweatshirt and her flashlight—went in another. She washed her hands again and stuffed the rest of her things from Boots into the suitcase, hoping that the bathrobes would look like a pile of dirty clothes on the X-ray machine. A final glance in the mirror confirmed that she looked a wreck. There'd been too little sleep and too much running both toward and away from danger over these past three days. A dab of her new makeup would help, but if she didn't hurry, she wouldn't have time to ask gate agents if they'd seen anyone matching Zara's description.

Forgoing vanity in pursuit of her target, Maggie hurried to the security line. Certain that there were video surveillance cameras watching the passengers, she studiously avoided looking at the K-9 dog who was headed in her direction. *You're bored, you're weary*, she told herself, *not anxious.*

She made a show of stretching her neck to the left and then the right and checking her watch.

The black Labrador and his handler were just feet away. Maggie tilted her head and smiled at the dog as if that would keep him from detecting what he'd been trained to sniff out. She exhaled after the dog paused briefly near her feet before trotting on down the line. Up ahead, she offered her passport and asked the security guard if she'd seen someone matching Zara's description. "My friend," she explained. "We got separated and she's not answering her phone." The guard shook his head and waved the next passenger forward.

As she made her way to the gate, Maggie stopped at the departures board, where she looked for flights to Washington, DC. One flight was in final boarding. "Excuse me. Sorry. Trying to catch my flight," she muttered as she ran around slow-moving travelers.

She arrived, breathless, at Gate 24 at the far end of the terminal, just as the jetway door closed. "Pardon me," she huffed to the gate agent, who ignored her as he typed something into a computer. "Excuse me, but I need to find someone on that flight."

The man, who had black hair with the spiked ends bleached white, raised his gaze from the computer screen.

Maggie glanced at his name tag. "Please, Oliver. A petite woman, early twenties, dark hair, green eyes. Really stunning. You must've noticed her."

He blinked. "Once that door"—he gestured to his left—"is closed, we cannot open it for passengers who are late."

"I'm not a passenger. I just need to find her."

Oliver folded his arms across his chest.

"It's personal."

He raised an eyebrow.

Maggie leaned her elbows on the counter. "If you must know, she's my girlfriend. We had a terrible fight and . . . and, she told me she was flying home without me." She pulled her ticket from her pocket. "See? We were supposed to leave on this flight to Washington."

He pursed his lips.

"She's not the most stable person. I'm worried."

The man sighed. "What's her name?"

"Ah, it's—" Maggie stammered. Zara would almost certainly be flying under a false name. It could be Betsy Ross for all she knew. "Zara Barayeva?"

He frowned and waved over another airline employee, who was chatting with a flight attendant. "Lydia, this young lady thinks her girlfriend may be on that flight. Do you recall checking in a gorgeous, young, dark-haired woman named Tara?"

"Zara," Maggie corrected.

He rolled his eyes. "I don't recall seeing any such Zara or Tara."

Lydia thought for a moment. "Maybe. I think so, but I can't be sure. I mean, there are over three hundred passengers on that flight. And it's the third flight I've checked in today."

Maggie's shoulders slumped. A quick glance out the oversized windows to her left showed the Boeing 777 pushing back from the jetway. "Can I see the passenger list?"

"I'm afraid not," Lydia replied.

"We don't call back airplanes because of a lovers' spat," Oliver added with a smirk.

Lydia threw him a dark look. "I'm sorry, miss. Is there anything else we can help you with?"

Maggie shook her head. All she could do now was give Roger the flight information and hope that Homeland Security would nab Zara when she landed. If—and it was a big if—she was even on that flight.

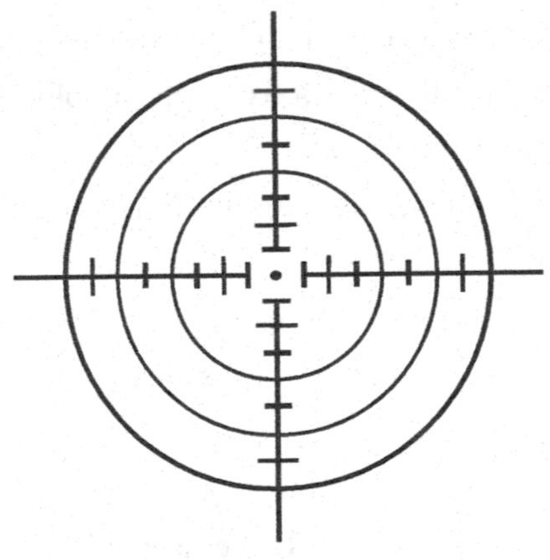

CHAPTER TWENTY-SEVEN

Vienna, Virginia
Saturday, September 4, 2004, 6:30 p.m.

Maggie paid the cab fare outside of her townhome in Vienna, Virginia. Although it was a Saturday evening, she half expected Warner and a CIA entourage to be waiting there to bring her to headquarters for a debriefing. Even if they wanted to question her tonight, she had nothing to add to whatever Roger already had told the Agency. And speaking of Roger, when she called the embassy in London after landing at Dulles, the night operator said that he'd left hours before. And when she called her cell phone, he didn't answer. She'd have to get in touch with Warner to see if Homeland Security had found Zara on that flight from Heathrow.

As she rolled the suitcase up the driveway, Maggie spotted Sam, her eccentric and slightly paranoid neighbor, plucking leaves from the hedges lining his tiny front yard.

She gave him a quick wave and bounded up the front stairs.

"Maggie, wait!"

Her shoulders drooped. She turned around on the top step.

"I didn't think you were due back so soon. Didn't you say six months?"

She nodded. "Change of plans."

"I started your Jeep for you three times already. Once a week, just like you asked me to. Hang on." He dashed into his garage, emerging moments later with keys dangling from his hand. "You'll need these."

"Thanks, Sam." Maggie set her suitcase down and descended the stairs.

His sharp brown eyes moved from the suitcase to her face. "So, where were you? You never told me where *they* sent you." He placed an emphasis on the word *they*.

"London." She took the keys. "Did I miss anything exciting around here?"

He rubbed his hands together, scanned the neighborhood, and whispered. "Strangest thing this afternoon. I looked out my back slider and saw a man in your backyard."

She frowned. "A man?"

"I didn't recognize him, so I went out front to see if maybe there was a service truck here for a routine maintenance check or something."

Steve had always handled those sorts of things. "And?"

"There was another man out front, up there." He pointed to the top of the stairs where her luggage stood. "It seemed weird, so I came out my front door to ask if I could help them." His eyes grew wide. "The guy didn't say a word. He just stared at me and it was like . . . I could tell he was dangerous. Then he watched me as he went down the stairs and got into a car. I don't think he blinked once."

Maggie swallowed but kept her voice steady. "What did he look like?"

Sam shrugged. "I don't want to stereotype or anything."

"It's okay, Sam, just . . . a general description."

He inflated his cheeks and exhaled loudly. "Dark hair. Tan, maybe. His skin was definitely darker than mine."

That wasn't hard. Sam had pasty white skin. "Middle Eastern?"

"I don't know. Maybe, but I can't say for sure. I didn't get a good look at the other guy. They were definitely up to no good."

"It was probably nothing," she replied, not so sure she believed it herself. Then again, Sam was a conspiracy theory afficionado. To him, nothing was ever as it seemed.

His eyebrows drew together. "Should we call the police?"

"I don't think that's necessary, Sam. Maybe they were checking on my HVAC system." She smiled, trying to reassure him. "I probably forgot that I'd scheduled a maintenance check."

He nodded, but didn't seem convinced. "Keep your doors locked."

"I will. Thanks, Sam." She trotted up the stairs and let herself in.

Everything in the living room and kitchen seemed in place. The windows and slider leading to the deck were all locked. Maybe Sam's imagination had gotten the best of him. Or maybe the Agency really had sent a team to bring her into headquarters. Or maybe . . . what if Zara had told Bukayev about her and he'd sent men to find her? No, that was too far-fetched, something Sam would come up with.

The answering machine blinked furiously. Three hang-ups from a restricted number and four missed calls from Warner asking her to call as soon as she got home. She grabbed a sleeve of saltines from the pantry and put on the kettle for tea before picking up the phone.

"Maggie?" Warner answered on the first ring, sounding breathless.

"Did they find Zara?"

"No. No one matching that description was on that flight."

"Great."

"Are you home?"

"Yeah. Just got in." She dropped a tea bag into her favorite mug, the one emblazoned with "Not a Morning Person." Steve had given it to her. Only a year ago. Maggie walked to the glass slider, stepped onto the back deck and surveyed the fence enclosing her postage stamp-sized yard below. The gate was shut tight and nothing appeared disturbed. "You sound a little tense, Warner."

"You haven't been answering my calls."

"I couldn't. Roger has my phone. And like I said, I just walked in the door."

"You need to come in. Immediately."

She twisted her torso and stretched her neck, trying to work out the kinks that had settled into her joints during the transatlantic flight. "To debrief them on Zara or to be interrogated?"

"Probably both. The Agency is not happy that you left Beslan. Or that you ran off to London. To say nothing of your escapades once you arrived there. I've done some damage control, but they have a lot of questions for you."

Great. She slipped back inside as the kettle's whistle began to chirp. "Did the Agency send a couple of guys over to my place this afternoon?"

"Not that I know of. Why?"

"My neighbor saw two men outside my house. Probably salesmen, or something." She poured steaming water into the mug and added a generous sprinkling of sugar. "Any word from Roger? Anything new on Zara or Bukayev?"

"No. No leads."

"I told you I overheard them talking about an operation in Washington, DC, didn't I?"

"Roger told me."

"Was there anything in Bukayev's documents about a terror cell meeting or plans for an attack?"

"Nothing like that. At least not yet. There's some financial transactions data, which could be interesting."

She sipped the tea. "Is this ever going to end?"

"Is what ever going to end?"

"The hunt for Zara. I was so close—"

"We'll get her eventually, Maggie. But your . . . obsession with her won't end until you accept that nothing you do will bring back Steve."

Her eyes stung with sudden, hot tears. "You think I don't know that?"

"Listen, Maggie, you've gotten us to this point. You proved everyone wrong. It's time to let the Agency take over."

"I—"

"You're young, with your whole life ahead of you. Steve wouldn't want you stuck in the past."

Her body bristled with anger.

How dare he presume to speak for Steve? "I have to unpack."

"They'll be waiting for you in Langley. Can you be there in an hour?"

"I'll try." She tossed the handset onto the counter.

The phone rang almost immediately.

"What now, Warner?"

"Maggie, it's Sam."

She suppressed a groan.

"The car's back. In the cul-de-sac."

"What car?"

"With the men. Look outside, but don't let them see you."

Her stomach lurched. She hurried to the living-room window and edged the sheer curtain aside. Sure enough, a gray sedan sat parked at the end of the street. Two men in the front seat appeared to be looking directly at her town house.

"See them?"

"You sure it's the same car, Sam?"

"Positive."

A spark of fear traveled from her shoulders down to her legs. Steve had always told her to trust her gut. "Can you let me in your backyard in five minutes?"

"Yeah," he whispered. "What's the plan?"

"I'll be over in a few."

She hung up and took the stairs, two at time. In her bedroom, she grabbed clean clothes from her dresser and peered out the window. The sedan was still out there. She clattered down the stairs, her arms full of clothes. She knelt, unzipped the suitcase with her free hand, and threw the clothes inside. She dashed back upstairs and retrieved her Glock from her bedside table and the ammunition from her bottom dresser drawer. She placed those in a pocket compartment inside the suitcase, flipped the cover closed, and tugged the zipper around its perimeter.

She rocked back onto her heels, stood herself and the suitcase up, grabbed her purse, and took a final look around before heading for the basement. Downstairs, she lugged the suitcase outside and paused at the gate, listening for a minute. The only sound in the fading daylight was the distant hum of cars and the buzz of cicadas. She tugged open the gate that led to a paved path separating the townhome development from a thicket of trees.

Stepping out of the safe confines of the yard, Maggie stopped again to make sure there was no sudden movement or rustling of leaves. She reached back into the yard for her belongings. If there was anyone watching, they'd show themselves now. She stared at the woods for a good thirty seconds. Still no movement or signs of life.

"Maggie!" Sam hissed as he poked his head outside his gate. "Hurry."

She rolled the suitcase down the path and onto the intricately patterned stone patio that Sam had laid himself. A wooden deck with no attached staircase floated overhead.

He ushered her into his basement. "Where are you going?"

"Away for a few days."

He swallowed. "Because of the men?"

"I have some things to do, including finding out who they are." She placed a hand on his arm. "But don't worry, they're not here for you."

A thin sheen of sweat formed along his hairline.

"I'm going to have some of my people check it out, okay?"

He nodded. "This is important national security stuff, isn't it?"

"Maybe, Sam."

"Well, I want to help, then."

"The most important thing you can do is tell nobody about this. If these guys are up to no good, we're going to have to catch them in the act."

"Good thinking." His eyes glowed with excitement.

"The other thing you can do is help me get out of here without them seeing me."

"How?"

Two minutes later, Maggie was curled up on the floor in the backseat of Sam's beloved, vintage Volkswagen Beetle. He was forever polishing and tinkering with the little bulbous white car, but he never drove it. Maggie didn't see the point of putting so much effort into a second vehicle you never used, but who was she to judge?

She couldn't remember the last time that she'd had the Jeep's oil changed. In fact, she'd never done it herself. That had been Steve's purview.

"Ready?" he asked from the driver's seat as he reached for the garage door remote.

"Yup. Just pull out and turn right."

Sam edged the car out of the garage and followed her instructions. Up ahead on the main road, he pulled into a neighboring development. Maggie popped out of the backseat and met Sam on the curb.

"Thank you so much for letting me use the car."

He chewed on his lip.

"I'll bring her back without a scratch or a dent. I promise."

He nodded. "I should get back. I'll sneak in through the basement," he added with an excited gleam in his eyes, "If anyone asks if I've seen you, I'll say no."

"Thanks, Sam. I'll be back in a few days," she called as he headed toward the tree line that would lead him to the backside of his house. "I hope," she muttered.

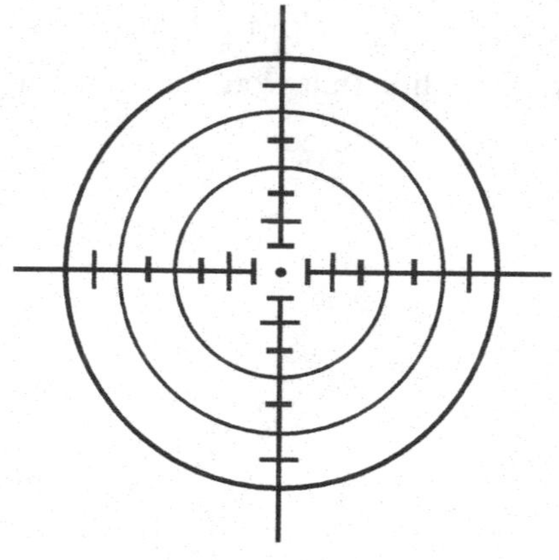

CHAPTER TWENTY-EIGHT

Warner set his cell phone on the dining table. Maggie should be in Langley by now, facing the wrath of Agency brass. He was willing to testify on her behalf, to be her character witness. He'd do whatever it took, call in favors he'd been saving—anything—to help salvage her career. Warner accepted a cup of decaf coffee from the waitress and watched tiny eddies of steam rise from the mug.

He glanced at the phone. It was too soon to expect an update from Jim Carpenter, and Maggie wouldn't be able to call. He'd offered—nearly begged, in fact—to help facilitate the meeting, but Jim Carpenter had turned him down. Yes, she'd gone AWOL, but

Warner wasn't sure she deserved being interrogated by the CIA's internal affairs squad. They were excellent at what they did, but they could be ruthless and relentless. A sense of unease rose inside him. As soon as he finished up at the café, he'd go to headquarters.

Warner looked up and nodded at Yuri as he ambled toward the table. He wasn't in the mood for the Russian, but maybe he had some information on Zara for him.

"Good evening."

With a grunt, Yuri squeezed himself into the chair. "Evening." He signaled to the waitress for a drink. "What's the matter, Warner? You look terrible."

"Tired. Lots going on." Warner studied the Russian. Since talking to Roger earlier today, he'd been trying to figure out whether Yuri had been behind the attempt on Zara's life in London. The Russian had reacted strangely at the vineyard yesterday when Warner brought up her name. But would he be able to pull off a killing that quickly? And why would he want to eliminate her? He couldn't seem to make sense of so many seemingly unrelated events.

The waitress placed a vodka martini in front of Yuri. "Can I get you gentlemen something to eat?" She slid two menus their way.

"Veggie burger on a bed of lettuce," Yuri grumbled without looking at the menu.

"Sounds appetizing."

Yuri scowled. "Doctor's orders."

"I'll have the barbecue bacon burger with fries, please." Warner poured a dollop of cream into his mug.

"Not very healthy, Warner."

"If a cheeseburger is what ends up killing me, Yuri, it means I've lived a boring life."

"Perhaps you're right, comrade. Make that two burgers."

The waitress nodded, leaving the men alone.

"You said you had something to discuss, Yuri?"

"I'm trying to figure out where you got your information about Zara being in London?"

Warner stiffened. He hadn't told Yuri that she had been seen in London. He'd simply said that Zara reportedly was close with Imran Bukayev. "What difference does it make where I got that information?"

Yuri didn't get the chance to respond before Warner's phone rang. It was a CIA exchange.

"Have you talked to Maggie?" Jim Carpenter, Maggie's boss, asked.

"Not since we spoke earlier."

"I don't know where she is."

"She didn't show up at the office?" Warner felt his stomach drop.

"No. She was supposed to be here a half hour ago. She's not answering her door or her phone and her Jeep's still in the driveway."

Warner pushed the coffee cup away. "I'm on my way over there now." He slid from the bench and dropped two twenties on the table. "Yuri, I'm sorry, but I have to run."

"What is going on?"

"It's nothing . . . just . . . I have to run."

"Maggie's like a daughter to you, isn't she?"

Warner nodded.

"Is she all right?"

"She's gotten herself in a bit of a mess at work."

"What kind of a mess?" Yuri seemed uncharacteristically curious.

"Nothing I can't handle."

Yuri stood. "I have resources at my disposal, as you know. I'll ask them to keep an eye out for her."

Warner frowned. "That's not necessary, Yuri."

"It's no trouble at all, Warner." The Russian smiled. "I'm happy to help."

After a quick trip to the store for some food, toiletries, and a disposable cell phone, Maggie turned onto the side street leading into an upscale community comprised of three-story brick town houses. She backed into a visitor's parking spot and double-checked Roger's driver's license. This was his place. She just hoped the key she'd found in his wallet stashed behind his credit cards was his house key.

She marched up the front steps of unit 1124 and inserted the key into the lock. It turned. Inside, she checked the walls for an alarm system. None in sight.

"Hello?" she called out, fairly certain that Roger lived alone. The town house smelled a bit musty, as if fresh air hadn't flowed through it in a while.

Roger's living room had a beige tumbled-marble floor and clean-lined, modern furniture. A mocha sofa was offset by a pair of crimson wing chairs centered around an iron-legged coffee table. Roger either had a good eye for style or a talented interior designer.

Maggie left the suitcase in the foyer and explored the dining room and the kitchen, where the stone floor gave way to gleaming maple. A pile of unopened junk mail sat on the counter next to an enormous Sub-Zero refrigerator containing a box of baking soda, a six-pack of ale, an unopened jar of dill pickles, and a bottle of ketchup. She unloaded the groceries and trotted upstairs to check out the bedrooms.

Each room was neat as a pin. The master bedroom was decorated in navy blue and gray. Boring but solidly masculine. The master bath featured a massive jetted tub. She swatted away an unbidden image of herself soaking in it with a glass of champagne in hand.

Back downstairs, Maggie called her answering machine. There were several frantic messages from Jim Carpenter and Warner. The final call from Warner was the only one that demanded immediate attention. She picked up Roger's home phone, blocked the number, and dialed.

"It's me, Warner."

"Open the door, Maggie."

"What?"

"That was me, pounding on your front door a few minutes ago."

"I'm not home."

"You could have told me that," he said, his voice rising in anger. "I thought something happened to you. You scared me to death."

"I'm fine."

"Are you at headquarters?"

"No. Something came up and I decided I should flee."

"Flee?"

"That might be too strong of a word." She explained the situation with Sam and the men in the car.

"I haven't seen anyone lurking around your neighborhood." He sounded skeptical.

"What if Zara told Bukayev about me being in Beslan and he sent a couple of his men to get me?"

"Sounds a little far-fetched, but—" Warner paused for a good ten seconds. "I'll have a couple of our security guys drive by your house every now and then."

"Thanks."

"You want to stay at my house until we figure out if there's a threat?"

"No, I'm good here, Warner."

"Where?"

"I'd rather not say. I just want to get some sleep and start fresh tomorrow."

"Maggie—"

"Don't worry. I'm safe."

"Fine." He let out an exasperated sigh. "Call me in the morning so we can set up a meeting in Langley."

"Okay." She heard a car door slam and ran to the front window where she caught sight of a taxi pulling away. Roger, head down, was pulling his luggage up the brick staircase. "Good night, Warner."

Outside on the landing, Roger bent down and flipped over the welcome mat. He scratched at his head in apparent frustration, then fumbled around in a large flower pot full of drooping weeds, eventually extracting a dirt-covered key from the soil.

Maggie opened the door. "You shouldn't hide a spare key in such an obvious place."

Startled, Roger straightened up. Bleary-eyed, he stared at her for a moment. "Is this a dream?"

She scanned the neighborhood over his shoulder. "No, a nightmare. Hurry up and get in here. I don't want anyone to spot me."

He dragged the half-open suitcase across the threshold. "What are you doing here?"

"Hiding out."

He looked outside then back at her. "From?"

"There were some strange guys hanging out in my back yard."

"Strange guys?"

She shrugged, suddenly feeling silly for fleeing her own house. "It didn't feel right, so I left."

"And you want to stay here so they can come get me too?"

"Warner's going to have security check it out. I figured I would hole up here since you weren't home."

"I'm home now."

"Don't worry, Roger. You'll hardly notice me. I'm quiet and neat."

He released the suitcase and watched it tumble to its side. Dirty laundry spilled out. "How did you get in here?"

Maggie headed for the kitchen, Roger trailing behind. "I found the key in your wallet."

"You have my wallet?"

"Yeah."

"I figured I lost it in London."

"Sorry."

"And you thought it was okay to keep it? And . . ." he waved a hand toward the front door, "take my key and make yourself at home here?"

"I said I was sorry, Roger. I didn't realize I had it until I was at the airport." She hoisted herself onto a stool tucked under the kitchen island. "You put it in my backpack before we snuck into Bukayev's house. Remember?"

Roger pulled her cell phone from his back pocket and slid it across the countertop without a word. He looked haggard. The bruise on the right side of his forehead resembled a smashed plum, dark under-eye circles betrayed a lack of sleep, and his silver-streaked hair sprouted in chaotic angles. The salt-and-pepper stubble on his face was a bit distracting, drawing attention to his dimples and full lips.

She focused on the unsightly bruise instead.

Roger crossed and uncrossed his arms. "I did the right thing and told the London station what happened with Zara and Bukayev and the hitman or whoever he was. I also downloaded Bukayev's document for them. And you know what happened next?"

Maggie shrugged.

"The embassy sent me straight to Heathrow. I wanted to help them find Bukayev, but they thought it would be better for British-American relations if I was no longer in the country."

He looked so pathetic that she felt a twinge of guilt for putting him in this predicament. "Sorry."

He glared at her and set to work making coffee. "You know what I want? I want to go to sleep. I want to forget the last four days. . . ." He grabbed a mug and slammed the cabinet door.

"There's creamer and milk in the fridge. I didn't know which you preferred."

He grumbled something unintelligible in return, grabbed a second mug, and prepared two cups of coffee. Standing across the island from her, he scratched his chin. How could someone this beat-up still look so . . . handsome?

"I completely lost Zara's trail in Heathrow," she said. "If she was headed to DC, why didn't someone spot her at Dulles?"

"Maybe she flew into another airport."

"Maybe. Even if she did, she's probably headed to DC."

He leaned his elbows onto the island. "There's no evidence for that, Maggie. You overheard a snippet of a conversation between

Bukayev and Zara under very stressful circumstances. Maybe you misheard or misinterpreted—"

"I know what I heard, Roger."

"Homeland Security, the FBI, everyone will be keeping an eye out for her."

That wasn't good enough. Not with Zara. Maggie took a sip of coffee and traced the pattern swirling through the granite countertop. "Do you think we're going to get fired?"

"I don't know about you, but I'm prepared to kiss some major ass to make sure I don't." He yawned and lifted his mug. "I was planning to go in tonight to see if I could begin the groveling process. Want to join me?"

"I can't."

"Why not?"

She sighed. "If I show up in Langley, the focus will be on me, not on finding Zara."

He topped off his coffee. "Why would it be about you? We'll explain everything. What happened at Bukayev's, the mosque—"

She raised her hand. "I already told you. They think I'm a loose cannon. Maybe even a bit disturbed."

"Hard to argue with that." He smirked.

"I'm serious, Roger. I don't care if I lose my job as long as . . ."

He came around the island and faced her. "As long as what?"

She shifted on her feet. "If we don't find her, she's not going to stop. She'll kill again."

Roger reached for her arm, then hesitated under the weight of her unblinking stare. "And you think you have to be the one to stop her. Because of what happened to Steve."

She averted her gaze. "I've let her get away three times."

Now his hand was on her arm.

She flinched, but he kept it there. "This is not your fault."

"I know."

His eyes met hers. "Do you? Do you really understand that none of this is your fault?"

She stepped back, lips pressed tightly together.

"Without you, we wouldn't know Zara was alive. That she was inside that school in Beslan. Or that she traveled to London."

"But she's still out there." Her voice was barely above a whisper.

He left her side and returned with the coffeepot, refilling both their mugs. "Maggie, I've done a lot of stupid things in my life, most of them when I was feeling hurt. Or lost. And I know what it's like to feel completely hopeless. It's a miserable existence."

"I'm sorry you've felt that way, Roger." Her tone was flat.

"Both Warner and I understand why this is so personal to you. Of course it is. But—" His hand rested on her arm again. "But nothing you do or don't do will change the past. I know because I've been through this. Ready to give up a career that I loved, not really caring if I lived or died—"

"I don't want to die," she retorted, her face growing red.

"Then please, Maggie, I'm begging you, please let the Agency take it from here. Steve would want you to be safe. And happy."

She closed her eyes, too tired to argue. If only she could sleep for a week, forget everything that had happened. Steve's smiling face flashed through her mind. "Give me two days, Roger. Two days to figure out what's going on."

He moved his hand to hers. "Two days."

"Okay." She smiled. "Unless I need more time."

"You're impossible." He rolled his eyes. "Look, I'll help you, but only if we play by my rules."

"Deal."

"You don't know my rules."

She withdrew her hand.

"Rule number one is that if we both get fired, you'll run away with me to a remote tropical island."

Maggie blinked at him.

"Rule number two—"

She raised a hand to stop him.

"I need to print Bukayev's documents. Maybe I can find something in them that the Agency missed." Maybe a word or a phrase would jump out to her in a way that other analysts might miss.

"Is reading Chechen among your hidden superpowers?"

"No," she conceded, "but maybe we can find a translator outside the Agency so I can dig into them."

He brightened. "I know someone. A former asset. A Chechen who knows several of the warlords."

Her heart skipped a beat. "What are we waiting for?"

"Maggie, this guy is very skittish." Roger frowned. "He'll clam up if I bring along someone he doesn't know."

"I'll wait in the car."

Roger considered the plan. "Let me call him."

"Great." Maggie grabbed her suitcase. "Do you mind if I take a quick shower first?"

"Make yourself at home." He shrugged. "Oh wait, you already have."

"Hey, at least you didn't come home to an empty fridge," she called from halfway up the stairs before returning to the kitchen. "While I'm getting ready, why don't you print the photo of Zara and the documents? Couple copies of each."

He gave a weak salute. "Yes, ma'am."

•★★★•

Ten minutes later, Maggie returned to the kitchen wearing mascara, jeans, and a Red Sox T-shirt. "Did you get in touch with your Chechen?" she asked.

"You're a hopeless romantic, aren't you?"

Maggie scanned Roger's face for more information. "Excuse me?"

"The Red Sox. You wear that shirt because you're eternally hopeful that someday they might win it all."

"They might. They'll make the playoffs this year." She crossed her arms over the red stocking logo. "Possibly."

"Yeah, keep dreaming." He swung an imaginary baseball bat. "Besides, they're cursed. They'll never get past the Yankees."

"Whatever." They could argue sports later. "Roger, your Chechen?"

"He's not answering his office phone and I don't have his cell number."

"I say we head over there anyway. He might be avoiding your call."

"Or he might be at home because it's nine o'clock at night."

"We have to get these documents translated."

"I know. When I finally go see him, you're not coming in with me. This is my source, not yours. Got it?"

"Absolutely, Roger."

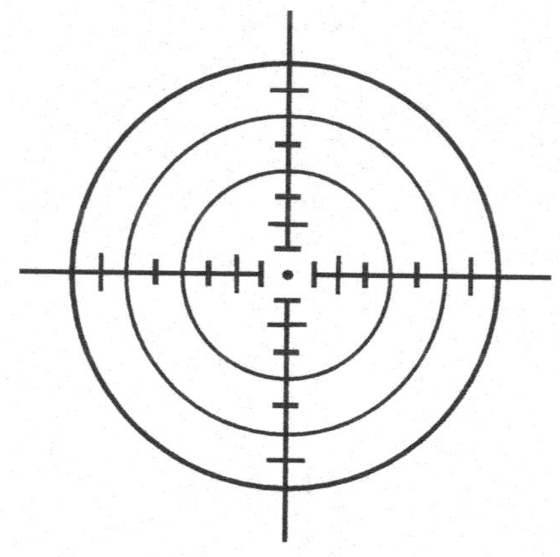

CHAPTER TWENTY-NINE

Washington, DC
Sunday, September 5, 2004, 10:25 a.m.

Daud peered out the window. The phone calls had triggered severe anxiety, keeping him up for half the night. Maybe there was an innocent explanation, but for the life of him, he couldn't imagine one. He'd known immediately who it was on the answering machine—Roger, his old CIA handler. Roger wanted to meet last night, but Daud didn't return the call. When Roger called again this morning, he'd finally answered.

He collapsed into the chair behind his desk. All the pacing was making his heart race. And his mind. If any of Daud's bosses found out, he was a dead man. Why would Roger call after three years?

The American hadn't said a word about Beslan, but the young Chechen didn't believe in coincidences. Too many masters. That was the problem. Daud answered to too many powerful people. He took a hearty drag from his cigarette. Smoking was banned in the building, but it was the only thing keeping him together at the moment.

If someone saw Roger enter the building, he'd say the American was an academic who wanted to discuss an upcoming research trip to Kazakhstan. After all, Daud needed to maintain his cover. He couldn't spend all his time funneling money and coordinating logistics for the Chechen Freedom Alliance.

Roger eased the silver Audi onto a quiet side street in northwest Washington, DC. Elegant brownstones stood on both sides of the tree-lined road. "Right there." He pointed out the window at a three-story brownstone.

Maggie handed him the documents and leaned forward to get a better view. "You think he's there?"

Roger reached for the door. "Don't go anywhere."

"Where would I go?"

He shrugged, closed the door, and jogged across the street.

If anyone found out he was meeting with his old asset, the one he'd been forced to sever ties with shortly before 9/11, he'd be job hunting by this time tomorrow. Daud wasn't a bad guy in the true sense of the word. He'd probably never killed anyone in his life. But he was friends with an awful lot of people who had. And therein lay the problem. Three years ago, CIA brass had ordered Roger to cut off contact with Daud, a man who'd been willing to provide intelligence on Arab fighters flooding into Afghanistan. Roger had gone to the mat for Daud and lost. Not even Warner had understood the urgency of the situation. And even after explaining the insight that Daud had about the growing Islamic threat, the Agency told Roger to cease contact with him until they'd fully vetted his background. Several years earlier, Congress had implemented restrictions on what kinds of people the CIA could recruit. Any potential asset who was suspected of a serious crime, particularly if that crime involved human-rights violations, had to be vetted by a CIA committee and reviewed by the chairs of the relevant congressional oversight committees.

It was an absurd policy, but the Agency stood firm. No further contact with Daud until they had fully vetted his background. Roger had ignored the directive and continued meeting with his asset. When the bigwigs on the seventh floor found out, they went ballistic. There'd been talk of an official reprimand, suspension without pay, or even termination. He beat them to the punch and resigned in August 2001.

Roger scanned the street and the windows of nearby buildings before disappearing through the front door. When he reached the second-floor landing, the door on the right swung open.

"Daud, my old friend. It's nice to see you."

Daud looked over Roger's shoulder and ushered him inside.

"What, no friendly greeting? No, hey, it's nice to see you?"

"I'm not your spy anymore."

Roger's eyes took in the brownstone's second floor, which consisted of a spacious central room with a small galley kitchen and bathroom at the back. An assortment of bowls and vases imbued with azure blues and bright yellows punctuated the bookcase that ran the length of the interior. Intricately patterned carpets of dark red, browns and black accented several areas in the space—the sitting area, the work area, and the kitchen.

"I like what you've done with the place." He thought he saw a tremor in the man's smooth hands. He hadn't aged at all. In fact, Daud, now in his early thirties, looked no worse for the wear since 2001. "You know I left the Agency because of you."

Daud studied Roger. "Because of me? What did I do?"

Roger walked over to a large bay window. Other than a woman walking her dog, the neighborhood appeared deserted. "Let's just say the bosses didn't like some of your friends."

Daud sat on a taupe chenille sofa. "But I was giving you excellent information. If they had listened—"

"I know." Roger had tried to warn the seventh floor, to no avail. Maybe Daud's information wouldn't have prevented the 9/11 attacks. But maybe it would have. And Jane would still be alive.

"Well, that was then. I'm no longer associating with such people." Daud nodded to a loveseat opposite the couch. "Please."

Roger sat. There was no way on Allah's green earth that Daud had cut off contact with his radical friends. *Someone* was paying him to run the Central Asian Studies Institute. "So how's business? Write any good white papers lately?"

"You didn't come here to ask me about my work."

Roger smiled. "No. Though I'm sure it's utterly fascinating."

Daud leaned forward, elbows resting on his knees.

Roger followed suit. "Daud, I need you to help me find someone."

• ★ ★ ★ •

Through a large bay window on the first floor, Maggie saw a woman grab her purse and coat. One minute later, she exited the building and walked a half block to a car. Once she drove off, Maggie slipped out the passenger door and followed Roger's path to the building. The ground floor housed a real-estate office. Beyond that, a wide wooden staircase curved up to the next floor.

Maggie crept along the edge of the stairs, trying to avoid the creaks inherent in an old building's bones. She'd grown impatient waiting in the car and wanted to find out if Roger was making any progress. On the second floor, she ran her fingers across the raised letters on the gold-plated sign—Central Asian Studies Institute—and pressed her head against the door. A low murmuring of voices penetrated the dark oak. She leaned in closer, and the door gave way, sending her sprawling into a room replete with Central Asian artifacts—carpets, pottery, and wall hangings.

Roger whirled around and scowled at her. "I told you to stay —"

She straightened herself and came face-to-face with a slight, olive-skinned man with jet-black hair.

"Hi, I'm Megan Franklin. Good to meet you."

The man shook her hand with a loose, timid grip. "Daud Chotkev."

Roger mouthed *Megan?* from behind Daud.

"I apologize for interrupting. We appreciate you meeting us."

"Well, Magg—um—Megan. I was just about to ask Daud if he'd ever heard of Imran Bukayev."

"Of . . . of course," Daud stammered. "Of course I've heard of him. He's a spokesman for the Chechen government-in-exile."

Maggie jumped in. "Do you know him personally?"

Daud shook his head vigorously.

Roger shot her a look and narrowed his eyes. "I've got this."

She ignored Roger. "What about his girlfriend?"

Daud looked confused.

"Her name is Zara Barayeva. Her family is rather well-known in Chechen circles. One of her brothers was killed in the Moscow theater siege a couple years ago. The other was killed in a hostage situation last year outside of Tbilisi. Surely, you've heard of this family?"

"I've lived in America for more than five years. I don't know many people in Chechnya anymore."

Maggie noted his evasive answer as she gazed out an oversized window to the street below. "Roger told me you have ties to some questionable characters back home." She turned to face him. "I thought you'd know this family."

The man's dark eyes darted from Maggie to Roger.

Roger cleared his throat. "Daud, do you know anyone who knows Bukayev? Maybe someone who knows where he might go if he ran into trouble or felt threatened?"

"I don't. I'm sorry." The younger man appeared stricken as worry lines appeared on his forehead.

Maggie pulled her phone from her purse and navigated to the photo of Zara in London. "Take a look at this."

The man drew near, squinted at the small screen, then jerked his head back.

"You recognize her?" Maggie asked.

Daud paled.

"Let's sit again," Roger suggested, throwing a sidelong glance her way.

Daud slumped into a tan upholstered wing chair, his back to Maggie.

She studied Daud's extensive book collection, which comprised mainly tomes about Central Asian art, culture, and history. At the far end of the bookcase, nearest to the kitchen, were dozens of classics from Russian literature neatly arranged by author. Several of the books on the top shelf were upside down, as if they'd been placed there in haste. She examined them one at a time. The last book was a worn, leather-bound Russian-language edition of *Crime and Punishment*.

She flipped through the dog-eared pages until she discovered a scrap of paper tucked in the middle of the scene where Raskolnikov confesses his crime to Sonya. Maggie glanced at the paper and hid it in her jeans pocket.

She reshelved the book. "Mind if I get some water?" she asked, heading toward the galley kitchen before either of the men could answer. Leaning against the counter between the coffee maker and the microwave, she fished around in her purse for the disposable cell phone and dialed the number she'd found in the Dostoyevsky novel.

"Hello?" The voice was low, gravelly.

Maggie listened, her lips pressed firmly together.

"Who is this? *Shto eto?* Hello?" the man said.

Maggie closed the phone. Definitely a Russian. Maybe she shouldn't be all that surprised. Daud probably had a network of Chechen and maybe even Russian friends in the DC area. But why go to such lengths to hide a friend's phone number?

She joined the men in the seating area. "You recognized Zara, didn't you?"

"Look," Daud began, "I don't know her personally. But, yes, I know of her. Through people in my network."

Maggie sat on the arm of the couch and leaned forward. "Zara and Bukayev may be planning some sort of attack. Any information, any leads, could help save lives."

Daud clasped his hands in his lap. "I would tell you if I knew."

"I know you would," Roger offered. "But maybe there's a way you can help."

Daud raised his eyebrows.

Roger continued. "We need you to translate documents that could reveal what Zara is planning next."

"Next?"

"You must know that she was in Beslan," Maggie chimed in. "And that she got away."

Daud's mouth fell open. "How would I know that?"

Roger leveled a gaze at him. "Come on, Daud, I know you have contacts with the rebels. You've told me yourself."

Daud jumped to his feet, turned himself in a circle and wound up behind the chair as if taking cover. "I had nothing to do with Beslan. No knowledge." He grasped the back of the chair, fingers digging into the upholstery. "I would not support an attack on children. Ever." His eyes bulged with anger.

Interesting body language, Maggie thought. The white knuckles plus the sweaty brow equaled one terrified Chechen. She felt a tinge of sympathy for the man. He might be telling the truth, but he sure wasn't telling them the whole truth.

"I believe you, Daud," Roger said, his tone soothing and sincere. "All we're asking is that you let us know if you hear anything. Anything at all about Zara or a possible attack in the US."

"I will."

"You're sure you don't know Zara?" Maggie asked again.

"I don't know her."

She pressed on. "Because we can find out through other sources."

He chewed on a cuticle. "I might have seen her in Grozny once. The last time I was there, but that was two years ago. My visit happened to coincide with the memorial for the Chechens who died in the theater siege."

"They held a memorial for the terrorists?" Roger asked. "Are you serious?"

"That's not why I was there."

Maggie made note of Daud's proclivity to answer questions they hadn't asked. Maybe it would be best if they let him stew about their visit for a day or two. They could always come back.

"The documents, Roger?"

"Right." He gathered up Bukayev's documents from the end table and offered them to Daud. "Can you translate these by tomorrow?"

The Chechen flipped through them, clearly relieved by the change of subject. "Yes."

"I'll call you," Roger said on the way out the door.

Maggie scampered down the stairs ahead of him.

"Wait up," he said with an edge to his voice.

She stopped several stairs down.

"I told you I would handle Daud."

Her mouth fell open. "I didn't mean to interrupt. I just wanted to hear what he had to say."

He glared at her. "You could've blown the whole thing out of the water."

"But I didn't."

"You got lucky." He pointed back up the stairway. "Daud is my source, not yours. I do operations, you do analysis. That's the only way this thing works."

"Really? Is that Roger's rule number two?" She turned and continued down the stairs.

He stomped after her.

Outside on the sidewalk, Maggie noticed a second-floor curtain move as if rustled by a breeze. Daud Chotkev was watching.

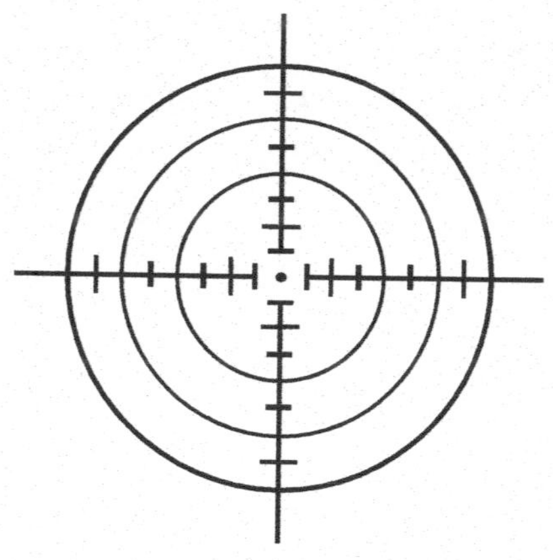

CHAPTER THIRTY

Washington, DC
Monday, September 6, 2004, 9:15 a.m.

Zara disembarked from the early train at Union Station in Washington, DC. The trip from Philadelphia had been an uneventful two hours. Following her fellow passengers across the concourse, she took the escalator to the Main Hall, a cavernous space whose soaring, coffered ceiling drew her gaze upward to a multitude of octagonal gold-leaf inlays that created the impression of hundreds of tiny skylights. Union Station wasn't at all like the extravagant, palatial train stations in Moscow, but its symmetrical, opulent design still stopped her in her tracks. As local riders rushed by and tourists bumped into her, Zara pulled her eyes from dozens of statues—Roman centurions—gazing down from their high perches along the granite walls. *Focus!* Fatigue was no excuse for gawking like a foreign tourist. She needed to blend in, garner no unnecessary attention.

Imran had originally planned for her to arrive late tomorrow, but after the unexpected developments in London, he'd scrambled to find an earlier flight landing somewhere outside of Washington. Zara couldn't really complain about the disruption. Having an extra day in Philadelphia to rest up was immeasurably better than being locked in a room in that oppressive mosque under the watch of the sulky, leering Omar. She couldn't get into the safe house for a few hours, which gave her the perfect opportunity to work on her personal mission, the one she'd promised Imran she'd abandon.

Twenty minutes later, Zara was inside a rental car. A quick inspection of the vehicle calmed her frayed nerves. The navigation system didn't look too complicated, and it would be invaluable in helping her get around. To her disappointment, the directions took her into a tunnel that deposited her on a highway leading into Virginia. She wanted to see the White House and Capitol Hill for herself as a reminder that even if she succeeded in her mission, there were many more targets waiting. She kept to the right lane in slower traffic, crossed a river, and exited onto Route 110 with signs for the Pentagon. Her pulse quickened. And then, there it was on her left. The center of it all. Where America formulated its deadly military operations. She slowed to get a better look at the massive building, garnering a symphony of honking car horns as a result. Reminding herself again to blend in, she accelerated away from the obnoxious drivers behind her.

When she finally reached the Beltway exit, it was another mile to the site. Zara slowed the car as she neared the address, then sped to pass a Metro bus before turning around at the next intersection.

On the second pass by the site, she saw the signal—a beat-up white compact car with a construction hat on the roof and a magnetic yellow "Support the Troops" ribbon on the bumper. The operation was still on schedule.

Fifteen minutes later, she drove past the second address. She couldn't help but gawk at the size of the house. It alone was larger than the entire apartment building she'd lived in as a child. After the third pass, she'd seen enough. Blood money had paid for this home. As far as Zara was concerned, it was time to call in the loan.

Zara surveyed the next neighborhood from inside the car. The two-story redbrick garden-apartment building looked nice enough, especially by Chechen standards. There wasn't a single blown-out window or mortar-shattered wall. She looked at the console clock a third time. *Where is he?* Her US contact, a man she knew only as Jalal, was supposed to meet her by the mailbox outside this apartment complex. She knew she was in the correct place. The rental car's computer told her so. If Imran had paired her with an amateur, he'd hear about it. Zara expected—no, she demanded—professionalism.

A man approached the mailbox, his eyes sweeping the surroundings. His slim build, the European cut of his clothes, the way he held his cigarette, none of it fit with the urban American setting. It had to be Jalal. Definitely not Arab. Perhaps a mix of Russian and Uzbek. She grabbed her small suitcase and climbed out of the car. He offered a broad smile as if delighted to see an old friend.

"Renata." He opened his arms for a hug.

Zara looked behind her to make sure he wasn't talking to someone else. She was Renata, a Chechen passing herself off as an Hispanic? What kind of cover was that? She let Jalal hug her.

"*Eto khorosho*," he whispered in her ear, a gesture far too intimate from a subordinate.

She wanted to shove him away, but instead answered with the preestablished protocol in English. "Yes, this is good."

Jalal led her to the apartment and left her to explore her temporary home. An old green couch and wood laminate coffee table faced a thirteen-inch television in the corner. The galley-style kitchen was drab but more than adequate. And the single bedroom contained a queen-sized bed covered with a faded blue comforter. A worn tan carpet ran throughout the apartment, including the bathroom.

Aside from the stale cigarette smell that clung to the furniture, she couldn't complain about her accommodations. If this was how the underclass lived in America, well, suffice it to say, they'd be shocked by how her family had lived. Of course, compared to Imran's posh home in London, this was a lowly residence. But Zara didn't need much, certainly not all the material things Imran seemed to put so much stock in. She only needed the knowledge that she'd set things right. Everything else was superfluous.

At the far end of the living room, Zara opened the glass slider that led out to a ten-foot wide patch of grass running the length of the apartments. Beyond the grass stood a weed-covered chain-link fence abutting a vacant lot. If anyone was watching the apartment from there, they'd be easy to spot. Back in the kitchen, she was pleased to discover that Jalal had stocked the refrigerator with some basics. Now she wouldn't have to find a store. The fewer interactions she had with the public, the better.

Zara had no tasks, no plans for the day. She hated being left in limbo. Moving, acting, making things happen—that's what kept her sharp and out of trouble. She powered on the prepaid cell phone Jalal had provided. He had a matching one whose number she'd already memorized. Such conveniences were very hard to come by in Chechnya unless you were a *mujahid* with connections. She tucked a strand of hair behind her ear, then did something she knew she shouldn't. She dialed the number.

"Hello?"

Zara disconnected the call. She'd already driven by the house once. Now she'd phoned. If she was going to succeed, she had to control her impulses.

Stick to the plan.

Standing outside Renata's apartment two hours later, Jalal took a deep breath. They weren't supposed to meet again until tomorrow, but Renata had claimed she had something urgent to discuss. It probably was nothing more than female hysteria. How could Bukayev have sent a woman to run this operation?

Seconds after he knocked, Renata opened the door wearing a towel around her chest. Jalal immediately averted his eyes. American women were immodest by nature, parading around in tight, low-cut shirts and miniskirts that left nothing to the imagination. He expected more dignity from a Muslim. "Get dressed. I'll come back in five minutes."

"No," she said, grabbing his arm. "You can't be seen loitering outside my apartment." She tugged him inside and slammed the door.

He refused to look at her. "Go put on some clothes. Then we can talk." This had to be a test. Maybe Bukayev was using the woman to check his fidelity to Allah and loyalty to the mission. He'd prove his worth by not giving in to her brazen vulgarity. But he turned his head too soon, catching sight of her walking away naked, dragging the towel behind her. She turned fully to him before shutting the bedroom door.

He steadied himself against the wall. She was exquisite. Maybe he should just leave. But what if there really was an urgent matter? He finally sat on the couch, knees pressed together, hands clenched in his lap.

To his relief, Renata emerged from the bedroom in baggy sweatpants and a long-sleeve T-shirt. Upon closer inspection, however, it was obvious she wasn't wearing a bra. He willed his eyes to focus on her face but found he couldn't look at her full lips. They were almost as tantalizing as her nude body. He recited a brief prayer in his head to center himself.

"What's so urgent, Renata?"

"I don't know if I can go through with the plan."

At her words, his shameful lust was overcome by panic. "Why not, what happened?" He couldn't imagine calling Bukayev with such news.

"Do you know the plan?"

He shook his head, humiliated by his ignorance.

"I need you to take some photographs for me. Can you do that?"

He nodded. "Of course. I do that kind of thing all the time for my imam."

"Wonderful." She gave him the details. "I need these today."

He hesitated. "But this isn't what I was told to do. And I don't have my good camera—"

"Use your phone, Jalal." She walked over to the kitchen.

He made an effort not to watch her.

She emerged from the kitchen with a glass of water and a small camera.

He stood. "What are you doing?"

She put the drink on the coffee table and in a flash her shirt was off. Then she backed into him with the camera in her extended arm. Before he could react, she snapped a photograph, then turned to him, a wide smile across her face. "Would you rather go take some pictures for me or would you prefer that I send this photo to Imran?"

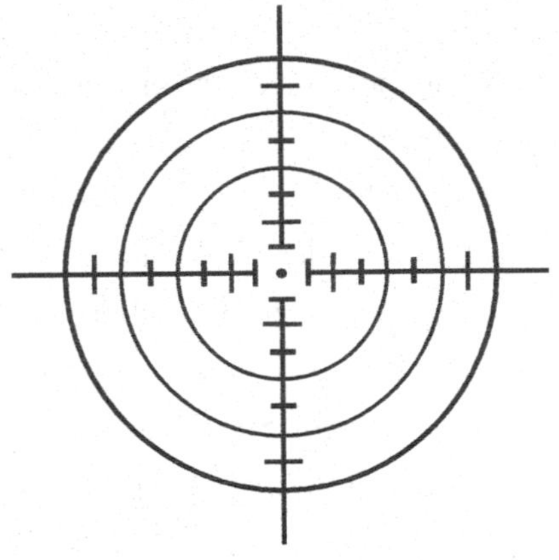

CHAPTER THIRTY-ONE

Zara was furious. Not every man fell into her arms, but most did. They were easy to manipulate if there was sex, or even a hint of it, involved. The way Jalal had ogled her, the perspiration on his face, indicated she had him on the hook. It wasn't that she'd wanted to sleep with him, but it would've been better to get blackmail photos showing a little more action. Still, the topless picture she'd taken should be enough to motivate him. Jalal's jihad career would be over if she emailed the photo to Imran. And Jalal knew it. He'd be back later with the pictures. The ones she might need as a decoy. Zara drove past the site several times before concluding it was safe to proceed. She parked on the far side of the building so the car couldn't be seen from the main road. Bulldozers and backhoes sat abandoned in the adjacent lot. A handful of the workmen were part of the operation, but she didn't know them by name or by sight. Yet. Zara wanted to meet them beforehand to ensure they could take orders from a woman. She wasn't about to walk into an operation where she wasn't fully in charge. Beslan would've been even more successful had the men listened to her from the get-go. She'd known all along that the government would not accede to their demand that Russian forces leave Chechnya immediately. But her fellow hostage takers were either too fanatical or too stupid to understand this. They'd even refused a Russian offer to send local politicians into the school in exchange for freeing some of the children. In one fell swoop, they could've executed several government officials who'd sided with Moscow against the long-suffering Chechen people. She'd tried to explain the benefits of such an exchange to the men in charge, but instead of listening, they'd told her to sit down and shut up. If Moscow refused to withdraw its troops, they said, they were obligated to fight to the death from inside the school. Zara wasn't afraid to die, but she wasn't going to sacrifice herself for absolutely nothing. That's why she'd fled at the first opportunity. There was too much left to do, too many wrongs to right.

She shook her head and brought her focus back to the current operation. There was only one vehicle in the parking lot. It probably belonged to the custodian, the only team member with full access to the building. At first, she was alarmed. Where was everyone else? Then she recalled that it was an American holiday today. Labor Day, they called it.

She walked to the rear of the building, her eyes committing every necessary detail to memory. Beyond the blacktop were scattered trees on a hill that led toward a dense thicket. Zara ascended the hill to get a better view of the rooftop. On the left side of the building, ladder rungs protruded from hatches on the roof, providing access to the heating and ventilation system. They'd make excellent escape routes, but they also could provide entry for police. Perhaps there was a way to lock them from the inside. She added that thought to her mental checklist.

Zara pictured herself fleeing while her martyr-minded cohorts blew themselves up or did whatever they'd intended to do for Allah's glory. She had no plans to join them in paradise. After she took care of her business, she'd disappear.

She trotted closer to the building. Not surprisingly, the door to the left of a dumpster was locked. If it was always locked, would opening it from the inside trigger an alarm? Would she need a key or pin code to exit the building from here undetected? If so, she could go out through the roof, jump down to the dumpster, and flee into the woods. If anyone saw her running, they'd probably mistake her for a civilian. Just like in Beslan. After all, who would suspect a beautiful woman like her?

A half hour later, Zara turned onto a quiet dead-end street. A row of modest but attractive brick town houses lined the left side of the road. Maggie Jenkins's house was the third one from the cul-de-sac. Zara's pulse quickened at the sight of a yellow Jeep parked in the driveway. She drove halfway around the circle and put the car into park.

Taking care of Jenkins wasn't part of Bukayev's plan. He knew that Zara had been involved in the murder of Steve Ryder last year in Tbilisi, but he didn't know that she'd been the actual assassin. Imran also knew that Zara had been in the Georgian farmhouse with Jenkins, but he didn't know that the American had seen Zara's face, never mind that they had spoken throughout the ordeal. He had no idea that they'd discussed their lives, their sorrows, and their losses. Or that Maggie had tried to help Zara save her younger brother's life after he'd been shot by Russians. Imran wouldn't understand how, under different circumstances, she and Maggie might've been friends. Far-fetched, perhaps, but if not for the war, everything would be different. Sometimes she dreamt that she was performing again, the prima ballerina floating across the stage. But those days were gone and her dreams were dead.

For months, Zara had considered whether to even target Jenkins. Ultimately, she'd decided it would be too complicated to try to run Bukayev's operation and kill the American in a single visit. Revenge would have to wait. Then came the events in Beslan. Jenkins knew too much. She had to go.

Zara slipped on a baseball cap and wraparound sunglasses. In her American jeans and Georgetown University sweatshirt, she could easily pass for one of Jenkins's friends. She pulled to the curb in front of her mailbox, shut off the car, removed the tops on two coffee cups, and gently unscrewed the caps on the small plastic bottles hidden inside. After placing the black plastic lids loosely on the cardboard cups, she got out of the car and gave the neighborhood a quick visual scan. All appeared to be quiet. She held one coffee cup in each hand and ascended the stairs.

Zara closed her eyes for a moment and focused on her next moves. When the front door opened, the initial phase of the attack would begin. Jenkins would be immobilized, then she'd move in for the kill. She couldn't wait to see shock animate the American's face.

Zara rang the doorbell and shifted on her feet. She rang the bell a second time, then lowered the cup in her right hand to the stoop. She knocked and strained her neck to see if there was any movement behind the windows. She pounded on the door, but there still was no answer. Was Jenkins home and just not answering? Or was she out for a walk? Asleep? Whatever the case, it was time to employ the backup plan.

Zara turned around on the stoop just as a black SUV made its way onto the street. When the car slowed in front of Jenkins's house, Zara gave a friendly wave that belied her sudden fear and trotted down the stairs. She was back in her rental car by the time the SUV turned around in the cul-de-sac. In the rearview mirror she saw a man in a gray suit emerge from the passenger's side and start toward her. She put the car in gear and drove away slowly, as if she were in no particular rush.

Before she turned onto the main road, Zara glanced to her left. The SUV was still idling at the curb, but the man in the suit was sprinting up the sidewalk toward her. It was then that Zara noticed there was only one coffee in the cup holder.

Warner pulled up outside Maggie's town house to find two Agency men huddled on her front stoop. A knot formed in his stomach the moment he got the urgent call from the CIA security team. *"Get to Maggie's house, stat."*

"Warner Thompson." He ascended the stairs. "What's going on?"

One of the men, a dark-haired, well-built thirty-something raised a hand. "Don't come any closer. This cup has some kind of acid in it."

"What?"

"We saw a woman approach the house," replied the second man.

"But it wasn't Jenkins," added the first. "Not tall enough."

"Who was she?"

"We don't know. Looked young. Petite. Black hair. We think she left this cup here."

The knot in his gut grew tighter.

"We need to get this liquid tested," one of the men said.

"Call headquarters first. They won't be too happy if you bring something toxic into the building."

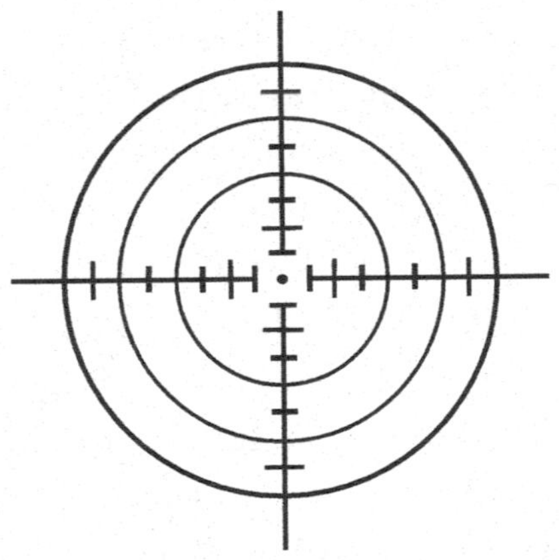

CHAPTER THIRTY-TWO

The buzz of the phone startled him. Warner flipped it open without checking the number.

"Hello, comrade."

Warner groaned to himself. He'd recognize the voice anywhere. "Hi, Yuri."

"Is everything okay?"

"Yeah. Of course."

"Good, good." The Russian paused. "Say, I was wondering if you found Maggie."

Warner's free hand gripped the leather-covered steering wheel. "Why do you ask?"

"I'm afraid I have some disturbing news for her."

The bottom dropped from his stomach. "What is it, Yuri?"

"There's no easy way to say this, so I'll just—"

"Out with it." Warner closed his eyes.

"According to one of my sources in Chechnya, an imam has issued a religious edict against Maggie. A fatwa. Someone wants her dead to avenge what happened last year in Georgia."

Warner hadn't been with Maggie when everything went down in the terrorist safe house, but he remembered every word she'd spoken in the debriefing at CIA headquarters.

"I don't know if I killed her." Maggie looked pale and small in the dimly lit conference room.

The young, stringy-haired interrogator took over, assuming the "bad cop" role. "Explain to me how you can't know whether you shot someone to death?"

"Look." Maggie sighed. "We've been over this a half dozen times. There was complete chaos, bullets flying everywhere. I was coming under fire myself."

Warner stood and loomed over the junior CIA officers. "Gentlemen, this is a waste of everyone's time. Maggie is the only witness we have and I believe she's told us the truth." He shot both interrogators a withering look. "And, I might add, if bullets from her gun killed any of the terrorists, she did the world a great favor."

"Warner, are you there?"

Yuri's voice snapped him back to the present.

"Yes, of course. What are you talking about?"

"Zara Barayeva."

Warner had to force himself to breathe.

"My source tells me that she's the assassin targeting Maggie."

Did this have anything to do with the men Maggie and her neighbor had seen outside her house? With the cup full of acid on her porch? Warner struggled for words. "Zara? When? How?"

"That's what we need to figure out. Where's Maggie now?"

"I don't know."

"We need to tell her, Warner. Make sure she's somewhere safe."

Yuri's sudden interest in Maggie's whereabouts was a bit unsettling.

As was his fixation on Beslan.

One of the Agency men approached Warner's car. "Hang on one second, Yuri." He put a hand over the mouthpiece and lowered his window.

"The FBI is sending a hazmat team to pick up the cup."

He nodded, put the car in gear and raised the phone to his ear, telling Yuri, "The Agency's going to want to talk to your source to determine if there's an actual threat against Maggie."

"I doubt my source will talk to the US government."

Warner turned from Maggie's street onto the main road heading east. It certainly was plausible that Zara would want Maggie dead, but he didn't trust Yuri. "Maybe we should have a conference call with Maggie. You can tell her about the threat."

"Perhaps telling her in person would be better. We can meet at my house. As you know, I have a lot of security here."

Indeed he did. Warner had seen it for himself at Yuri's sixtieth birthday party earlier that year. But better security could not possibly be why he wanted them to meet at his house. *What are you up to, Yuri?* "I'll let you know."

• ★ ★ ★ •

Maggie and Roger both slept late without intending to on Monday morning. They'd been up late the night before, arguing about how to proceed, how far to push Daud.

Over coffee, Maggie resumed the discussion where it had left off just after midnight. "Daud knows more than he's letting on, Roger."

He glanced up from the sports page. "I know."

"Then why didn't you press him for more information?"

"I told you. He does better with gentle persuasion than with demands."

"I know, but—"

"He's my asset, Maggie. I know him. Period." His eyes went back to the paper.

Maggie fumed as she paced the length of the kitchen, pausing only to answer her phone.

"Good morning, Warner."

"You okay?"

"Yeah, why?"

"I have some news."

She could hear the strain in his voice. "What is it?"

"I just got off the phone with a Russian source who claims a Chechen imam has issued a fatwa against you."

"Against me?"

"Because of what happened in Georgia last year." He paused. "He claims the assassin is Zara. This could be why she's here. *If* she's here."

Was that the operation she'd overheard Zara and Bukayev discussing? An operation to kill her? Maggie steadied herself against the counter. "I don't know, Warner. I don't think Zara would come all this way just to kill me. After Beslan, wouldn't they want to do something equally if not more spectacular?"

"Maybe it's both. Maybe Zara's after you *and* she's planning a separate operation."

"Maybe." She caught Roger peering around the newspaper watching her. "How reliable is your source?"

"I'm not sure," Warner replied, "but I think he may be onto something."

She lowered herself into a kitchen chair across the table from Roger. "What do you mean?"

"The Agency guys I have patrolling the neighborhood saw a woman at your front door this morning."

Maggie gripped the edge of the table.

"What she'd look like?"

Roger folded the paper and set it beside his mug.

"Petite. Dark hair. Young. She left a cup full of some sort of acid on your front stoop."

"Acid?"

Roger's mouth fell open.

"Yeah. Maggie, listen, why don't you come stay with me so I know you're safe. I could shuttle you to and from headquarters."

"I'm safe where I am, I promise." She felt Roger's eyes on her.

"Are you sure?"

She didn't respond.

"I think we should talk to my Russian source, find out if he knows more. I could pick you up and we can meet him in person."

"Well, I need to shower and then I have to—" she stopped, realizing that Warner might be trying to figure out where she was hiding. "You know what? Just give me the address." She checked her watch. "I can be there in an hour."

"I'd rather we go together."

"I have something I need to do after," she lied.

"Fine, Maggie. I was going to tell you this in the car, but since you're traveling solo, you leave me with no choice."

Her grip tightened around the phone.

"Carl Manning died."

"Carl Manning? Steve's colleague?"

Roger looked up at her over the brim of his mug.

"How'd he die?"

"Apparent suicide."

"Suicide?"

The mug slipped from Roger's hands, hit the edge of the table, and crashed to the floor, where it shattered, spewing coffee in every direction. He sprang from the chair and grabbed a roll of paper towels from under the sink, his face screwed up as if he were in pain.

"What was that?"

"Nothing. I dropped something," Maggie lied again. "I'm sorry to hear about Carl. He was so kind to me after Steve died. He knew what it's like to lose someone so suddenly. His wife, what was her name again?"

"Jane."

"Jane, that's right. I remember Steve telling me that Carl was confused about why she even was on that flight on 9/11. She was supposed to be in New York on a business trip."

"Yeah. Poor guy. He kind of faltered since then. I just put him in charge of an interagency task force on the Beslan attack, hoping that would give him some purpose. Maybe that was a mistake. All those deaths, the terrorists, maybe it was too traumatic for him to handle."

"Sounds like he never recovered from losing his wife." She paused, her voice catching. "I can relate."

Beside her, Roger sat on the floor, stock-still, unmoving, staring at the mess he'd made.

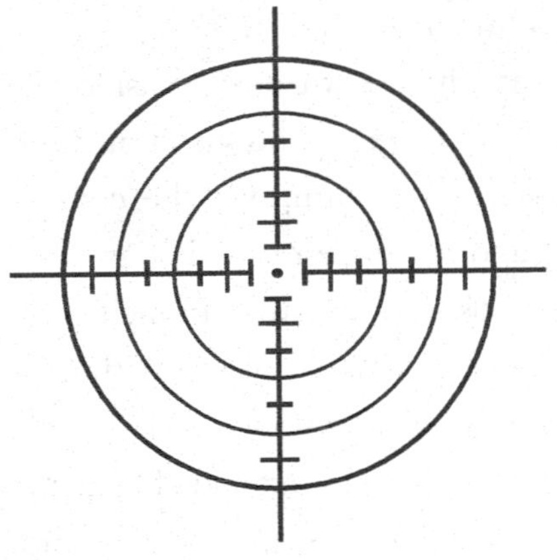

CHAPTER THIRTY-THREE

Zara had been trained to check and recheck every facet of an operation. Despite that training, she'd screwed up badly today. If the man in Jenkins's neighborhood didn't notice the coffee cup she'd left on the stoop, Jenkins surely would. And since there was no way she could return to retrieve it, Zara had to cover her tracks. She'd returned the car at Reagan National Airport, taken a cab to a rental agency in the District, and obtained another vehicle using a second false identity and credit card. The authorities might find the original rental, but the trail would end there. As for Jenkins, Zara hadn't given up on an alternate plan involving a minor fender bender, a sedative, and the Potomac

River. But for the moment, Zara needed to focus on the primary mission, which was why she was back outside the building. As far as she was concerned, there was no such thing as overpreparation.

From the base of the dumpster, she counted twenty strides to the grass and another fifteen to the edge of the tree line. She trotted into the woods, swatting away branches and trying to avoid the brambles grabbing at her ankles. Within two minutes, she discovered that the woods weren't so deep after all. They gave way to an office-building complex surrounded by a large parking lot. It was the perfect place to leave her car for the escape.

Through squinted eyes, Zara thought she saw surveillance cameras mounted on the office buildings. There was no reason to concern herself too much with them. If she made it this far, she'd almost be home free. And even if she were caught on film, it would be hours, if not longer, before the police thought to check cameras this far from the scene. Zara smiled.

It was all working out, the way she always knew it would. If only Bukayev were here to see it come to fruition. She could call him, but she didn't want to breach operational security. And besides, how could she apprise him of her latest plans when she'd sworn to stick to his?

If she ever saw him again, she would make certain he understood that it had been her meticulous planning, her brilliant strategy that had resulted in such great success.

Maggie parked the Beetle at the top of the street and took a swig of diet soda. For a moment, she contemplated whether this meeting was a trap. Perhaps Warner's friend's house was filled with CIA security officers waiting to escort her to headquarters. She rubbed at her bleary eyes. He wouldn't do that to her. Would he?

Outside the car, she called Warner's cell phone.

"I'm parked up the street. Where do I meet you?"

Maggie listened to Warner's muffled voice for a moment. "At the end of the driveway."

She clapped the disposable phone shut and bent over to tighten the laces on her running shoes. Then she slung her purse across her chest and trotted past three sprawling mansions before spotting Warner standing with a short, heavyset man. Was that who she thought it was? Maggie slowed and squinted at the men.

"Don't make us wait out here all day," Warner called. "Yuri's a busy man."

Maggie took a moment to catch her breath. This definitely wasn't a CIA setup, not with the infamous Yuri Markov involved. Then it dawned on her. If Markov, with all his Russian intelligence connections, had information about Zara, it could all be true. Zara's operation, might, in fact, be directed at her.

She walked slowly toward the men, all the while taking in the Baroque-style mansion looming behind them. It seemed Yuri Markov had done very well for himself since the demise of the Soviet Union.

"Thank you for meeting us, Maggie," Warner said. "I'd like you to meet Yuri Markov. Yuri, this is Maggie Jenkins."

His voice was thick and low. "Hello, Ms. Jenkins. I've heard so much about you."

Maggie locked eyes with the aging Russian spy. What was Warner doing associating with the likes of him? Not only was he a former KGB official but he was also reputed to be involved with the Russian mafia, which might explain how he'd amassed a fortune great enough to afford his sprawling house. "And I've heard a lot about you." She glanced at Warner and back to Yuri. "So, tell me about the fatwa."

"Please, let's go inside." Yuri nodded toward a hulking man with a blond crew cut who'd materialized from inside a security booth partially concealed behind a tall hedgerow. "We're making Boris here very nervous lingering outside."

The man nodded to his boss and turned his eyes to Maggie. As he stepped toward her, Yuri raised his hand. "No need to search Ms. Jenkins, Boris. I consider her a friend."

Maggie smiled and tried to appear relaxed. If he was going to stare, she might as well give him something to look at. She threw her shoulders back and drew the purse strap tighter across her chest. "Nice to meet you, Boris."

The young Russian nodded, his cheeks blushing pink.

Warner raised his eyebrows, then frowned at her. She shrugged. She was wanted by the CIA for questioning and apparently being hunted by a terrorist. You never knew when having an armed Russian thug on your side would come in handy.

Maggie let her eyes linger on Boris as the trio walked up the driveway. He kept his gaze trained firmly on her, even as his hand fumbled for something inside the security booth. Suddenly, a large, wrought-iron gate swung shut across the end of the driveway. Maggie waved to Boris and turned her attention to the house.

Up ahead, the driveway split in two, encircling an obscenely ornate fountain modeled after the People's Friendship Fountain in Moscow. Fifteen gilded statues of voluptuous maidens, one for each of the former Soviet republics, stood watch over Yuri's lush estate. To the left was a five-car garage. Maggie was disappointed to see only a Cadillac Escalade and a black Mercedes parked inside.

The garage's empty bays would be a great place to house a replica of Lenin's tomb to go along with the ridiculous Soviet fountain. Ahead was the home's main entrance, an arched wooden door that looked strong enough to hold back an invading army. The only thing missing was a moat.

"Nice place," Maggie offered.

They entered a grand, white marble foyer dominated by a coffered dome, an enormous crystal chandelier, and a sweeping staircase with a wrought-iron balustrade.

"You like my little dacha?" asked the Russian.

Maggie realized she was gawking. A dacha, indeed. She cleared her throat. "It's lovely, Mr. Markov."

"Please, call me Yuri."

Maggie offered a weak smile and followed the men to the library, which had an entirely different yet equally impressive atmosphere.

Every inch of the room was covered in mahogany. Floor, ceiling, and walls. Recessed lighting was enhanced by yet another, albeit smaller, crystal chandelier. She studied a display of framed photographs on the wall, one of which was from Dominion Elementary, a local school.

"My granddaughter's the pretty blonde in the front row," Yuri commented.

Maggie leaned in for a closer look. The little girl had white-blonde pigtails and large blue eyes. She was a beauty.

Across the room, Warner studied Yuri's framed "Hero of the Soviet Union" medal. "She's a cute little girl. About the same age as my girls, Maggie. In fact, Yuri and I often find ourselves seated together at school assemblies and dance recitals."

"Oh?" Exactly how chummy were Warner and Yuri?

"Yes. Perhaps we should set up a . . . what do you call them, Warner? A playdate?" Yuri chuckled and gestured to a soft leather chair beside the fireplace. "Please, have a seat, Maggie."

Yuri sat opposite her and cleared his throat. "As you probably know, I'm retired from intelligence. But I have many contacts all over the world who share information with me. And last night, I learned that a cleric in Chechnya has declared a fatwa against you."

Maggie folded her hands together and dug a thumbnail into her palm.

"It's because of what happened last year in Georgia. They want revenge for the death of their comrades. Or should I say jihadists?"

"I didn't kill any of them."

"You know that this doesn't matter to them. They often blame others for self-inflicted catastrophes."

Maggie nodded and bit down on the inside of her cheek.

"I'm told that they've dispatched a woman, someone who doesn't fit the profile of an Islamic terrorist, to carry out the fatwa. She was one of the Beslan terrorists." He glanced at Warner, who hadn't taken his eyes off Maggie. "I asked my source, '*Shto eto*? Who is this woman?'"

Shto eto? Maggie tried to keep her expression neutral even as her breath caught in her throat. There was something about Yuri's voice, its cadence, the tone.

"And"—his deep, raspy voice cut through the cavernous room —"I'm sorry to inform you that it's Zara Barayeva."

Maggie exchanged glances with Warner, who gave her a subtle nod. "The CIA says she's dead. How could she have been in Beslan? How can she be trying to hunt me down?"

"Your intelligence gets many things wrong. Always has." Yuri chuckled, but there was no amusement behind it. "Funny. I thought you, of all people, would be tracking this woman. After all, she killed your fiancé."

Maggie blanched. The Russian was testing her. But why?

Warner broke the silence. "As I said earlier, we'd like to talk to your source. Off the record, of course. Maybe between the three of us, we can figure out where Zara is."

"Assuming she's really alive," Maggie added, testing for Yuri's reaction.

Yuri narrowed his light blue eyes at her. She looked away. "Tell us what you know about Zara. No detail is too insignificant. Anything she—"

The telephone on his desk interrupted him. He raised a hand in apology and answered. "Hello?"

That voice. The guttural way he pronounced *hello*.

"Okay, yes, I will call you later." Yuri hung up. "My apologies. Where were we?"

Maggie needed a moment. "May I use your bathroom?"

Yuri gave her directions to a nearby powder room, which was on the far side of the foyer, near the main kitchen. Maggie pulled the disposable cell phone from her purse and dialed the number she'd found hidden inside Daud Chotkev's volume of *Crime and Punishment*.

"Hello?" the man said.

She cracked open the door and said nothing in reply.

"Who is this? *Shto eto*?" The same voice on the phone was echoing from the library. She powered off the phone, leaned against the sink, and splashed water on her face. Yuri Markov knew Daud Chotkev. Were they working together in secret? Why would Daud have Yuri's number hidden in a Russian novel if not to conceal his association with the KGB man? And since Daud knew Zara, perhaps Yuri did too. And if he did, it was possible that Daud and Yuri knew more about Beslan than she had realized.

She took several deep breaths and returned to the men.

"You okay?" Warner's brow wrinkled in concern. "You look pale."

"I'm not feeling well. Must've been something I ate."

"You should probably go home and rest." Warner advanced toward her.

"I'd be happy to drive you home, Maggie," Yuri stepped closer.

She retreated toward the foyer. "Thanks for the offer, but I'll be okay. Just need some antacids. Maybe a nap."

"Let me know when your source is willing to talk," Warner said to Yuri. "We can meet again then."

Yuri nodded and addressed Maggie. "Be very careful, Ms. Jenkins. Zara Barayeva is a dangerous woman."

Maggie opened the front door and hurried out without a glance behind.

Warner scrambled to keep up. "Maggie, wait. What just happened in there?"

Maggie stopped when she reached Warner's BMW. She should tell him about Daud having Yuri's phone number, but that would reveal that Roger was back in contact with him. And he wasn't supposed to be. "I need to do a little more digging to confirm things, but suffice it to say that Yuri knows Chechens with possible links to Beslan. And maybe even to Zara."

Warner appeared taken aback. "Wait. What? I need details."

"I'll get them to you." Just as soon as she talked to Roger.

"Yuri hates the Chechens. Hell, he was the driving force behind targeting civilians in the first Russian-Chechen war. Why would he associate with them now?"

Over Warner's shoulder, she caught sight of Boris approaching. "Bye, Boris." She gave a friendly wave and lowered her voice. "I'll call you when I know more." With that, she trotted up the street to the car. When she glanced in the rearview mirror, she saw Warner leaning out his driver's side window, staring at the Beetle in confusion.

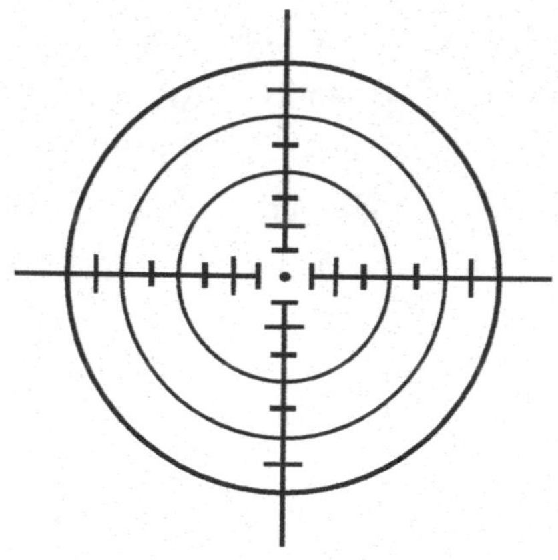

CHAPTER THIRTY-FOUR

Back at Roger's house, Maggie found a note on the kitchen counter.

Had to go into work. Call my office phone.

First things first, she went upstairs to check her email on Roger's computer. "Thank you, Tamaz," she murmured. He'd found the missing camera chip in his flat and emailed her the contents. She printed off the photo of Zara outside the Beslan school and hurried back to the kitchen to call Roger.

He picked up on the second ring.

"You okay?" she said. He hadn't said a word to her after her call with Warner this morning.

She hadn't known him long, but silence wasn't one of his personality traits.

"Well, they haven't thrown me in the dungeon or waterboarded me yet. Of course, it is Labor Day. Even CIA torturers get the day off."

"I mean the news about Carl Manning."

"Oh, that. Yeah, poor guy." He cleared his throat. "They asked me to take over the Beslan task force now that he's . . . gone."

"Well, that's good. Maybe you can find some classified information on Zara. Or Bukayev. Or chatter about an impending attack."

The clattering of a keyboard filled the line. "Yeah."

"You sure you're okay?"

"Just busy. And tired of answering questions about whether I know where you are."

"Listen, I learned something new this morning. It's kind of urgent."

"What is it?"

"Not over this line. Hurry up and get home."

His voice was suddenly muffled. "One second. Just getting off the phone with my lady." His voice returned to normal. "Okay, my love. We'll talk over dinner. You cook, I clean. We drink. Heavily. Gotta run."

Maggie stared at the receiver for a second before grabbing her keys and heading for the door. There was no sense in wasting time.

• ★ ★ ★ •

Yuri looked at the image of Maggie Jenkins in the Grozny market for what felt like the hundredth time. Did Warner know she'd been to Chechnya? And that she was only pretending to believe that Zara Barayeva was dead? After his men, whom he'd tasked to keep an eye on Jenkins's comings and goings, reported that she seemed to have vanished from her house sometime between Saturday evening and yesterday morning, he'd concocted the fatwa story, hoping it would draw the American out. Maybe he could gain her trust, or at least her fear, and have her confide everything she knew about Zara. But it hadn't gone well just now. The woman had outright lied to his face. Questions swirled in his head in an endless loop. What had Maggie learned from the terrorist's aunt in Grozny? Had anyone discovered his role in funding the Beslan attack? Zara? Maggie? Or worst of all, Warner?

He drummed his meaty fingers on the desk. As soon as he took care of one problem, two others sprouted up. Like that ridiculous carnival game his granddaughter liked to play. Whac-A-Mole or some such thing. His men had drugged and hung Carl Manning. That took care of one loose end. But then there was Daud. It was time to apply the screws.

Yuri smashed out the cigarette that lay smoldering in an ashtray, grabbed his keys, and headed outside. He had an entire organization under him—businessmen, retired Russian intelligence and military, and hitmen. Yet nothing was going his way. How did the old saying go? If you want something done right, do it yourself.

A half hour later, Maggie parked around the corner from the building housing the Central Asian Studies Institute, Daud Chotkev's think tank. When he opened the door, his jaw dropped.

"Miss—"

"You can call me Megan." She pasted on her broadest smile. "I have a couple more questions."

He remained motionless in the doorway. "I already told you everything I know."

Maggie tilted her head and stared at the Chechen. "How do you know Yuri Markov?"

Chotkev staggered, as if he'd been hit in the gut with a two-by-four. "How dare you bring up that man's name. He's responsible for the deaths of tens of thousands of my countrymen."

She slipped past him into the office. "What do you mean?"

Daud closed the door behind him. "Yuri Markov was the KGB man behind the first Chechen war. Because of him, the Russians bombed apartment buildings, schools, stores. He destroyed my country. My family."

Maggie ran a hand through her hair. His story sounded a bit like Zara's. So much death and destruction. "If he's so bad, then why do you have his phone number?"

He stared blankly.

"On a slip of paper hidden inside one of your books?" She gestured toward the bookshelf.

"I don't know what you're talking about."

Maggie marched over to the top shelf at the far end of the bookcase. When she flapped the pages of *Crime and Punishment*, a scrap of paper fell out and fluttered to the ground. She snapped the paper from the floor. "Does this ring a bell?"

He crossed his arms. "I inherited most of these books from the institute's previous director."

"So the previous director knows Yuri Markov?"

"I have no idea." Daud's voice rose. "No idea!"

Maggie slipped the scrap back into *Crime and Punishment* and reshelved it. "In case you need it." Running a finger along the spines of several other books, she added, "Roger doesn't know I found Yuri's phone number here. I guess I should tell him."

Daud's gaze darted from Maggie to the bookshelf and back.

"He seems like a nice guy. Wouldn't hurt a fly, right? But let me tell you, Roger is the most cutthroat person I've ever met. If I tell him about your connection to Yuri, he'd make sure you got deported. He doesn't take kindly to deception and disloyalty."

"I'm not deceiving anyone."

She looked at the Chechen with what she hoped was a sympathetic expression. "Can you imagine what it would be like for a known Russian collaborator to live in Chechnya?"

Daud frowned. "What do you want from me?"

"I want to know about your relationship with Yuri Markov. If you don't want to tell me or Roger, I'll have to call in the FBI. They have a very thick file on your Russian friend."

Daud crumpled onto the sofa, head in his hands. His voice was soft, weary. "Yuri's blackmailing me. My brother's been in a Russian prison for a year. If I don't do Markov's bidding, he says my brother will die."

His sudden sobbing chipped away at Maggie's resolve. She took a moment to steel herself. "What kinds of things do you do for Yuri?"

Daud took a few deep breaths to calm himself. "I funnel money to people."

"What people?"

"I don't know." He dropped his head back into his hands, moaning. "I'm just the middleman. I send the money to a contact. I don't know where it goes after that."

"Are you sure about that? Because I have a strong suspicion that I might find your name in those documents Roger gave you to translate."

"I don't know where the money goes after I transfer it. I swear!"

"Where's your contact?"

He looked up and blinked at her. "In . . .in England."

"Is it Imran Bukayev?"

He stood and walked to the window. In a voice not much louder than a whisper, he added, "Yuri will kill me if I . . . oh, no." He whirled around, wild-eyed. "He's here."

Maggie dashed to Daud's side. "Who?"

"Yuri."

Out on the sidewalk below, she watched as Boris opened the rear door of a black Cadillac Escalade with tinted windows. The portly Russian lumbered out onto the sidewalk.

Daud froze then seemed to snap out of it. He hurried over to his desk, pulled open the top drawer and pressed a key into her hand. "The tenant upstairs on the third floor is out of town. I'm supposed to water his plants." He cracked open the door. Voices rose from the first floor. "Go!"

Maggie didn't hesitate. She took the stairs up two at a time and managed to slip into the empty office before Boris and Yuri caught sight of her from the landing below. She cracked the door and listened. A loud pounding—probably a fist against the door—was followed by Yuri's booming voice.

• ★ ★ ★ •

Yuri took a minute to recover from the effort of climbing the steep stairs before banging on the door again. Finally, Daud opened the door, his dark complexion a bit ashen, probably a result of Yuri's surprise visit. The Russian plowed past him into the office. Handwoven carpets from Azerbaijan, similar to ones Yuri owned, added much needed color to the drab room.

"Some coffee?" Daud offered in Russian.

"*Nyet.*" Yuri wasn't there for a kaffeeklatsch.

"Please sit." The Chechen gestured with a trembling hand toward the sofa behind Yuri.

"We alone?"

"Yes." He licked his lips and wrung his hands together.

Yuri sank back into the couch and folded his hands on his lap. As much as he hated being here, dealing with a Chechen of all people, there was something enjoyable—or maybe *nostalgic* would better describe it—about the situation. Nothing was more pleasurable than making subordinates squirm.

He watched the Chechen fidget for a moment. "Well, Daud?"

"Is there something wrong, Mr. Markov?"

"Where are they?"

"Who?"

Yuri struggled to his feet. "Zara and Bukayev!" he boomed.

Boris was now within arm's reach of Daud. "Honestly, I don't know."

"Did you tell them that I'm the financier?"

Daud shook his head violently. "I've never spoken to either of them. I just transfer the money to the designated accounts. And even if I did know them, I—I—I wouldn't," he stammered.

"How do you think Bukayev would react to learning that a powerful KGB boss is funding these attacks? To learn that he's acting on my behest, not on Allah's?"

Daud looked like he wanted to flee.

Yuri smiled. Little did Daud know that once his goals were achieved, or if the Chechens became too much of a liability—or both—Yuri would eliminate them all. And in the end, he'd be cheered by patriotic Russians for his success in ridding the country of such dangerous extremists.

The Chechen shifted from one foot to the other. He opened his mouth as if to speak before shutting it again.

Yuri tugged on his waistband. "Surely you know people who know where Zara and Bukayev are."

Boris advanced another step closer.

"Bukayev lives in London, doesn't he? I could find his address for you, I could—"

"He hasn't been seen there in two days. What if he's gone to the British authorities and told them everything he knows about you?"

Daud balled his hands together.

"If it turns out that either Zara or Bukayev know about my involvement in Beslan, you'll be the first to pay for that security breach. Understand?"

The Chechen blinked back tears. "Yes."

"Good." Yuri smiled to put Daud at ease. It had been a while since he'd been able to toy with someone this frightened. "I thought my friend Boris would have to do a little bit of convincing." He studied the slight young man. "Maybe we should preview what awaits you if you fail to get the information I want. What do you think, Boris?"

A crooked smile broke across the bodyguard's wide face.

Daud raised his arms in defense. "No, no, I'll do whatever you say."

In a flash, Boris's right fist connected with Daud's nose. He collapsed into a heap on the floor, blood running down his face, his core exposed. A swift kick in the gut led to howls of pain between desperate gasps for air. Boris lifted his foot as if he were going to stomp on Daud's head. Instead, he kicked him in the thigh and nodded to Yuri.

"You have twenty-four hours, Daud. Find them."

With that, the Russians left the Chechen moaning on the floor.

Upstairs, Maggie ran to the window. As soon as the SUV pulled away, she clattered down the stairs and burst into Daud's office. He was on the floor by the couch, motionless, his face a bloody mess.

She squatted next to him. "Daud?"

He moaned in reply.

"What did they want?"

He seemed to be flickering on the edge of consciousness. He needed help and she had to disappear before help arrived. "Hang in there, Daud. I'm calling 911."

She should tell the police who did this. But then, if Yuri got arrested, he'd lawyer up. She might never learn more about his connection to Daud or any other Chechens, Zara included.

She used Daud's office phone to report a serious physical assault by unknown assailants. Then, scooping up the documents they'd left for him to translate, she slipped out of the building and hurried around the block to the car, where she waited until the ambulance arrived.

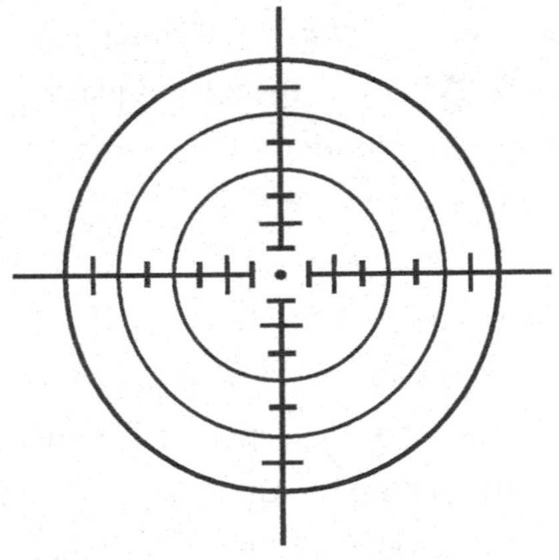

CHAPTER THIRTY-FIVE

Inside the mall, Maggie flipped through a rack of dresses near the store window. Roger arrived first. Then Warner. She watched the men settle at a corner table in the pub across the way—Roger facing the widescreen television and Warner slumped in an adjacent chair, arms crossed, jaw set, bad mood written all over his body. Just wait until he heard the latest.

Maggie left the clothing store and scanned the length of the mall, looking for suspicious activity at the adjacent stores. It didn't look like anyone from the CIA had followed the men to the pub. Everything seemed normal. Just a gaggle of teenagers yapping on cell phones, mothers pushing strollers, a few power-walking senior citizens.

Maggie approached the table. "Gentlemen." She slid into a chair between them. "Any news from headquarters?"

Roger shook his head. "I met the Beslan task force team today. They weren't happy about coming in on a holiday, but I had to bring them up to speed on Zara."

Warner flipped through the drink menu. "Now that British intelligence has finally confirmed that Bukayev went missing after being seen in the company of a suspected Beslan terrorist, I should be able to get the Feds to raise the threat level. Of course, I could've gotten it done sooner if you'd come into the office for a debrief."

"I know. It's just . . . I'll go in tonight, okay?"

"Good." Warner's face relaxed. "I'll go with you."

Roger signaled the waitress. "Round of drinks on me. Beer, whatever you have on tap. Your best scotch, neat, for the gentleman here. And for the lady?"

"Just a diet soda," Maggie didn't want alcohol to cloud her mind. "I think Yuri knows far more about Beslan than we realized."

"Who's Yuri?"

"Markov," Warner said. "Former KGB officer turned mafia boss."

Maggie nodded. "I found a phone number in Daud's office, Roger."

It was Warner's turn for confusion. "Wait, the same Daud from three years ago?"

"Well, now that cat's out of the bag." Roger scowled at Maggie. "Yes. The same one."

Warner squinted. "You're not supposed to be in contact with him."

"Yeah, I know. But it was an emergency. Just like before 9/11. When the Agency refused to make an exception for him."

"Roger, I tried—"

"Well, maybe if you'd fought a little harder for me, I could've gotten more information from Daud and maybe three thousand people wouldn't have been mass murdered a month later."

Warner's mouth pinched closed. Everything he had accomplished in his illustrious career mattered little to him because of 9/11. He felt personally responsible, which Maggie never quite understood.

It had been a systemic bureaucratic failure, not the fault of a single man.

"Look, can you two fight the last war later?"

The men retreated to their corners, Roger sulking, Warner steaming.

"The phone number I found in Daud's office belongs to Yuri. I confirmed that today when we were at his house, Warner. I called it from the bathroom."

"So, you weren't actually feeling sick?"

She shook her head. "No. But I had to get out of there and get to Daud."

Roger lowered his beer mug with an angry *thunk* on the tabletop. "I told you I would handle him."

"You were in meetings. I didn't think it could wait. I needed to ask him about Yuri." Maggie leaned forward against the table. "I think he's funneling money to Chechen terrorists."

"What?" Warner and Roger said in unison.

"Daud admitted to me that he funnels money to organizations all over the world. He claims not to know who gets the money or for what purposes, but when I pressed him on his connection to Yuri, he confirmed that he has handled financial transactions for him." Maggie paused a moment to let the bombshell sink in. "Daud does

Yuri's bidding because Yuri has threatened to kill his brother, who's been in a Russian prison for the past year."

"Wait a minute," Warner interjected. "Are you saying that Yuri's money goes to Chechen terrorists?"

"I don't have hard proof," she confessed, "but Yuri showed up at Daud's office when I was there."

Warner blanched. "Did he see you?"

"No, I managed to hide."

Warner shook his head in disbelief.

"What did he want?" Roger prompted.

"He wanted to know where Bukayev and Zara are."

Warner's expression morphed from anger to disbelief. "Are you sure?"

"He's not a quiet man, Warner. I heard him correctly."

The waitress appeared. "Are we ready for appetizers?"

"Potato skins and nachos, please," Maggie replied. Once the woman was out of earshot, she continued. "We've learned two things about Yuri. First, he funnels money through the Central Asian Studies Institute to unknown recipients. Second, he seems desperate to find Zara and Bukayev." She took a long sip of diet soda. "My theory? Yuri's money funded the Beslan attack. He probably didn't expect any of the terrorists to survive the school siege because, let's face it, Chechen militants are fanatical. They don't seem to care if they die. But Zara is different. She's not like the others."

Both men nodded, fully caught up in the scenario.

"Imagine Yuri's shock when he learned that not only had Zara escaped but that she is tight with Bukayev, the man who planned the school attack. That had to make him nervous. I mean, if anyone was privy to information on who was funding the siege, it would be

Bukayev. And given Bukayev's relationship with Zara, she might also know about Yuri's involvement."

"And that's why he's looking for them," Warner suggested. "They could potentially expose him."

Roger nodded. "That explains the assassin in London."

"And the men watching Zara's aunt in Grozny."

Roger scooped a potato skin into his mouth and signaled the waitress for another beer. "But why would he, the architect of the first Chechen war, fund Chechen terrorists?"

Warner sipped his scotch. "The other day, Yuri claimed he had evidence that Putin was behind Beslan. That the attack was meant to garner public support for an all-out military assault on Chechnya." He narrowed his eyes. "Maybe that's actually Yuri's motive. He opposed the Russian-Chechen peace treaty back in 'ninety-seven. And if I recall, a couple of years ago, he put out a public statement calling for Moscow to put an end to the insurgency once and for all."

Maggie nodded. "I think you're onto something, Warner."

Roger wadded up his cloth napkin. "I want to talk to Daud."

"Oh," Maggie lowered her fork. "There's more to the story. Unfortunately, Yuri's thug beat Daud to a pulp. I called 911 and left right before the ambulance arrived."

Roger winced. "Do you know what hospital he was taken to?"

Maggie shook her head.

"Why don't we tell the cops who attacked Daud?" Warner suggested.

"Yuri will lawyer up," Maggie said, "and then we won't be able to watch him, see what leads he has that we don't."

"What a mess," Roger muttered.

"I'm afraid it gets worse." Maggie pulled several documents from her purse. "Look what I found on Daud's desk."

Roger and Warner leaned forward to read the Central Asian Studies Institute's *Cultural Happenings* newsletter. Maggie chewed on a piece of ice. "A Chechen dance troupe is due to appear at several elementary schools in the region."

"And?" Warner prompted.

"Zara trained as a dancer."

"So, she's a graceful terrorist," Roger snorted.

"Check this out." Maggie pointed to the first page of the untranslated documents. "The number eight followed by this word. The number nine followed by the same word. Maybe like dates on a calendar? Maybe it means September?"

The men listened intently.

"I scanned a little farther down in the document until I found this." She pointed to a phrase. "It's written in Russian. Near as I can tell, it says 'Capitol Day School.'"

"I don't get where this is going," confessed Roger.

"Capitol Day School is where the president of the United States sends his children. The secretary of state's kid goes there. And the Russian ambassador's. And who knows how many other dignitaries. Which brings us back to our dance troupe. Guess where it's performing in two days?"

"The Capitol Day School?" whispered Warner.

"Holy shit," said Roger.

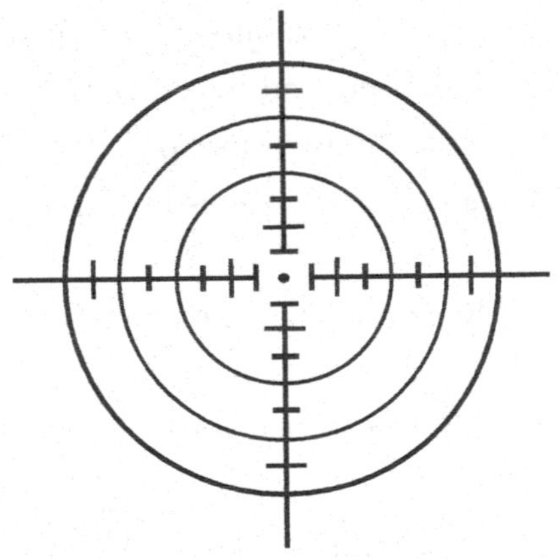

CHAPTER THIRTY-SIX

Maggie rode with Warner on the way to CIA Headquarters. The BMW's leather seats were chilly against her exposed skin on this cool September evening. "How do you know they aren't going to confiscate my badge and suspend me?"

"Because of what you've uncovered. The Agency needs you."

She glanced in the side-view mirror. Roger's silver Audi followed close behind. "Who's going to be there?"

"The director, of course. FBI, Secret Service, Homeland Security." He sniffed. "They won't be happy. My call to headquarters disrupted more than a few holiday weekend plans."

Ten minutes later, they pulled into the executive parking garage underneath CIA headquarters and took the elevator straight to the seventh floor. Maggie caught a glimpse of herself in a hall mirror. A purple V-neck top and a denim mini-skirt. *Yeah, sure, these men will take me seriously.*

"Hey, wait up," Roger called as he closed the gap with a hurried gait.

The trio entered the conference room in the director of Central Intelligence's office suite. The heart of the country's national security apparatus sat around the table. The DCI himself. The head of the National Counterterrorism Center. The Director of Homeland Security. The FBI director. And another man who Maggie assumed was Secret Service based on the pin in his lapel.

Maggie tugged on her skirt, suddenly aware of all the eyes on her.

The DCI stood. "Warner, Mr. Patterson, Ms. Jenkins, please have a seat." There was only one empty seat at the conference table. Several empty chairs were set along the opposite wall.

Warner gestured toward the table. "Maggie." Five pairs of eyes watched her settle into the leather office chair.

"We understand you have some information you'd like to share with us, Ms. Jenkins. I'm told it's rather time sensitive."

Maggie cleared her throat. What if she was wrong? What if she'd read too much into Bukayev's documents? She sipped from the water glass before her and took a deep breath. "We have reason to believe that one of the terrorists who was at the school in Beslan is in the Washington, DC, area."

"Who's we?" asked the director of Homeland Security.

"Warner, Roger, and me."

The director sighed and dropped his pen on the notepad in front of him.

She locked eyes with Roger, who gave her a nod.

"Zara Barayeva, a known Chechen terrorist, was spotted fleeing the school in Beslan. Less than forty-eight hours later, she turned up in London at the home of Imran Bukayev, a spokesman for the Chechen government-in-exile and a suspected terrorist mastermind himself."

The conference room door opened. Her boss, Jim Carpenter, and Dr. Hansen, the Agency psychiatrist, stepped in. She glanced at Warner. He shrugged.

"Where did we get this information, Ms. Jenkins?" asked the DCI.

"From me. I saw Zara in both Beslan and London."

Dr. Hansen slipped the DCI a note. He read it and frowned. "Ms. Jenkins, as I understand it, the Agency believes that Zara Barayeva died last year in Georgia a few weeks after killing your fiancé?"

Confusion clouded the faces at the table.

She bit down on her tongue and clenched and unclenched her fists.

"The truth is, she's not dead."

The DCI turned to Warner. "A word outside?"

Warner reached into his suitcoat, pulled out a folded eight by eleven-inch piece of paper, smoothed it open and handed it to the DCI. "This is Zara Barayeva at Imran Bukayev's London home on Friday."

Maggie reached down into her purse and unrolled the pile of documents inside. She slid a printout of the photo she took of Zara in Beslan toward the DCI. "And here she is fleeing the school siege last Thursday." She glanced at the shrink and smiled triumphantly. Jim Carpenter, standing behind him, paled.

A murmur arose around the table. The DCI cleared his throat. "Let's assume this really is Zara Barayeva. How do you know she's in the US?"

"I overheard her and Bukayev discussing an operation in Washington, DC. And I followed her into Heathrow Airport."

"She could be anywhere in the world," objected the FBI director.

"Yes," conceded Maggie, "but the evidence points to DC. And a woman matching her description left a cup full of acid on my front steps earlier today."

"This is the delusional thinking that I've documented," opined Dr. Hansen to no one in particular.

Warner cleared his throat. "You might want to check with the FBI lab before you try to diagnose her again."

Maggie bit down hard on her lip to keep from smiling. When no one challenged her, she continued. "These documents came from Bukayev's safe. And this document," she held up the Cultural Happenings flyer from Daud's office, "references a Chechen dance troupe that will perform at several local elementary schools beginning tomorrow."

"I don't understand," said the DCI.

"The documents from Bukayev's safe are mostly written in Chechen. The Agency has a copy and has determined that at least some of the information pertains to financial transactions. I've also taken a look at them and discovered references to September eighth, ninth, and tenth."

"The runup to the 9/11 anniversary," noted the Counterterrorism director.

Maggie nodded. "And I found something written in Russian in the sentence referencing the eighth. Capitol Day School. The

Chechen dance troupe is performing at that school Wednesday. The eighth."

"My niece goes there," said the FBI director.

"And the president's children. The secretary of state's. The Russian ambassador's," Maggie added.

The men sat in stunned silence before the Secret Service director broke in. "You think they're going to pull off a Beslan-style attack at the most secure elementary school in the country?"

Truth be told, she had no idea how Zara would get past all that security. There had been none in Beslan, which had made it an easy target. "I think they're going to try," Maggie responded.

"We'll close the school, then," the Secret Service chief suggested.

"Wait just a second," the Homeland Security director objected. "Closing the school will send this Barayeva woman and her network underground. The threat will remain."

The Secret Service man's face flushed. "My job is to protect the president and the first family. We aren't going to use all those kids as bait for some speculative counterterrorism operation."

The FBI director interjected. "We need to take this to the president. It's his call."

"If we close the school and word gets out that it's because of a terrorist threat, the entire country will panic. Schools will close indefinitely." The Homeland Security director shook his head. "Parents will have to stay home from work to watch their kids. The economic repercussions will be massive."

"The repercussions of dead children would be even worse," the Secret Service director barked.

Maggie felt like a spectator at a barroom brawl. From the corner of her eye, she saw Jim Carpenter speaking with the DCI, who then returned to his seat at the head of the table.

"Maggie," he began, "You said there were several performances this week?"

"Yes." She pulled the dance troupe flier from the pile of papers. "Thursday is Madison Elementary in Bethesda. Friday is Dominion Elementary in Great Falls."

"What?" Warner gasped. "My girls go there."

Maggie's hands flew up to her chest. "Warner—"

The DCI spoke next. "Clearly, many of us have a vested interest in determining if this threat is real and what to do about it. First, let's figure out who will brief the president. I suggest that all the department and Agency heads present join me."

Side conversations sprang up around the table.

"Has anyone spoken to the dance troupe?" Maggie asked above the rising din of competing bureaucrats.

All eyes turned to the Secret Service director. "We run background checks on every Capitol Day School visitor." He flipped through a folder. "So, I'm sure we did that for this group. But we don't normally talk to visitors unless a concern surfaces."

"Sounds to me like a concern just surfaced," said the CIA director.

The Secret Service director frowned. "I'll call my ops center."

He stood and others followed suit. Maggie joined Roger and Warner across the room. Warner looked pale.

"Nothing's going to happen to the girls. Zara will go after the highest-profile target. And that's not the girls' school."

He nodded but didn't appear convinced.

Next to Warner, the Secret Service director was on a secure phone set on a small table. Maggie slid over a few steps and glanced at the notes he was scribbling on a notepad. *The Regency Hotel. Bingo.*

Jim Carpenter approached. "Maggie, we need to talk."

"I know. But can it wait until this is all over?"

Over Jim's shoulder, she saw Roger subtly wave toward the exit.

"Security wants to debrief you now."

"Okay." She saw Warner and Roger exchange nods. "I need to use the ladies' room. I'll be right back."

Just then, Warner put an arm around Jim's shoulder and began peppering him with questions about the Beslan task force. Maggie slipped into the hall, where Roger was waiting.

"You were amazing. Now let's blow this joint before security shows up." He grabbed her hand and tugged her down the hall to the elevator.

• ★ ★ ★ •

Inside Roger's Audi, Maggie rattled off the name of the hotel where the Chechen dance troupe was staying. He plugged it into the car's navigation system and sped through the security gate at the rear of the CIA compound. The hotel was in Tysons Corner, just up the road in McLean, Virginia.

"Do you have any idea how badass you are?" He beamed at her.

She laughed. "I'm not sure being a badass will get me another job after the CIA fires me."

"They won't. You'll be all right." He squeezed her left hand. "We both will."

Maggie blushed and looked out the window as Roger weaved around traffic on the George Washington Parkway.

Roger broke the awkward silence. "I wonder whose dragnet will be bigger—the one for Zara or the one for Maggie Jenkins, rogue CIA analyst?"

She laughed. "It felt great to see the expression on the shrink's face when we produced the photos of Zara."

"We should make him a T-shirt that says, 'Always Believe Maggie.'"

"Now that would be funny." She glanced at him. "But, Roger—"

"Yeah, Mags?"

Her breath caught in her throat. Steve was the only one who ever called her that. It took a moment to recover. "What if the attack is against one of the other schools? " *Warner's daughters' school?* "Or what if the schools aren't the target at all? What if I'm wrong about everything?"

"I don't think you are." He paused. "In fact, I'm going to get me an 'Always Believe Maggie' shirt, too. I could start a fan club—"

"Roger, I'm serious. There's no way Zara can get into a school protected by the Secret Service."

"And there was no way terrorists could hijack four passenger planes."

She took his point in silence. Something wasn't right. "Maybe once we talk to the dance troupe, it'll start to make sense."

His lips drew together in a thin line. "I hope so."

Inside the hotel lobby, piano music floated over from the restaurant at the far end. Crystal chandeliers cast a bright light on the gleaming marble floors.

They headed for the front desk, where a young man in a navy-blue suit stood eying them expectantly.

"Good evening." Roger wrapped his arm around Maggie's waist and pulled her close. "My wife and I would like—"

Maggie stepped on Roger's foot. "I'm a reporter with the *Washington Post*, here to do a story on a group of your guests." She smiled broadly.

"Oh?" The clerk tilted his head.

"Yes, there is a dance troupe here from Russia. They're expecting me."

The young man furrowed his brow. "Your name?"

Just then, a gaggle of petite preteen girls with enormous red bows securing their ponytails hurried past to the restaurant.

"Ah, never mind, there they are." Maggie turned and looked over her shoulder. "You joining me, darling?"

Roger waggled his eyebrows and caught up to her. "You sure that's them?"

"The Soviet Union may be long gone and the Chechens may hate Russia, but those red bows are a dead giveaway."

The maître d' sashayed over to them. "Reservations?"

"No, we're joining friends, right over there." Maggie waved in the general direction of the girls, who were gathered around a table in a dim corner.

"Very well."

As they approached, Maggie's heart beat wildly. Zara might be just feet away.

"*Dobryy vecher*," she said to a dark-haired, heavyset older woman who met her gaze across the table. Across from her sat another woman, a blonde, her back to Maggie. No sign of Zara.

"*Dobryy vecher*," responded the older woman. The blonde turned to look. She was tall, with elegant Slavic cheekbones, full red lips, and the lithe carriage of a trained dancer.

"Can I help you?" the dark-haired woman asked.

"Yes." Maggie reached into her purse, and fished out her CIA badge and the photo of Zara. "I'm with the FBI," she lied, flashing the badge quickly so they wouldn't notice the absence of the words *Federal Bureau of Investigation*. "I have a few questions."

The women exchanged glances. The older woman spoke in rapid Russian to her blonde colleague, who got up and settled the young dancers around a nearby table.

"Irina's the troupe leader. She's doesn't speak very good English. I'm her translator," the first woman explained as she too stood.

"I see." Maggie extended her hand. "My name's Maggie Jenkins."

"I'm Olga Prokovskaya." Her eyebrows drew together. "What do you want from us?"

"Please don't be alarmed. I only need a minute of your time, Ms. Prokovskaya." Maggie unfolded the picture of Zara. "Is this woman traveling with your troupe?"

Irina and Olga stepped closer to examine the photograph. Olga asked Irina few questions in Russian, which Maggie pretended not to understand. Irina shook her head "no" to each question.

"We don't know this woman. Why do you think she'd be traveling with us?"

Maggie ignored Olga's question. "Does the name Zara Barayeva sound familiar?"

The women shook their heads again. "No." Olga glanced at her watch. "Look, Ms. Jenkins, the children need to eat and get off to bed. Tomorrow is rehearsal and Wednesday is our first show. Is there anything else we can help you with?"

Maggie felt an odd mix of relief and despair. Based on the women's reaction to the photograph, it didn't seem like they recognized Zara. Of course, it was possible they were part of the plot. She tucked that disturbing possibility away for the moment. "No. Thank you for your time." She pulled a scrap of paper from her purse, tore it in two, and scribbled her cell phone number on both halves. "If you see the woman in the photo, please call me immediately. It's rather urgent."

Olga handed one slip of paper to Irina and stuffed the other into the pocket of her blazer. "I will. Are you coming to any of our performances?"

"I'd love to, but—"

"Definitely," Roger chimed in from behind her. "Maybe Thursday."

"Wonderful. The children are quite talented."

Maggie looked over at the dancers giggling and whispering to one another. "I'm sure they are."

And if her analysis was correct, these girls were in as much danger as the American students at the three schools.

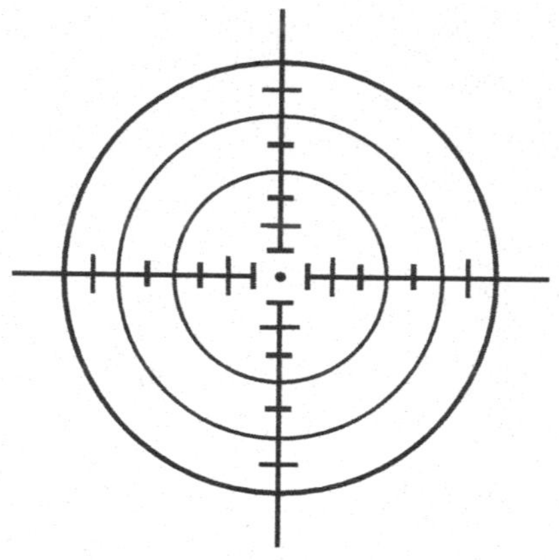

CHAPTER THIRTY-SEVEN

Northern Virginia
Tuesday, September 7, 2004, 12:30 p.m.

Yuri checked his email and phone again. Still nothing. His men in London hadn't updated him since this morning. Last he'd heard, Bukayev hadn't returned to his home on Lennox Place. This afternoon, his local security team reported that the government car was still parked outside of Maggie Jenkins's town house. No one seemed to know where on earth, literally, Zara Barayeva was. And Daud was in the hospital. Doped up into unconsciousness, he hoped.

He stretched his arms overhead. His chest felt like it was being squeezed in a vise. His stomach was in in turmoil. This was no time to get sick. If that Jenkins girl gave him a bug . . .

Yuri rolled the chair away from his desk. As he stood, a sharp pain struck at his chest. He staggered back toward the chair but missed it by a couple of inches and crashed to the floor.

Jalal scanned the website of a Turkish carpet company. Clicking on carpet number seven's red diamond downloaded an embedded, coded message from Bukayev. With trembling fingers, he flipped through the thin pages of his *Qur'an*, translating the code into instructions. The pencil dropped from his mouth. *Proceed with the operation.* If everything went according to plan, he'd surely get a promotion. Bukayev might finally send him to the camp in Pakistan, and he'd be one step closer to becoming a real jihadist instead of a lowly messenger.

The message further instructed him to contact the individual cell members. All except Renata were to provide him with discrete, prearranged code words. If they didn't know the code words, Jalal was to call Bukayev immediately. Otherwise, once he had all the words, Renata was to recite them back to him. Then he was to send Bukayev a message confirming completion of the task. All within four hours, or there would be unspecified consequences.

Jalal tugged credit cards from their slots in his wallet. The list of cell members was in there somewhere. He was supposed to have memorized and destroyed it, but he'd never been good at such mental exercises. Finally, he found a piece of paper jammed between two faded receipts.

First, he would update Renata, then he'd visit the six men. Jalal gnawed on his lip. None of the men had ever seen him in person. What if they didn't believe he was who he said he was? He'd carry a gun, just in case. He said a brief prayer, pocketed the hotel key, and slipped into the hall.

• ★ ★ ★ •

A half hour later, Jalal circled the block around Renata's building for the third time. There was so much congestion—both cars and people—that it was impossible to tell if anyone was following him. Finally, he gave up, parked, and walked to her apartment. He braced himself for what he'd find when the woman answered the door.

"Jalal, come in."

"Thank you, Renata." He was pleasantly surprised to see her dressed modestly. She was still stunning, a fact he could appreciate this time because he didn't have to avert his eyes from her bare flesh. Perhaps she'd realized that her stunt hadn't worked.

"Have a seat." Renata left room for him beside her on the couch.

Jalal remained standing. "Everything is in place. I will go to the others, collect their code words, and bring them back here for you to verify."

Zara smiled. "Excellent."

"There is one thing." The young man shifted on his feet. He was supposed to tell her this during their initial meeting, but her outrageous behavior had flustered him so much he had forgotten. "Imran asked me to make clear that you are not to be inside the building when the attack begins. Once it launches, you are to make a phone call and get in place." He didn't know who Renata was supposed to call or what "in place" meant, but he could tell by the serious look on her face that she did. "He asked me to confirm that you understand."

She smirked. "Oh, I understand perfectly. Tell Imran not to worry." She stood. "Did you take the photos?"

He nodded.

"Show me," she demanded.

He flipped open his phone and showed her the pictures he'd snapped of the designated sites.

"Very good. When will you return?"

"Three or four hours. Once you have confirmed the code words, everything is a go. There is no backing down."

"There never is." Her face betrayed nothing but intense, cold calculation.

"I wish you luck, that all will go according to plan, *inshallah*."

She laughed but said nothing. Instead, she stood and embraced him, slipping one hand to his lower back, the other onto his chest. He backed away, but not before her lips brushed his.

"Good-bye, Renata."

"Until we meet again, Jalal."

Zara scanned the computer screen in the Patrick Henry Public Library. *Damn.* She needed a library account to access the internet. When the woman across from her got up to use the restroom, Zara grabbed her library card from atop a stack of books. The man at the adjacent computer frowned. Zara smiled. "My friend was holding my card for me."

He nodded and went back to his work.

Zara typed in the card's identification number and returned it to the stack. There was nothing in the news about an elevated terrorist threat. No articles about her anywhere, which meant one of two things. Either Maggie Jenkins hadn't told the CIA she was on the loose, or the government—American or Russian, or maybe both—were secretly trying to find her. Perhaps they would. Perhaps they were closer than she suspected.

After jotting down a few notes, she gave in. Zara navigated to the email account, the one she was supposed to access only in case of emergency. There was no emergency, but maybe Imran had emailed anyway. The inbox was empty, as was the draft folder. She drummed her fingers on the table, drawing another glance from the nosy man. This time she glowered at him until he looked away. She started typing.

> *If I don't see you again, I wish you much happiness. Don't become so blinded by your new friends' fervor (and money) that you forget what our battle is about. Your fight for Allah and mine for revenge aren't much different. Our goals, at least, are the same—destruction of the enemy. My family were martyrs, just like your jihadists. After this week, the world will understand that our fight is global and our resolve is endless.*
>
> *Yours, Z*

Zara's index finger hovered over the mouse. If she sent the email now and Imran happened to check the account, he'd be furious. But what could he do from London? Get Jalal to take her off the mission? He could try, but he'd fail.

Jalal gripped the steering wheel, trying to control his shaking hands. He hadn't expected so much hostility. They were all Muslim brothers, working together for Allah's glory, weren't they? The first team member on the list, Ibrahim, a gruff young Arab, had yanked Jalal into the apartment and pinned him against the wall with two beefy, callused hands. Only after Jalal had explained who he was a second time did the man release him and offer some tea. *Strange people, those Arabs.*

Jalal scribbled down the first code word—*their*—which he'd asked Ibrahim to spell three times. There was no room for error. *Their* seemed like an odd code word, but he didn't dare anger the Arab by questioning him again.

Jalal consulted the map. The next cell member lived about five minutes away. So far, he was on schedule.

Jalal received similar greetings at the second and third stops. All three men were Arab. And hostile. None seemed as if they'd take well to a woman ordering them around, especially one like Renata. If she were as immodest and sacrilegious around them as she'd been with him, they'd probably kill her ten minutes into the operation. The prospect of it almost made him smile.

A few blocks before the fourth man's apartment, he pulled over to jot down the first set of code words: *their, and, women.* They made no sense. He checked his watch. Still plenty of time to meet with the rest of the men and get the information to Bukayev.

Jalal had all the code words. The only thing left to do was confirm them with Renata and transmit the message back to Bukayev.

He prayed in the car for five minutes, maybe more, until some punk rapped on the hood and leered at him. There was no avoiding it. He really despised this woman, but maybe she'd prove her worth in the attack. He got out of the car and trudged to her apartment.

When she opened the door, Jalal blurted out. "I have the code."

A smile flashed across her face. "Excellent." She waved him into the apartment. "Wait until you see how the world reacts. This attack will scare the hell out of everyone."

Jalal winced at her vulgar language, but he couldn't help but smile. He was part of something great, something glorious.

Inside the apartment, Renata sat, perched on the arm of the couch. She was drinking a clear liquid over ice. A sudden urge for alcohol seized him. He hadn't had a drink for almost five years, not since he'd learned it was *haram* for Muslims. He didn't want to do anything forbidden, but maybe celebrating a little would be okay. "What are you drinking?"

Renata smiled. "Vodka. Like a good little Russian." She popped up and rustled around in the tiny kitchen.

Jalal rubbed his eyes and stood. The clink of ice hitting glass echoed into the living room. "Do you know the phrase?"

She sidled up to him with a glass in each hand. "'We kill their women and innocent.' Osama bin Laden, October 2001."

The force of her words—bin Laden's words—cut through him. The phrase had sounded familiar, but he hadn't known why until now. Was he really working for Osama bin Laden? No words could describe how honored he felt. He dialed the number he'd been given and left the message. "*Eto khorosho.*"

Zara smiled and handed him a glass. He took a sip. It burned the entire trip to his empty stomach. The second sip slackened every tense muscle in his body. "*Allahu Akhbar,*" he murmured.

Renata ran a hand across his chest.

Jalal took a third sip and found himself smiling as Renata pulled off her shirt. He didn't remember alcohol affecting him this quickly. She seemed to float to him, guiding him to the bedroom. Then she held the glass to his lips, encouraging him to drink more. He complied and sank onto the bed.

The last memory Jalal would ever have was of Renata pulling off his clothes.

After checking into the hotel in Tysons Corner, the first thing Zara did was shower off Jalal's scent. There was nothing like breaking down a man's resistance. Imran had always tried to resist her. That's why she couldn't stay away from him. She loved a challenge. When he was *just* a leader of the Chechen resistance, she'd been an acceptable lover—maybe a bit young for him, but otherwise fine. It wasn't until he'd started falling under the sway of the Saudis—for their riches—and al-Qaeda—for its commitment to destroying the secular world—that she'd become problematic for him. He'd begun refusing her advances, citing verses from the *Qu'ran*, of all places. Her willingness to participate in Beslan was the spark that had rekindled the affair. But even then, Zara had made it perfectly clear that she'd never be a martyr for Islam. As for Imran, he never gave up hoping that she'd change her ways.

After the shower, Zara balled up her clothes. She'd have to dispose of them tomorrow. There'd been more blood than she'd expected, but then again, she didn't have experience killing with a knife. She'd seen videos of jihadists decapitating infidels, but couldn't imagine taking it that far. After having sex with the drunk and drugged Jalal, she made one long, curved slice across his throat and left the gurgling, blood-oozing man to his death in the bathroom. Before departing the safe house, she made sure everything was in place. With a final glance back, she shook her head. The poor fool would soon learn that the promise of a virgin-filled paradise was nothing but a lie.

Zara sat on the hotel's queen-sized bed and turned on the television. There was no way in hell she'd sleep. Soon, months of planning would come to fruition. Revenge would finally be hers. And if she died in the process, so be it. At least she'd be dying on her own terms. Whoever the cell members were, she was certain they'd be in it for Allah, to demonstrate their power and reach to the nonbelieving *kuffar*. Zara didn't believe in their God, but she'd been wronged by the same forces that had turned them into eager martyrs. In that sense, they were on the same team.

The cable news droned on about the upcoming election. On another channel, a panel of policy wonks bemoaned problems afflicting the families of 9/11 victims. She understood. Every day was like 9/11 in Chechnya. She clicked over to a music video channel, catching an overly bleached blonde gyrating to a techno beat. Next, she found a television evangelist praising the good Lord while a 1-800 donation number scrolled across the screen. She left that channel on. He was the most entertaining thing she'd seen since arriving in the States.

Zara hopped off the bed and pulled the pistol from her bag. There would be plenty of guns stashed in the building, but she wanted a familiar weapon the others wouldn't know about, just in case. Her hand fit perfectly around the Walther PPK grip. She preferred the Makarov PM but hadn't been able to find one in the US on such short notice. The man who'd sold her the Walther didn't blink twice when she purchased additional cartridges and bullets. Americans had no idea how dangerous their freedoms were.

Zara released the cartridge and checked the chamber. In front of the full-length mirror, she practiced drawing the pistol from the back of her waistband. Then she combined drawing with dry firing. As she shot at herself, she pictured her targets. Adrenaline coursed through her. She couldn't wait to see their faces.

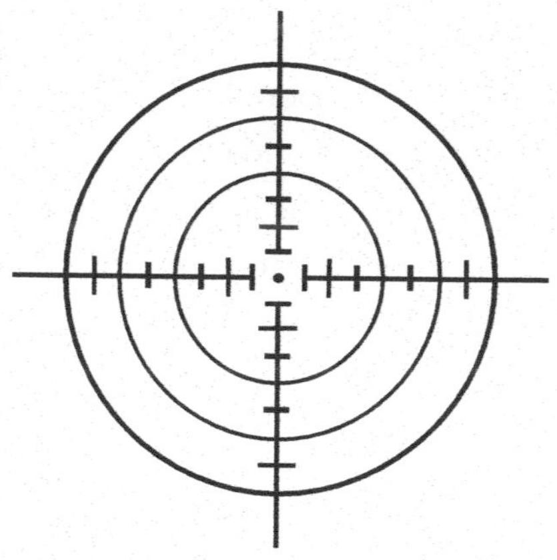

CHAPTER THIRTY-EIGHT

Capitol Day School, Great Falls, Virginia
Tuesday, September 7, 2004, 3:45 p.m.

Maggie bounced on her toes outside the school building. The buses had left a half hour ago. The afternoon pickup line was empty. Now, they were waiting for the teachers to leave. Ever since Warner called late last night to tell her that the president wanted Capitol Day School to remain open and the dance troupe to perform on Wednesday, she'd been running on adrenaline. And fear. It'd been a sleepless night. She'd never wanted to be so wrong in her entire life.

That morning at the CIA, she'd gone to see Jim Carpenter to try to smooth things over with him.

"Jim, I'm sorry for all the chaos."

"We're going to have to fully debrief you and decide whether—never mind. I've been told to let you focus on the current situation."

She'd thanked him and jumped right to work, which included watching several days' worth of surveillance footage from the Capitol Day School's security cameras. She and several analysts from the Beslan Task force had divvied up the footage and sped through it until someone or something appeared on camera. Then they slowed the video to study it more closely. In the end, they found absolutely nothing out of the ordinary. She also scanned through the teachers' and staffs' Secret Service files. Again, nothing of note. But she still couldn't relax. She couldn't shake the feeling that she was missing something.

The FBI and Department of Homeland Security teams coalesced in separate groups at the side of the school, leaving Maggie, the sole CIA representative, alone in the front parking lot. Just then, the Secret Service director emerged from the building and waved them in.

"Bring the K-9s," he called. "We're doing a full sweep to clear the school for tomorrow."

Maggie hung back, giving way to the tactical teams and their equipment. She stole a look at her watch. *Where are you, Warner?* When she couldn't wait any longer without getting locked outside, she scurried across the parking lot. Inside the school atrium, the headmaster, an older man with a waxy complexion and angular features, explained the schedule for the next day.

When he was done, the FBI sent its K-9 dogs and handlers off in every direction. Several men in Homeland Security jackets carried power drills that they used to screw small black devices inside two large trashcans and on the underside of the metal detector they'd rolled into place for the next day's events.

A sudden banging broke through the commotion. It was Warner trying to get someone to open the door. Maggie turned to let him in, but was cut off by a Secret Service agent whose right hand rested on the grip of his Sig Sauer handgun. "I know him. That's Warner Thompson. deputy director of Operations. CIA."

"ID," the agent demanded through the windowpane. Warner raised his badge and was let in.

"I miss anything?" From the looks of it, he hadn't slept well either.

"No. The FBI is doing their thing. DHS is doing theirs."

"Ms. Jenkins?" It was the Secret Service director.

She walked over and nodded to him before introducing herself to Theodore Ashforth, the headmaster.

"Please, call me Theodore."

She smiled politely. "I'd like to walk the route that the dance troupe will take tomorrow."

"Of course."

Warner and several of the federal agents tailed along.

"We expect the troupe to get here around noon. As we understand it, the girls will need time to get in their costumes and warm up and stretch and so forth."

Maggie took in the marble floors and bright white tiles along the walls. The drop ceiling tiles weren't like the dingy fiberglass ones she remembered from her school days. These were decorative tiles reminiscent of the antique tin that might be found in a Victorian home. As lovely as they were, they also were functional. Between them and the building's roof was space for pipes, wires, and the like. A perfect place to conceal weapons. "You're checking the ceilings, right?" she asked one of the agents.

"Of course."

The classrooms on either side of the hallway were bright, with ergonomic desks and chairs for every student. Bookshelves, closets, and desks would be checked for explosives, chemical and biological agents, guns, knives, and anything that could be used as a weapon. Up ahead was the performance center, which put to shame Maggie's old high-school auditorium. Modern lighting and sound systems hung from walls and ceilings that were covered in sound-absorbent panels. A state-of-the-art control room hovered over the rear of the auditorium.

Theodore took the group backstage to the dressing room and a small, mirrored room where the girls would do their warmups. "That's about it for the tour," he said. "All doors and windows will be locked. No visitors will be allowed in for this performance. The Secret Service assures me that security will be airtight."

"Will there be a security detail outside your house tonight?"

Theodore recoiled. "Is that really necessary?"

An FBI agent scribbled something down on a pad of paper.

"You can't be too safe these days," Maggie said.

"I suppose not. Let's head back, shall we?"

Warner sidled up to Maggie. "What do you think?"

"There are a million places to hide weapons and explosives in this place. But the problem is access. They'd already have to have weapons in here, unless they're planning to storm the building tomorrow."

"And that wouldn't go well, with all the firepower here."

"True." Maggie continually scanned the hallway as they walked. "And they'll be sweeping every corner of this building throughout the night."

"Does it sound terribly selfish to hope this is the target?" Warner shook his head. "Wait, of course it does."

"I know what you mean, Warner. If this is the target, and we catch Zara, then it's over. Your girls are safe. Everyone is safe."

"Exactly. Are you going to be here tomorrow?"

"Yup."

"I'll see you then."

"If you're coming just for me, you don't have to." Maggie gestured toward the teams of FBI and DHS officials. "I think they've got it covered."

"I hope you're right, Maggie."

"Me too."

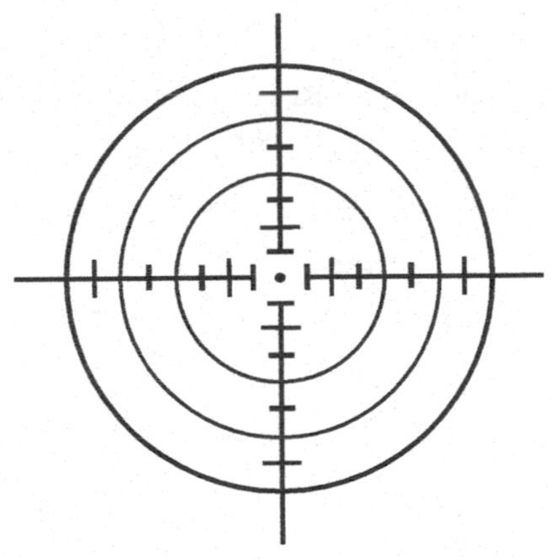

CHAPTER THIRTY-NINE

McLean, Virginia
Wednesday, September 8, 2004, 5:22 a.m.

Maggie rolled over and opened one eye: 5:22 a.m. Despite the anxious buzz permeating her body, exhaustion had taken the upper hand several hours ago. It didn't feel like she'd fallen into a deep sleep. More like she'd hovered somewhere in the twilight stage between consciousness and dreams.

She tottered downstairs to find Roger standing at the coffeepot, a day's worth of salt-and-pepper stubble framing his jawline. "Did you sleep?"

"A bit. Maybe three or four hours."

The bruise on Roger's temple had faded to a light mocha. Maggie fought a sudden urge to touch it.

Instead, she accepted a cup of coffee from him.

"To foiling the bad guys." Roger raised his mug.

Maggie raised hers in return. "To doing whatever it takes."

Roger clicked his mug against Maggie's and sipped, watching her over the brim. "Bacon and eggs?"

"I'm not really hungry, but I probably should eat something before I head over to the school."

He scratched at the stubble on his cheek. "Do you really have to go? There's going to be plenty of law enforcement there."

"But no one knows Zara the way I do. I just hope they'll listen to me if I sense something or—"

"Just be a major pain in the ass and they'll have to listen. Works for me."

She laughed but sobered quickly. "Do you ever think that if the Agency had listened to you, had let you work with Daud, that maybe 9/11 could've been stopped?"

"I don't know if Daud knew anything specific about the attack, but had I been able to pursue some of his contacts, who knows? Maybe we could've stopped them." His azure blue eyes darkened. "So, yeah, I think about it every single day. The what-ifs."

The what-ifs were the worst. They could paralyze her for an entire day, keep her wide awake at night. "It's not your fault, Roger. You know that, right?"

He averted his eyes. "There was one death that day that was my fault."

She frowned. "What do you mean?"

He swallowed. "I've never told a soul."

She touched his arm.

"You won't tell anyone?"

She shook her head.

"I lost someone on 9/11. A woman I loved very deeply."

"Roger, I'm so sorry."

He nodded, lips drawn together.

"What was she like?"

"She was beautiful. And funny. So smart." His eyes focused on a point across the room. "She was the best and worst decision I ever made."

Maggie wanted to ask why, but stayed silent.

"The best, because, well, because she was Jane, and I loved everything about her." He turned his gaze to Maggie, pain lining his forehead. "The worst because she was married. When she finally decided to leave her husband, I suggested we meet for a celebratory vacation. And on 9/11, she boarded flight 93." His head dropped into his hands and a sob shook his shoulders.

She wrapped her left arm around his back. "Roger, I'm so sorry."

"I ruined three lives. Mine, hers, and Carl's."

The name hit Maggie like a thunderbolt. Roger's Jane was Jane Manning, Carl's wife? The same Carl who had just hung himself, nearly three years after 9/11. "Did Carl know about you and Jane?" she asked, her voice barely above a whisper.

Roger took a few deep breaths to get himself back under control. "I don't think so. I saw him a few times after I returned to the Agency earlier this year and he acted normal. I mean, he was a shell of his former self, but I didn't sense any anger directed at me." He sniffed and straightened himself. "I can't believe I just told you that. Now you know what a miserable snake I am."

"You're not a miserable snake."

"I'm the most miserable, venomous snake on the planet."

Maggie laughed.

She laughed until tears streamed down her face.

"What's so funny?"

She tried to catch her breath. "Just . . . picturing . . . you slithering around the CIA—" she burst into laughter again.

Roger joined in and they laughed until they were both crying.

He wiped a tear from her cheek. "I never thought I'd meet anyone—"

"Roger," she whispered. "I don't . . . it's only been . . ."

He searched her eyes. "I know." He lowered his hand. "How about breakfast then?"

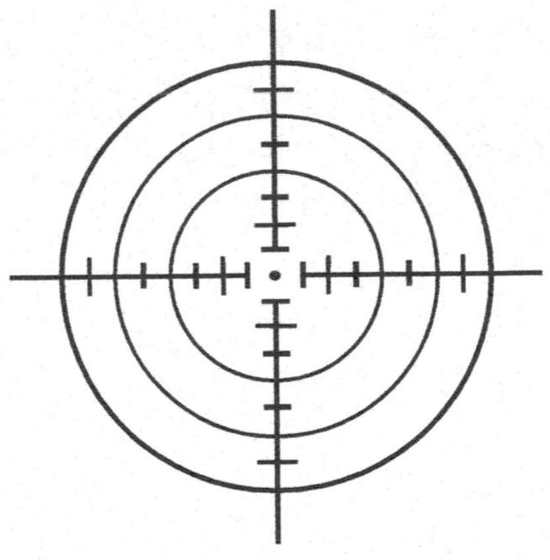

CHAPTER FORTY

Maggie arrived at Capitol Day School at 7 a.m. She parked in the side lot with the government vehicles, a few spots away from Warner's BMW. She clutched her travel coffee mug with one hand and shoved her other into her sweatshirt pocket to stave off the cool morning air. Outside the entrance, she scanned the small crowd for Warner but didn't find him. Then the Secret Service director began his briefing. Teachers were scheduled to arrive in a half hour. Students thirty minutes after that. The plan was to run every employee, student, and visitor through metal detectors and past chemical and biological sensors that were concealed inside new trash bins placed in the school's foyer. The car drop-off line would be patrolled by additional Secret Service and their most experienced service dogs. To cover for the enhanced security, parents had been sent an email about the school testing upgraded metal detectors and serving as a training site for new service animals.

"Think they'll buy the security story?" Warner said, sidling up to her.

"Who, the parents?"

"Yeah. Lot of defense and intelligence officials' kids go here. They might suspect something is up with all the extra security measures."

She sipped the still-steaming coffee. "Don't forget, a lot of these parents have the nanny drive their kid to school."

"Excellent point."

"Did they run background checks on the nannies?" Her pulse rate accelerated as she pictured Zara undercover as a nanny.

"I don't think so, but no one can get into the school if they don't have a background check already."

"Right." She tried to steady her breathing.

"By the way, we got the tests back on the coffee cup left on your porch. Muriatic acid."

"What's that?"

"Basically hydrochloric acid," Warner explained. "The stuff was highly concentrated. Probably would've burned your eyes beyond repair."

She shuddered. Where do you think she got it?"

Warner nodded to an FBI agent he knew. "You can pick it up almost any hardware store."

"So it's pretty much untraceable?"

"Yes, when bought in small quantities."

"Great."

"And speaking of not-so-great news, I tried calling Yuri last night and again this morning. He's not answering. That's unusual for him."

Maggie watched as several large German shepherds walked by with their handlers. "If you keep calling him, he might figure out that we're on to him."

"I realize that, but I need to keep him close. If he runs off to Russia, we'll never get the full story on Beslan." He eyed her coffee. "It's been so long since I've done fieldwork that I came totally unprepared."

"I saw people getting coffee at the FBI truck over there." Maggie nodded toward the parking lot.

"It's probably not up to my standards, but desperate times call for desperate measures. Be right back." He trotted away.

Maggie watched as the Secret Service director headed her way.

"Good morning. Everything in place?"

"It is. I'd like you to be inside the school entrance, watching every person who enters. Maybe act like a mother who's dropping off the lunch her child forgot at home."

Maggie gave her outfit a once-over. Between the jeans, the sweatshirt, and the running shoes, she didn't exactly fit the part of a wealthy suburban mother.

"If you see anything—and I mean anything—that appears out of the ordinary, get my attention. I'll be right there, playing the part of a volunteer parent."

"Got it."

"Let's get in place. The first teachers should be arriving soon."

Inside, Maggie settled on a bench to the side of the metal detector. Ten minutes later, the first teacher appeared. She seemed taken aback by the security equipment, even though an email had gone out to all staff the prior evening. One by one, more teachers arrived. None of them looked remotely like Zara. The headmaster nodded to each one in greeting, as he'd been instructed to do. If someone he didn't recognize tried to enter, he was supposed to scratch his head. He never did.

By 7:45, all staff had arrived. Outside, cars had begun to pull into the drop-off line. Two K-9s paced back and forth, checking every vehicle, much to the excitement of the children inside them. At 8:00 a.m., the bell rang and children lined up to enter the school. Excited shouts and giggles filled the atrium as the kids placed their backpacks on the X-ray conveyor belt. Most of them, probably seasoned travelers all, walked through the X-ray machine itself like pros.

Maggie found herself yawning when Warner appeared with a fresh cup of FBI coffee for her. "Thanks."

"Anything yet?"

"Not a thing."

He lowered himself next to her on the bench. "What are you supposed to do between now and the dancers' arrival?"

"I don't know. Maybe they'll let me take a nap with the kindergartners."

He laughed but quickly sobered. "Look at us. I can't believe we're actually sitting here in an elementary school, looking for a mass-murdering bunch of terrorists."

"The world's gone mad, Warner. Ever since—" She blew on her coffee.

"It was mad well before Zara killed Steve."

"I know." She watched two little girls skip down the hall. "I'm just afraid it will never feel normal again."

He leaned forward, elbows on his thighs. "It will. Once you decide it's time to move forward."

She nodded and averted her eyes.

Just before noon, Warner returned with sandwiches. Maggie had spent most of the morning reading to children in the library. But time had crept by, even with Roger's three calls to check on her.

"Thank you," she said, resuming her post on the bench near the metal detector. As soon as the silver minibus carrying the dance troupe pulled up, her appetite vanished.

"You ready?" Warner said, squeezing her hand.

She swallowed and nodded vigorously.

Hulking men in full tactical gear slipped into restrooms just off the atrium. From this moment until the time the dance troupe left the school, no children would be allowed in classrooms or within fifty feet of the school's entrance.

Outside, two K-9s prowled around the bus. Inside, a nervous-looking music teacher tugged on her blouse sleeves. The teachers had been told that the dance troupe had requested extra security after receiving an unspecified threat. The dance troupe had been told that this level of security was normal for a school like this.

Maggie stood and cracked her knuckles. The first person out of the bus was Olga, the group's translator. Next came Irina, the dance troupe instructor. One by one, the girls exited carrying large garment bags that presumably held their costumes. Several of them looked up in wonder at the school's gleaming glass-and-steel edifice. Once inside, they passed through the X-ray machine with little trouble, although Irina fretted over the costumes wrinkling as they passed through the machine.

Maggie stared at Olga, who narrowed her eyes in confusion before widening them in recognition.

"Hello," she called.

"Good luck today," Maggie called, her eyes trained on the woman's face. She seemed entirely calm and relaxed.

Irina didn't notice Maggie, as fixated as she was on getting each costume bag to the correct dancer. Even so, she too seemed to act normally.

Two female FBI agents appeared, dressed as teachers, to escort the group to the dressing room. The music teacher tottered along behind them.

A Homeland Security agent secured the front entrance. "No one enters or leaves the building until the troupe has left."

"I'm going to the dressing room, Warner."

"I suppose I'm not allowed in there, so I'll grab a couple of seats for us."

Maggie planned to spend the performance alternating between the auditorium and the hallway. "I'll see you in a bit."

The dressing room was aflutter with taffeta, silk scarves, and hair bows in an assortment of bright colors. Female FBI agents watched from a corner as the girls slipped into their costumes and did each other's hair. Irina went around to each child, applying a dab of blush and lipstick to their faces. Maggie approached Olga, who was speaking with the music teacher about the origins of their folk songs.

"Excuse me, I'm sorry to interrupt. Could I steal Olga for a minute?"

"Of course," said the teacher.

Olga followed Maggie into the hall. "How's your stay been?"

"Fine. I never saw that woman you showed me."

Maggie exhaled. "Good." She smiled. "The girls are adorable."

"They're very excited. Most of them have never traveled outside of Chechnya, never mind to the United States. This may be their only chance to go on such a trip. It's so expensive."

"How did you get the money? Fundraisers, or—"

"No, there is some group or foundation or something that gave us the money." She smiled broadly. "And we don't have to pay it back. It was all free."

Maggie's insides seized. "Do you know the name of this group?"

Olga shrugged. "I don't remember."

"Was it the Central Asian Research Institute?"

Olga tilted her head. "Maybe, but I'm not sure."

Maggie fought to keep her tone even. "If you remember, give me a call. You still have my number, right?"

Olga frowned. "In my purse, yes. I hope there's nothing wrong with our funding."

Maggie pasted on a smile. "Nothing wrong at all. I hope you have a wonderful visit."

At 1:45, the dancers performed a final encore to loud applause. By 2:15, they were out of the building. Maggie sat with Warner in the back row of the auditorium. "I thought this was it. I really did." She sank back in the seat and drew her knees up to her chest.

"We all figured this was too hard of a target, right?"

"Yeah," she muttered.

"Now we need to ensure that the other schools are secure too."

She turned her head his way. "Are you sending the girls to school on Friday?"

"Honestly, I have no idea." He sighed.

She dropped her feet to the floor and sat up straight. "The only thing about today that didn't sit right with me was when the troupe's translator told me the entire trip had been paid for by a foundation. She couldn't remember the name of it."

"Maybe you can ask her again?"

"Bukayev's documents." Maggie jumped up. "The Agency translator needs to go back through it to search for anything related to a dance troupe. If Daud's foundation paid for this trip, was it a legitimate expense, the sort of cultural exchange they normally fund?"

"Great question."

"We should get back to headquarters.'

Just as Warner stood, a group of FBI, DHS, and Secret Service officials entered the auditorium and filled the seats around them.

Maggie and Warner sank back into their seats.

"Excellent job today, everyone," began the Secret Service director. "But apparently a false alarm." He leveled a gaze at Maggie. "We will write up our usual after-action report and request input from everyone."

Warner raised a hand. "There are two more schools on the dance troupe's itinerary."

"We're all aware of that, Warner. I think it's smart to have some security outside these schools, to keep an eye out for suspicious behavior. And we should brief local police and the school-system leadership."

"Public schools are soft targets," Maggie pointed out.

"Yes, but also low profile. If this terrorist of yours was going to make a big splash, she'd want to do it here."

Maggie clenched her teeth and exchanged a glance with Warner. "You don't know what Zara's capable of doing."

"Assuming you're correct about this woman being a Beslan terrorist, Ms. Jenkins, I think we all know full well what she's capable of."

"She's always a step ahead," Maggie protested. "It's like she hides behind one threat to plan the execution of another. Zara will never stop, she'll—"

The Secret Service director raised a hand. "Point taken. But if she was planning to use this dance troupe as cover for an attack, she would've done something today to these VIP children."

Maggie jumped to her feet. "That's easy for you to say. Your protectees are safe. What about the children who go to the other schools?" She glanced at Warner. "Like Warner's kids."

All eyes turned to Warner. He stood and cleared his throat. "Kindly include us in the planning. As you yourself have already acknowledged, Maggie knows this terrorist better than anyone else here."

"Lot of good that did us today," someone a few rows in front of them commented. A few people laughed.

"Include us or the DCI will be on the phone with the president before any of you pour your evening drink," Warner said as he got up to leave.

Maggie stared down the agents, who returned their attention to the Secret Service director. "See you in the morning, gentlemen." With that, she followed Warner out.

• ★ ★ ★ •

Back at headquarters, Jim Carpenter was waiting at her desk. "The director wants to see you."

"About what happened today?"

"More about what didn't happen."

Heart in her throat, she checked her office phone for messages and took the elevator to the seventh floor.

"Maggie, dear, it's nice to see you," said Priscilla, Warner's long-time administrative assistant.

"Great to see you, too, Priscilla." Maggie leaned her head into Warner's office. "Is he around?"

"He's in with the director. They're expecting you?" It came across as both a statement and a question.

"Thanks." She turned to the short hall leading to the director's suite, taking a deep breath before entering the outer office. His assistant wasn't at her desk. "Might as well face the music," she muttered before knocking on the director's office door.

The DCI himself opened the door. Over his shoulder she caught sight of Warner, who wore an expression somewhere between irritation and exasperation. "Come in, Maggie. We were just beginning."

"Thank you, sir."

He closed the door behind her.

"Please, have a seat."

She and Warner took the chairs opposite the director's desk. "The president wants to know what the hell happened today."

"Nothing, obviously, but—" she began.

"Maggie, let me—"

She widened her eyes at Warner and continued. "Nothing happened, probably because Capitol Day School has too much security, even on an ordinary day. But I still think that Zara Barayeva is involved with this Chechen dance troupe. Maybe she's using it as a decoy to distract us from some other attack. Or maybe she's planning to hit one of the other schools."

"The intelligence is very weak, Maggie."

"It's incomplete, to be sure, sir. But we can't let our guard down, especially not when it involves children."

The director walked around to the near side of his desk and leaned against it, arms folded across his chest. "The president does not want to alarm the American people. He has directed us not to show up in force at either of the remaining schools."

"So we leave the kids out there like"—her voice rose an octave—"like sitting ducks?"

"Sir," Warner interjected. "What sort of presence will we have in these schools?"

"Local police, three FBI agents, and two Homeland Security personnel."

"What about me?" The words escaped Maggie's mouth before she could stop them.

The director studied her and narrowed his eyes.

"What I meant to say was that I would recognize Zara instantly. Even if she disguised herself, I know the way she moves. I know her voice."

"Warner, your thoughts?"

Warner cleared his throat. "I would like Maggie to be at the schools in an observational capacity. She would recognize this woman before anyone else."

The director walked back behind his desk and picked up a folder stamped Top Secret. He flipped it open and read before speaking. "If I allow you at those schools, Maggie, know that one false step," he raised his index finger, "just one, will result in your termination from the Agency."

She fought to keep her expression neutral. "I understand, sir. I appreciate your willingness to let me help. But what about Warner? And Roger Patterson?"

"You'll be in excellent hands with the other law enforcement and intelligence officials. The CIA can only participate in domestic operations in an advisory capacity anyway, so one of you there is more than enough." He glanced back at the Top Secret folder. "I have a pressing issue to attend to. Warner, keep me apprised of developments tomorrow."

The DCI didn't acknowledge Maggie again, so she stood, said, "Thank you," and exited the office ahead of Warner.

The men exchanged a few words she couldn't hear before he joined her as they walked to the elevator.

"I can't believe they're not sending more people." She punched the down button repeatedly. "What the hell is wrong with this thing?"

"Nobody is more concerned than I am." A flash of pain crossed his face.

She headed for the stairwell with Warner trailing behind. "Nothing is going to happen to your girls," she said over the echoing thud of their footsteps. "I won't let it."

"You realize the DCI is serious about firing you if you step out of line?"

"Of course, but it would be worth it if it meant stopping Zara."

He grabbed her arm on the fourth-floor landing. "Just do your part and leave the rest to the people trained for this sort of thing."

"Okay, I will," she conceded.

"I'll hold you to that." He released her arm and continued his descent. "Any luck with the Chechen translator?"

"He's almost done with the documents. Some of the words were code words written partially in Chechen and Russian. Says he's never seen anything like it." She clambered down the stairs to catch up with him. "Did you ever hear back from Yuri?"

"No."

"Maybe he fled, Warner. Maybe he was afraid Daud would talk to the police."

"Maybe, but something feels off."

"I know the feeling, Warner."

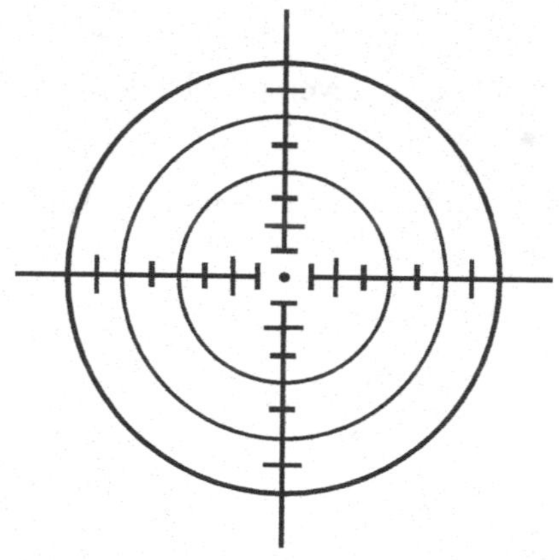

CHAPTER FORTY-ONE

Bethesda, Maryland
Thursday, September 9, 2004, 6:50 a.m.

Maggie pulled into the school parking lot at 6:50 a.m. Unlike yesterday, there wasn't a crowd of federal agents milling around outside. In fact, all she saw was a state trooper talking to a police officer. Roger had wanted to join her, but he knew the director would have his head on a platter if he showed up without authorization.

Finally, at 7:00, an FBI van pulled up along with a single K-9 vehicle.

She took a final swig of coffee and joined the group. She introduced herself to the officers and nodded to the three FBI agents, who she'd seen in action at the Capitol Day School.

"Same drill as yesterday," one of them began, "but at a smaller scale. We'll have the dog inside to pick up any unusual scents. One law-enforcement officer will stay inside the school, and the other outside."

"I'll keep an eye out for the female terrorist or any other unusual activity," Maggie chimed in.

"Great," he said with little enthusiasm. "Let's go inside and look around. The students arrive at 8:30, the dance troupe at 9:30. The assembly begins at 10:30."

At 11:15, the curtain fell and the students filed back to class. Fifteen minutes later, Maggie was in the car, seat belt on, engine running, trying to avoid what she knew was coming: another dressing down from the DCI.

She threw the car into gear and eased out onto the main road. Traffic was lighter at this time of day, but it still took almost thirty minutes to get back to Langley. Neither Warner nor Roger had called her yet. They probably already knew that the dance performance had gone off without a hitch. Besides, what could they say? She'd been wrong. Completely wrong.

Upstairs, on the fourth floor, she avoided conversation, instead heading straight for her desk. The monitor hummed to life as she checked her work phone. No messages there either. She clicked through the emails cluttering her inbox, stopping only when she spotted one from the translator. He'd attached Bukayev's translated documents.

Maggie searched the documents for "Capitol Day" and found it translated as she'd expected. Same for Madison and Dominion schools. At least she'd been correct about the schools. And the dates. But she couldn't find anything about the dance troupe. Maybe it was listed under some sort of official name. But what? She'd muttered in frustration as she scrolled through page after page of financial transactions data.

If the donation to the dance troupe was hidden behind a bank routing number, she'd never figure out who paid for the girls' trip to the United States.

She continued to scan the documents. "What's this?" she murmured. An address in Falls Church. For a one-month rental property. Starting September 1. She jotted down the address and hurried across the hall to where Roger sat with the Beslan task force.

"Hey, how'd it go?" he asked. His expression revealed that he already knew.

"Can I talk to you?" She jerked her head toward the hall. Roger followed.

"Nothing happened at the school. But I finally got the translated documents and found something potentially interesting." She handed the paper with the address on it. "Look at this. A one-month rental that began on September first."

"And?"

She folded her arms across her chest. "Why would Bukayev have a document with an American address on it? For a one-month rental? Might be worth checking out."

"I suppose," Roger conceded.

"I'm going to head over now. You want to join me?"

He made a face. "I can't, I have two meetings this afternoon." He looked at his watch. "We could go after work. Maybe grab a bite to eat?"

Maggie's face fell. "Yeah, sure. I'll catch up with you later." She turned away without another word and headed back to her cubicle. On the way, she ran into her boss.

"I was looking for you," Jim Carpenter said.

Her heart sunk. "Looks like you found me."

"Let's step into my office for a minute."

She followed. He closed the door behind him.

"Have a seat."

She stood.

"I don't know how else to say this, Maggie. So I'll come out with it. Everyone has abandoned the school attack theory."

"I'm not surprised."

"It was absolutely right of you to bring it to our attention. Can you imagine if we knew about an attack targeting the children of prominent government officials but did nothing about it?"

"Nightmare."

"Exactly. But now that nothing has happened twice, you need to focus on other things."

"Jim, someone left muriatic acid on my porch."

"I know. But maybe you have a crazy neighbor. Or a stalker."

"Have you talked to Warner about this?"

Jim leaned against the back of his chair. "He agrees that some fresh eyes on the intelligence might be helpful."

Maggie swallowed. She was *not* going to cry. She bit down on her lip and blinked. "Should I even bother to come in tomorrow?"

"Of course. You're not suspended or anything. And if Zara pops up somewhere, we'll need your expertise."

"Right." She closed her eyes for a moment. "Do you mind if I take the rest of the afternoon off?"

Jim offered a sad half smile. "Not a problem."

She nodded and retreated to her desk, where she powered down the computer, grabbed her purse, and left.

Maggie slowed the car as she neared the brick row houses that ran along both sides of a busy road in Falls Church, Virginia. She pulled into the first empty space she found and fed the meter. Within minutes, she'd located the unit, the second from the end. A woman sitting on a nearby stoop watching her child play in the sparse grass eyed her warily. Maggie continued to the end unit and peered around behind it. She dashed past the barred ground floor windows of the first unit and came to a halt at the edge of the next one. Nothing was visible through the nearest window. The next window looked into a sitting area featuring a green couch, a wooden coffee table, and small television on a flimsy-looking stand. Worn tan carpet appeared to run throughout the small space. To the right was a glass-paned door. Locked. Maggie squinted. There appeared to be dark stains on the carpet off to the left. But with the lack of lighting and the apparent age of the carpet, it was hard to tell if the stains were fresh.

Maggie returned to the front of the apartments and approached the rental's front door. A smear of something discolored the knob's chrome finish. Dirt? Blood? The woman two houses up spoke harshly to her child in Spanish. Maggie pulled out the photo of Zara and approached.

"Excuse me. Do you know this woman?"

The woman took the piece of paper, studied it, and shrugged before handing it back.

"Is she staying there?" She pointed to the unit in question.

Again, the woman shrugged.

Maggie reached into her purse and pulled out a twenty-dollar bill. The woman raised her eyebrows. Maggie retrieved another twenty.

"Yes. I see this woman," she said in heavily accented English. "She leave two days ago. Big hurry."

"Has she come back?"

The woman shook her head.

Maggie folded up the photo of Zara and sprinted for her car.

Inside, she dialed. "Roger?"

"Hey."

"I found where Zara was staying."

"What?"

"I think she's gone, but we've got to get in there."

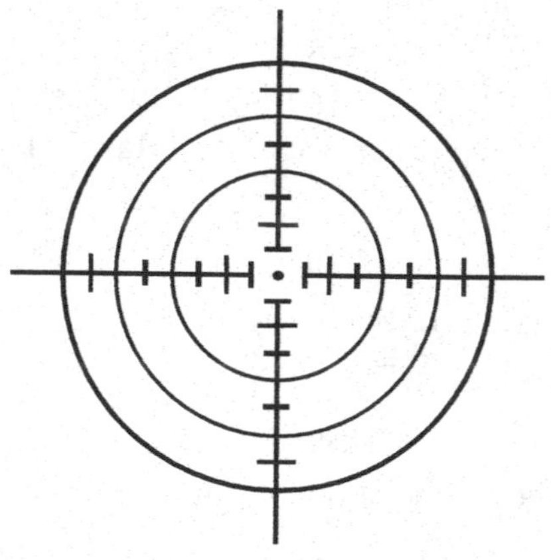

CHAPTER FORTY-TWO

Zara tucked her hair into a baseball cap, slid a pair of cheap drugstore readers onto her nose, and headed to the lobby. She sat in a maroon wing chair and pretended to read a copy of the local newspaper. As expected, a group of preteen Chechen girls, accompanied by two women, soon emerged from the elevator and turned toward the restaurant. The sight of the girls, vivacious and naïve, sent a pang of sadness through Zara. It hadn't been that long ago that she'd been that young and innocent.

Six months ago, when she'd heard about this dance troupe raising money for a trip to Washington, a plan started to come together in her head. It took a little bit of convincing, but Imran had finally seen the genius in her scheme. Bukayev arranged for the Central Asian Studies Institute to finance the trip, provided that the dance troupe agreed to the institute's itinerary, one that Zara created. Over a shared email account, where they left messages for each other in a hidden draft folder, she and Bukayev had hammered out the details.

Only, he didn't know that she intended to diverge from the plan. If it all went well, his top target would be taken care of, but not until after hers were destroyed.

She made a show of rifling through her purse, then rose from the chair. Over at the concierge desk, she smiled demurely at the young man behind the counter. Donning a Russian accent, she pouted and explained that she'd forgotten her key in her room.

"I am so excited to see Washington, DC, that I ran out of my room without checking my purse."

"Your name?"

"Olga Prokovskaya."

"Room number?"

She leaned forward and smiled. "Oh, I didn't even pay attention. I got off the elevator and turned right. And then it was down the hall."

He frowned at her.

She glanced at her watch. "My friend will be here soon. I'd rather get the key now instead of later in case we have a wild time." She winked. "Will you be here later tonight?"

The pale young man blushed. "Yeah. Until midnight."

"Do you bring room service to interested customers?"

His jaw fell open.

A stout older woman with garish red hair emerged from a door behind the counter. "Is there a problem, Billy?"

"Nope." He smiled at Zara, his eyes glistening. "Just helping Ms. Prokovskaya with a new room key. Room 312."

Zara accepted the key card, letting her fingers linger on his a moment too long. "Thank you, Billy."

With that, she turned for the elevator, glanced back and mouthed, "Later."

Upstairs, she slipped into Olga's room. An open suitcase sat on the bed. In the bathroom was an assortment of toiletries. Toothbrush, travel-size toothpaste, an assortment of Russian-made cosmetics. Nothing remarkable.

The only thing to do was wait.

"Finally," Maggie muttered as Roger and several FBI field agents showed up at the housing complex.

Roger rushed over. "You okay?"

"Yeah. Why wouldn't I be?" she snapped, instantly regretting it. The stress was getting to her. Roger appeared just as tired and drawn.

"What do we have, Ms. Jenkins?" An agent approached, squinting at her in the afternoon sunlight.

"I believe this is a safe house that someone rented for a wanted terrorist."

"What evidence do you have?" the agent asked.

"We've obtained documents full of financial transactions from the home of another suspected terrorist. That's where I found this address."

The neighbor who'd identified Zara earlier stepped out her front door. When she saw the men in FBI windbreakers, she slid back into her house and closed the door.

Maggie nodded toward her door. "That woman's the one who identified the suspect. Don't let her skip out."

A second FBI agent took up station closer to the neighbor's unit.

The third agent spoke as he scribbled notes. "So, if this is a safe house, who's living in it?"

"Zara Barayeva."

"And she is?"

"A Chechen terrorist who is here to—" She exchanged glances with Roger.

"We think she's here to lead a terrorist attack in the DC area," he offered.

The first agent chimed in. "Isn't this the woman who was supposed to attack the Capitol Day School yesterday?"

"Yes," Maggie conceded. "I think she backed off that plan once she discovered how tight security would be. But she's dangerous, so I had to follow up on this lead."

"This isn't the CIA's purview, Ms. Jenkins."

She ignored his admonition. "The neighbor recognized Zara from a photo. Said she'd left Tuesday night and hasn't returned. And then there's the blood on the front doorknob."

All heads turned toward the door. Two of the agents approached to get a closer look. One examined the top of the knob, the other knelt and peered up. "Could be blood, but that's not enough for us to enter without a warrant. And there's no blood trail leading away."

"Well, then get a warrant."

"Based on what?" said the first agent.

"Based on the fact that I have reason to believe a terrorist stayed here. There could be evidence inside. We could figure out—"

"I'm sorry, Ms. Jenkins, but that isn't sufficient cause." The first agent nodded to the other two. "Let's get rolling. Call us if you get a real lead."

She scowled at the men and turned to Roger. "Look, come see this doorknob."

He shrugged and followed her.

"See? Right here?"

Roger studied the two dark reddish-brown smudges. "I don't know, Maggie." He looked at the FBI agents, who were standing on the sidewalk next to their shiny, black SUV. "Let's get dinner. Have a few drinks. Just forget about today."

Heat rose up Maggie's neck to her face. "You don't believe me, do you?"

"No, it's not that, it's just been a long day and at some point, you . . . we just have to take a break."

She tugged at her hair and looked away. "Fine. Just give me a minute."

He nodded and walked toward his car.

Maggie took the bottom edge of her T-shirt and used it to grip the doorknob, careful to avoid the dark smudges. The knob turned and the door swung in.

"Hey!" one of the FBI men shouted. "What the hell are you doing?"

She ignored him and stepped inside. Her gaze fell immediately on a large, dark stain on the carpet ahead. The stain continued down a hallway. Maggie tiptoed along the edge of the hall to avoid stepping in it.

With her foot, she nudged open the partially closed bathroom door. Inside the tub lay a man, his head seemingly hanging on by a thread, his naked body covered in dried blood.

• ★ ★ ★ •

Within ten minutes, the chaos at the scene drew dozens of curious onlookers. The Falls Church police roped off the front and back of the unit with yellow crime-scene tape. After one of the FBI agents shouted and cursed at Maggie for disturbing a crime scene, she noted that they wouldn't have known it was a crime scene had she left without trying the front door.

After he suggested she line up a lawyer, she sidled up to the forensics team, which had gathered the man's clothing inside a plastic tarp that now lay on the front lawn.

"Check the pockets," Maggie urged.

"We will, miss," a thin, bespectacled man with mousy brown hair said, "as soon as we figure out whether this is the FBI's jurisdiction or the local police."

"This is a national security—"

"We found something." A policewoman decked out in white protective gear emerged from the unit. "A slip of paper next to the bed. It's clean, no blood."

Maggie dashed over. "What's on it? Does it say anything?"

The FBI agents and a police detective circled around the officer. "Yeah. 'We kill their women and innocent.'"

A sudden throbbing filled Maggie's ears. "That's Osama bin Laden. It has to be her."

Had she said that aloud? No one seemed to hear her. "Osama bin Laden." Now she was shouting. "These are bin Laden's words." She pointed to the man's clothing. "We have to identify him, now. He's a member of a terrorist cell."

Two of the FBI agents conferred, then called over the lead police detective. "Search the pockets," the detective ordered.

One of the FBI agents powered on a camcorder and focused it on the tarp. The officer in protective gear squatted next to the faded blue jeans, patting the front pockets with her gloved fingertips. When she got to the back pockets, she paused, inhaled, and retrieved a worn brown wallet, which she laid next to the jeans. A hush fell over the law-enforcement personnel while the crowd, oblivious to the wallet discovery, buzzed with excitement when a TV news truck arrived.

The officer pulled a set of tweezers wrapped in cellophane from a pocket in her billowing white coveralls. Gently, she used the sterile tweezers to open the wallet. "License belongs to Jalal Badawi. J-A-L-A-L." She spelled out his last name and address. "Date of birth twenty December, 1980."

Maggie felt lightheaded. She inhaled slowly and held it for a count of five. "You okay?" Roger appeared and slipped an arm around her waist. "What's wrong?"

"Why do you keep asking me that?"

"Because I want to make sure you're okay."

"Stop asking. Please. I'm fine." In truth, every moment this week had been a battle. As had every day since Steve died. She closed her eyes for a moment, wanting to lean into Roger. Instead, she straightened and edged away.

To their right, the FBI agents huddled together around a phone. The note-taking FBI agent looked over to her, astonishment written across his broad face.

"They found something, Roger." They hurried over to the agents. "What is it?"

The agent cleared his throat. "It turns out that we have a file on Jalal Badawi. We know he attended a radical mosque not too far from here. He had no job, no visible means of support, but he appeared to live relatively comfortably. In addition, his file includes a report about him filming federal buildings, monuments, and so on."

"That's no crime," Roger said.

"No, it's not. But his videos focused on security personnel at those sites." He frowned. "Enough to keep him on our watchlist, but not enough for an arrest."

Maggie's phone rang. She stepped a few feet away. "Warner?"

"I just heard. What the hell is going on?

She filled him in.

"Why would Zara leave this guy's identification on him?"

Maggie thought for a moment. "Maybe she wants us to know who he was."

"But why?"

Another commotion erupted at the front of the house. The female officer announced another find. "Cell phone on the floor behind the bedroom door."

"Warner, hang on."

They gathered around the officer. She read out the incoming and outgoing phone numbers for the previous twenty-four hours. One of the agents immediately called them into FBI headquarters.

"Check his photos," Maggie said.

The woman squinted at the phone's tiny screen. "Long distance shot of the White House. And . . . this photo looks like Arlington National Cemetery."

Maggie looked over the woman's shoulder. "I think that's the Pentagon Memorial."

"September eleventh is Saturday," said someone behind her.

"Holy shit," one of the FBI agents breathed. "They're going to hit the 9/11 memorial services. Get these people out of here!" he shouted to the police officers. "Block the road and evacuate all of these units." He waved his arm up and down the row of brick-faced apartment units. "We need to sweep the entire place for explosives, weapons, anything and everything. We have a little over forty-eight hours, max, to stop this."

Maggie raised the phone to her ear. "Did you catch that, Warner?"

"My God, Maggie, you were right."

She shook her head. "But Warner, Zara doesn't care about 9/11. This . . . it has to be something more personal."

Several voices filled the background from Warner's end. "I have to jump into an emergency meeting. Keep your phone on. We may need you."

Roger hurried to her side. "You're incredible, you know that?"

"Aren't you going to ask me what's wrong?"

"You told me not to ask you that anymore."

"Well, you should've. Because something is definitely wrong."

As soon as she heard voices in the hall, Zara jumped from the bed and slipped into the closet between the bathroom and the bedroom. A faint buzz and click emanated from the doorway. Other than the sounds of Olga entering, bolting the door, and humming to herself, the room was silent. *Good.* No roommate. Two people would've increased the risk of failure exponentially.

Voices and cheering suddenly filled the room. The TV. Volume high. Also good. Zara slowly lifted the purse from across her chest and set it on the closet floor. The bathroom door clicked shut. The rushing sound of water followed. She squatted and pulled a large butcher knife from the purse. A dried bit of Jalal's blood tinged the tip.

Slowly, quietly, she pushed the closet door open and looked to her right. The bathroom door was shut. She studied herself in the full-length mirror on the opposite wall. The black sweatshirt she'd put over her blouse and the sweatpants she'd pulled over her jeans would conceal the blood from afar. If it got too messy, she could simply discard them in Olga's room before heading to her own suite down the hall.

The water cut out. Zara stepped away from the mirror and flattened herself against the wall. Two minutes passed. Then three.

Zara bounced on her toes. Better to strike before the adrenaline wore off. She pushed the chrome bathroom door handle down. When the door opened, Olga shrieked. A hand flew to her mouth and she fumbled for a towel to hide her pasty rolls of fat. Zara raised a finger to her lip, and in one swift move, slid behind the larger, heavier woman, The blade of the knife flashed in the artificial light.

"*Nyet!*" Olga shrieked, her eyes wide in horror in the bathroom mirror. "*Ny*—"

Her voice cut out as the blade sliced across the carotid arteries from the left to the right side of her neck. Blood spurted in what seemed like every direction. Spray spattered across the mirror, the walls. Olga slumped forward, hitting her head on the edge of the vanity. It took every ounce of Zara's strength to keep her from falling to the floor with a thud that might raise the curiosity of people in neighboring rooms. She lowered the woman slowly to the blood-slicked tile floor. As the woman gurgled, Zara grunted and spun her around. She grabbed the woman's short black hair with one hand and a fleshy arm with the other and heaved her torso over the edge of the tub. The mess was unavoidable, but she didn't want to risk the blood finding a crack in the floor and staining the ceiling on the floor below.

One look in the mirror told Zara that her outer layer had to go. She rinsed the knife and her hands in the sink and used a washcloth to clean her face and neck. Next, she peeled off the sweatshirt and the sweatpants, which landed with a soft splat in the tub. She removed the baseball hat and readers she'd bought at the local discount store and threw them into the closet. Then she tousled her hair, retrieved her purse, and tucked the knife inside of it. For a moment she debated keeping the television on, but decided it might raise questions in the morning. Off went the gameshow featuring contestants buying vowels or some such idiocy.

A quick glance through the peephole showed an empty hall. She cracked the door and peered out. All clear. In one swift move, she put the "Do Not Disturb" placard on the outside handle, closed the door with a soft click, and hurried off to room 324.

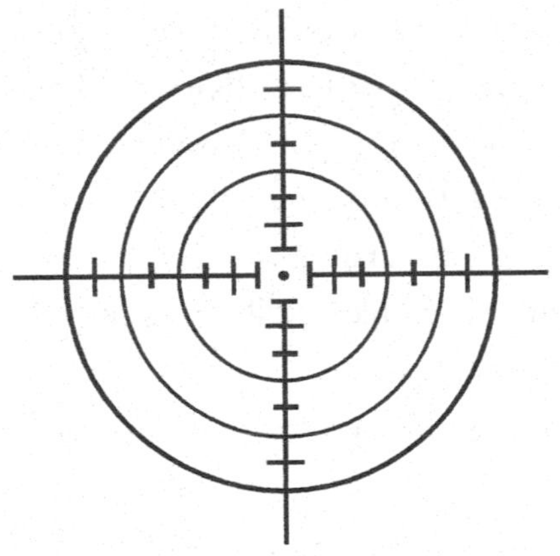

CHAPTER FORTY-THREE

After the police ordered everyone to evacuate the area around the building in case there were bombs or other explosives inside the apartment, Maggie headed to Roger's. She beat him to his place by ten minutes, which gave her enough time to clear the breakfast dishes they'd left out.

"Afghan food," he announced as he opened the front door. "Hope that's okay."

It was her favorite.

Actually, it had been their favorite—hers and Steve's. How could she share their favorite meal with another man? "I'm not very hungry."

Roger pulled four still-steaming cartons out of the first bag, naming the contents one by one. "Kibbeh. Lamb kabobs. Rice. And of course, hummus with pita bread." From the second bag, he pulled a bottle of Chardonnay and an assortment of plastic utensils. "I can't possibly eat all this myself."

Maggie's stomach rumbled. "I'll have a little." *Steve wouldn't care*, she told herself. It was just food.

He plopped into the kitchen chair across from her and proceeded to peel the covers off the containers. After a few seconds, he was back on his feet, rummaging around in a cabinet. He returned with paper plates, plastic cups, and a corkscrew.

Maggie folded and unfolded her hands while Roger served the food and poured the wine.

"There's nothing like cheap wine to enhance a fine dining experience."

Maggie followed his lead, taking a sip. The wine wasn't horrible, but she'd had better.

He dug into his meal, still keeping his eyes on hers. "Aren't you going to eat?"

Maggie nodded and poked a plastic fork into a chunk of lamb. She scooped some rice onto the meat and tasted it. The spices were at once foreign and familiar.

"Good?"

Maggie's eyelids flew open. She hadn't realized they were closed. She swallowed and nodded. "Quite."

Roger continued to watch her, trying to maintain eye contact. Little alarm bells rang in her mind. A change of subject was in order. "I'm really sorry about Jane, Roger."

His eyes clouded over. "Yeah, I know. Sometimes life sucks. As you know."

"Yeah."

He poured himself another glass of Chardonnay. "The best you can do is hope that the bad stuff will lead to—" He raised his glass. "Better things."

Maggie got the distinct impression he was referring to their meeting each other. Her mouth went dry. She busied herself putting lids on the food containers. "Thanks for dinner."

He watched her intently. When she carried the containers to the kitchen, he followed.

Maggie couldn't look at him. If she did, he might notice that her face was burning, that her skin was warm to the touch. *This will pass*, Maggie told herself. The air between them was alive, pulsating, but it wouldn't last.

Nothing lasted.

Roger touched her arm. "Did I do something wrong?"

"No." It hadn't even been a year since Steve had died. "I . . . this isn't right."

Roger's voice softened. "Maggie, if you want to tell me you're not ready for dating or that I'm the most annoying man you've ever met, that's one thing. But if you want to live conforming to what is and is not considered right, then you're going to miss out on some of life's greatest moments." He took a carton of rice from her and set it on the counter. "You don't have to play the martyr or the grieving widow." He shook his head. "Take it from someone who's been there. You can't stop living."

Maggie blinked. She wasn't sure what felt wrong—the fact that she might actually like Roger or the fact that she'd forgotten about Steve for a few minutes.

He stepped closer.

"Roger—"

"Take a risk, Maggie." He ran a hand across her hair, wrapping his fingers in her curls. "Live a little." He moved in, his lips brushing hers, lightly at first. And then, more urgently.

Maggie sank against Roger, giving in to the attraction and the fear and exhaustion of the past week. Before she knew it, her hands were on his face, around his neck, across his back. She lost all sense of time and place. It might have been five seconds or five minutes later when her ringing phone pulled them apart.

"Warner?"

"Listen, Maggie, they checked surveillance videos at the site where this Jalal character took photos. He was there just a few days ago, on Monday. Now all of DC is on alert for Saturday. These have to be the targets. It's September eleventh."

"But Warner, I think there's more to this than meets the eye. It's almost too obvious. The ID, the photos on the phone. Zara's not sloppy."

"It's all we've got to go on. And it makes sense with the 9/11 anniversary."

"What about the girls' school?"

"It's not the target, Maggie. But just in case, the same team will be deployed there tomorrow."

"Including me?"

There was a long pause. "You're not on the list."

"I should be. I could keep an eye on Emma and Abigail."

"They won't be at school. I asked their mother to keep them home."

"Under what pretext?"

"I said my uncle is passing through town Friday morning and would love to stop by to see the girls."

"Did Shannon buy it?"

He nodded. "She complained, of course, but said she'd keep them home for the morning."

Maggie chewed on her lip. "There's a part of you that thinks the school might still be the target, isn't there?"

"I can't rule it out completely, but think about it, Maggie. Why would Zara go after a school when there are 9/11 ceremonies on the White House lawn and at Arlington National Cemetery?"

He had a point.

"We've alerted authorities in New York City and Shanksville as well." He paused. "Maggie, this was all you. You never gave up."

"But—"

"Assuming we find Zara and stop this attack, you will be responsible for saving countless lives. I'm so proud—"

"Let's just make sure we find her."

"Keep your phone on in case I need you."

"I will." She hung up and turned to Roger. But the moment had passed. "I'm going to try to get some sleep."

He approached and placed his hands on her arms. "It's going to be okay, Maggie."

"You don't know that, Roger."

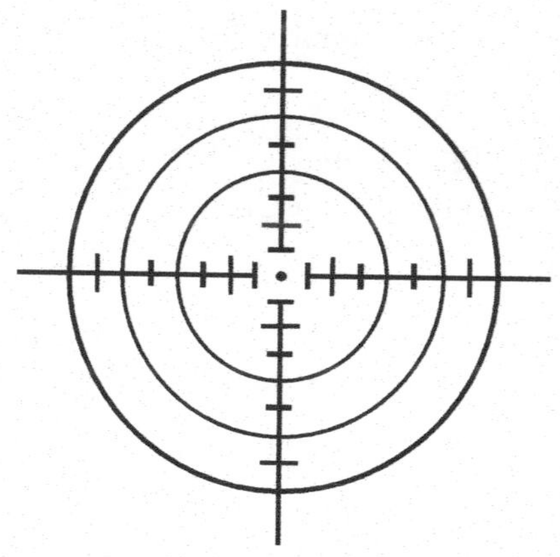

CHAPTER FORTY-FOUR

Dominion Elementary School
Great Falls, Virginia
Friday, September 10, 2004, 7:00 a.m.

Maggie trudged over to the familiar team assembling in the school parking lot. She'd hardly slept the previous night and her head was pounding. One of the FBI agents caught her eye.

"What are you doing here? You're not on our list."

"That has to be a mistake. I'm supposed to—"

"I'm sorry Maggie, but we can only let authorized people into the school.

"I need to be in that school."

"Unless your boss calls our boss, you can't come in."

She felt heat rising in her face.

"I'll get the authorization," she called over her shoulder as she headed for her car. As she slid into the driver's seat, her phone rang.

"Maggie?" It was Jim Carpenter.

"What's the hell is going on, Jim? I need to be in that school when the dance troupe arrives."

"There's a nine-a.m. meeting at headquarters about the threat against the memorial ceremonies. The DCI wants you there after what you uncovered in Falls Church yesterday."

"Oh, so now I'm needed again?"

Jim ignored the sarcasm in her tone. "Nine sharp, Maggie."

"Okay." She tossed the phone on the seat and rummaged around in her purse for some headache medicine. "Great," she muttered when she discovered that she'd left her Glock in the bag since yesterday's school operation. She'd have to drop that off at Roger's before going to Langley. The assembly began at 9:00, which meant the dance troupe would be at the school by 8:30. That gave her enough time to drive to Roger's and return before the dancers arrived.

She threw the car into reverse, spun around, and headed for the main road. Not ten minutes into the drive, her phone rang again.

The voice on the other end babbled incoherently. It took Maggie a moment to realize the woman was speaking Russian. It took another thirty seconds to figure out that it was Irina, the Chechen dance-troupe director she'd met at the hotel.

"Irina, slow down. I can't understand you," Maggie replied in Russian.

The woman did her best to steady her voice. "Olga is gone."

She slammed on the brakes to avoid hitting the car in front of her. "Gone? What do you mean, gone?"

"There was a note under my room door on hotel paper. Apparently she told the concierge to write and say that she became ill and went to the hospital."

Maggie pulled into a strip mall. "What hospital?" she asked over the *click-clack, click-clack* of the blinker.

"I don't know."

"Was she sick last night?"

"No. The note said it was her heart. Chest pain."

Maggie swatted at the blinker. "Does she have heart problems?"

"Yes."

Maggie ran a hand through her hair. "Where are you now?"

"We are leaving the hotel."

"Have you seen anyone who looks like the dark-haired woman I showed you? Anyone at all?"

"No."

A wave of nausea passed through her stomach. Olga's sudden disappearance could be nothing. A middle-aged, overweight woman with a history of heart problems. She drummed her fingers on the steering wheel.

"Can you find her? Find the hospital?" Irina pleaded.

"I'll be at the school when you arrive to make sure everything is okay. Then I'll find Olga. Okay?"

"Thank you, Maggie. I'm so worried about her."

She wasn't the only one.

Zara hurried to her rental car. The original plan had been for her to arrive at the same time as the dance troupe and introduce herself as the substitute translator sent by a Chechen official. That plan had changed when a man who said he was calling on Imran's behalf provided her with new instructions.

Twenty minutes later, she pulled into the nearby office-building parking lot. Nodding politely to a middle-aged man as he stepped out of his sedan a few spots away, she pretended to be looking for something in her purse. Once he disappeared into the building, she made her way through a thicket of trees to the top of a hill overlooking a playground. Her contact was supposed to unlock the door at 8:00 a.m. sharp. If there was a problem, he would leave a mop outside the door on the far right.

There was no mop.

With a furtive look at her surroundings, she descended the hill, her kitten heels sinking into the soft ground. She leaned her ear against the metal door. Not a sound. A quick glance through the door's narrow windowpane revealed an empty hallway inside. Slowly, she twisted the cool metal knob to the right. It clicked softly as she pulled the door toward herself.

Everything was still.

Proceeding to the first door on the right, she inhaled and opened it. Before she could step inside, a man curled his arm around her neck and dragged her into a large supply closet. Zara's instinct told her to fight, but his voice stopped her.

"*Assalamu'alaykum*," he said, hesitant, questioning, as if he'd never spoken to a woman.

Zara twisted, freeing herself from his arm. "*Alaykum assalam*," she replied with a knowing smile and a flip of her hair. *Peace be upon you, indeed.*

A slender, olive-skinned man stared at her, disbelief contorting his features. He tried to put some distance between them, but janitorial supplies scattered around the floor got in the way.

"Were you expecting someone else?" She smoothed her hands along the sides of her tight black skirt, enjoying his obvious discomfort. "I got the call. About the police."

"I am Ibrahim." He blinked and seemed to gather himself. "I don't know if I can get my men inside. The police, the FBI, they are searching the entire school."

She lowered her voice "Do they know?"

"I don't know." He clasped his hands together. "Why else would they be here?"

Zara cracked open the door and listened before closing it again.

"They already searched this end of the building. But how do I get the men into the gym with the police here?"

"Where are the others?"

"Outside. In a construction van."

Zara ran a scenario through her head. She and Ibrahim would slip into the gymnasium, killing whatever law-enforcement officers they encountered along the way and taking hostages to fend off any other officers. The rest of the team, meanwhile, would rush the school and overwhelm the remaining police.

It could work.

"I think we should abort."

"No, Ibrahim. This is our only chance."

"But the weapons are in the van," he protested, desperation creeping into his voice.

Heat rose in her face. "The weapons are supposed to be inside the school, you fool."

"The men were about to bring them in a side door when Samir spotted the police driving into the parking lot."

Zara shook her head. She hadn't come this far to give up now. "Here's the plan."

Ibrahim listened, arms crossed across his chest.

"You are supposed to leave the building before the attack begins," he said. "Follow the plan and go to the other target."

Indeed, this was the moment when Zara was supposed to leave and take up a position outside of the private school a few miles away. When news broke of this school siege, she'd snipe out children of the elite as they evacuated their school. She'd promised Imran, but agreeing to his mission had been a ruse, her way to get here to carry out her own. "No."

"I'm in charge here."

"I'm not going anywhere." Reaching into her purse, Zara pulled out the Walther PPK.

Ibrahim's eyes grew wide.

She pointed the gun at his chest. "When I say go, your men will storm the building and take out the police. Understand?"

He stared. Then nodded.

By the time Maggie pulled into the school parking lot, she'd already tried to reach Roger and Warner. She'd even called Jim Carpenter. None of them answered. She needed their help to find Olga. Someone to go to the hotel and confirm the story about her being ill. Someone to check the local hospitals. She tried Roger again. No answer. "Damn it!" she shouted as she pounded the steering wheel.

She pulled into a spot on the far right side of the school, a few spots away from where the team's vehicles were parked. Grabbing her keys, purse, and phone, she trotted toward the main parking lot in front of the building and peered around the corner. Children streamed from two buses, passing a police officer and one of the Homeland Security agents on their way inside.

Maggie hung back at the side of the school until the silver minibus transporting the dance troupe turned into the lot.

The Homeland Security agent frowned at her as she approached. “Maggie?”

“I just want to make sure everything looks normal.”

He sighed and rolled his eyes.

The minibus door whooshed open. Maggie studied each of the girls. There was no difference in their demeanor from the previous two days. Irina was the last one off the bus.

She caught sight of Maggie and rushed over.

“Did you find Olga?” Her lips pinched together tightly.

“Not yet, Irina. But we’re working on it.” She smiled, hoping it would reassure her. “Did anything else happen? No one tried to get on the bus? No one gave the girls a package or anything?”

Irina shook her head, worry creasing her forehead.

Maggie touched her arm. “Good. I’ll call you as soon as I find out how Olga is.”

“Okay,” She looked over her shoulder. “I better go.”

Maggie nodded. “Good luck.” She watched as the Homeland Security agent followed the troupe inside before approaching the officer. “Are you going inside?”

“No, ma’am. Once the dancers start getting ready for their show, we’ll lock up the school so no one else can enter and be on our way.”

Maggie’s jaw dropped. “You’re not staying?”

“One of us is. Kevin the other police officer. He’ll stay until the end of the performance.”

Maggie strode past him.

"Hey, where do you think you're going?"

She ignored him, but by the time she reached the door, his arm was on her wrist.

"I have my orders. No one enters the school now that the dancers are inside."

Maggie struggled against his grip. "Let me go."

The officer slid between her and the entrance. "If you try to enter the building, I will have no choice but to detain you."

Maggie shot him a glare, whirled around, and stormed back to her car. Inside, she tried to calm herself down. Zara hadn't come near the dance troupe. The team had searched the building. They'd lock it tight when they left. An armed officer would be inside. It was already 8:30. If she didn't leave now, she'd be late getting to headquarters. Jim Carpenter would be furious. The director might be waiting to talk to her.

She decided to wait until the security team left the building, to make sure they were all accounted for and acting normally. Ten minutes later, all but one—the local police officer named Kevin—exited the building. She waved at them as they headed for their vehicles and watched as they drove off one at a time.

Maggie sighed, started the car, and moved her right hand to the gear selector. Images of Zara flashed through her mind, unbidden and unwelcome.

Zara outside the school in Beslan, carrying the gravely wounded child as a decoy.

Zara escaping in Imran Bukayev's car.

Zara vanishing in the airport crowd.

She pulled the key from the ignition. A flat tire. That would be her story. In twenty minutes, she'd call Jim Carpenter, explain that she was waiting for the service truck to arrive. They wouldn't fire her for getting a flat tire. And once this knot in her stomach eased, she'd be able focus on the upcoming 9/11 memorial ceremonies. It wouldn't be long until the dancers made their final bow.

In the school's music room, Zara greeted the music teacher and Irina, whose hands visibly trembled when Zara explained that she was filling in for the troupe's translator. Chechnya's cultural minister, a family friend, she said, had called early this morning and asked her to help due to Olga's sudden illness. In Russian, Zara promised Irina that they'd visit Olga at the hospital as soon as this morning's performance ended. The troupe director lowered herself into a chair, eyes brimming with tears. Killing Irina wasn't part of the plan, but if she didn't get her act together, she would attract unwanted scrutiny.

Zara turned her attention to the girls, explaining to them that as a former dancer herself, she was thrilled to be part of the troupe, if only until Olga recovered. She pasted on a smile as each of the preteens introduced themselves to her. They were in full ethnic costume—crisp white capes over vibrant turquoise silk dresses—and clearly excited to show off their culture and talent. She checked the clock on the wall.

The men in the van had called Ibrahim ten minutes ago to report that the police officers had all left. It was a good thing she'd refused to abort the mission.

Everything was falling into place, but she had to admit that she was nervous this time. There was a lot more at stake, not least because she was disobeying Imran's orders and couldn't be sure that the men would go along with her.

She considered praying for success, but didn't know who or what to pray to.

"The assembly begins at nine sharp," the school music teacher said. "Would you like to take the girls backstage now?" She gestured to an open door that led to a windowless hall. "The stage is right through here."

Zara smiled—all sweetness and light—and translated the teacher's words for Irina and the girls. Irina's hands shook and her lips were drawn into a thin line, but at least she'd stopped asking about Olga. The young dancers fell in behind their leader, who trailed the music teacher.

Zara waited until they'd disappeared before hurrying down the hall to the supply closet.

Maggie fidgeted in her car. She could use some more coffee. Her phone rang.

"Roger?"

It wasn't him.

"Irina, slow down. I can't understand you," Maggie said in Russian.

The woman did her best to steady her voice. What she said next had the opposite effect on Maggie.

"You're sure it's the woman in the photograph, Irina?" Every muscle in her body was tense.

"Yes." Her voice rose an octave. "Oh, dear God, Olga's dead, isn't she?"

Maggie gripped the steering wheel. This couldn't be happening. "Irina, is there anyone else with this woman?"

"No."

"Okay." She fumbled for words. "Get everyone out of the school, okay? I'll come find you."

Zara passed through the short hall from the music room to the stage, which stood at the end of the school's gymnasium. It was similar to the one in Beslan, only this one was about fifty years newer. Bleachers were pushed flush against the wall. *Good.* Fewer places for people to hide. Several dozen plastic chairs lined the perimeter of the gym, probably teacher seating. The children must sit on the floor. *Even better*. Nowhere to take cover.

At 8:55, the first little bodies filtered into the gymnasium. They looked wholesome and earnest, as American as apple pie, as the saying went. They followed their teachers' commands and sat dutifully, the youngest close to the stage, the older children farther back.

The performance began with a delightful folk dance full of twirls and dips. When the second dance ended, precisely at 9:11—Zara loved the irony of it—Ibrahim darkened the rear entrance to the gymnasium, then vanished back into the hall. She patted her oversized purse—the Walther was secure—before returning to the music room to make the first call.

The woman who answered the home phone insisted that he couldn't be reached. "It is an emergency. A development in Moscow," Zara said in her most official-sounding voice. "He will be very angry if you don't give me his number." The ruse worked—the woman gave Zara the cell phone number. And what she said to the Russian when he answered sent him into a panic. Zara smiled. Everything was going as planned.

She hurried toward the supply closet, where five young Arabs stood waiting with Ibrahim, who distributed black ski masks and 9mm Glocks to everyone. Several of the men leered at Zara. Ibrahim spoke. "You are supposed to leave now."

"Change in plans." Zara locked eyes with him and snatched an AK-47 from the large trash bin the men had rolled into the school from the back of their truck. "Let's go."

The men nodded and lowered their masks. As she stepped into the hall, one of them lobbed an Arabic pejorative her way. She smiled and responded in kind. If she survived, she'd leave every one of these misogynist animals bleeding and crying for mercy. They might be on her side today, but she was everything they loathed in women—independent, free-minded, strong, and yes, disobedient. They could all rot in Gitmo as far as she was concerned.

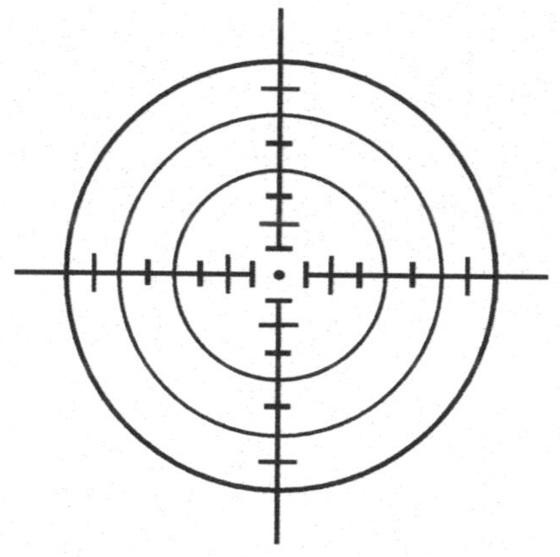

CHAPTER FORTY-FIVE

"Roger, Zara's at Dominion Elementary. Where are you?" Maggie struggled to get the words out. "It's Beslan all over again." She disconnected and dialed 911. "There's a terrorist at an elementary school."

"May I have your name and address?"

"Maggie Jenkins. Dominion Elementary. In Great Falls."

"You say there is a terrorist?"

"Her name is Zara Barayeva. And she might not be acting alone."

"Please spell the name."

"Call the FBI, get the SWAT team. Just hurry!"

She hung up, jumped from the car, and ran to the front of the school, her eyes settling on the large sign above the main entrance. There was something about Dominion Elementary gnawing at her.

She dialed Warner's office phone, silently pleading for him to answer.

"Warner Thompson."

"Zara's here," she blurted out.

"Maggie? Where?"

"Inside the girls' school."

"What?"

"Thank God, you kept them home. But"—she swallowed—"all the—"

"I just listened to a message from Shannon," Warner interrupted. "She forgot about a hair appointment and took them to school."

Maggie's skin stung and pulsated as if shards of glass were raining down on her. "You sure?"

"Yes, that stupid—" Warner was clearly struggling to suppress a few choice words for his ex-wife. "I was pissed but . . . the security team reported that the school got the all-clear, so I thought it was okay. That selfish—" He was yelling into the phone. "A hair appointment? What the—"

"Warner, listen, calm down. There's a police officer inside."

"That's supposed to calm me down?" he shouted.

"I'm going in to help him, Warner. I'm getting the girls."

In the music room, Zara did some deep breathing, trying to relax to the strains of the Chechen folk song echoing from large speakers in the gym. If she let herself go for a moment, she could dance in time with the children, not missing a step. But not now and definitely not here. She slipped down the hall to the rear of the stage behind the dancers. Irina, who was gesticulating wildly to a teacher, froze when she saw Zara.

Her expression morphed from confused to alarmed in a split second. She gasped when Zara raised the assault rifle and lowered the ski mask over her face.

"Ladies and gentlemen, boys and girls, pardon the interruption. The performance is over." Zara nodded toward the rear door. Her six accomplices entered and casually pulled AK-47s from the trash bin, which one of them had wheeled in. Within seconds, a man stood from where he'd been sitting on the floor among a group of older students. A police officer. He drew his gun, but before he could choose a target, bullets tore through Officer Kevin Vincent's intestines, shredding the life from him.

Stunned silence turned to shrieks as blood leached from under the lifeless man. An older boy screamed, "Dad!" from somewhere nearby. Teachers gathered children into their arms. Little girls wailed.

"There is no need for further bloodshed," Zara shouted. "Remain calm and no one else will get hurt." She nodded at the men again. They laced chains through the handles of three sets of double doors, blocking off escape routes. "I need your computer teacher onstage, now."

Heads swiveled in the audience, but no one uttered a word.

"Very well," Zara said. "You, Mrs. Principal. If you don't tell me who the computer teacher is, I will kill one child every ten seconds. Maybe starting with the front row." She swept the AK-47 across a row of five-year-olds.

The middle-aged principal stood and turned to face her charges. "Boys and girls." Her voice was trembling and soft. "Boys and girls," she started again, more firmly, "do as I say and we'll keep you safe."

"Counting down, ten, nine, eight—"

"Ms. Cooke!" the principal shouted.

A young waif of a brunette rose unsteadily from a chair. "I'm the technology teacher." Tears were streaming down her face as she shuffled toward the stage.

Ms. Cooke climbed the stairs slowly, then stood before Zara, unable to make eye contact. Zara used the tip of the AK-47 to lift the woman's chin. "I need a computer with internet access. And a web cam. You have five minutes to bring them to me."

"But we only have desktops and there are no modems in here." The woman's tone was pleading.

"I'm sure you'll figure something out." She pushed her with the butt of the assault rifle. "Muhammed, take her. If she tries anything, kill her."

One of the terrorists stepped forward. *There was always a Muhammed*, Zara thought, smiling to herself under the ski mask. Zara didn't know who was who. She only knew their names—Muhammed, Yasin, Samir, Khaled, Rashid, and, of course, Ibrahim.

"Remember, five minutes, or a child dies." She made a show of checking her watch. "Now, everyone, take out your cell phones. That includes the students." Everyone knew Americans were rich, but children carrying cell phones was obscene excess. Hands reached into purses and pockets. "Hand them down the rows to the center." She watched as everyone appeared to obey, encouraged to do so by the pacing men brandishing fully loaded firearms.

The men gathered the phones and dumped them in a canvas tote purloined from a teacher.

"Excellent." The phones would be left on. When panicked loves ones started to call, the incessant ringing would heighten the hostages' anxiety.

Soon, Ms. Cooke reappeared, pushing a cart carrying a desktop computer. Zara ordered Muhammed to help the woman carry it up the stage steps. "I want this online and the webcam going." The streaming video had been Bukayev's idea. Zara thought it was an unnecessary complication, although she had to concede that the propaganda value would be priceless. She pictured Imran sitting in his lounge, staring at the computer screen. He'd be shocked to see her face, because she was supposed to have left by now.

Ms. Cooke warned Muhammed to move slowly so the computer didn't tumble off the cart. Once the ensemble was onstage, the teacher set about booting up the machine. "I'm going to try to pick up the wireless signal from the main office," she explained to Zara. "I had to take a modem and a router from two other computers, so it may not be configured correctly."

"I'm sure you'll figure it out." Zara instructed Muhammed to stay with the teacher and slipped backstage to make the next call.

Maggie ran back to the car and grabbed the Glock and a thin canister of mace. Tucking the gun into her waistband and the mace into the front of her bra, she slammed the car door as her phone rang.

"Maggie? Where are you?" The panic in Roger's voice was unmistakable.

"Did you talk to Warner?"

"Tell me you're not at that school."

"I am. I have to get Warner's girls out, Roger." She felt calm, certain, and almost serene.

"Maggie, leave. Just drive away. There's a SWAT team on the way. Hostage rescue too. Let them handle it. Please."

In the distance, sirens wailed. "I can't let her do this again, Roger."

"If you go in, she's going to . . . look, just wait for me. I'll be there in fifteen minutes."

"I can't wait." She leaned against the car. The morning sun felt warm on her face. "She'll kill Emma and Abigail and all the other kids."

"Maggie, please don't."

The sirens grew louder. "I have to go." She hung up, turned the phone to vibrate, and sprinted toward the back of the school. As she peered around the corner, the phone buzzed.

"Roger, please stop—" she whispered hoarsely.

"Hello, Maggie." The voice was female, the accent British.

It felt as if every last molecule of air had been sucked from her lungs. "Who is this?"

"I have a proposal for you, Maggie. If you come to Dominion Elementary School, I'll let one hundred children go."

"How did you get my cell number?"

"I had a nice conversation with your mother."

Maggie froze, clutching the phone so tight that her hand began to cramp.

"Very naïve woman, your mother. I told her I was a neighbor and that I needed to reach you immediately to inform you that someone had tried to break into your house."

She placed a hand against the brick building to steady herself. "What do you want, Zara?"

"Come to the school. My men will let you in. Once I see you in person, I will release one hundred children as a gesture of goodwill."

Goodwill? Maggie almost laughed. "What's the address?" She needed to buy time.

"Dominion Elementary. You're a smart girl. I'm sure you can find it."

"Zara? Zara!" She'd hung up. Maggie peered around the back of the school again just as the first police car came screaming into the parking lot. Behind the building, a twisted jump rope lay abandoned in the grass. A swing swayed lazily in the warm morning breeze. A few dry green leaves skittered across a hopscotch board painted on the pavement. To the left, a classroom window was covered with bright drawings of flowers and birds. Maggie leaned forward to scan the artwork for Emma and Abigail's names. The fourth drawing from the left on the bottom row caught her attention. A big yellow flower and a smiling bumblebee. The name, written in red crayon below, was Elena Markova.

Markova?

"Yuri," she gasped. The photograph of the pretty little blonde girl in Yuri's home library. Right, this was her school, too.

She checked again for Warner's girls' names, but they weren't on any of the pictures. She straightened and followed a concrete path leading to a door with a narrow vertical glass pane running the length of it. *Locked.*

She quickly ran to a soccer field situated on a rise above the playground and surveyed the back of the school. The security team had locked down the entire building. The only way in, it seemed, was through the hatch on the roof. Heading back, Maggie ran for a green dumpster that stood a few feet from the building, grabbed a metal bar on the side of it, found a foothold, and yanked herself halfway up. The smell of rotting food greeted her as she peered over the edge into the trash below. Holding her breath, she scrambled atop the edge of the dumpster, only to find that the school roof was about three feet out of reach.

She peered down into the garbage, bent over, and grabbed a five-foot long plank of wood that rested on a mountain of trash bags. She placed one end of the board on the edge of the dumpster and the other end onto the roof, forming a crude bridge.

Here goes nothing, Maggie thought. She lowered a knee onto the board and reached up to grasp the sides of it. The plank wobbled precariously under her full weight, but didn't roll or snap. Slowly, an inch at a time, she made her way across the gap between the dumpster and the roof. When her first foot hit the roof, the board slipped and clattered noisily against the dumpster before falling to the concrete below. So much for coming out the way she'd gone in.

Maggie stood and surveyed the area. From this angle, she couldn't see the front half of the parking lot but she could hear multiple sirens seemingly competing to wail the loudest. She dropped to her knees. If the police saw movement on the roof, they'd shoot first and ask questions later. She crawled across black tar paper to the hatch, which to her relief, wasn't locked. Inside, several ladder rungs protruded from the wall. Beyond the first few feet, it was pitch-black.

Maggie swung her legs into the hatch, maneuvered her feet to the first rung, and began her descent. Motors and fans hissed and boomed through metal ducts like an out-of-sync brass band. After the seventh rung, Maggie's foot found nothing but air below.

She let herself drop several feet to the floor, where she crouched in the dark and listened a moment before running her hand along the wall in search of a doorknob. Her fingers soon found cool, rounded metal. Maggie whispered a prayer and pushed gently on the door, which opened into a room stuffed with janitorial supplies and folding chairs.

Just then, her cell phone vibrated in her pocket.

"Roger?" she whispered.

"I'm on my way. The cavalry should be there by now."

"Zara called me."

"What?"

"She said she'll let a hundred kids go if I come to the school. I'm inside now."

"Maggie, get the hell out of there."

"I'll do some recon and text you in a few minutes. Pass it on to the police."

"Maggie, no."

"Roger, I have to go." She lowered her voice even more. "I hear something."

Before Maggie could hang up, the door leading to the hall flew open, revealing a slightly built man in camouflage coveralls and a black ski mask. As she reached for the back of her waistband, the man threw himself at her, sending her reeling against a metal shelf lined with industrial-sized rolls of toilet paper.

"Terrorists, Roger," she yelled toward her cell phone, which had slipped from her hand and clattered to the floor.

Zara walked to the center of the stage. "Is it ready?"

Ms. Cooke nodded.

Muhammed, the group's computer whiz, shoved the teacher aside and began typing furiously. He accessed the designated website and made sure the camera would sync up and broadcast in near real time.

Zara checked the computer screen. The video was somewhat grainy, but it would suffice. And once she called the local media, the entire world would be transfixed by the spectacle unfolding inside the school. She twisted the camera mounted on top of the computer, pausing on each of the terrorists. Then she pointed the lens back at the children.

Enjoy the show, Imran.

Zara showed Yasin and Samir a photograph she'd printed off the internet. At first, they objected to the change in plans, but relented when she explained that bringing the man in the photo here was part of the plan, approved by Imran Bukayev himself. Imran had agreed with Zara's suggestion to target this particular school, but he didn't know she was going to lure this individual to the building.

It was a risky move, messing with a powerful man that way, but as far as Zara was concerned, if she was going to put her life on the line, she was going to make it worth her while.

The man in camouflage kicked the phone out of reach, produced a silver semiautomatic pistol, and leveled it at Maggie's forehead. She raised her hands, shifted her left foot backward, and judged the distance between her right foot and his hands. A snap kick would do it.

"Please don't shoot. I'm just a teacher." Maggie felt her hands trembling. She'd practiced this kick dozens of times at the dojo before leaving for Moscow, but dislodging a loaded gun from a terrorist's hands was entirely different from kicking a padded dummy for fun. Even so, she couldn't let it end now, not after she'd tracked Zara two thousand miles and back again.

Maggie leaned into her left leg and took a deep breath to center herself, but before she could execute the kick, a second, identically dressed man appeared behind the first, the black tip of his assault rifle staring at a point on Maggie's throat.

They spoke gruffly in Arabic. Then the first terrorist stepped forward, seized Maggie's right arm, and twisted it behind her back. Their hands were all over her in an instant, frisking and patting. When they found her Glock, the second terrorist shoved her against the metal shelves and jammed the tip of the pistol against her temple. Maggie closed her eyes and saw Steve's face—the dark hair, the bright blue eyes, the all-American-boy smile.

She opened her eyes. "If you kill me, Zara will kill you."

The men exchanged a brief glance, but the Glock stayed in place.

"Zara is the woman running this operation. I have a message for her."

The men spoke to each other. Maggie silently cursed herself for dropping out of Arabic class midway through the first semester. They nodded almost imperceptibly, then each grabbed an arm and forced her into the hall. One of the terrorists shoved her forward, the tip of his gun resting against her shoulder blade. Papier-mâché masks grinned out from a display case on the left. Children's self-portraits brightened the walls on the right. The halls were silent, the classrooms empty.

"Did you know Zara killed all her accomplices in Beslan?" If she could plant a few seeds of doubt, maybe these men would turn on Zara.

The second man grabbed her left arm with one hand, and raised his handgun to her cheek with the other. She squeezed her eyes shut. *Hail Mary, full of grace—*

The man shoved her so hard, she stumbled but managed not to fall. Up ahead, outside a set of double doors, he holstered the gun and pulled Maggie's hands together at the base of her spine.

The second man rapped the butt of her Glock against a narrow glass pane. Yet another man, a near clone of the first two, appeared at the window and opened the door.

"Move," one of them barked as he forced Maggie into the school gymnasium.

Hundreds of children, babies practically, sat on the floor, huddled with their teachers. Frightened, tearstained faces stared up at her. Maggie had nothing to offer in consolation. It was Beslan all over again, and she was just as helpless here as she'd been outside that school.

Soft whimpers weakened her knees. Waves of panic coursed through her. She slowed her breathing. *Focus. Analyze.* Maggie tore her eyes from the children. She couldn't help them until she dealt with Zara. And the others.

A wheeled cart holding a computer stood on the stage. At the far side of the room sat a group of bewildered preteen girls dressed in bright costumes—the dancers. Irina sat with them, arms around the nearest two girls, her eyes squeezed shut. Maggie counted six men in camouflage and black ski masks, including the two who'd discovered her. There were two entrances into the gym from the hall, and a double door on the far wall that led outside—all the doors except the one she'd just come through had chains looped around the handles.

A sudden movement about seven rows back caught her eye. A girl with long black hair jumped up to get Maggie's attention. *Emma.* A teacher threw her arms around Warner's daughter and struggled to restrain her. Maggie locked eyes with Emma and mouthed "No," but not before one of the terrorists noticed and strode toward the girl.

"Where is she?" Maggie shouted. "Where is Zara Barayeva?"

The man stopped just feet from Emma. All eyes turned to Maggie. Whispers and shifting bodies stirred the air.

"Boys and girls, it's going to be okay. I'm here to help, but you have to stay calm."

The broad side of the AK-47 came at Maggie's head. She twisted an arm free and ducked, only to be tackled to the ground by two of the terrorists.

"Let her go," a woman's voice ordered.

Maggie's chin and nose throbbed from the impact with the gymnasium floor. She tasted blood. Someone pulled her to her feet.

The woman before her stood in stark contrast to the other terrorists. Her black hair was smooth, her makeup light but expert. And her petite figure was hugged by a tight black skirt and a cream-colored sweater. If it weren't for the assault rifle dangling from a sling on her shoulder, Zara could pass for a high-powered Senate staffer.

Her heart pounded erratically, but Maggie forced her voice to be steady. "Hello, Zara."

A flicker of irritation flashed across Zara's face. The terrorist who'd noticed Emma moments ago leaned over to whisper in Zara's ear. She studied Maggie for a moment, then smiled. "Maggie is going to pick a child to release to demonstrate our goodwill and our willingness to negotiate."

"You said one hundred children."

Zara shrugged and nodded to the man who was standing at the end of Emma's row.

In three swift steps, he was beside Warner's daughter. He yanked her and the boy sitting next to her to their feet. The boy was sobbing. Emma's eyes were pleading.

Someone shouted, "Emma!"

Maggie caught sight of Abigail, Emma's twin, standing on the other side of the gym, tears streaming down her cheeks.

"The boy or the girl," Zara commanded. "Which one?"

A wet patch crept down and across the boy's pant leg. Emma blinked rapidly. The boy started to wail. Several children seated nearby broke into sobs. Two AK-47s were raised, aimed at the boy's chest.

They're going to kill him. They wanted calm and this poor little freckle-faced boy was hysterical. *Forgive me, Warner.* "The boy." The words came out as a whisper, but Emma heard. Her eyes grew wide and filled with tears. Maggie pursed her lips, trying to hush the girl, who collapsed onto her teacher's lap.

Then Zara was at the crying boy's side. "Maggie wants us to free the boy." She marched him by the elbow to the front of the collapsed bleachers. Struggling to catch his breath between sobs, he wiped his eyes with the green sleeve of his shirt.

Zara studied the face of the young boy. He had that wholesome look, what with the freckles, the tousled sun-streaked hair, and the blue jeans. But there was something familiar about him as well. She bent down and studied his wide, brown eyes. That was it—the fear, the same fear she'd seen in the Beslan children's eyes, the same fear she'd seen in her brothers' eyes the night her family had barely escaped their apartment being shelled by Russian troops.

If this boy were to die here today, surely his family would grieve the way Zara had grieved after each of her losses. But fear, pain, and loss were all part of life, weren't they? And children born into certain circumstances, like those in Chechnya, learned that at an earlier age than others. Until today, this child's worst fear probably had been monsters under the bed, or maybe a house-shaking thunderstorm. Zara felt a certain kinship with the boy. She had been that young and innocent once. So had her brothers. They'd only just emerged from childhood themselves when they were killed.

Zara pulled her gaze from the boy. He probably had siblings, and even if he didn't, his parents could always have more children. She, on the other hand, couldn't produce a new mother, or father, or brothers. What was about to happen to this boy was hardly equivalent to the injustices she'd suffered all her life.

Maggie watched Zara step away from the boy. Relief swept over her like a wave of warm water. Maybe she wasn't going to kill any children today. Maybe Beslan had been enough.

"Why are you doing this, Zara?"

Zara's mouth curved into a smile. She raised her right hand over her head. As she dropped it down, two shots screamed upward from the muzzle of an AK-47. Shards of glass and plastic rained down from the overhead lights. The boy stumbled backward against the bleachers, eyes wide, mouth open in a silent scream. Urine trickled from the hem of his pantleg.

Children shrieked. A woman shouted, "Tommy!" The terrorist unleashed another volley of bullets at the ceiling. The shrieking ceased. The crying didn't.

Maggie's shock gradually gave way to rage. It slowed her voice, her heart rate, her breathing. "If you hurt a single one of these children—"

Zara laughed. "Don't waste your breath, Maggie. You won't be around to see the finale."

Outside, Warner paced before the makeshift operations center that the FBI and county police had set up. Some FBI hothead who didn't know him wanted him removed from the scene. They'd have to drag him away in handcuffs before that happened.

"Let me get this straight, Mr. Thompson, you're CIA?" Agent Barrett's gaze shifted to Warner's CIA badge.

"Yes."

"Well, that's fantastic. But this is our jurisdiction and only essential personnel are permitted here. There appears to be a serious situation inside that school. We can't have any distractions or outside interference."

Warner pulled off his sunglasses and fought to control his voice. "I'm fully aware of the situation. In fact, I'm the one who called the FBI at the behest of the CIA director. And I know a hell of a lot more about Zara Barayeva than the rest of you."

The other FBI agents turned their attention to Warner.

"And you should know that there's a CIA analyst inside the school."

"Hey, everyone listen up!" A young man wearing headphones jumped from the side of an unmarked black van parked several spaces away. "We've picked up some audio from inside the school. We just heard automatic gunfire and screaming. Sounded like children."

Warner's lungs felt like they'd been punctured. He steadied himself against a folding chair. *Please . . . not the girls.*

There was little time to recover. FBI agents swarmed him.

"Why is there a CIA analyst in the school?" shouted one man.

"Who is it?" demanded another.

Warner forced his daughters' faces from his mind. "Her name is Maggie Jenkins, and she has single-handedly worked to track down Zara Barayeva since the Beslan attack." He pulled the picture of Zara from his pocket and handed it to an agent. "That's her. Zara."

The buzz of questions rose to a crescendo. "That's the woman we've been looking for at several local schools," offered one agent.

"Yes." Warner nodded as he told them all he knew. Then he leaned against the unmarked van and tried to catch his breath. Maggie, Emma, Abigail. Gunshots. He wasn't going to let them die. No matter what it took.

"Mr. Thompson, we have more questions," someone shouted.

Warner stepped away from the crowd of excited federal agents when his cell phone rang.

"Thompson."

"Warner, did you hear?"

"About the school? I'm right outside it, you sonofabitch."

"Warner—"

"Shut up, Yuri. I want the truth. Did you have anything to do with this?"

"Warner, I have no idea what you're talking about."

"Don't give me that BS, Yuri."

"Warner, a woman called me about fifteen minutes ago. She said she's in the school and that I need to get there or she'll kill them."

"Kill who?"

"Elena and Svetlana." Yuri's voice wavered. "They're all I have and they're inside the school, Warner."

With my babies. Warner wanted to unleash a string of expletives but forced himself to focus. "Was it Zara who called?"

There was a long pause.

"Yuri, you still there?"

"*Eta nevozmozhno,*" he whispered, slipping from English to Russian.

Warner stared at the single-story brick building. "Where are you?"

"I'm on the big street. The police won't enter me, even though I say who I am." The Russian's English was faltering. Too much stress, too much fear.

"I'll be right there."

"Hurry, Warner."

• ★ ★ ★ •

Zara and one of the men forced Maggie onto the stage. She struggled to free her arms, finally giving up after the man clamped handcuffs on her. Another man adjusted the computer cart so that the web camera faced Zara.

"Where is Svetlana Yuryevna Markova? Ms. Markova?"

Children's heads turned in unison to a woman with high cheekbones and blonde hair pulled back in a sleek ponytail. She stood, her young charges encircling her, looking up at her with wide eyes and tearstained faces.

"And where is your daughter?"

Svetlana Markova shook her head.

"Mama!" cried a petite child with eyes the same shade of blue as her mother's.

Maggie looked from the woman to the child and back again. The girl must be Elena. She looked just like the child in the photo hanging in Yuri's library. And the woman—a teacher?—had to be Yuri's daughter. Her mind raced. Was Zara going to let them go? Was Yuri in on this siege too?

"Bring them to me," Zara said to no one in particular. One of the men seized Svetlana by the arm. Another snatched her daughter from the floor.

"Mama!" she wailed.

Svetlana's face crumpled.

The men deposited her and her daughter next to Maggie.

"I know your father," Maggie whispered.

Svetlana looked at Maggie, blue eyes wide and pleading. "What is going on?"

"Excuse me." Warner slid through a throng of cops. The scene beyond the police car barricade was chaotic. Parents were yelling, begging for information. Television cameras were everywhere. He stood on his toes, searching for Yuri's bald head.

"Yuri Markov!"

A woman, somebody's mother, noticed the Agency badge around Warner's neck and rushed him.

"My son's in fourth grade. About four foot eight, brown hair." She started to cry. "He plays baseball."

"Ma'am, I'm CIA, not police. I'm sorry."

"He's a good boy. Really bright," she insisted as tears rolled down her face.

Warner took the woman's hand. "We'll get everyone out." He looked over her shoulder and spotted Yuri leaning against a television van. "Yuri, over here."

The Russian broke through a line of people. "We have to hurry."

A stout policewoman stopped Yuri and Warner. "No one's allowed through."

Warner lifted his badge. "I'm Warner Thompson, deputy director for operations, CIA. And this is Yuri Markov with Russian intelligence. He has vital information on the terrorists and must be let in. I can vouch for him."

The woman folded her arms across her ample chest. "What'd you say your name is?"

"Warner Thompson."

She turned her back to them and spoke into a police radio. After a few painful seconds, she waved them through.

Yuri struggled to keep up with Warner, wheezing with every breath. Warner kept the pace brisk. "I've been trying to reach you for two days."

Yuri raised his left arm. A white hospital bracelet encircled his wrist. "I was too sick to answer your calls. Heart attack." He stopped and tried to catch his breath. "I checked myself out when Barayeva called."

"How do you know her?"

"I've never met her. I swear." The Russian's sweaty red cheeks faded to white. "I need to get Elena and Svetlana. The rest can wait."

"Tell me everything or I won't let you into that school. I'll have you arrested on the spot."

"You can't," Yuri protested, his voice weak.

"Oh, I most certainly can. And I will."

"But my daughter—"

Warner jabbed a forefinger into Yuri's chest. "You know my daughters are in there, too, you sonofabitch. Along with one of *your* Beslan terrorists. So you *will* tell me everything. Or they're all going to die."

Yuri used a white handkerchief to mop the sweat from his gleaming forehead. "I gave the Chechens money and intelligence about the regional police and military. Their numbers, their tactics. That's all."

"That's all?" Warner forced a laugh. "You let them kill hundreds of children. Russian children, Yuri."

"Russia needs to wake up to the Muslim threat." He didn't sound like he believed his own words.

"So you became a terrorist yourself to demonstrate the threat?"

Yuri's eyes narrowed. "I did it for my country."

"For your country, huh? Any regrets that one of your terrorists is holding your family hostage?" He sniffed. "Or did you fund this attack, too?"

"How dare you," Yuri spat. "This is nothing but another American intelligence failure. If my family dies in there, I will hold your government responsible and expose its incompetence to the world."

Warner ignored Yuri's empty threat and resumed walking. The old commie bastard would pay beyond his wildest nightmares for what he'd done. But first things first.

At the FBI table, Warner made Bureau jaws drop again when he introduced Yuri, whose shirt was now drenched in sweat. "Mr. Markov has critical information on the Beslan attack and on the female terrorist inside the building. He's willing to submit to a full debriefing, but first, we need to get his daughter and granddaughter out of the school."

Yuri stood silent, wringing his hands.

The most senior agent stood, ready to defy Warner. "We can't let him go in there."

"I'm afraid you have to. Zara Barayeva called Yuri a while ago and demanded his presence."

Yuri spoke, his voice low and shaky. "She's supposed to call back," he glanced at his watch, "in two minutes."

This revelation set off a flurry of conversation among the agents. How can we get someone else in the building with the Russian? Will we have a clear shot at any of the terrorists? Can we trust this guy to negotiate with Barayeva?

Yuri's ringing phone ended the discussions.

"Put it on speakerphone," someone ordered.

"I don't know how." Yuri was suddenly just a pathetic old man, a shadow of his former fearsome self.

"Everyone shut up," Warner commanded. He grabbed the phone from Yuri's hand and found the speakerphone button. He pushed it and nodded to Yuri.

"Hello?"

"Is this Yuri Markov?"

Yuri confirmed that he was outside the school. "*Da. Ya zdes.*"

Zara spoke rapidly in Russian, instructing him to walk to the front door of the school, alone, hands in the air. She said she was releasing his family as a sign of goodwill.

Warner translated for the FBI agents then turned to Yuri. "Don't do anything stupid." He lowered his voice. "We'll work out a deal with the FBI when this is over."

Yuri walked unsteadily toward the school, stopping briefly when a particularly violent cough racked his body. He felt dazed, as if this were all a dream. Bad things simply didn't happen to Yuri Markov. Losing the Cold War had been devastating, but that cataclysmic shift hadn't been his fault. Far from it, in fact. He'd fought with every tool at his disposal to prevent the Soviet Union's demise. But this—this threat to his own family was terrifying and unfamiliar ground. With every step, the question, *Is this my fault?* reverberated through his mind. Had his own money put his beautiful family at risk?

He raised his hands over his head as he stepped onto the curb. *Damn*, his chest hurt. Things had always gone according to plan for Yuri, but not this time. Never had he imagined being on the receiving end of such a nightmare.

One of the blue double doors leading into the school opened slowly. Yuri stopped beside the flagpole. Above him, the American flag undulated in a soft breeze. The flag's snap hooks pinged against the metal pole, breaking the stillness that had descended over the parking lot.

A pretty, diminutive girl stepped through the door. Yuri dropped his arms and smiled broadly. Elena was like a baby doll with her blonde curls, bright blue eyes, and bow lips. He started toward her, then stopped suddenly. Behind Elena, a masked terrorist forced a tall, blonde woman—his dear Svetlana—outside. The terrorist had a Glock in his right hand, and in his left was a large hunting knife placed strategically near Svetlana's carotid artery.

"*Otpusti ikh. Pozhaluyysta.*" Yuri repeated the request in English, hoping the terrorist would understand one of the languages. "Let them go. Please." Seeing his own flesh and blood teetering precariously between life and death made breathing difficult. The sidewalk felt as soft as sand underfoot. He stumbled, but regained his balance. He'd trade his life for theirs without hesitation. He'd confess to everything about Beslan and Carl Manning's death. He'd pay for his actions, so long as Svetlana and Elena were spared.

Elena looked from her mother to her grandfather, bewildered. Svetlana closed her eyes.

"Your attention please." A woman's voice—Zara's, Yuri assumed—boomed from a speaker mounted on the building. "Yuri Markov, in his years with the KGB, was responsible for innumerable atrocities against innocent people. Among the most heinous of his acts was the campaign of terror he helped wage in the bloody and endless war against the Chechen people. I hold him directly accountable for the murder of tens of thousands of my fellow Chechens who only wanted an independent homeland."

Yuri brought a hand to his pounding heart and locked eyes with Svetlana.

"Today, he is going to pay for his crimes."

"*Ubejte menja,*" Yuri yelled up at the speaker. "Kill me, not them. They've done nothing wrong."

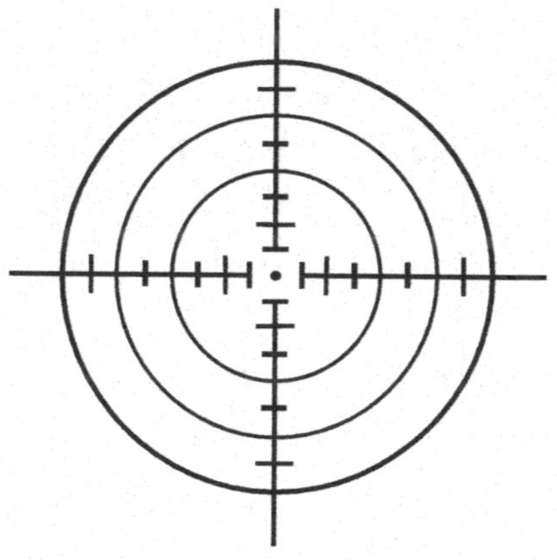

CHAPTER FORTY-SIX

Roger had called Maggie's phone a couple dozen times since their call was disconnected. Each time, he hoped against hope that she'd answer. Every message he left was the same— "Maggie, please call me. Please." The texts he sent were similar—"You okay? Call me!"

The phrase *Don't die, don't die*, ran through his head like an absurd, hopeless mantra.

Roger ran to the far end of the parking lot and sprinted along the side of the school.

"Stop or we'll shoot," someone yelled from a treelined hill near the rear corner of the lot.

Roger stopped and squinted up at the trees. Within five seconds, four SWAT team members materialized from atop the hill, weapons drawn and aimed at Roger's chest. He raised his hands over his head.

"I'm CIA. Maggie Jenkins, my coworker, is inside that school."

A man in black Kevlar who was built like a tank jogged to a position closer to Roger, his gun still leveled at him. "We understand that there's a CIA employee in the building. We certainly don't need two of you in there."

"But she's—"

The man stepped close by and signaled for his colleagues to join him. "You need to go back to the parking lot immediately. It's not safe anywhere else."

Roger remembered the way Maggie's lips felt against his. He loved her obstinance, her independence, her vulnerability. He realized he loved everything about her. "If you guys aren't ready to go in," he began as he tried to make a run for the rear of the school.

They were too fast, too strong, and too well armed for him. Before Roger got fifteen yards, they'd tackled him to the ground. He closed his eyes, and for the first time in a long time, Roger Patterson prayed.

· ★ ★ ★ ·

Zara and one of her men had been gone for five minutes. Maggie could hear Zara's voice echoing faintly from somewhere outside the gym. "This is your chance to get away," she said to the terrorist standing guard in front of her. "That door over there leads outside."

He grabbed a chunk of her hair and jerked her head back. "Shut up." His breath was foul against her face.

Hundreds of little eyes watched Maggie stumble. Handcuffs dug into her wrists. Her mind, besieged by the same paralyzing fear she'd felt as Zara's captive in Georgia, struggled to formulate a plan. If she got herself killed, it wouldn't do anyone any good. If she waited too long to act, all the hostages might die. Maggie looked back at the terrorist.

"I need to use the bathroom."

He shook his head but didn't speak.

"She didn't say no bathroom breaks."

She saw his black eyes narrow through the holes in the mask. He signaled to another terrorist, who jogged to the stage. They exchanged a few words in Arabic, then her minder yanked her down the stage stairs and into the empty hall. Zara's voice was louder here, but Maggie still couldn't make out her words.

The man glanced toward the school entrance, looked at Maggie, then down the hall again.

"What's the matter? You can't act without a woman's permission?" He rewarded her insult to his manhood with a backhanded slap. Maggie absorbed the blow to her jaw and locked eyes with him. Then she pushed open the bathroom door with her shoulder. He followed her inside.

"Um, if you don't undo the cuffs, you'll have to help me with my pants."

He grunted and freed her hands.

"Thanks." She spun her wrists in circles and rolled her shoulders. "Could I have a little privacy?"

"The door stays open."

"Fine." Trying to appear more calm and confident than she felt, Maggie smirked at him as she hitched down her jeans. As soon as the waistband reached her hips, he turned to the side, but remained in front of the open stall. Maggie lowered the jeans with one hand while she slipped the other under her sweatshirt and into her bra. She palmed the slender mace canister and sat. Using her thumb, she twisted canister cap open.

"Done," she announced. He glanced at her and quickly averted his eyes as she pulled her panties and jeans into place. "Can I wash my hands before you cuff me?"

He nodded and peered into the hallway. As he turned back to face her, Maggie depressed the mace trigger, setting loose a stream of burning chemicals. The handcuffs clattered to the floor as his hands flew to his face.

A swift kick to the back of his knees sent him sprawling headfirst into the edge of a white ceramic sink. He collapsed in a heap on the floor. Maggie pulled the AK-47 from his arm and slung it over her shoulder. Then she grabbed the handcuffs, looped them around the pipe under the sink, and clamped the shackles around both his wrists. Terrorist number one wasn't going anywhere for a while. She tugged off the ski mask, revealing a steady stream of blood flowing from a gash in his forehead. He was young—early twenties, maybe. She pried open his mouth, stuffed the mask inside, and pulled the pistol from his holster—it was just like her Glock, a familiar old friend she could use just about now.

Yuri whirled around as if looking for Warner or someone, anyone, willing to help him. Everyone remained frozen in their positions, M-16s trained on the terrorist's forehead, the only part of him visible behind the shelter of Yuri's daughter.

Zara was silent, but her words hung in the air.

Warner kept his eyes fixed on the man holding Svetlana, who struggled suddenly. The terrorist responded by making a small slice in her neck. "*Nyet*!" Yuri shouted. "Svetlana!"

Then Zara's voice returned, preternaturally calm.

"Yuri Markov is a murderous criminal. I've been debating whether I should kill the man who has murdered so many innocents, or let him rot in prison for his crimes."

Svetlana shouted something in Russian. Elena nodded and ran toward her grandfather.

Warner watched Yuri lean forward, arms extended for his granddaughter. The terrorist suddenly shoved Svetlana to the concrete pavement, and slipped back into the school. Yuri lumbered toward Elena just as the tip of an AK-47 edged out the door opening.

In an instant, five bullets tore into Yuri's chest. The muzzle disappeared and the door shut as Yuri collapsed to the pavement just feet from little Elena.

"Damn it, Yuri!" Warner ran to his former foe, whose blue eyes stared vacantly up at the school flagpole.

SWAT team members dashed from car to car, working their way closer to the school. "Svetlana!" Warner shouted at the woman who remained on the sidewalk as if frozen in place. "Run!"

The SWAT team edged forward. Someone yelled for Warner to take cover. But he had a better idea. He snatched the pistol he saw holstered around the Russian's left ankle and slipped through the unlocked front door. He ducked into the first classroom on the right in the split second before the terrorist returned to rechain the main door. He crouched behind the teacher's desk, his finger on the trigger of Yuri's Makarov PM, a Russian firearm he'd trained on years ago, at the Farm.

The sound of gunshots propelled Maggie from the bathroom to the nearby music room. Inside, she rolled the piano in front of the door and collapsed into a chair.

She took a minute to catch her breath. *One down, six to go*. The odds weren't in her favor. Maggie ran to the windows and lifted the blinds. Four police officers stood at the edge of the parking lot, their backs to her, about a hundred yards away. She unlocked the window and pushed it out. It opened only about eight inches. She tapped on the glass as loudly as she dared. Not a single officer flinched and she didn't dare shout and give away her location to the terrorists.

She couldn't very well sit around waiting to be rescued. For all she knew, the good guys might be working their way into the building. Or they might not be. Wherever they were, it was up to her to take out the terrorists. And settle the score with Zara.

Warner waited a full two minutes before daring to stick his head out of the classroom. The terrorist was nowhere in sight. In the parking lot, he'd seen a map of the school. The gym was to the left, but it'd be too risky to take the direct route. Instead, he ran to the right, away from the gymnasium—away from Emma, Abigail, and Maggie—to a corridor at the far end of the school.

He paused before every classroom, the muzzle of Yuri's gun leading the way. The rooms were abandoned—which one was the girls'? Meet-the-teacher night was supposed to be next week. He shook their little faces from his mind. He had to be the Warner

Thompson of twenty years ago, the one who'd run circles around the enemy, who'd never let fear take the upper hand.

At the end of the corridor, Warner took a left into a long hall that led toward the center of the school. Every step took him closer to the gym. He stopped about twenty yards from the end and ducked into a classroom to call Roger.

He whispered, "It's me," then described the sequence of turns he'd taken.

Roger confirmed that the rear entrance to the gym was at the end of the hall. "You're insane to go running in there, Warner. The Feds are having an absolute fit. I just had a little misunderstanding with the SWAT team myself. You don't want to mess with these guys."

"What are they going to do, kill me?"

"It should be me in there."

"Well, it's not. Have they picked up any more audio from the gym?"

"Yes, but it's mostly garbled noise."

Warner could hear people firing questions at Roger. "I'm going to find Maggie."

"You should wait for the SWAT team. They're climbing onto the roof as we speak."

"Would you wait?"

"No."

"Then we're more alike than I thought, Roger."

Maggie sat on the top of the piano and put her ear to the door. Shouting echoed from the gym into the hall. It wouldn't take the terrorists long to find their guy clamped to the bathroom sink. Maggie hopped down and paced the perimeter of the room. She had to act quickly before Zara found her. On her second loop, she noticed a door partially hidden behind a tower of stacked chairs.

Maggie squeezed behind the chairs, pushed the door handle, and peered into a windowless corridor. She slung the AK-47 over her shoulder and gripped the pistol, careful to keep her finger off the trigger. Zara's shouting was growing louder. Ahead were three stairs leading to a door labeled STAGE. Maggie grimaced—she'd been sloppy. And lucky—lucky that Zara hadn't ambushed her through this door.

Maggie crept up the stairs and passed through the stage door. She ducked behind a heavy curtain, held her breath, and listened.

"If someone doesn't tell me where Maggie Jenkins is, I will kill five children. Then five more. And so on, until I find her."

The students were crying louder now.

"Where is she?" Zara screamed in Russian at the men. She repeated the question in crude and halting Arabic.

Maggie parted the curtain and leveled the pistol at the back of Zara's head, trying to focus on the front sight and steady her frantic hands. She'd never shot a target from this far away, never mind a live human. Despite her weekly practice at the range, she'd probably miss. Maggie let her finger fall to the trigger and began applying pressure. She froze at the sound of two muted, but distinct blasts. *Gunshots?* In response, Zara ran down the steps, out of Maggie's line of sight.

"Where are they?" Zara's voice carried through the gym. "Khaled! Rashid!"

Maggie crept along the left side of the stage, moving closer to the front. One of the men was standing thirty yards away near the door leading to the hall. *Still too far.* She retraced her steps, ducked behind the back curtain, and emerged on the right side of the stage. From here, she could see groups of children huddled together with their teachers.

Maggie inched forward, using the side curtain to conceal herself. Zara screamed orders—two men were to stay in the gym, another was to go with her. But what about Khaled and Rashid? Had they been shot? Or had they shot someone?

From her position between the curtain and the wall, she could see a terrorist's back. He was only ten yards away, still farther than she liked but close enough to make it possible. The man was pacing, alternating between staring at his captives and stealing furtive glances into the hall.

A second terrorist was at the rear of the gym, his assault rifle aimed at the assembled children.

Maggie tried to steady her breathing. She raised the pistol in the space between the curtain and the wall, but her hands shook so violently she couldn't shoot. She lowered herself to one knee, rested her elbow on her right thigh, and retargeted the gun. *Much better.* She followed the terrorist through the sights, willing him to stop moving for just a few seconds.

He did, pausing to shift the AK-47 from his left to his right shoulder, then cracking his knuckles. Maggie held her breath, aimed at his upper torso, and pulled back on the trigger. The recoil knocked her slightly off balance, but she kept herself upright as she watched the man collapse.

Little fingers pointing toward the stage. The terrorist in the rear of the gymnasium sprinted forward, firing wildly over the children's heads. Maggie had nowhere to go but down. She flattened herself against the cold, hard floor, trying not to inhale the unsettled dust swarming around her head like so many angry bees. Bullets ricocheted off concrete walls and tore through velvet curtains and brightly painted props.

At the sound of feet pounding up the stage steps, Maggie sat up, her back against the wall, legs bent to her chest, arms extended, finger on the trigger. He stood, not five feet away, panting, wild-eyed. But he was focused on the rear stage door, probably thinking she'd escaped through it. Maggie pulled the trigger again, knowing this time she was plenty close. The shot ripped through his neck, sending him and his weapon clattering to a heap on the stage floor. A spent shell rolled to a stop next to her foot. Maggie stood on shaky legs, keeping the pistol trained on him as she grabbed his AK-47 and his Glock. She ran to the front of the stage.

Children were sobbing, clinging to their teachers. Maggie clambered down the stage stairs and lowered the weapons to the floor. "Who can fire a gun?" An older man raised his hand. A young woman did the same. Maggie began barking orders. "Take these guns. Get that chain over there and secure the door behind me the best you can. And the door to the music room. Pull out the bleachers and hide under them. Stay away from the doors so they can't see you. And someone grab a cell phone and call 911."

Maggie jumped over the dead terrorist sprawled on the floor. She couldn't look at him—it would slow her momentum. She peered into the hall, then looked back at the male teacher who was clutching one of the Glocks. "I'm going out there. Don't let anyone in."

He nodded, silent, eyes moist, and secured the door behind her.

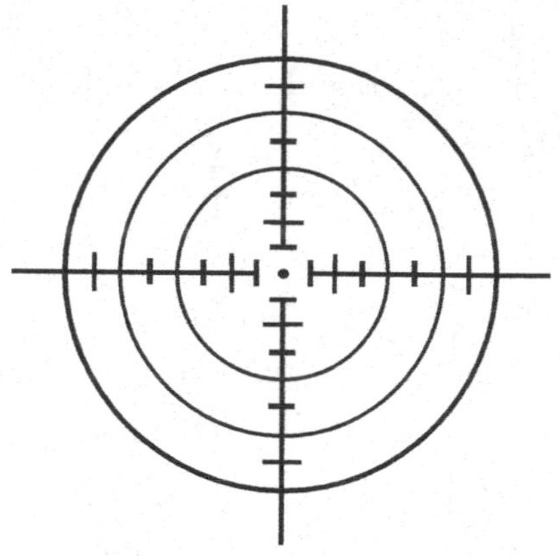

CHAPTER FORTY-SEVEN

Down the hall to the left, two terrorists lay dead. Was the SWAT team in the building? Only two hundred feet stood between her and the front door. She could make it. Let the professionals do the rest.

Maggie looked both ways, like a little girl crossing the street alone for the first time. With the Glock leading the way, she flattened herself against the wall and crept down the hall. Twenty feet from safety, Maggie glanced back toward the gym and said a silent prayer for the children and teachers. The squawk of a police radio beckoned from outside, followed by absolute stillness.

Click.

Maggie whirled around, gun raised. More silence. The door on the left—wasn't it shut tight a few seconds ago? Her legs were like lead, her mouth like sandpaper. She edged closer. Just outside the room, she stopped and listened, unable to hear anything above her thumping heart. She crouched and peered in through the six-inch gap between the door and the frame. Steadying the gun, she stood and kicked the door wide open.

Stained-glass butterflies cast rainbow light along the windowsill. Paint-splattered smocks hugged the backs of chairs. Maggie sank against the art teacher's desk and exhaled. After five deep breaths, she stepped back into the hall and started toward the gym. What had she been thinking? She couldn't leave yet. Not until she knew it was really over. It would only take a few minutes—fifteen, maybe—to check every classroom. Zara wasn't getting away this time. She'd left too long of a bloody trail. It had started with Steve. It would end with a gymnasium full of children. Alive.

The first two rooms were clear. Up ahead on the left was the gymnasium. Beyond that, the custodian's office and her phone. Maggie sprinted down the hall, pausing only to check the intersecting corridor. There was no one in sight. Leading with the Glock, Maggie kicked open the custodian's closet door. *Clear.* She snatched her phone, stuck it in her jeans pocket, and proceeded down the back corridor. Once she was safely inside an empty classroom, she'd call Roger.

Maggie peered into a light-filled kindergarten classroom whose walls were covered with oversized cutouts of primary-colored letters and numbers. Half-eaten crackers and pint-sized milk cartons were scattered around the children's tables. A maple rocking chair sat empty before a bright yellow rug that was anchored by a dozen tiny beanbag chairs.

As she stepped into the room, the door suddenly slammed against her head, sending her stumbling sideways. Before she could recover her balance, someone tackled her from behind, and Maggie fell to the floor, losing hold of the Glock. She gasped and blinked away the haze clouding her eyes. Standing over her, aiming a Walther PPK at her chest, was Zara. She closed her eyes and silently pled for mercy.

Please, no, God. Not yet.

"You know, Maggie, you showing up here made my day considerably easier." The Chechen smiled, but her eyes remained cold. "I've been looking for you. Thanks for saving me another trip to your house."

Zara stood between Maggie and the hall, the only escape route. And her Glock was out of reach on the floor over by the children's coatrack. Maggie swallowed hard and concentrated on keeping her voice steady to mask the fear that pumped through every nerve in her body. "It's over, Zara. Your men are all dead, the hostages are safe." She propped herself up on one elbow. "You failed."

"My men, as you call them, aren't all dead. But even if they were, it wouldn't matter." She shrugged. "My mission is just about accomplished."

"Your mission?"

"I came to the States to accomplish one thing—to avenge the murders of my family."

"If you're talking about Dhokar, you know no one could've saved him."

Zara took a step closer. "Shut up."

Maggie pressed her fingertips into the floor to steady her shaking body.

Zara raised the gun toward Maggie's forehead.

A tremor ran through her voice. "The Russians killed your brothers. And your mother. It wasn't me."

Zara's hand flinched slightly.

"How can you do this after what happened to your mother?"

"You know nothing about her," she spat.

"You told me Zara. Last year when we were in the farmhouse. You told me she was killed in her own classroom by a Russian airstrike. And now you've targeted schools. You're no better than the Russians."

Zara's eyebrows drew together and her lips tightened into a thin line.

"Your brothers are a different story. If they hadn't become terrorists, they'd still be alive today, wouldn't they?"

A flush passed over Zara's face. "My brothers weren't terrorists. They died for freedom." She squinted her eyes shut for a moment. "They were killed in cold blood. And today, I got my revenge."

Maggie let her right arm drift to her hip. If she could just reach her cell phone and hit redial, Roger would hear everything. He'd get help to her. "How does killing American children constitute revenge against Russia?"

"I wasn't targeting the children."

"Then who?" Maggie breathed.

"Yuri Markov. Dead." She sniffed. "Maggie Jenkins." She smiled but her eyes were dark, empty. "Soon to be dead."

"You've got me, so let those children go." She strained to cover the fear in her voice. "You're not going to get out of this school alive." Her fingertips reached the top seam of her pocket.

"Put your hands where I can see them," Zara snapped.

Maggie glanced behind Zara into the hall. Where was everyone—the SWAT team, FBI, Warner, Roger? The cold reality of the situation was a blow to the gut. No one was coming to save her. But that didn't mean it wasn't worth buying more time. "You took over this school to get revenge on Yuri Markov?"

Zara nodded. "He ran intelligence operations during the first Russian war on Chechnya. So many dead. My grandparents, cousins, uncles. And Markov trained the men who stormed the Dubrovka theater. Maybe he didn't pull the trigger, but he is responsible for all those deaths. For Ramzan's death."

Under different circumstances, Maggie might have felt a twinge of sympathy, but not now, not for the woman who'd murdered Steve. "You're no different than Yuri Markov. In fact, you're worse. You've killed people who had nothing to do with the war."

"Still not over your fiancé, I see." Zara tilted her head. "One of the biggest thrills of my life was killing a CIA spy." She frowned at Maggie. "Do you realize that if you hadn't come to Tbilisi and asked so many questions, we never would've met? And you wouldn't be here today."

Killing Steve was a thrill? Maggie's fear gave way to anger. "If you hadn't murdered Steve, I never would've gone to Tbilisi. And if I hadn't gone to Tbilisi, Dhokar would still be alive. It all comes back to you, Zara. You've destroyed everything in your life that was good and real."

Zara shook her hair away from her face, then smoothed it with her free hand. In a quieter voice, she said, "I never figured out how you knew I was in Beslan, but it doesn't really matter, does it? Even before Beslan, I knew I'd see you again. You had to pay for killing Dhokar."

Maggie stared into Zara's enormous, almond-shaped olive eyes, and it struck her—Zara Barayeva would never stop seeking revenge. She'd always blame someone else for her pain and live a life driven by an obsessive desire for vengeance. It was her sustenance, the only thing that kept her from dying a slow, agonizing death of despair, loneliness, and grief. It suddenly all made sense because that's what she'd been doing too. But it ended now.

"You're right, Zara. It doesn't matter how I found you. The only thing that matters is that you don't have anything left to live for."

Zara shifted on her feet and shook out her arms, as if trying to keep herself loose.

"Not even those Friday-morning phone calls with your sweet Aunt Natalia. She was the last one left, wasn't she?"

"What—"

The expression on Zara's face showed Maggie she'd hit a nerve. "I suppose you'll blame her death on me too."

Zara blinked slowly. "My aunt is alive and well."

"You didn't hear?" She nodded toward her pocket. "My cell phone's in there. See for yourself. I took pictures after we met last week in Grozny."

Zara blanched. "I don't believe you."

"I'm sorry to break the bad news. Your aunt was shot and killed at the marketplace in Grozny." The next few seconds would reveal whether Zara had heard from Natalia since the shooting.

"Liar!" Zara shouted as she lunged at Maggie, kicking her in the gut and then on the side of her head.

Maggie curled into a ball and tried to protect her stomach with one hand and her head with the other. "It's true," she protested between gasps. "I have proof." Natalia Barayeva wasn't dead, but she sure looked it in the photographs.

Zara smoothed her hair with one hand, reached over Maggie's hip, and tugged the phone from her pocket. She took two steps back, keeping the gun trained on Maggie.

"Push the camera button, then click galleries. See for yourself." Maggie watched as Zara's expression morphed from anger, to surprise, to crumpled grief.

"When?" she said without taking her eyes from the phone's tiny screen.

"A week ago."

"No," Zara said softly. "No," she repeated, her voice rising to a shout.

Zara felt the weight of a thousand bricks pressing down on her heart. She dropped the phone, covered her eyes with one hand, and wailed, "*Moja dorogaja tetja* Natalia."

She raised her head just in time to see Maggie roll to her side and sweep her right foot into the back of her leg. She buckled, pitched forward, and landed on her knees. The Walther flew from her hand. Before she could grab it, Maggie kicked it away and snatched the Glock from under the coatrack.

Zara looked up at the American, who stood with her feet apart, both hands on the Glock, the muzzle pointed directly at her. "Did you kill Natalia?" she whispered hoarsely.

"No, Yuri Markov did." Maggie shifted her body so she could see into the hall.

Zara's head throbbed.

"I'm going to call my friends outside. They'll be here in a minute, so don't move, or I'll kill you."

Zara shrugged. "I'm not afraid to die."

Now that Natalia was dead, there really was nothing left, except perhaps for Imran. To be sure, he might want nothing to do with her after today's disastrous performance, but she'd win him back.

She always did.

"Your mission failed, Zara. Everyone you ever cared about is dead. It's over. You've lost." Maggie bent over and reached for the cell phone, never taking her eyes or the gun off Zara.

As Maggie stood, Zara noticed a shadow fall across the floor out in the corridor. A moment later, she thought she saw someone duck into the room across the hall. This was her chance. "It's not over," she said with a grin. "Not by a long shot." She paused, then shouted, "Samir!"

Samir? Maggie followed Zara's gaze. The door to the classroom across the hall was wide open.

"Samir, she has a gun," Zara yelled.

Maggie leaned slightly into the door frame and tried to make out shapes in the darkened room. She edged the muzzle of the gun forward, threw a quick glance back at Zara, and steadied her hands. As soon as she saw the outline of Samir's body, Maggie fired three shots in rapid succession. The man stumbled and fell forward into the hall.

She turned the gun back to Zara, who smiled broadly up at her. "Well done, Maggie."

Maggie glanced into the hall at Samir. Only it wasn't Samir. A wave of horror slammed against her. "No!" She ran to the man, who lay softly moaning on the cold, white tile floor.

"Warner," she cried, her eyes already stinging with tears. "Warner!" She dropped to her knees, grabbed his shoulder, and rolled him onto his back. Blood oozed from his arm, but nowhere else, not that she could see.

He opened one eye. "I'm okay," he whispered as he closed his eyes.

"No!" She fumbled for his wrist, seeking a pulse, to make sure he was really okay. But before she could steady her hands, the cold, hard muzzle of the Walther pressed against her temple.

"I take it you know this man well, Maggie," Zara said as she squatted next to Maggie and pulled the Glock from her hand. "So why'd you shoot him?"

Maggie closed her eyes and waited for what would come next.

"Now you know what it's like to kill an innocent person." She laughed. "I guess you could say we're not so different after all, are we?" Zara removed her gun from Maggie's temple and stood. "Tell me, how will you live with yourself?"

Maggie closed her eyes, bracing for the inevitable. Warner twisted his wrist. There, his pulse. Steady and strong. "Looks like I win again, Maggie," Zara mocked her as she began to back down the hall. "Perhaps we'll meet in the future under better circumstances."

Maggie made a show of grieving over Warner as she slid her hand under his back and extracted a gun from his waistband. With an almost imperceptible shift, she turned her head and peered to the right through the hair that cascaded over the side of her face. She slipped her index finger to the trigger, quickly sat up on her knees, and pumped two bullets into Zara's chest.

Zara stumbled back a few steps, then reached unsteadily for the wall as she looked down at her chest, surprise written all over her face. Blood leeched quickly across the white sweater, spreading in spiderweb-like patterns. Zara leaned against the wall. The blood from her back painted red swirls on the white tile as she sank slowly, almost gracefully, to the floor.

Maggie lowered the gun and breathed in the acrid mix of gunpowder and metal. After a moment, she stood, weapon raised, and approached Zara. She kicked the Walther away and felt her neck. "She's gone." She took several steps back, leaned her head against the cool tile wall, and sank to the floor. Absent was the joy and relief she thought she'd feel if this moment ever arrived. There was only emptiness and exhaustion.

Down the hall, Warner sat up, his bleeding right arm tucked gingerly against his stomach. "Thank you for saving your good aim for her."

She smiled. "You're welcome."

"Are you sure they're all dead?"

"All but one. He's cuffed to the bathroom sink. Then I killed two in the gym, plus Zara."

"And I shot two," Warner added.

"So yeah, that's six."

"I thought there were six men plus Zara."

Maggie's eyes widened as she mentally counted the men she'd seen in the gym. "Samir?" she whispered.

They stood. Warner motioned for her to hide in a classroom.

She shook her head and signaled for him to check the classrooms on the left, while she took the ones on the right.

He frowned but joined her as they crept forward. All the classrooms ahead were clear. They neared the end of the hall, where it intersected with the hall that led to the gym. Maggie peered around the corner to the right. Then Warner did the same to the left. All clear. There were no classrooms here, so they picked up the pace, glancing behind them every few steps. To the left were two restrooms set apart by a large window that overlooked an interior courtyard. Warner kept watch in the hall as Maggie searched the girls' room. She did the same for him as he searched the boys' room. As Warner emerged, a glint of light flashed on the windowpane.

"Warner!" she shouted as the glass shattered and a bullet screamed by.

Warner dropped to the ground. Maggie turned, locked eyes with Samir and fired until the chamber was empty. She rushed to Warner's side, her feet crunching on broken glass.

"I'm okay." He moaned as he sat up. "Other than your bullet in my arm," he grunted.

Maggie threw her arms around him.

They waited in the hall as the SWAT team swept each classroom, until finally, they gave the all-clear and let Maggie and Warner into the gym, where teachers and students were hugging and crying.

Warner spotted Emma first. Then Abigail shrieked, "Daddy!" and came running.

Maggie blinked back tears as the two little girls—one in a black denim jumper and the other in pink overalls, fell into their father's arms.

An FBI agent climbed onto the stage and asked the teachers to gather their students, make sure all were accounted for, and exit the school by grade, beginning with the kindergartners. As each teacher did so, Maggie sank onto the bleachers, too tired to move. She closed her eyes.

"You're Maggie Jenkins, right?"

She looked up at a man in an FBI windbreaker. "I am."

"We need to debrief you while the details of what happened are still fresh in your mind."

"Okay." As if she'd ever forget a moment of this day. Or anything that led up to it. She followed the agent out of the gym. At the end of the front hall, near the main entrance, stood Roger.

"Maggie!" he shouted as he sprinted toward her.

He wrapped his arms around her and burrowed his face in her hair.

"She's dead, Roger. Zara's really dead."

He pulled back, pushed an errant curl from her face, and kissed her.

"Ms. Jenkins?" The FBI agent stood by the exit, waiting.

"Let's go." She slipped a hand into Roger's and stepped outside into the brilliant September morning.

ACKNOWLEDGMENTS

To the team at CamCat Books, thank you for taking a chance on me with *The Wayward Spy*, the first book in this series. And thank you for believing in Maggie and her story enough to publish the sequel—*The Wayward Assassin.* Special thanks to CamCat's founder and CEO, Sue Arroyo, for believing that readers will want to "live in" these books. And to Helga Schier, editorial director extraordinaire, whose insight and direction have, once again, elevated my storytelling beyond my greatest expectations. And to the entire production and marketing team who have worked tirelessly to get this book ready for its readers—thank you.

Many thanks to my wonderful agent, Steve Hutson, at Word-Wise Media Services and to Ruth Hutson for your keen eye and guidance along the way.

For my husband, Dan—thank you for continuing to support my writing dreams. And to my children—thank you for always asking about the books and understanding when I need time to write.

Finally, thank you to everyone who read *The Wayward Spy*. Your enthusiasm for my debut novel kept me motivated to finish *The Wayward Assassin*. I think you will love it!

ABOUT THE AUTHOR

Susan Ouellette is the author of *The Wayward Spy*, a thriller that *Publishers Weekly* calls a "gripping debut and series launch . . . Ouellette, a former CIA analyst, brings plenty of authenticity to this fast-paced spy thriller."

Susan was born and raised in the suburbs of Boston, where she studied Russian language and culture and international relations at both Harvard University and Boston University. As the Soviet Union teetered on the edge of collapse, she worked as an intelligence analyst at the CIA, where she earned a commendation for her work done during the failed 1991 Soviet coup.

Subsequently, Susan worked on Capitol Hill as a professional staff member for the House Permanent Select Committee on Intelligence (HPSCI). There, she participated in several overseas staff and congressional delegations focused on intelligence cooperation with allies and classified operations against adversaries. She also played an integral role in a study about the future of the post-Cold

War intelligence community. It was there, during quiet moments, that Susan conceived of Maggie Jenkins, an intrepid female character thrust into a dangerous situation borne of tragedy. Next came the threads of a plot, and from that blossomed her first espionage thriller, *The Wayward Spy.*

Susan lives on a farm outside of Washington, DC, with her family, cats, chickens, turkeys, and too many honeybees to count. In her spare time, she loves to read, root for Boston sports teams, and spend time staring out at the ocean on the North Carolina coast.

FOR FURTHER DISCUSSION

1. Do you have any sympathy for Zara? In what ways is she like Maggie?
2. Maggie, Roger, and Warner are, in part, driven by a sense of guilt. Do you think they are responsible for the deaths that haunt them?
3. What is next for Maggie? Is she ready to move ahead with her life?
4. There is obvious chemistry between Roger and Maggie. However, they bring a lot of baggage to their relationship. Do they have a future together?
5. What part of the story left you on the edge of your seat?
6. Which plot twist surprised you most?
7. If you could write a different story ending, what would it be?
8. Did you guess the ending? If so, at what point?
9. What surprised you most about the book?
10. If *The Wayward Assassin* were made into a movie, who would play each of the lead characters?

AUTHOR Q&A

Q: What are some common misunderstandings about CIA work? Did you find yourself seeking to address any of those in your series *The Wayward Spy* and *The Wayward Assassin*?

A: Common misunderstandings about the CIA tend to focus on negative characterizations. To some, the Agency is an overly powerful, world-manipulating, evil organization. To others, it's an incompetent, bloated bureaucracy that can't predict, much less stop devastating events. Neither is entirely true. The CIA has done some incredibly bold things throughout its history that have ensured our national security. It also has been accused of failing to predict major world events and of engaging in illegal acts. I don't address misunderstandings about the CIA directly in *The Wayward Spy* or *The Wayward Assassin*. Rather, I show that CIA is comprised of every kind of human, including the heroic, the cowardly, the conniving, and the honest. It is a complicated organization filled with complicated people.

Q: You have two very strong female characters in both books in the *Wayward* series. What made you write them? And what do you perceive as their strengths and weaknesses?

A: *The Wayward Spy* originally featured only one strong female character—Maggie Jenkins, my protagonist. With a career path and a personality much like mine, she was a natural choice for me to write. I knew what she'd think, say and do in every circumstance—including tragedy—I threw at her. Maggie is persistent, loyal, and highly analytical. Her instincts almost never fail her because they are based not on emotion but on her innate ability to analyze situations from every angle. Maggie's greatest weaknesses are fear (of failing, of being wrong, of angering others) and a lack of confidence in herself. I love that her weaknesses diminish and her strengths grow as the story progresses.

When I first began writing *The Wayward Spy* many years ago, the antagonist was Osama bin Laden, someone few had heard of outside of national security circles. But after the attacks of September 11th, I decided he should have no role in the story. I started playing around with the idea of a female antagonist, a character Maggie could relate to despite vast cultural and geopolitical differences. Zara Barayeva was just that woman. A young Chechen who also had endured great tragedy, Zara is on her own quest for justice. Only for her, justice doesn't necessarily mean finding the truth. It means vengeance. Like Maggie, Zara is persistent, intelligent, and loyal. Zara's greatest weakness is her hubris. Convinced of the justness of her cause, she harbors no self-doubt. Maggie is both appalled by and sympathetic toward Zara. I'm convinced that under different circumstances, they'd be friends.

Q: What was the greatest challenge about writing *The Wayward Assassin*?

A: The greatest challenge was making sure that Maggie Jenkins grew as a character. She couldn't remain stuck in her past, but she also couldn't act and feel like her old self. Finding the balance between those two "Maggies" was critical to making this story work.

Q: What would you consider the key theme of this book?

A: At its heart, *The Wayward Assassin* is about the decisions we make in the wake of tragedy. While the grieving process is different for every person, at some point, a person must decide what path they will take forward. Will they choose destructive behaviors as a way of coping or "righting" a wrong? If so, what are the consequences of such a choice?

Q: What is the hardest thing about being a writer?

A: For me, it's making the time to write when there are other obligations and diversions. I think most writers struggle with this issue. There's no easy solution. You just have to make the time and get it done!

Q: What would you consider your superpower?

A: Well, according to my editor, my superpower is writing scenes where characters are hiding or fleeing from a dangerous situation. Those scenes are so fun to write. I love to put myself into the character's shoes and figure out how I would get away or where I would hide.

• THE WAYWARD SERIES •

If you've enjoyed Susan Ouellette's
***The Wayward Assassin*,**
we hope you will consider leaving a review
to help our authors.

Also check out another thrilling read from CamCat:
Bryan Johnston's *Death Warrant*.

PREFACE

"*Jesus*," thought Joey, stopping to catch his breath while simultaneously chastising himself for using the Lord's name in vain. They'd said the hike was challenging, even by hardy Norwegian mountaineering standards. But he didn't realize "challenging" was code for "your lungs will be bleeding." He supposed it wouldn't have been too demanding for a younger person, but he grudgingly admitted he no longer fit that demographic. Those advancing "middle-years" made his little adventures even more important to him. He took a swig from his water bottle and checked his watch. He'd been making good time. "That's why you trained for six months, dummy," he reminded himself for the umpteenth time, not that anyone could hear him. He'd seen a few hikers coming back down the mountain but to his surprise he hadn't seen anyone else making the assent.

He'd purposefully picked the least touristy season that didn't include several feet of snow to make his bucket list trip, but still, he expected to see a few more people. Not that he was complaining; he was enjoying the solitude. With one last cleansing breath and the taste of copper dissipating from his mouth he got to his feet for the final push.

On the climb he'd taken to talking to himself, carrying on conversations out loud, playing the part of all parties involved. He'd found it highly entertaining and helped keep his mind off the lactic acid burning in his thighs over the five-hour climb.

"Why in heaven's name does it have to be Norway? It's so far away," Joey said out loud in the closest resemblance of his wife Joanie's patented exasperated tone. He'd had thirty years of marriage to fine tune it.

"Because that's where the Trolltunga is, hon!"

He vividly remembered when the holo-brochure had arrived. "Have you ever seen anything like it?" he'd asked her. She hadn't. The 3D image projected by the brochure had been impressive, and even his wife couldn't deny that. The Trolltunga was a rock formation that sprang two-thousand feet straight up above the north end of a Norwegian lake Joanie never could pronounce and was topped with a cliff that jutted out preposterously far, like an enormous plank of a pirate ship.

Watching the image slowly rotating over the brochure on their dining table had sealed the deal.

Joey could taste the copper again but powered through. He knew he was almost there.

"Should have brought the stick, genius," he grumbled to himself. "That's what hiking staffs are for." But he'd been afraid some careless baggage handler would damage it. The staff had been too important to him. The entire Boy Scout Troop had carved their names into it along with the final inscription, "Thanks for all your years of service." He wasn't sure who was prouder of the gift, him, or Joanie. Regardless, the staff would have been a help.

His research showed that the round-trip climb would be just under 22 kilometers—45,000 steps—and the equivalent of climbing and descending 341 floors. He guessed he was right around floor 170. Almost there.

As he rounded a large boulder, he thought back on all his training, preparation, and admittedly, the inconveniences he'd put Joanie through. "Joey Dahl, I swear you will be the death of me," she tease him. But then what he saw stopped him in his tracks. At that moment Joey felt complete validation. He also instantly understood what made the Trolltunga such a draw for thrill seekers. The cliff's edge reached out so far that the photo op was one for the books. It would make for the type of picture you frame and hang in your den. A conversation starter. Bragging rights. Oh, was he going to brag. The other church deacons were going to be sick of hearing about it.

"Oh, babe," Joey said more to himself this time, "I wish you were here to see this." But even six months ago he knew that was never going to happen, what with her condition, but she was never going to begrudge him this trip. He'd been dreaming about it for years.

• • • • •

It took a certain person, one immune to heights and vertigo to walk to that cliff's edge and look out. Joey was one of those people. He set up the small, portable tripod he'd brought and mounted his mobile device, his optic, to take pictures and video remotely. He couldn't wait to show it to Joanie and the kids. Through a little trial and error, he eventually got the framing right and strode out to the edge. He turned to face the camera and spread his arms wide in a "look at what I achieved" pose. The optic's camera lens clicked once, twice, three times.

• • • • •

And then the bullet hit him right above the left eye.

Joey Dahl dropped like a puppet whose strings had been cut, toppling backwards off the cliff, falling into space. And falling. Like a base jumper, but one without a wingsuit or parachute. His body tumbled down the sheer cliff face, yet he never quite hit the side. His body stayed just clear of the rocky wall, due to the sharp drafts racing up from the lake below. The constant pushing, away from the wall, managed to keep him undamaged, bullet wound aside, until he finally met the ground below, by a lake with a name Joanie never could pronounce. By then, however, he'd been long dead.

• • • • •

Six thousand miles away, a room full of people in finely tailored suits and skirts were watching intently, applauding their approval. One of them, a woman with severe bangs, all business, smoothly pivoted from the wall of monitors, her eyes drawn to another, smaller screen where a series of numbers were appearing in real time. Her eyes on the screen, she allowed herself a trace of a smile. The ratings were in. Perhaps not matching those of the pop star's demise from last summer but still better than management had expected. Enough to trigger her bonus. Maybe she'd take the kids to Six Flags.

CHAPTER ONE

January

If you're going to be summarily executed, you'd at least want the place that's arranging it to have a couple of nice rugs. Just for appearances. Nobody wants to be offed by some fly-by-night outfit that considers Ikea the height of corporate décor. As it turns out, I needn't have worried. Coming in I really didn't know what to expect; they don't show the offices in the commercials. I knew it probably wouldn't be like walking into a notary office in a strip mall—some tiny space filled with cheap furniture, all pleather and particleboard. It is anything but, and instantly fills me with a good vibe, reinforcing my belief that I am making the right choice. The entry doors are an artistic combination of rich amber hued wood, glass and burnished metal, most likely brass, but buffed dull to appear understated. Looks classy. You feel like you are walking into a place of importance, where critical decisions are made on a by-minute basis, which I guess they are. Upon entering I'm greeted by a kindly gentleman with open arms.

"Welcome, Ms. Percival, we're so pleased to see you," he says with utter sincerity. "Our receptionist will take care of your every need."

It takes me a second to realize the man is a hologram. I take a step closer and poke at it, which the holographic gentleman tolerates with a smile. Only the subtlest flicker gives away its true identity. From more than a few feet away you'd swear the man was flesh and blood. Holos are common these days, but this one takes the cake. Clearly, the technology at work here is top shelf stuff. Based on the intimate greeting, they had me scanned and identified the moment I stepped through the front door.

I immediately pick up on the smell: lavender. It's subtle but noticeable. The perfect scent, as it's probably the world's most relaxing smell. Smells have a stronger link to memories than any of the senses and I can feel myself imprinting the scent with the experience. What did my high school teacher always say? Smells ring bells. True that. I'll probably go to my grave associating that smell with this place. Ha, go to my grave, bad choice of words for this visit.

The lobby floor is a combination of real hardwoods and Persian rugs so soft you instantly want to take your shoes off and pace them for the sheer sensory experience. The space feels more like the lobby of a four-star hotel: tasteful, elegant, contemporary without pressing the issue. The woman behind the reception desk is perfectly in line with the ambience. She is probably in her late thirties, attractive but non-threatening. I like the cut of her jib, as my mom used to say. Her clothes are professional but still fashionable. If I were to guess, they were most likely chosen for her by a consultant, like news anchors' clothes are chosen to project an image of trustworthiness. When I approach the desk, her face lights up with one of the most endearing smiles I have ever witnessed. I lean in a bit and squint to make sure she's real. Yep, carbon-based life form.

"How may I help you?" she asks, and I absolutely believe she means it.

"I'm here to get whacked." I mimic guns with my fingers, firing off a couple of rounds at her before blowing the non-existent smoke from the barrels. When I'm nervous I say stupid stuff. Stupid or snarky. Stupid, snarky, or sarcastic. I've been attempting to pare it down to just one for the last ten years with mixed results. I try to sound like being here is no biggie, but my voice sounds shrill in my ears, and I seriously doubt my anti-perspirant is up to the challenge.

The woman is unfazed by my cavalier attitude and nods with a soft, endearing smile. "Of course. You can speak with one of our sales associates. Please take a seat. Someone will be with you in just a moment."

She gestures to a cozy waiting area with a half-dozen comfortable looking chairs, where a distinguished looking woman is sitting, idly paging through an issue of Vanity Fair, one of the last media hold outs that still clings to the quaint notion of publishing on paper. At a glance I can see an A-list actress of some substance gracing the cover, dressed in a bold red riding jacket, khaki jodhpurs and knee-high boots. I can practically hear the baying of the hounds. The actress is currently all the rage and the expected shoo-in come award time for her role in a recent high-profile drama that has captured the country's imagination. A period piece that boasted betrayal, star-crossed love, and overcoming staggering odds in the face of adversity. Or at least that's what the trailers led me to believe.

I turn back to the receptionist. "So, how's it work?"

"Pardon?" she asks innocently.

"I mean, do you get to choose? Sniper shot? Blown up? Dropped into a vat of acid? There was one episode, brutal, they dropped a piano on the guy, like in a cartoon." I also yap when I'm nervous.

The receptionist's smile doesn't waver. "I remember it well." She gives me a polite nod and says, "Your sales associate will answer all of your questions."

I don't even have a chance to pick up the magazines strewn about before my appointed sales associate arrives to greet me. If there ever was a physical embodiment of warmth and compassion, he stands before me. He introduces himself as Benjamin and I can no sooner call him Ben than flap my arms and fly to the moon. To call him Ben would be an affront. This is Benjamin, the type of man who walks one step behind his wife, who enters a room of strangers with his hand on the small of her back to let her know he's right there with her. Benjamin is clearly a man who listens more than he speaks and gives careful consideration before he does. This is my three-second impression.

Benjamin appears to be maybe a decade older than me, in the early throes of middle-age with salt and pepper hair, receding, in baseball terms, at the power-alleys of his forehead.

He wears a nice-fitting suit of deep blue with the thinnest of pinstripes. His shoes, brown, match his eyes. It's the eyes that support everything. His whole demeanor, the warmth, radiate from those dark twins. But I can see upon further review that the smile that rides along with them is what seals the deal. The smile and eyes work in tandem. One without the other, strong, but together, unimpeachable. I would buy a Rolex out the trunk of this guy's car.

OTHER THRILLERS FROM CAMCAT BOOKS

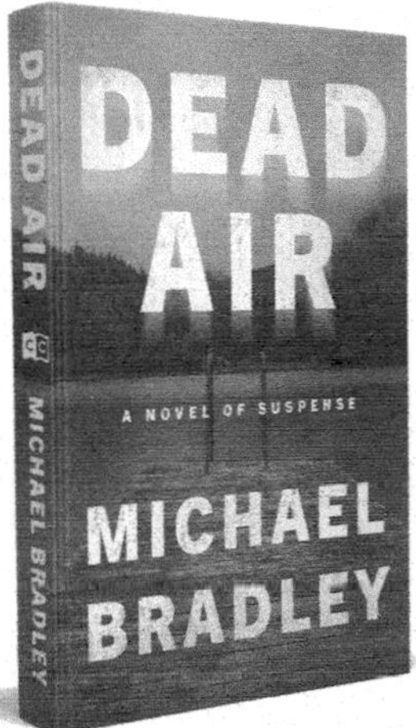

Available now, wherever books are sold.

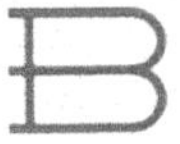

CamCat
Books